Dolores Stewart Riccio

The Divine Circle of

LADIES ROCKING THE BOAT

The 6th Cass Shipton Adventure

ISBN: 1-4392-5887-2
ISBN-13: 9781439258873

BookSurge Publishing
7290-B Investment Drive
North Charleston, SC, 29418

Also by *Dolores Stewart Riccio*

SPIRIT

CIRCLE OF FIVE

CHARMED CIRCLE

THE DIVINE CIRCLE OF LADIES MAKING MISCHIEF

THE DIVINE CIRCLE OF LADIES COURTING TROUBLE

THE DIVINE CIRCLE OF LADIES PLAYING WITH FIRE

To Marilyn Mastrostefano,
good friend and faithful reader…

With loving acknowledgement
of my dearest editor and loyal advisor, Rick,
who makes everything possible…

and special thanks
to my dedicated proofreader, Anna G. Morin.

Dear Reader,

This is a work of fiction. The characters, dialogue, events, businesses, love affairs, criminal activities, herbal remedies, love potions, and magical spells have been created from my imagination. Recipes for dishes prepared by the Circle, however, may have been taken from actual kitchens, probably my own; Plymouth, Massachusetts, is a real place, but some of the streets and locales in the *Circle* books are my inventions. Greenpeace, too, is a true crusading organization, but the ship *Gaia* and its misadventures are fictional.

In a series, families keep growing, changing, and becoming more complicated with time, so that even the author has to keep copious notes. For my sixth *Circle* book, therefore, I'm including a cast of primary characters, their families, and their animal companions—to be consulted when confusion reigns. It will be found at the back of this book, along with a few recipes from the Circle.

– DSR

PROLOGUE

and as you read
the sea is turning its dark pages,
turning
its dark pages.

– Denise Levertov "To the Reader"

The bride was still conscious as she fell through the starlit night. She could taste blood in her mouth, taste the blackness of the scream that consumed her. Her arms flailed to catch onto something, anything, her legs thrashed for a foothold in the frigid air under the cold high moonlight of an October Eve. As she fell, the tatters of her dress flapped around her like torn flags, the shrill treble of her cry was lost in the commotion of the waves. Quick and smooth as a knife, her body sliced through the icy water, her open mouth drank in the origin of all things.

Only once she bobbed back to the surface, took in a great gasp of breath, the last to fill her blue lungs. Then she was gone. The dark sea closed over her head as if she had never been on earth, a mermaid returning to her coral reef and the sea worms who longed for the taste of her flesh.

Above the unmarked ocean where she perished in freezing darkness, there was orchestra music, dancing and laughter, guests in bright colors floating around the midnight buffet, cakes and ices, cocktails and pink champagne. The ship's small casino bustled with men and women buoyed up with the hope of winning, pushing coins and chips toward the all-consuming turn of Fortune's wheel.

The groom was slumped in a shadowed alcove of an unfamiliar deck. He had been drinking steadily all day, merry-making with his new buddies, the cheerful, joking blond trio, their faces as scarred and hard as soccer players, who had somehow disappeared, leaving him to find his own way back to the lavish stateroom. Right now, huddled in his evening jacket, chilled to the bone by the wet, salty air on deck, it didn't seem worth the effort to move. Trying to remember the bitter quarrel with his bride only made his head ache worse. But one thing he knew, she would not be waiting for him, looking up with a welcoming smile from the glittering dressing table or the luxurious bed. He might as well take a little nap first. The honeymoon was over.

PART ONE – THE CRUISE

CHAPTER ONE

Fifteen men on a dead man's chest,
Yo ho ho and a bottle of rum...

– Robert Louis Stevenson

"A Samhain cruise through the Bermuda Triangle. On the good ship *Norse Goddess of the Sea.* How can you resist such an enchanting prospect, Cass? It's simply pregnant with possibilities. Oh the sea, the sea...how it enhances every psychic sense!" Heather poured a healthy measure of dark rum into two blue dolphin mugs, added a lemon twist, a dollop of honey, and a cinnamon swizzle stick. "Best not to dilute the rum too much," she murmured, adding a little boiling water from the cast iron kettle on the hearth. The cozy fire outlined her patrician profile and highlighted the chestnut hair she wore in one long braid down her back.

The toddy's heart-warming aroma swirled around us in the snug paneled library, my favorite room in the handsome Morgan mansion, built by her great-great-grandfather Nathaniel Morgan whose portrait hung above the mantel. The fortune he'd made in the China trade still supported my friend and her pet sanctuary, Animal Lovers of Plymouth. The sweet little fireplace was surrounded by tile-portraits of historic naval heroes.

I curled up in a maroon leather chair, too comfortable and warm to entertain adventurous thoughts of the open ocean.

"Need I mention that October is right in the middle of the official Atlantic hurricane season?" I said. "Wouldn't it be more sensible to plan our trip for spring instead?"

"The word 'sensible' is not in my grimoire—and it's certainly not in yours. Listen, Cass, I've been to Bermuda a few times, and in different seasons, so I can tell you that there's really no reason to fret. My voyages have always been as smooth as a silk chemise. Those mammoth cruise ships are built to withstand the pitch and roll of the waves. You won't even know you're traveling over water unless you look out from a porthole, my dear."

"So...what's the point then? And don't try to becloud my reason. It isn't as if Joe hasn't regaled me with a thousand tales of the unpredictability of sea travel." My rugged husband Joe Ulysses works as a ship's engineer for Greenpeace and is the veteran of many voyages on ships not equipped with stabilizers and other niceties that made today's cruise ships more like sleek floating hotels. In really bad weather, he'd told me, the incidence of seasickness could be close to one-hundred percent, though insisting that he himself has never been so afflicted. A macho boast, but nevertheless, I'm convinced he's nearly as tough as he thinks he is.

"And all that stuff about the Bermuda Triangle," Heather continued her spirited defense of this latest wild idea. "Well, *Fate Magazine* subscribers may believe every fairy tale about strange disappearances in calm waters, but Lloyd's of London declares the Triangle no more dangerous than any other part of the ocean. And if an insurance company doesn't seize on an opportunity to raise its rates..." She propped her feet up on a venerable ottoman and took a long swig from her mug. Two of her resident refugees, Trilby, the ancient bloodhound, and

Honeycomb, a golden retriever and so-called therapy dog, wandered in and took their ease on each side of her chair, like guardian lions.

"What about our families? Are we just to abandon them for nearly two weeks? How does Dick feel about this scheme?" I realized that I was down to the bottom of the barrel of plausible excuses for not enjoying a fall vacation in Bermuda. Dick, who was Heather's fourth husband, gave proof to that old adage *if at first you don't succeed, marry, marry again* by being a big sweet teddy bear of a man. No way would he deny any wish of Heather's heart.

"Oh, please...you know Dick," Heather laughed affectionately. "And how many times has Joe abandoned you while he sailed the seven seas with the green crusaders?"

"Well, there are the doggies—and Freddie's preggers." My insouciant canine companions, Scruffy and his offspring Raffles, valued their creature comforts, and my daughter-in-law depended on me as a doting grandma-to-be and a watch-witch over her considerable psychokinetic power.

"Your mutts can stay here with the gang, cared for by my darling Dick, best vet on the South Shore, and Freddie's not due until Yule. The actual Norse Goddess of the sea, by the way, is Gefjon, who's also the goddess of fertility."

"Yes, well, that reminds me...I'm not sure that Deidre can afford ...."

"Deidre will be invited as my guest. She's the chief reason for this jaunt. What that girl's been through this past year would have driven a lesser woman over the edge. It's because of Deidre needing a life-affirming change, a luxurious treat, a lift of heart, for Goddess's sake, that I've planned all this. And Fiona is absolutely in favor."

I succumbed to the growing forces marshaled against me. "Oh, well...if it's for Deidre...anything."

"And who knows, maybe she'll meet someone..."Heather mused.

"Oh, Sweet Isis...she's still officially in mourning. I draw the line at matchmaking." Deidre's husband Will Ryan, a firefighter, had died last spring of sudden cardiac arrest, leaving his widow with four young children to raise. "Are you sure she'd be willing to leave those bereaved youngsters?"

"No prob. Jenny and Willy will come with her. The Norse Cruise Line is quite family friendly, with a delightful roster of activities especially designed for the kiddies. Bobby and Baby Anne will stay with Will's mom and Deidre's au pair, the redoubtable old Betti."

"'Delightful roster,' indeed. *Now* you're beginning to sound like a travel agent. But what about Fiona? You know she never goes anywhere without her beloved grandniece, and Laura Belle is Bobby's age, rather too young."

"Ah, but you know how all barriers fall away when the universe is in favor. Laura Belle's mommy is coming back from The Hague for the holidays—*her* holidays, Thanksgiving and Christmas—and therefore Fiona's darling will be returned to the maternal and grandmaternal bosoms until the first of the year."

"*Not good!* Fiona will be lost. You remember how she was the last time those two decided to part her from the child? Fell right back into living in Chaos Cottage," I said.

"Yes, the nerve of those MacDonalds!" Heather smacked down her mug on an antique Chinese panel table that ornamented the library "Honestly, how Fiona's family takes advantage of her loving nature whenever they need a nanny for that beautiful little doll. Then, whenever it suits, they snatch the child away. It makes me so cross, I would just like to hex them. Something minor, of course. An infestation of ants, maybe. But that's only for spring, isn't it?"

"*Stop right there*, Heather," I commanded, "and *banish that evil impulse*. We don't do hexes."

"You're right—you *are* a watch-witch, not to mention a worry wart. But I do think we should be allowed the occasional fit of psychic pique."

"Hexes rebound threefold," I continued sternly, "and I hate to think what sort of infestation would be two up from ants. Fleas, ticks, and ringworms?"

"*All right, all right*. But you do agree that the five of us will celebrate a spectacular Samhain this year in balmy Bermuda?"

"Or a balmy Samhain in spectacular Bermuda." Actually, I was beginning to think it might be a refreshing change to sail far away from the terrors we'd recently endured with the arsonist and other sociopaths who had ranged through Plymouth. I imagined a ship filled with well-dressed, well-heeled, good-natured vacationers whose darkest desire was to revel in the midnight chocolate buffet. A restful prospect for a clairvoyant like myself who was frequently afflicted with glimpses into malevolent souls.

Even though the idea was appealing, I groaned a bit, draining the last of my excellent toddy. "I suppose I'll need some new outfits, and you know how I hate clothes shopping."

"Yes, you're an entirely a-typical female. Of course, there will be formal dinners on board, and you'll need some good stuff for Bermuda as well. So forget about L.L.Bean online—I'll take you shopping at Neiman Marcus in town. Did I tell you I that my cousin Brooke knows the *Norse Goddess* captain?"

"Why am I not surprised? Does that mean we'll get special seating?"

"You can bet your witch-hazel wand it does!"

~

On the way home from a sodden afternoon with Heather, I was thankful for the neat sturdiness of my new RAV4, which I had equipped with a sachet of safe-traveling herbs (mint, fennel, rosemary) as well as a small crowbar under the driver's seat in case I ever drove off a Cape Cod bridge and needed to break a window. *Better paranoid than sorry*, I always say.

Even though I'd refused Heather's offer of another rum toddy, it seemed wise to stop off at Phillipa's for a jolt of caffeine. Not that Joe was a critical type like my first husband, but I didn't want to push it. I found Phillipa in her airy kitchen, surrounded by open cookbooks, reading the tarot at the long marble table that served as her work-island.

"Coffee," I moaned, "I must have plain black coffee before I go home, the stronger the better."

"Had lunch at Heather's, did you?"

"How did you guess? What's this? Looking for culinary inspiration in the cards?"

"Be still. This is serious business. Kona or Columbian?"

"Kona. What's up?"

Phillipa glided over to her Miele altar and did something intricate with a coffeemaker so sophisticated it did everything but harvest the beans. The wonderful aroma of freshly ground coffee tantalized me, followed by the steamy fragrance of brewing. Intent as a high priestess at a sacrifice, Phillipa watched over this process, occasionally pushing this or that button with a slim graceful finger, until she was ready to fill two gently warmed white stoneware cups. I contemplated the actual price-per-cup; even Starbucks was probably cheaper. On the other hand, every upscale piece of equipment in this state-of-the-art kitchen, from the Viking restaurant range to the SubZero side-by-side, would be tax deductible for a cookbook author.

Wordlessly, Phillipa put the perfect brew in front of me, then turned another card of the Ryder deck, laying it face up.

Her well-fed black cat oozed into the room and brushed herself against Phillipa's legs, hinting for a handout.

"Later, Zelda. Mommy's busy. Ah, the Hanged Man," Phillipa said, leaning intently over the tarot spread so that the dark wings of her hair fell forward. The silver pentagram she wore with her black cashmere pullover dangled over the cards. "Always a sacrificial figure. Glad to serve and save others. Who can he be? Surely, not one of us. Of course we're as giving and generous as Wiccans are bound to be, but not to the extent of sacrificing ourselves or giving up something dear to our hearts."

"But he's upside down, Phil. That is, right side up when he's *supposed* to be upside down. Doesn't that change things?" I asked. Many tarot readings at this table had taught me a few of the basics.

"True enough. This particular Hanged Man is not operating on a higher spiritual plane, alas. He may appear to be one who gives of himself, but underneath he's arrogant and egotistical. Mired in his physical desires. Maybe even gone over to the dark side. No one we know comes to mind. Must be someone we've yet to meet. Perhaps on this cruise of Heather's. Quite the clever organizer, isn't she?"

"So...are you in favor of her Bermuda scheme, then?" I savored the steaming coffee, hoping it would clear my rum-soaked brain. "And what about Stone? Is he resigned to your gallivanting off with your Wiccan pals while he deals with murder and mayhem on the South Shore?"

"Stone has been urging me to go, what a darling. He claims to anticipate a peaceful hiatus for the Plymouth County Detective Unit. Apparently he harbors the notion that somehow we attract crimes, as if it's our karma. Do you think he's getting to be a true believer?" Phillipa smiled, the rare lovely smile that softened her sharp features and made her suddenly beautiful. "But hey, a Samhain cruise to hibiscus island just as New England is turning dark and dreary—what's not to like? As a matter of fact, I was just laying out the tarot with our trip as the subject. See?" She pointed to the significator, center of layout, for which she had chosen the Six of Swords, a journey by water.

"Yes, well it's all in the interpretation, isn't it? What else have you got?"

"Four of Wands here, a promise of festive pleasures. Just look at those merry dancing maidens—that's us! High Priestess—that figures. Fiona, probably. Then that old spoilsport, the Hierophant, whom you'll notice we're leaving behind us. The Devil—well, what's a cruise without a bit of carnal temptation?" Phillipa's graceful hands pointed to each card in turn. "The Fool, that's innocent choices. Nine of Cups, wishes come true. The Hanged Man, could be read as a sacrifice. And now, the *final outcome...*" She turned over the tenth and last card with a flourish. "*Oh, shit.*"

It was the Ten of Swords; it depicts a prone form with ten swords sticking out of his torso. There was no way to pretty up this one. I waited with interest to see how Phillipa would deal with its chilling portent.

She drew herself up like a good soldier. "I'm going anyway," she vowed. "If only to keep the lot of you out of trouble."

"You see," I said, "you're feeling sacrificial already. Just remember what Alice of Wonderland said."

Phillipa grinned and with the flat of her hand pushed all the cards together into an indistinguishable heap. "*Who cares for you? You're nothing but a pack of cards!*"

"That's the spirit," I said, but at the back of my mind an unwanted picture was forming, small and clear like a tiny film clip, a shrouded figure falling silently though darkness. A girl, I thought. I felt the twist of nausea that often follows a clairvoyant spell. Deliberately, I shoved the vision aside as Phillipa wrapped up the tarot deck in its protective red silk bag. "We'll have a great time, I just know it," I declared.

Thoughts are things, as my grandma always told me. I would keep thinking those good thoughts.

CHAPTER TWO

I must go down to the seas again, to the vagrant gypsy life;
To the gull's way and the whale's way, where the wind's a whetted knife..."

– John Masefield

"We'll be gone ten days, but you needn't feel you're tied to the house dogsitting all that time," I explained to Joe as we walked along the shore. It was a perfect September evening, just crisp and breezy enough to qualify as autumn. The Atlantic was a darkening blue with flashes of silver, richly scented with salt and weed. Gulls carried the last of sunset's reflections on their wings, stitching the water to the sky.

"Hey, we're family now, sweetheart. I'll be glad to man the home fires, take care of the pups, watch over the house and whatever nefarious herb concoction you've got brewing in that workroom of yours." Joe's muscular arm went around my waist with a reassuring squeeze. When we paused to rest, he pulled up my jacket collar snuggly. His fingers were warm, lingering on my neck. We were almost the same height, so his Aegean blue eyes were gazing straight into mine. A lingering kiss naturally followed.

Scruffy, who was plodding along behind us, gave a disgusted snort.

"The only problem is Spain," Joe said.

"Really! Inquisition? Conquistadors?"

"No, just a simple case of greed run amok again. There's a chance I'll be called in to help our Spanish wing denounce their country's tropical timber industry," Joe said as we continued our walk, "in which case..."

"In which case, the pups can be parked at Heather's. You know she never has less than six or seven needy dogs at her place, so what's a couple more? And besides, she offered. On Dick's behalf, of course."

Like many of his species, Scruffy was ever alert to conversations that concerned him and had been listening to every word, while Raffles galloped ahead nosing seaweed, rocks, crab shells, with all the enthusiastic innocence of canine youth.

Me, a pure-bred French Briard forced to push and shove with that ill-mannered horde? And you know what those mutts get to eat? That stuff tastes worse that the bottom of Ishmael's bird cage.

Somehow, I always heard Scruffy's thoughts almost as if they were spoken aloud. "Oh, come on, Scruffy, it won't be that bad," I said. "Besides, you're only half Briard. The other half is plain old mutt."

Hey, Toots, there's no need to be insulting. You'll notice that I've inherited the double dewclaws of my Briard ancestors. And the distinguished lift of my ears.

"Yeah, yeah. Well, you're not too noble for the dog pack experience, fella. And don't forget that Honeycomb will be there as well. *She* is very well-bred indeed." I held out the ultimate lure. Honeycomb was Raffles mother, but since that not-exactly-blessed event, the golden retriever had rarely given Scruffy as much as a friendly nosing.

Hummph...that moody blonde bitch. Scruffy ran into the narrow waves at the edge of the shore to cool his paws and change the subject. He was greeted with glad woofs by his offspring.

"You know, some guys might feel insulted if their wives held long conversations with the dog instead of begging for details about his next adventure on the high seas." Joe's tone was more resigned than aggrieved.

"*She loved me for the dangers I had passed*... So, tell me, then... what's the dark side of the lumber trade this time?"

"Not only ecological damage along the Ivory Coast but their illegal logging is funding armed conflict between the rebels and the government."

"Ivory Coast? You mean as *in Africa*? You'll be sailing along the African coast? Is that, like, *Somalia*?"

"No, sweetheart. Somalia is on the Indian Ocean, the Ivory Coast is on the Atlantic. Not to worry."

My grasp of geography has never been exactly firm, but since I've known Joe I've been constantly tutored on environmental hotspots from one end of the globe to the other. Always someplace remote and dangerous, I've noticed, with bizarre crusades such as rescuing the Pategonian toothfish or boycotting Frankenfarm soybeans.

"It may not come to actually shipping to Africa, Cass," Joe said. "We may just end up in some European port painting bootlegged logs with political slogans as we did before."

"Oh, sure. My first real vacation since our honeymoon, and I just know I'm going to be worrying about your being captured by some pygmy headhunters with a Weyerhaeuser contract."

"*Jesu Christos*, I hope that's not one of your clairvoyant whammies."

"Naw, just kidding." I tucked my hand into his, and we turned to start home.

I didn't tell Joe about that unexpected mind's eye image of a girl's body falling into the ocean. That kind of vision is like glancing into the window of a passenger train hurtling down the tracks, destination unknown. It happens so fast that

I might be inclined to shake my head and dismiss the whole thing if experience hadn't taught me to pay close attention. The evil that I see is often the evil that later comes to pass. The curse of clairvoyance, always a warning, never a winning lottery number.

~

A young widow with four children, Deidre Ryan did not appear to be her usual perky prolific self, and no wonder. Her mop of blonde curls was plagued with odd bits sticking out here and there, and there were smudges of fatigue under her pale blue eyes. Always unsparing of her own energy, she now drove herself relentlessly to keep her doll shop, Deidre's Faeryland, afloat in the piratical competition of Massasoit Mall. Her husband's unexpected death had not exactly left her destitute. Mortgage insurance had paid off the pretty garrison Colonial house. Will's life insurance as a small town firefighter had provided a decent settlement, but hardly a fortune. Deidre was recovering, too, from being attacked by the crazed stalker of a young friend last year. Work had always been her therapy, but now she was going at it like the sorcerer's apprentice.

Bearing two cappuccinos accompanied by Colossal Cinnamon Explosion Frosted Pecan Buns from Sweet Buns Coffee Shop, guaranteed to pick us up with a rollercoaster sugar high, I'd dropped into her shop with the intention of finding out whether she really wanted to take this cruise or was being shanghaied by Heather. I found her turning out little Conan Doyle faeries-on-a-stick at top speed. They were clothed in gossamer dresses of mauve, azure, primrose, and other exquisite colors that sparkled with every motion.

"Positively enchanting," I said, lifting a fey Victorian faery into the light. When I turned the doll, her long green sleeves turned silver like poplar leaves before rain. "I predict they'll sell like crazy, Dee. Are they for kids, or...?"

"You'd be surprised, Cass. A fair number have been bought by women as decorative items for the home. In fact, when I saw that, I sent a few samples to *Home Elegance* and got favorably reviewed in their "Nouveau Decora' column. Now I'm playing catch-up-with-the-orders. But you know what that's like. A wildly successful product can be a mixed blessing to small business. Say, don't get your sticky fingers on that fabric, dearie." Deidre caught me reaching for another faery, an irresistible violet number. "So...do you want to tell me what's brewing under that pointed hat of yours today?"

"About this cruise of Heather's," I said. "I just want to be perfectly sure..."

"Oh, it's an absolutely delicious prospect, Cass. But I just don't know how I'm going to tear myself away from home, the shop, *the babies*. You know. And the orders inspired by *Home Elegance*, of course."

"Knowing you, I bet you've got some midnight crew of little people lined up to paste together your new faeries in no time. When it comes to accomplishing miracles, you always leave the rest of us in the dust."

Deidre grinned with a hint of her former gamine self. "I love it that you all wonder how I do it, my time thing. Yes, I suppose I can manage. It certainly would be a treat for me and my two oldest. Jenny's over the moon, but Willy's not so quick to react—much like his dad, you know, so a true junior." The light went out in Deidre's eyes, and the grief darkened her. Guilt, too. Will had always been a bit slower on the uptake than mercurial Deidre. Often, she'd been restless and impatient with him. Only in that last year when his health was in jeopardy had she realized how much she'd always loved Will.

Wanting to see her brighten again, I would have said any dumb thing. And I did. "Phil read the tarot for our voyage. Predicted we'll be dancing up a storm. Oh, and the Fool turned up. New choices and opportunities for all of us."

"Oh, sure. Haven't you noticed that our feet are pretty well encased in domestic cement these days?" She stabbed her swift sharp needle into a red-haired faery in a flowing pale blue frock. "Not so easy to trip the light fantastic anymore. So then, what was the final outcome of the reading? You know, the last card."

I swallowed. *Uh oh.* "Well, I'm not saying there will be... but there might be...someone...you know, injured, or maybe deeply depressed."

"Holy Mary, Mother of God." Deidre's Catholic roots still gave her comfort, or at least oaths of feeling. "The Ten of Swords?"

"Well..."

"A little shipboard mayhem, like?"

"Makes a change?"

"Like hell it does. *Same old, same old* for us. Ever since we began to celebrate the Sabbats, it's been one neighborhood crime watch after another. Thievery, arson, poison, murder—why can't we be like other witches and just dance around the woods sky-clad and brew a few love potions?"

"Personally speaking, I'm a little too old and thin-blooded for streaking through the pines," I said. "It's just a karma thing, don't you think? We replay like a TV series. *The Avengers* meets *Bewitched.* So...do you think a Samhain cruise for the five of us might be pushing our luck? That we ought to keep our dancing feet right on *terra firma?*"

"Hey, no way. I was a bit afraid that the cruise would turn out to be a lot of shuffling off to shuffleboard, but if there's going to be a mystery...well, that's what I call an intriguing prospect."

"Dee, you never fail to surprise me. It's a go, then."

"You bet. *The devil and the deep blue sea.*"

"Yeah, he turned up in the Phil's tarot spread, too. Satan, however, has never been one of ours. Invented by fearful priests, employed by misogynistic witch-hunters."

"Alive and well, however, in the children's catechism." Deidre made a wry face. In deference to Will and her mother-in-law, Mary Margaret Ryan, the young Ryans were attending Sunday school at St. Timothy's.

"We'll have to do something about the children," I murmured, thinking not only of the Ryans but also Laura Belle and my lovely grandchild-to-be. Maybe with Fiona's guidance...a few classes...some real mythology...include them in Esbats and Sabbats.

"Very carefully," Deidre said. "I don't want to run afoul of the Ryan family's religious sensibilities, and I wouldn't want Fiona to get into trouble with her bunch, the MacDonalds. They might just snatch away Laura Belle forever. Let's just keep a low profile, I say."

"Okay, but I doubt that's in the cards for us." Wrapping up the sticky papers from our coffee klatch, I was, at that moment, feeling quite grateful that my own three children were adults now, and I need answer to no one for my choices. I threw the refuse into the wastebasket and wandered over to play with the Faeryland dollhouse, the centerpiece of Deidre's shop. The table-size cottage had once housed a little family of woodland "brownie" elves with all their miniature belongings. Today it was set up to display the life style of a Green Witch and her family. The downstairs rooms were crowded with bookshelves, and there was a tea set on the coffee table with a plate of scones. The witch doll was reading an arcane leather volume smaller than a matchbox. Leaning against the reading chair was a tiny green reticule. In one upstairs room, the bed was made up with tartan blankets. A tiny gray cat reclined on the cushions with the regal demeanor of Omar. The other room was a duplicate of Laura Belle's, the walls decorated with magical animals.

"Wow! Has Fiona seen this?" I asked. I adjusted the wee quilt on the napping "Laura" doll.

"Not yet. It's fun, isn't it?"

"It's also a spell, I'd say. A poppet play to suggest a happy outcome."

"I have to admit, while putting this together, I did say a few prayers for Laura Belle's return to Fiona. And why not? What good is being a witch, if you can't help out a friend?"

CHAPTER THREE

Of Neptune's empire let us sing,
At whose command the waves obey...

– Thomas Campion

Beginning life as an unplanned pregnancy, Laura Belle, the little girl with morning glory eyes and a rosebud mouth, had been fostered by her grandaunt Fiona Ritchie while her mother Belle MacDonald finished law school. We had watched in awe as the arrival of Laura Belle completely transformed our untidy friend's way of life into an orderly child-centered existence. But whenever the little girl was whisked away by her mother and grandparents, our remarkable Fiona, who'd lived widowed and alone for many years, fell into a profound disorder.

Chaos Cottage had returned indeed. I entered her front door sideways to avoid *The Golden Bough*, the 1935 original in twelve volumes, piled against the entry's wall along with stacks of the magazine *Punch* circa 1920. Her fish-net draped home in Plymouth Center might be considered the rare-books annex of the Black Hill Branch Library where she was librarian, crammed as it was with obscure texts and esoteric pamphlets. But chaos or not, Fiona could always put her hand on whatever archaic tome or ephemeral pamphlet was wanted. Whether she dowsed with her crystal pendant or browsed through the internet, she was, in fact, our official "finder."

It was Fiona who had initiated the Black Hill Women's Studies program where we five had met. Eventually, in that workshop, as we moved through myth, magic, and matriarchy, we'd realized that we shared an appreciation of the spirit in all things, that we were natural mystics. We'd been inspired to form our own circle. The more we traveled back into the past, the more we longed to celebrate earth's natural cycle and its ancient deities, especially the long neglected and maligned Divine Female, and to practice a little high-minded magic in the Wiccan way. There being no dogma or college of theologians with whom we had to contend, we'd found our own path, not exactly a primrose one. Then, because of my clairvoyant abilities, we'd fallen like Alice through the rabbit hole into a dark world of mystery and murder. We'd been transformed into crime-solvers, sometimes crime-savers. This sidetrack didn't prevent us, however, from thoroughly enjoying our newfound power as Wiccan women.

"We ought to pay more spiritual attention to the Great Horned God," Fiona declared when she and I had settled ourselves on her sofa (having shoved to one side the Sunday New York Times and a stack of Wonder Woman comic books).

"Any special one?"

"In any of his manifestations, Herne the Hunter, Pan, Osiris, Dionysus, Cernunnos, the Green Man. The celestial father image." As Fiona poured steaming lapsang souchon tea into thistle cups (none too clean, I observed), the many silver bangles on her plump arms tinkled musically. Her resident companion, the Persian cat Omar Khayyám, walked gracefully along the back of the sofa, eying the tray, noting the location of the shortbread tin.

"Should we really? Funny, I was just discussing the devil with Deidre apropos of our Bermuda voyage."

"Oh, piffle. The devil has nothing to do with our horned god. Just another Judeo-Christian invention to discredit simple traditional country rituals. I feel we have been giving the majority of our attention to the Great Mother, which is natural enough, we being women, She being the creator of all things. But we need the phallic input. Spiritually, you know. Green Jack, that raucous old fellow. John Barleycorn. Robin Goodfellow. The legend of Arthur. The element of change, risk. The great catalyst. Now this trip we're taking...that's the thing."

"That's what thing, Fiona. You're leaving me behind here." Fiona's leaps of pixilated logic often left me shaking my head like a Mexican jumping bean.

"Neptune," she said succinctly. "Shortbread, dear?"

"No, thanks. The tea is lovely." There were two dark cat hairs balancing on the tin's edge. Omar leaped gracefully onto the coffee table and was rewarded with a cookie corner. "Neptune is not one of the horned gods, and certainly not one of the leafy woodland fellows," I pointed out.

"Well, dear, there's the trident. That's horny enough. Let's keep in mind that all divine manifestations are one when you get right down to it. Or up to it. And we're going to need the Great Father on our side as we traverse the Bermuda Triangle. Neptune. a.k.a. Poseidon." She looked at me earnestly over her half-tracks. Two pencils were stuck in her coronet of carroty-gray braids, the sign of a mildly stressful day. "I have a pamphlet you should read."

She reached into the green reticule always kept by her side and drew forth a yellowed booklet with a wrinkled, chipped cover. I read the title: *The Seven Pagan Prayers for Highly Successful Voyages.* Suppressing a smile didn't fool Fiona.

"What do you know about methane hydrates?" she demanded. This time she reached into the bookshelf behind her for a paper published in 1981 by the United States Geological Survey.

"Okay, lay it on me," I said.

"A very interesting survey, dear." She patted it affectionately. "It posits that periodic eruptions of methane hydrates off the Southeastern United States coast could produce frothy waters that are no longer capable of providing adequate buoyancy for ships. Furthermore, the air above these regions is not as dense as normal air and might interfere with the lift needed to keep airplanes flying."

"Sort of makes you rethink the whole Devil's Triangle thing, doesn't it?"

"Just a theory, dear. But scientists have been able to reproduce these conditions in the lab. Heavy bubbling of the water did cause the model ships to sink."

I imagined a group of white-coated, gray-bearded men sailing their toy boats in the lab water tank. *Typical!*

"Think how interesting it will be to celebrate Samhain aboard ship," I offered a distraction to Fiona's dour Scot fixation on sinking ships.

She brightened immediately. "Oh, it will be rather different, won't it? But actually we'll be in Bermuda on the 31st. So I'm working on finding us a suitable outdoor site, perhaps one of the pink-sanded beaches. Not as cold there as it would be here in Plymouth. Perhaps others from the ship will want to join us. You know, it could be like one of the onshore excursions, only not so over-priced. We wouldn't mind sharing the Sabbat, would we? That's if we make it there in one piece. Or should I say five pieces?"

"Fiona, we're going to be just fine. Stop worrying. I'm sure one of us will get a cosmic nudge if we really shouldn't take this trip. Otherwise, let's just go and enjoy ourselves. The worst thing that will happen is we'll probably gain a few extra pounds hitting the midnight buffets."

Nevertheless, she pressed the Pagan missal into my hands before I left and added another little pamphlet, *Feng Shui Your Stateroom*.

~

The cruise was a go! And with Joe's wholehearted encouragement. But then, what else could he have said after all those times I'd waved good-bye to him as he sailed off on some exotic adventure leaving the little woman at home to keep the altar fires burning? Still, he was a most understanding guy, and I loved him for it.

The only thing left to do was to call my children with the news.

Becky, my reliable oldest child, was easiest and therefore first. Noon seemed a likely time, and so it was. She answered from her office at Katz and Kinder, where she was having a lunch snack. "Oh, good for you, Mom," she said warmly, then went right on to tell me about her latest win in court, a difficult custody suit, and her new boyfriend, "a real family guy, you'll love him." Before we could get back to my plans, she had to hurry off to an urgent appointment with a distraught wife.

Later that day I received a lovely *Bon Voyage* bouquet from Becky delivered to my front door. Fortunately, the dogs alerted me to the suspicious object or I might never have found it until spring, since like most New Englanders, the front door is opened only to welcome visiting clergy or to take away a dead body.

Adam answered the phone in his Lexus; he was driving his very pregnant, very young wife to birthing class. "Way to go, Ma," he managed to say before Freddie commandeered the cell.

"How cool is that!" Freddie crowed. "You five witches sailing through the Bermuda Triangle at Samhain—now that's what I call a cosmic event! We're both thrilled, thrilled, thrilled for you! And I suppose we can count on hearing about a catastrophe or two en route? High crimes on the high seas? Exorcism of the entire Norse Line when you disembark?"

I laughed indulgently. "Dear Freddie, the only worry I have is *you.* I'm counting on being home for my grandchild's arrival, so don't you dare disappoint me with an early debut. As for us witches, as you insist on calling us, we're planning to enjoy a relaxing time-out, a thoroughly pampered vacation away from the stress and strain of our regular lives."

"Yeah, sure, Cass. See you on CNN!" was her parting shot. I could hear Adam's deep chuckle all the way through our conversation. I loved it that Freddie had brought so much laughter into his life. And mine, too, for that matter.

That left Cathy, my youngest, who with her partner Irene, was seeking her big break into stardom in Los Angeles. Since she was never parted from her cell phone, I was sure of reaching her—and of a very short conversation.

"Mother!" she exclaimed. "You're going *where?* Irene, Mother's going to Bermuda with the gang? Isn't that a hoot? Listen, Mother, I can't talk long. We're expecting an *imminent* call back from, *now hear this*, Tarantula's new production, *Ghouls of Galilee.* We're reading for the banshees. Oh, I know, it's just another horror flick, but it's a foot in the Universal door. So...*gotta go now.* Have a marvelous cruise, darling! *Kiss-kiss!* Irene sends a kiss, too. Oh, and here's the big news—we *will* be coming East when Freddie delivers our new niece. Or nephew. Adam sent us the airfare—isn't he a dear? And Irene won't let me touch a penny of it. Of course, if *Ghouls* works out, we'll have to fly in and out in a flaming hurry."

"The baby's due around Christmas. Perhaps Tarantula will find it in his heart to allow you a half-day off ?"

"Ha ha, Mother. Cruise carefully, and all that."

~

Taking a cruise means never having to dash with your carry-on across an interminable airline terminal, and schlep baggage from taxi to hotel to taxi. The unsophisticated traveler is thus encouraged to pack three times as much luggage as she would for the grand tour of Europe. One thinks nostalgically of Louis Vuitton steamer trunks as big as walk-in closets from the good old days of luxury travel aboard the *Queen Mary* or the *Titanic*. Not surprisingly, the five of us and two children somehow managed to accumulate enough baggage to fill a bus. So that's what we decided to do, hire a bus to take us to the Port of New York, from which that good ship of Liberia *The Norse Goddess of the Sea* was departing.

Heather did the hiring, however, so the "bus" turned out to be a white Hummer limo with two plasma TV screens and a mirrored ceiling with starlights that changed color as we sped along.

"If they're going to do stars," Fiona said, having flattened her swivel chair into viewing position, "it's a pity they didn't do constellations in the Northern Hemisphere, an excellent opportunity to educate young travelers like Jenny and Willy."

I doubted that very many children would be expected to travel in a limo with several bar areas and a parquet floor suitable for dancing. The young students in question were at that very moment being mesmerized by a huge Discovery channel show in which creatures were snacking on other creatures with obvious relish.

"Are there alligators in Bermuda, Mom?" Willy asked.

"No, dear, but there's a lovely aquarium." Deidre shut off Discovery with a firm hand and turned on a music channel—Songs of the Seventies. *Like a Bridge Over Troubled Waters* seemed to be belting out from all directions at once on some hidden super woofers.

"I'm guessing that this limo is generally used to transport The Rolling Stones or similar," Deidre said, adjusting the volume to less than deafening.

Heather was busying herself opening bottles and filling flutes with Vive Cliquot. "Now we must have a toast!" she declared.

Phillipa stood up looking lean and magical in her black silk shirt and black linen slacks. She raised her glass and, like Cyrano, composed a verse on the instant.

"May our tarot always turn the Nine of Cups,
May the ships we sail never be bottoms up."

"I recognize that one, or the last part of it," Fiona said. "A famous nautical toast. A favorite of my poor dear Rob Angus Richie whenever he was in a reveling mood. Then a sixty-foot wave took him down with the *Fiona Fancy*, alas. Perhaps not the best of omens, dears."

"Oops. So sorry, Fiona," Phillipa said. "Banish that sad memory. Here's another, then.

Drink up, drink deep, as we begin these rites,
For we do trust they'll end in true delights."

"Ah, paraphrased from *As You Like It*," Fiona said. "Now that's perfect." She drank her champagne straight down as if it were a hit of vodka, ending with a barely audible ladylike hiccup. Wearing her favorite coat sweater of many colors and carrying the essential green reticule (always a source of whatever was needed at the moment, whether hankies, candies, or lock-picking tools for breaking and entering), she looked the very picture of a faery godmother.

"Is there any quote she doesn't know by heart," Deidre whispered to me.

"What she doesn't already know, she can find in a twinkling," I whispered back. Willy leaned on Deidre's lap, his eyelids heavy. "Driving in a car always does him in," she explained. "That's okay, honey. You can nap, if you want. It will be hours before we get to the port."

"I wish Daddy was going with us," he said, crawling up beside her on the leather banquette.

Deidre sighed. "Yes, honey, I do, too. But Daddy is in Summerland, which is the most beautiful, peaceful place you can imagine. And we're on our way to Bermuda."

"At Sunday School, Sister Firmina said Summerland was all wrong. Daddy is in Heaven not some amusement park. She said we're all going to join him there someday." Willy nestled himself into a more comfortable place against Deidre's side.

Deidre sighed. "Someday, yes, honey. But it's not our time just yet. No one on our ship is going to Heaven on this voyage."

A chill not at all reminiscent of Summerland slid like an ice cube straight down my collar from neck to coccyx. In a flash, I saw in my mind's eye a man's hand roughly grasp someone's shoulder. A girl's shoulder, her dress a shimmering rainbow. He spun her around. She tried to scream but instead slumped down as if fainting.

It's not possible to drown a water nymph. I had no idea where *that* thought came from, but it hardly mattered when the image faded as instantly as it had appeared. I took another delicious sip of champagne and put the disquieting vision out of my mind.

~

Heather was not to be trusted to make prudent, economical arrangements, which was one of her charms. Although Deidre was her guest (over some weak protest), Phillipa, Fiona, and I had each paid for lovely first class cabins with window views, no lifeboats or posts obstructing. Reservations made by our "cruise director," however, upgraded the lot of us to the Penthouse Deck, two decks below the Blue Vista where there was a jazz band playing nightly. Our staterooms were called Owners Suites; there were six of them. (Were there six owners who were conveniently absent?) These luxurious accommodations were clustered around a courtyard with a small private pool, a hot tub, a sauna, and a spa room with fitness equipment. Heather and Fiona were sharing a suite, Deidre and her two children another, and Phillipa and I the third.

Modern staterooms, rightly called cabins, are generally Lilliputian, but these suites offered a luxurious taste of the grand era of cruise travel and were even decorated with an Art Deco flair. Living rooms with desk alcoves, small but private twin bedrooms (each with a comfortable single bed hiding a pull-out cot a child might use), walk-in closets, real marble bathtubs, floor to ceiling windows opening onto balconies, a VCR as well as TV, and an actual butler on call were just some of the amenities. Phillipa and I agreed we felt entirely pampered. The luxurious ambiance had quite dispelled the awful slowness and shabbiness of moving with long lines of passengers with all our gear through the cold, drafty embarkation building to board the *Norse Goddess*.

It was after four when we sailed out of New York harbor. Our party clustered on the Promenade Deck to watch the fun—music blaring, everyone singing, drinks with *Norse Goddess* swizzle sticks being consumed all around the pool. Jenny and Willy were not the only ones who cheered and waved as we steamed past the Statue of Liberty. It was a moment to lift the heart of a gal like myself who hadn't been out of Plymouth since our New Zealand honeymoon two years ago, and before that, Goddess knew when. I was not a world traveler like Joe; I had been immersed in the quaint and brooding New England atmosphere my whole life, and now I was thinking that I could, after all, acquire a taste for the exotic and expansive—in a discreet, ladylike, middle-aged way, of course.

Dismissing the waitress offering us a tray of piña coladas, Phillipa was not amused. "Don't drink that weak, tepid stuff, Cass. This mob gaiety is just too, too much. Let's go see if they're serving any decent Earl Grey inside." She elbowed me sharply out of my simpleminded pleasure at the merriment around me and dragged me away to the Mayfair Tearoom where afternoon tea would be served every day of the voyage. Within the lounge, the music blasting outside was dulled a few decibels, and we could look out from a superior distance at the raving hordes.

Phillipa bustled around finding us a waiter to bring a pot of tea and a plate of cakes and pastries. "Ah, this is the life, *far from the madding crowd*," she said, propping her feet up on an empty chair.

"Not as much fun, though." I gazed at her lean black-clad form. "I can hardly wait to see what you've brought with you in all those bags. I know it's your signature color, but is your entire wardrobe black?"

"Wait and see. Black is the traditional Wiccan color, not the rainbow of pastels in which the rest of you waft about. In fact, I think it's time we all got ourselves some long black velvet hooded robes. Or at least, deep purple. And speaking of rainbows, turn around casually and have a look at the gal over there on the windowseat. I wonder why she isn't out there swinging with the swingers."

As a general rule, there's no surprising a clairvoyant. I knew what I'd see before I turned around. It was the rainbow girl in my vision. Nevertheless, I turned as though looking around for a friend, which in a way, I was. "Lovely, isn't she. The gypsy colors suit her. I hope she'll be all right."

Phillipa paused in the act of pouring a decently steaming brew. "You've seen her before, haven't you? Don't tell me..."

"Okay."

"Belay that. *Do* tell me. *Inquiring minds need to know.*"

"It was just a glimpse. You know. But I remember the dress. A man's hand heavy on her shoulder. Then she seemed to slump down or faint. No idea what happened next." I sipped my tea, feeling slightly out of touch with the room, all my senses turning inward. "We'll meet her later," I said dreamily. "If there's a warning to be given, I'll find a way to give it."

"Of course you will. But consider this, the man may have been trying to help not harm her. Especially since she fainted. Have one of these little pastries. The lemon ones look half-decent." Phillipa examined the sweets critically, as she did all foods not produced in her own kitchen. "And put some sugar in your tea. You need sweets when you're in one of these moods."

"I wonder who the heavy-handed man is. I have a rather apprehensive feeling about him."

"And to think we took this cruise to *get away from it all*, as the song goes," Phillipa said. "Well, if you're not going to speak to the young lady now, let's go get changed for dinner. Goddess only knows what grand table Heather has commandeered for this evening."

~

When we returned to our small, elegant courtyard, we found that the Ryans were there already, Jenny and Willy dogpaddling merrily in our private pool. Reclining in a deck chair, Deidre was embroidering mermen and maids on a silk pillow cover, her tiny needle quick and sharp, while she watched the children closely. I noticed that she was wearing half-track glasses—that was something new—looking up over them at every splash and delighted scream.

"Wait till you see..." she called to us, pointing to our stateroom. "That Heather..."

Uh oh, I thought. We waved and ducked into the door of our suite.

Resting against a bronze vase holding an exotic arrangement of lilies and bird-of- paradise blooms was an envelope with the blue and gold crest of the Norse Line. Phillipa held it to her forehead and grinned. "Now let me do an Amazing Kresgin-Cass thing here. Penetrating this thick white envelope with my third eye, I read the words, *The Captain cordially invites Ms. Phillipa Stern and Ms. Cassandra Shipton to have dinner with him...* etc. etc."

"Uh oh," I said aloud this time. In fact, like Phillipa, I had already figured out that the occupants of the six Owners Suites would be prime candidates for dining at the Captain's table. No slouching into the dining room in comfortable casual attire for me. "Guess it's time to unpack the satin dresses and tiaras, then."

Phillipa, who had slipped the invitation out of the envelope, said, "Yes, indeed. Well, at least the wines will be excellent. I wonder..."

"What?"

"I'm getting that *déjà vu* feeling, you know what I mean? As if there's something fateful or fated about this voyage. What *are* you chuckling at? I'm baring my innermost spiritual feelings here."

"Sorry, Phil. I'm just wondering how the Captain and whatever officers are dining with us will react to Fiona, our aging hippie."

Phillipa giggled and unzipped the garment bag hanging on the closet door. She proceeded to shake out and hang her evening outfits. I was pleased to see that, although shimmering black prevailed, at least one cocktail dress was a brilliant scarlet.

Morticia steps out, I thought. "Wow, so chic," I said aloud. "Well, wait till you see what Heather had me buy. They're like bridesmaid dresses—I'll probably never get an opportunity to wear them again. I mean, really, can you see me wearing this anywhere in Plymouth?" Reverently, I removed the green silk Caroline Rose tunic with cape from my own bag. I would save that for the final *Goddess* gala.

"I see what you mean. It's a bit over the top for *Bert's Cove* or the *East Bay Grille.* But that's why the goddess made attics. You may take another cruise one of these days, and like Miss Haversham, you just brush off the cobwebs, and there you are."

"You are such a comfort, Phil."

"I know. So...who's first for the marble tub?"

CHAPTER FOUR

Sigh no more, ladies, sigh no more,
Men were deceivers ever,
One foot in sea and one on the shore,
To one thing constant never.

– William Shakespeare

Captain Lars Johansson was as looming, vigorous, and bearded as a Viking, with deep-set eyes of the particular dark blue of the Atlantic at sunset. He towered above us all, smiling fiercely. I could just hear him thinking, *Another friggin' dinner party. Public relations, be damned!*

Feeling trussed as a roasting chicken in my new Donna Ricco cap sleeve cocktail dress (conservative beige, almost the color of my sandy hair) I projected my attention outward beyond my discomfort. If I could stop thinking about myself while introductions were being made, I might be able to register those names and faces.

Along with the Captain, the ship's doctor, Daniel Simic M.D., was also present at the pre-dinner cocktail party in a reserved corner of the Atrium, both gentlemen looking splendid in uniform, although Simic was a head shorter, swarthy, with warm brown eyes and tightly curled dark hair.

I couldn't help wondering what Joe would have looked like in sharp dress whites with lots of gold braid instead of his usual Greenpeace sweat shirt and Greek cap. It was an exciting thought. *Oh, why wasn't Joe here tonight, with or without the sweatshirt? Who cares about logging in Africa? Don't they have plenty of trees anyway?* How I wished I were making this romantic voyage with Joe, sharing the insistent presence of the sea, the uninterrupted vistas of light, the shipboard kisses.

Phillipa nudged me out of that pleasing reverie, none too gently. "*Earth to Cass, Earth to Cass...*" I realized that, while I was *in a galaxy far, far away,* the social hostess, Ulla Nobel, pale gold and as curvy as a mermaid, had been introducing our dinner partners to each other.

The occupants of the other three Owners Suites proved to be as varied as the expression "shipboard acquaintances" would suggest. Ignoring the agony of wearing what were aptly termed "killer heels," I concentrated on committing my dinner companions to my unreliable memory.

A British psychiatrist and his wife, Tony and Lindsay Grenville; he was gray-eyed with a wicked smile, rather piratical. His back was hunched, but that was somewhat hidden by his beautifully tailored single-breasted tux. His wife was a well-preserved, perfectly-groomed, striking ash blonde who probably sat on several museum boards, or at least was a Friend of the London Symphony Orchestra.

Also sharing our private courtyard, a couple from Pennsylvania who had achieved the desirable status of Frequent Cruisers, Rudy and Muffy Koch from Poughkeepsie, New York. He was a broadly built professor of cultural anthropology at Vassar whose piercing ice-blue eyes, unruly thick brown hair, and strong square chin must have revved up interest in *Coming of Age in Samoa* among his gal students. His tux was not as elegant as Grenville's, but his muscular shoulders filled it out heroically. Muffy (*short for muffled?*) had the prim, fragile, colorless air of a perfect handmaiden.

A fantasy author, Jason Severin, traveling with his mother, Madeline, (whom he affectionately called "Mad"). Aesthetic and intense, they both appeared to be somewhat haunted, as if they were escapees from some Tennessee Williams play. His lambskin blazer and white cashmere sweater conceded little to the formality of the occasion. Her well-cut, shoulder-length hair was strikingly white against a slash of red lipstick. I made a mental note to check for Jason Severin's books in the ship's library. I hoped they wouldn't be about dragons, though. I'd had enough fire-breathing last year.

Among the other notable guests from the Penthouse and Riviera decks joining the captain (*Good Goddess help us*) was Boston's Bishop Aiden Guilfoyle in full regalia, his eyebrows as thick as two black caterpillars, being seated next to Fiona!

The traditional newlyweds, occupying the Romance Suite, Tyler and Paige Bratton, both tall tan blonds with taut abs, were leaning together as if already three sheets to the wind. *Or maybe drunk with love?*

The stylish Japanese Tea Master, Ken Ogata, was as lean, pale, and gray as one who had survived too long on artfully arranged but minimalist meals. *Occidental eyes. His mom, no doubt.* Wearing a formal black silk Japanese haori jacket, he moved with economy and grace, and yet wasn't in the least self-effacing. *Not easy to read, even for me. A man to watch, and watch out for,* my sixth sense suggested.

And our gypsy girl, her flawless skin a Caribbean almond-brown, was introduced as Calypso del Mar, a novice reporter on cable TV's weather channel, whose companion Rob Negrini, an investment advisor, was absent. I would have said there was a dark cloud surrounding her, but I really don't see auras. Just the barest shadowy impression.

"A touch of seasickness perhaps," Calypso said, and was urged by Dr. Simic to seek his professional care for her boyfriend. *Instantly I could see the guy, smooth and handsome in the nondescript way of catalog models, but a man of secrets and worries. The casino lights were up and had drawn him like a moth. Not an illness the good doctor could cure.*

Also absent was Ken Ogata's teen-aged nephew, Rikyu Ogata, who'd opted for meeting friends his own age at the Starfish Sushi Bar. Deidre's children, too, had dined separately on burger specials at the Terrace Cafe. Exhausted by non-stop glee, they were now tucked up in bed under the care of a ship's "nanny," hired by the Norse line as a Youth Counselor.

The statuesque Ms. Nobel shepherded us smoothly to the captain's table, which was set with crisp white linens in the grandest of the *Goddess's* restaurants, *Le Consulat*. The first course was served, choice of smoked salmon with condiments or escargot in garlic butter, while the wine steward filled our glasses with a crisp Sancerre.

Looking around at our new friends, Phillipa was not impressed with their compatibility. "Jumping Green Jacks," she whispered in my ear. "Is this the dinner party from Hell or what?"

Exchanging a few words in Swedish with the captain, her tone commiserating, Ulla had probably drawn the same conclusion as Phillipa. She undulated off to other duties without discernible regret.

"Yeah," I said. "*No Exit*. And, hey, look at Heather. *What is it that* she's doing with her eyes. Looks like some kind of crazed signal."

Phillipa leaned my way to explain, *sotto voce*: "I believe she's drawing our attention to the fact that Fiona has been dowsing her snails with a crystal pendant. Don't look now, but she seems to be leaning *over* Heather to explain to Jason Severin that the pendulum detects poisons. I don't know what Heather thinks we can do about Fiona, but not to worry. It isn't as if we're traveling on a train where Captain Johansson can put her and her pendulum off at the next station. Thankfully, we are non-stop to Bermuda. And besides, Deidre's caught the scene and is distracting Bishop Guilfoyle very nicely. Dare I hope she's pinning him down on the ordination of women?"

As if I could refrain from wheeling around to watch this tableau! Severin was listening to Fiona's friendly chat with the startled expression her presence often inspires in strangers. *The fantasy writer meets the real thing.*

Calypso, who was seated on my other side, asked me what my friend Fiona was doing with the crystal. "In Jamaica where I was born some of the old ladies get into stuff like that, but not my family. We are Catholics. My grandmother is very devout and would not allow such things. Do you suppose there's anything to it?"

"You must ask Fiona yourself," I said. "Fiona Ritchie. She'll be glad to explain how she uses the pendulum." And Goddess knew what else she'd reveal about the lot of us. "It's just her little ritual before eating. Sort of like saying grace."

"I guess the escargot passed muster," Phillipa muttered, arranging salmon on a toast point. "I trust she won't go through that rigmarole with every course."

"Maybe it's just snails she doesn't trust," I said. "You never can tell where they've been."

Fortunately, that proved to be the case. As we wound our way through the rest of the menu, from entrees, Atlantic Haddock in Saffron Sauce and Beef Wellington, to desserts, Profiteroles and Pomegranate Sorbets, only the haddock was subjected to Fiona's "field test." To her credit, in the past I've seen how the pendulum goes neurotic in her hands when dangled over poisoned food. This has proved to be a useful survival tool.

Ken Ogata at the opposite end of the table from Captain Johansson was explaining Wabi Sabi, an appreciation of the impermanent, imperfect, and aged, to Muffy on one side of him and Paige on the other, not the ideal audience for the contemplation of Zen precepts. Paige's eyes were glazed; she drank Pommard steadily but barely nibbled at the Beef Wellington on her plate.

Although Dr. Simic glanced her way speculatively as if waiting for the young woman to slip under the table and be in need of rescue, he seemed much more interested in carrying on a conversation with Phillipa, describing restaurants that were "not to be missed" in Bermuda. The attentive way he was inclining toward my friend in her plunging black gown made me wonder if soon he would be offering to escort her himself to Bermuda's fine inns. Would he be deterred if he knew she traveled with a circle of Wiccans?

"I don't trust doctors," Paige blurted out, apropos of nothing we were talking about. "They can do anything they want to a girl with drugs," she confided to Muffy across the table.

"Not to my girl, he won't." Tyler pounded on the table with a feeble fist, sloshing red wine. His fine cleft chin sagged low over his stained shirt.

An embarrassed silence descended broken only by Muffy's nervous giggle. I took a long fortifying drink of wine. As Phillipa had predicted, the Sancerre was to die for.

"Such a cliché, date-rape drugs," Jason Severin broke the impasse. "But then real-life predators are so rarely creative."

"Unlike fictional scoundrels?" Phillipa said.

"Ketamine, that's one of them," Heather said thoughtfully. "Vets use Ketamine as a sedative. A drug often stolen in break-ins."

Fiona, who had apparently found her Atlantic Haddock harmless and was sopping up the last of the saffron sauce with a bit of bread, changed the subject adroitly by asking Captain Johansson if he gave any credence to the myth of the Devil's Triangle, otherwise known as the Bermuda Triangle. All conversation stopped while the rest of us listened.

The captain laughed *basso profondo*. "My dear lady, you must realize that I am asked that question on every voyage. As one who's been sailing this route for several years now, I can assure you that you are as safe on these waters as you are in any other part of the Atlantic."

"Hardly reassuring," Phillipa murmured quietly to me but Dan Simic heard and smiled sardonically.

"The Bermuda Triangle or so-called Devil's Triangle," the Captain continued, "is a figment of some writer's weird imagination."

"My Jason's work-in-progress is on that very subject, isn't it, dear?" Madeline Severin smiled fondly at her son who scowled in return. "That's why we decided to make this voyage. Nautical gossip, local color, the Sargasso Sea and so forth. A research trip."

"Not to mention a tax deduction as well." Phillipa was still speaking quietly for the amusement of me and the doctor. His spaniel eyes gazed at her with more than avuncular interest.

Phillipa's earlier tarot reading sprang into my mind. She'd turned up the major arcana card called The Devil, dismissing it with, "What's a cruise without a bit of carnal temptation?" If my clever friend had an Achilles' heel, it was her susceptibility to male charm. Even an apparently contented wife may be vulnerable to shipboard romance. But Phillipa's husband Stone was a wonderful man, caring and intelligent. And she loved him devotedly.

"Be that as it may, I rest easier knowing that we have Cass here, our own clairvoyant traveling with us," Fiona was telling the captain confidingly, oblivious to looks of interest and alarm around the table.

Tony Grenville smile was mocking. "I've treated women with psychic abilities. Inevitably, they prove to have a talent for rapid calculation based on empirical evidence. Nevertheless so-called witches abound in the West Country of Britain."

"Just another bloke who wouldn't know a real witch if he fell over her broomstick," Phillipa said sweetly.

I kicked Phillipa's foot and shook my head at Fiona warningly.

Deidre stepped in to salvage the social situation, her eyes mischievous. "I, for one, have no fear of the Devil or his triangles. We have Bishop Guilfoyle to pray for us, although I believe St. Christopher, patron saint of travelers, has been demoted. We have one of the foremost captains in the Norse fleet with an impeccable safety record. *And* we're sailing on a state-of-the-art floating hotel with every modern safeguard. Relax, Fiona."

Captain Johansson smiled at Deidre, the first genuine smile that had crossed his public face this evening. "Well said, young lady. Let's have a toast then. To a safe and splendid voyage in excellent company!"

We raised our glasses. "So must it be," said Phillipa and I in unison.

CHAPTER FIVE

For whatever we lose (like a you or a me)
it's always ourselves that we find in the sea.

– E. E. Cummings

Later, with Heather ordering what she called a *"liqueur digestive,"* the five of us gathered at the Blue Note, a jazz bar on the Blue Vista deck. The waiter brought the bottle with several small glasses. Immediately, we fell to gossiping about the Captain's dinner guests.

"I had a most interesting conversation with the Bishop," Deidre said. "He sees dead people. He says he's been seeing specters his whole life, and this aberration—his word, not mine—actually contributed to his call to the Church. While his superiors aren't thrilled about his specialized perceptions, he's not being sent to some half-way house for possessed priests either. In fact, he's on the roster of Catholic clergy who are allowed to perform exorcisms. Inspired to confront Satan, you know."

"I'm surprised he let *that* cat out of the bag," Fiona said.

"Well, the subject of 'glamourous powers' naturally came up after you began waving that crystal over your food," Deidre scolded "Perhaps keeping a low profile at the Captain's Dinner might have been a more discreet course of action, Fiona!"

"*As if...*" Fiona laughed, her booming, full-bodied, irresistible laugh that got us all going. "So, what ghost on the ramparts has the good Bishop seen recently, Dee?" she demanded.

"Well, my dears...there was a tragic event on this very ship. Yes, last year on the *Norse Goddess of the Sea.* Don't you remember?" Deidre asked quietly. "The bride who disappeared? Christy Callahan, I believe her name was. Her husband was detained by the Brits in Bermuda for more than ten days, and the FBI got in on it, too."

The light dawned over Marblehead as all of us made the connection. The disappearance had been a major news story, with a great deal of suspicion focusing on the groom, Bobby Callahan. He'd admitted to quarreling with his new wife, but claimed to have been drinking with some buddies he'd met on board at the time of her disappearance. After initially supporting his story, the bride's family gradually became estranged from the young man and complained that the FBI's investigation had not been sufficiently thorough. There was even talk of a civil suit naming Bobby as the defendant; But there hadn't been enough evidence to proceed.

"Are you saying that Bishop Guilfoyle saw the ghost of Christy Callahan," Phillipa demanded.

"No, I did." Deidre's voice had gone even softer, and she was whispering now. "*I saw something like a spectral figure in my cabin* while the children were at the Terrace Cafe. Not really a ghost, you know, more like a brief glimpse of white lace and a veil. I just thought if I confessed this incident to the Bishop, he might set my mind at rest. Catholics don't encourage that sort of thing, you know. And who needs a ghost in her damned fancy Owners Suite, for Goddess' sake? I'd counted on the bishop to assign me ten Hail Marys with a warning to stop hitting the

Irish whiskey, but no such luck. Instead he tells me, *he sees them, too*. Ghosts. Dead people."

"There's a lesson in there somewhere. You're looking in the wrong place for psychic support," Phillipa said, putting her arm around Deidre's slender shoulders. "I tell you what. Tomorrow, Heather will pin down the lovely Ulla on exactly which cabin the Callahans occupied on that fateful voyage. Maybe yours, maybe not. More likely, the Romance Suite where the Brattons are bunking in splendor. But for tonight, you'll put the eerie bride out of your mind and, like Peter Pan, *think lovely thoughts* so you can fly. Remember this is meant to be a merry vacation for us hard-working sisters in crime."

"And that means *thou shalt not see drowned women materialize in thy cabin!*" I added.

"Okay," Deidre said in a small voice. "It was probably just a trick of the light anyway."

Fiona's eyebrows rose in disbelief at Deidre disavowing her own sixth sense, but instead of delivering her usual homily on following one's intuition, she changed the subject. "Speaking of brides, that was a strange remark Paige made," she said.

"Almost as if she wanted to skewer poor Dan Simic, who was terribly taken aback. After all, he'd never met her before tonight," Phillipa said.

"In her condition, past and present get muddled. Perhaps she was recalling a previous experience, not necessarily her own," I said. "Ironically, alcohol can rob a gal of her inhibitions as well as other drugs do. Better for the would-be ravager, even, because it's all perfectly legal."

"Simply can't hold her liquor, poor gal," Heather said, filling glasses liberally all around.

Deidre tasted hers and made a terrible face. "Eeck. Tastes like hair tonic. Frankly, I don't know how you can drink this stuff. I'll just have a nice cup of Irish coffee, if you don't mind, Heather."

"This *stuff*, as you call it, is a secret blend of healthful herbs that has enabled the monastery of Chartreuse to devote themselves to meditation and prayer since the 17th century," Heather declared loftily.

"And it's110 proof, don't forget that," Phillipa said, examining the bottle.

"Elixir of Long Life," Fiona declared, reaching into her reticule and drawing out a green pamphlet that proved to be *The Story of Chartreuse*. Fiona's ability to unearth a relevant item from that magic carryall was a source of constant amazement. Besides butterscotch candies, rosemary and sage oils, smelling salts, and the odd banishing charm, Fiona's reticule had even been known to hold a pistol given to her by the late Rob Angus Ritchie, but I breathed a sigh of relief knowing she couldn't possibly have spirited that one past the port's security personnel.

"Hmmm," Phillipa mused, studying the story, "Did you know, Heather, that there are 130 plants, herbs, roots, leaves, barks, along with your basic brandy in this marvelous Elixir of yours? Says here that only three monks know the entire recipe, and they are never allowed to travel together. So I wonder if it's a good idea for us five to travel on the same ship. Surely the world couldn't handle such a loss." She laughed darkly, her wicked stepmother laugh. "Well, Cass ought to be able to decode the secret recipe, if anyone can, being both an herbalist *and* a clairvoyant."

I was about to make my stock speech that clairvoyance wasn't "on call"—it comes and goes without conscious control. But just then, Tony and Lindsay Grenville wandered in, chatting with Rudy Koch. They sat in the shadows of the Blue Note where through long windows the moon could be seen rising high over choppy silver-tipped waves. The steady vibration of the engines was more noticeable here on the top deck. *We're at sea*, I thought, with a thrill of wonder, *a ship of souls alone on a vast ocean.*

"Oh, let's join Rudy and the rest," Heather enthused. "I want to catch up on the latest news from my alma mater. I'll bet Rudy draws droves of coeds into his lectures on obscure primitive rituals. If those Vassar gals still go for iceberg eyes and a superhero jawline, that is."

We drifted over and sat around in a casual crowd. I noticed that Heather and Fiona had their heads together, our two loose cannons on deck.

The jazz musicians returned from their break and began a soulful rendition of *Night and Day,* drowning out the subliminal sounds of ship and sea. One of the ship's young officers, who had just come off duty, strode purposefully over to Deidre and asked her to dance. She'd been sitting quietly, gazing into space, half-listening to our babbling. With an abstracted smile, she got up and let him lead her onto the diminutive dance floor. I had the feeling if he'd asked her to accompany him to a walk on the plank, she'd have gone like a sleepwalker without protest.

Fiona elbowed me in the ribs and smirked. "We hummed him over here. Heather and me." she murmured. "Deidre needs a bit of enlightening up."

Humming is a nice quiet, useful little spell that Fiona has taught us. And when the five women hum under their breaths with a shared intent, it's surprisingly effective. Sympathetic vibration, enchantment "across a crowded room."

Does it work? We've seen it accomplish wonders in a courtroom, unsettling an abusive husband. I hadn't thought of it as an attractor. Perhaps that fresh-faced young officer with the nearly invisible blond buzz cut just happened to catch sight of pretty, petite Deidre and was overcome with the desire to dance with her. *And then again...* We never really know if we're working magic or if the universe just happens to be falling in with our wishes coincidentally.

Deidre was looking up at her partner (whose name, we learned, was Gerry Leary) as if surprised to find herself dancing. They made an attractive couple, he in his crisp white uniform and Deidre in soft blue chiffon and sparkling silver shoes, dancing well together to the romantic medley that the musicians were playing with occasional riffs of improvisation. (Did I actually hear *That Old Black Magic*, or imagine it? Why has no one written a song for *That Old White Do-no-harm Magic*, I wondered.) Lighting in the jazz bar was moody, changing colors, shifting shadows. Deidre laughed at something her partner said, and the sadness of this past year seemed to fall away for a brief interlude. A sleepwalker came awake to the moment. We watched and smiled.

Believing is seeing.

◆

"Muffy doesn't care for night life," Rudy Koch explained his solo sojourn in the bar. "Jazz now, that's an anthropologist's kind of music, and this trio is rather good, don't you think?"

Heather wanted to know what was going on at Vassar these days. Coed dorms already had been old hat in her day, and political outrage had diminished with the end of the Vietnam Conflict. Koch said that the real activism now was in religion not politics. Besides Christian fellowships and Jewish unions, there was even a Pagan study group. Fiona got into the conversation at that point, and between her and Heather, Rudy Koch soon had a full report on our own Wiccan circle and activities.

"Are cultural anthropologists interested in the upswing of Pagan religions?" I asked.

"My own fascination has been with the Caribbean religions. Cruising is my way of combining a vacation with a field trip. Usually we go to Jamaica or Haiti, though. The British have pretty well sanitized Bermuda. Ask Grenville, he knows. Still, there are elements worth investigating." Koch had swerved away from a direct answer, but I felt he was indeed interested in us Wiccans. Anything he believed to be a walk on the wild side would attract him, Santeria and the like. Suddenly, as happens to me sometimes, I saw another Koch superimposed on the real flesh-and-blood man before me. He was wearing a colorful big-sleeved shirt, and something syrupy and red was pouring down the side of his face. As fast as it had appeared, the image vanished, and again I was facing the icy eyes of the handsome professor, now in ordinary attire, without a tie, his dress shirt open at the neck, casual. I looked away quickly, hoping the pupils of my eyes had not widened as they do when I get an instant vision.

Alas, something had sparked between us which he was mistaking for sexual interest. He smiled. The jazz trio pursued the Cole Porter theme, *It Was Just One of Those Things*. "Care to dance?" he asked me quietly. Almost without volition, I found I was on my feet and in his arms.

What a suffocating experience! Touch has always told me much more than I ever wanted to know about other people. At that moment, dancing with Rudy Koch, his hand on my back, his cheek not pressed against mine but so close I could feel its heat, his chest against my thin beige silk, I felt only an overwhelming desire to escape before this man would find a way to control my thoughts. *What was wrong with me!* Couldn't I dance with anyone but Joe? How ridiculous. I forced myself to breath deeply and slowly, dispelling my frantic foolishness. Clearly, what I was picking up was Rudy's relationship with Muffy. He the controller, she the controlled. *Yes, that must be it.*

Chance favors the disturbed witch. One of my fabulous heels caught against the leg of a pedestal cocktail table, and I went skidding right out of Rudy's arms, flew across the room under swirling lights, and landed in the lap of Tony Grenville. Fortunately, he caught me in his arms before I could tumble to the floor.

"Well, hello," he said coolly, very James-Bond British.

"Oh, hello. I mean, sorry. I haven't hurt you, have I?" I disentangled myself awkwardly and fell into a nearby chair. Rudy strolled over to see if I'd twisted an ankle, and I was aware of my friends' concerned faces turned toward my fiasco.

"I'm okay, everyone. I think my darned heel cracked in two. I'll just catch my breath here for a moment, if you'll forgive me, Rudy." He bowed gallantly and moved off to visit his spellbinding charm on Heather.

Calypso del Mar came into the bar, lighting it up in a shimmering dress of yellow and red. Her wild mop of chestnut hair was twisted up on her head, a few tendrils escaping, long gold hoops dangling from her small neat ears, showing off a bare neck both graceful and vulnerable. All heads turned, especially Rudy's. I couldn't help wondering why such a high-testosterone type had married the pale, wistful Muffy. How badly did he need someone he could control? The choices love makes are often so astonishing to outsiders, the inner truth of a marriage so impenetrable (unfortunately, not so much to me).

I wrenched my attention back to the Grenvilles. "Lindsay, please forgive me for crushing your husband. I don't know how I managed to gain so much momentum."

Lindsay sipped a crème de menthe frappe and smiled vaguely. "I dare say he enjoyed it," she said smoothly. "Didn't you, darling?"

"Makes a welcome change, my dear," he replied, patting the back of my hand. "No permanent damage, I assure you," he said to me. His touch informed me. Whereas Rudy's physicality had been suffocating, Tony's vibes were dark and secret like an underground river.

"Pity. A little shaking up might do you good," Lindsay said, looking not at her husband but at the youthful, uniformed Gerry Leary dancing with Deidre, something hungry in her eyes.

I didn't have to be a clairvoyant to feel a kind of poisonous atmosphere surrounding the Grenvilles. I could have sworn right then that the chief sport of these two people was one-upping each other in every way, including sexually.

If I hoped to enjoy this voyage among a mass of strangers, I was definitely going to need to screen out some of these discomforting intuitions. Something that worked like sun block, I decided. A lotion to keep out harmful thought-rays and prevent psychic burnout. As an herbalist, my mind immediately leaped to which essentials oils might do the trick. Well, sage for sure. Fennel. Wormwood. Camphor, but who wanted to go around smelling like mothballs? Luckily, I'd packed an herbal first aid kit for just such emergencies. Protectors, restoratives, energizers, attractors, and banes to avert evil. Fold-up wand in a carrying case. Comfrey for safe travel, ginger to prevent *mal de mer*.

"You dropped in just in time to lift me out of the doldrums, Cassandra." Tony brought me back to the moment. He had a wonderfully deep voice, theatrical and mesmerizing. "Was it true what your friend claimed? Do you have the powers of the mythic Greek Cassandra? And what are you drinking? Let me order another..."

"Heather has got us a bit high on Chartreuse, and I've definitely had enough alcohol. Perhaps an espresso, if that's available. But to answer your question, maybe it's like you said earlier. I read the subliminal clues very quickly. As do psychiatrists, I believe."

Lindsay laughed. A perfectly musical laugh appropriate to Ascot and the Queen's Garden Party. "You're wrong there, my dear Cass. If ever a man were completely clueless..."

The clueless one was signaling to the waiter, who nodded *si* to *due espresso* and hurried off to fulfill the request.

Just to say anything that would interrupt this Noel-Coward brittle banter that obsessed the Grenvilles, I blurted out, "Speaking of clues, if I were to read you two, I'd guess that you met in a theatrical production. Something Shakespearean, perhaps?" So desperate was I to avoid being their bone of contention that I continued to rattle wildly on before either Tony or Lindsay could interrupt. "Oh, let me just take a wild swing. *As You Like It.* That was it. Or maybe *The Taming of the Shrew.* I bet you'd have been wonderful together in that—so spirited and venomous—but if it wasn't a college production, what was it? Oh, I *am* seeing such a lot of ivory roses." And I was. With my third eye, the invisible one in the middle of the forehead. Many bouquets of long-stemmed creamy roses.

"Brilliant!" Lindsay said. "It was amateur theater, but a very decent one with a devoted following. We were dedicated to the Elizabethans. An occasional well-known actor gone dotty would join the cast for a bit of slumming." She almost smiled, remembering, and took another sip of her frappe. "Tony used to smother me in ivory roses, didn't you, darling? I felt he was visualizing me as a dead body. A touch of necrophilia, you know. We did *Othello*, too, as it happens. Do you tell fortunes, too? I'd thought of asking that little gypsy over there, the one dancing with Rudy, if she read palms or something, but you are clearly the amazing one. Aren't you confounded, Tony?"

Tony's gray eyes were steely. "I believe there were a number of write-ups about our Elizabethan theater. Some mention of us as well. We were quite well received. Perhaps you read something about us, Cassandra? Strangely enough, the theater was called

The Bermuda. Scholars supposed Bermuda to have been the inspirational source of Prospero's island in *The Tempest*, can you imagine? There were accounts of its discovery in Shakespeare's time. 'Bermuda or Isle of Devils, Silvester Jourdain, 1610.'

"Synchronicity," I murmured.

"I was in my thirties, fresh out of psychiatric residency," Tony continued; crinkles of pleasure appeared around his eyes. "I'd fooled around in theater before, at Oxford, and liked it. After my hospital experiences, I felt I needed an antidote to the real madness I'd encountered as a resident, and *The Bermuda Theater* seemed to be just what the doctor ordered. You'd have forgotten reading about us, of course, Cassandra but everything is forever imprinted on one's subconscious."

"Yes, that must be it," I agreed at once. "I'm sorry, Lindsay, I don't tell fortunes, and I doubt very much that Miss del Mar does, either. It might even be against the ship's regulations, like card sharking or something. I wouldn't want to disappoint Captain Johansson."

"Pity. But I understand perfectly, my dear," Lindsay said. "Speaking of disappointing our rugged Viking captain, what do we have here? Is this the famous invisible escort come to claim his gypsy?"

It was the first any of us had seen of Rob Negrini. The image I'd had of a male model was accurate enough, though—those classic features and expressionless gray-blue eyes, those wide shoulders and tapered waist, and of course, the sexy shadow of a one-day beard. His appearance had certainly brought Lindsay to life. She watched his every move avidly as he cut in on Rudy and Calypso. Negrini danced her showily around the dance floor, while she clung to him and sang softly in his ear. Soon he swirled her out of the bar and onto the deck awash with midnight moonlight.

Lindsay sighed. Tony laughed. Like Cinderella, I got out of there before all the magic had turned to ashes.

CHAPTER SIX

...so all the night-tide, I lie down by the side
Of my darling, my darling, my life and my bride.

– Edgar Allan Poe

"Jesus, Mary, and Joseph, I saw her again," Deidre said at breakfast the next day.

Jenny and Willy, having demolished plates of scrambled eggs and strawberry waffles, had run off eagerly to the Lido Deck Kids Center to join the scheduled 7- to 12-year-old ship's tour. We grown-ups had ambled more slowly through the buffet, marveling at the largesse, contemplating heaped plates with hungry anticipation.

"The briny bride?" Phillipa asked, poking at her made-to-order mushroom omelet as if judging an omelet contest. She put a fragment on her fork and tasted it experimentally. "Tarragon, I think," she said. "Not bad. I'd like to see their kitchens."

"You should have gone with the kids, then," Deidre said. "Listen, I could almost make out the bride's face this time. Under bunches of veil. And I think there were fronds of seaweed hanging off her." She shuddered delicately. "You know, this kind of thing never happened to me before Will...before last year. Do you think being a widow...?"

"You've had more than one emotionally wrenching experience," I said. "It's not surprising that your psyche might have been jolted into a new place with new sensitivities. Like one of those stories where the hero has a near death experience and comes back to life with an unexpected paranormal power."

"Yeah, well who needs it? I'd like to put this gift right back into Pandora's box or wherever it came from. I only wish all of you could have seen that disgusting mildew-green bridal gown."

"Christy Callahan was wearing a rose satin cocktail dress when she went over the side of the *Norse Goddess* last year. With matching shoes. One of which was left on the International Deck outside the ballroom," Phillipa pointed out the flaw in Deidre's vision. "Ulla wouldn't say a word, and Dan was rather reluctant to discuss the matter—the Norse Line's gag rule, I don't doubt—but I had the whole story from Simic's nurse, Kirsti Hansen."

"Psychic visions are often symbolic. What you see is archetypical," Fiona reminded us. "What do you think, Cass? Isn't this ripe papaya to die for?"

Not sure which question to answer, I ploughed ahead. "Heavenly papaya. Ghastly ghost. But I'm a clairvoyant. I don't see spectral stuff, which is what is happening here. My visions are usually spot on, slices of reality, sort of a psychic surveillance camera," I said. "Trouble is, I only catch part of the action. Interpretation is the tricky business. But in Dee's case..."

"You know I'm the one who usually tries to keep us out of whatever trouble Cass is getting us into," Deidre interrupted. "But this specter seems to be pointing at me, beckoning to me. Do you think that means I'm meant to do something about her?"

"Like what?" Heather asked curiously, just as if we'd never been involved in crime before. "I wonder if they make mimosas in the morning." She looked around for a waiter, and one appeared at her elbow almost at once. *Must be something they learn at Vassar,* I thought.

"Might be like solving what they call a cold case," Deidre said.

"A very cold case indeed," Phillipa said, picking apart a croissant critically. "And besides, by tomorrow we'll be in Bermuda and have our hands full of hibiscus or whatever. And incidentally, I'll be having dinner with Dan Simic at this very swank restaurant owned by a major film star." She smiled like Zelda with a dish of crème fraiche.

"Girls, girls. You're not paying attention here. This is serious," Fiona scolded us, the Wiccan headmistress with her unruly charges. "Dee is seeing what is probably the image of a girl who may have been murdered on this very ship. She's responding to some very real karmic energy. Energy that should not be allowed to roam freely on board, doing Goddess-knows-what damage. How many frightening stories have we all read about the harm caused by haunted ships? No, no...this bride business has come to our attention for a reason. Dee's instincts must be respected, this is a matter we should and will investigate."

"Sure, and it's *much* more stimulating than the bridge tournament in the Promenade Deck games room," Phillipa said.

A waiter with a drink-laden tray loomed over us. "Oh goodie, it's our mimosas," Heather said. "Slosh them around to everyone, please. Just the thing to brighten us up."

"Oh, gee, that's right—we'll be in Bermuda by tomorrow," Deidre said, taking the frosty glass that Heather pushed her way. "What is this? Orange juice and seltzer? How much can we find out once we're docked? There'll be all those excursions. The aquarium, the perfume factory, the caves, and, Goddess help us, the shopping in Hamilton! And I thought I heard that you, Fiona, would be involved in some kind of demonstration this afternoon in the Mayfair Tearoom."

All heads swiveled toward Fiona, who smiled modestly and sipped her effervescent drink. "Oh no, nothing special. Ken Ogata is giving a Japanese tea ceremony during regular tea time in the lounge, and I'm going to be his 'honored guest of the spirit.' Some of the ship's crew have knocked together the outline of a tea house from wooden slats. Inside every tea house is a small alcove, *tokonoma*, where a poem painted on a scroll and other art objects are displayed. The honored guest is seated there to—I don't know what you'd call it—maybe channel the spirit. Mind, heart, and spirit are the essence of the tea ceremony. Ken and I had a long talk about that, and other Zen matters. Should be fun."

Dee grinned impishly, a good thing to see in a subdued widow. "Maybe when you're channeling the spirit, you'll catch sight of my ghost Christy and tell her to *begone, foul spirit,* or whatever you do to exorcise them. Now let's all drink up our juices and go for a bracing jog on deck."

"You and Heather jog, I'll stroll," Phillipa said. "I'm saving my strength for the pink sands of Bermuda. And Samhain. And by the way, since the wall of mist between worlds is thinnest at Samhain, maybe that will be the time to really channel the drowned bride."

"I'll stroll with Phil. I'm not sure it's seemly to jog at my age, all that flapping of flesh." I said. "But here's the thing, Dee...if it was murder and not some sort of accident, I don't know how we can solve a crime that took place months ago on another voyage."

"*You* could," Fiona said. "If you'd just get your clairvoyance under control."

"In your dreams, Fiona. You have no idea how ill that makes me. Rather like seasickness of the soul." Just thinking about deliberately courting visions made me long for a piece of candied ginger. I'd brought several pounds of it to ward off nausea, but so far, all of us had been great sailors, even the kids.

Deidre and Heather set off at a brisk pace up the stairs to the jogging track on the Skyline Sports Deck. Deidre, small and quick, wearing blue and white running shorts and t-shirt, blonde curls bouncing; Heather, tall and graceful, in a russet jogging suit, bronze braid swinging from side to side.

It had been a mistake even to talk about the possibility of a clairvoyant vision. I'm susceptible to glaring light, and as I watched my two friends' ambitious departure, the morning sun hitting the metal railing was like an arrow straight into my subconscious mind. I felt myself eddying away from the present time into a darkened world of vision. It was night. No moon, but the stars were brilliant overhead, and loud upbeat music was drifting out from the dance floor, a big band sound, not the jazz bar. The music covered the noise of a struggle going on in a shadowed alcove. A girl with her back to a hulking lifeboat was making an ineffectual effort to push away a man. Somehow she was unable to scream. Was his hand over her mouth? I couldn't quite see because his back was toward me. He had pushed up the girl's skirt and was savagely thrusting himself into her. A beam of circulating light touched the girl's face, a wilted flower, her eyes closed. Was it Calypso? I had the fleeting idea that her hair was lighter than Calypso's, the mouth fuller. The beam moved on before I could be sure. The girl must have been unconscious to be so passive to the man's brutality.

When I came back to myself, I was in a deck chair with Phillipa patting my hand and Fiona hanging over me with the smelling salts she always carried in her reticule. The many silver bangles she wore on her arm tinkled musically, reassuring me before I even opened my eyes. Nevertheless, I was cross.

"Oh, put that noxious thing away, Fiona. This is all your fault, you know," I said. "What you call exercising conscious control is like trying to ride the Minotaur to me."

"So...never mind the kvetching, Cass. Tell us what you saw," Phillipa demanded.

I described what I'd seen to my two eager friends, and in as much detail as I could remember. I've learned that in visions, as in dreams, important pieces of the picture fade incredibly fast if you don't either write them down or speak them aloud.

"And you think it *might* have been Calypso," Phillipa pressed me.

"Calypso is the name of an enchanting sea nymph." Fiona could always be counted upon to produce odd bits from her eclectic memory as well as her reticule "The one who delayed Ulysses on her island for seven years."

Just speaking the name *Ulysses* made me yearn for Joe, always my best medicine for the psychic whim-whams. *Oh, why isn't he here with me? What if some enchanting sea nymph got her clutches into him?* I shook both my hands to be rid of that negative thought. Time to concentrate on the problems here and now, as no doubt he was doing, the wretch.

"I *wish* I could be sure it was she," I said. "Some moving beam of light touched her face for a nanosecond and then moved on. I couldn't even tell the girl's race for sure. Calypso appears to be a West Indian type, named for their music, don't you think? Those fine-boned features and that burnished skin. And yet... although I've been afraid for Calypso ever since I first saw her, the girl in the vision seemed to be a little lighter in coloring. Anyway, whoever was in the clutches of that rapist, I got the impression that she might have been drugged. Now, isn't that crazy! But, remember Paige Bratton's unfortunate diatribe at the Captain's Dinner? I guess one of us ought to talk to Paige, try to find out what was really going through her mind."

"I certainly hope you won't allow that drunken girl's ranting to make you suspicious of our ship's doctor. I'm just as psychic as the next witch, and I feel that Dan's a very decent and interesting guy," Phillipa protested.

"Oh, sure you do," I said. "And, besides, he knows all the good restaurants on Bermuda."

"No moon you say?" Fiona brought us back to the matter at hand. I nodded. "That could mean either late at night after the moon has set, or at the dark of the moon, which is tomorrow or the next day. But if your fears are right and that was Calypso, it means two things. *One*, the attack will happen on this voyage. *Two*, we've got to find some way of protecting the girl."

"And *three*, this time we're dealing with a hot case not a cold one," Phillipa said.

CHAPTER SEVEN

The rude sea grew civil at her song,
And certain stars shot madly from their spheres
To hear the sea-maid's music.

– William Shakespeare

We gathered in the lounge at four to watch Ken Ogata demonstrate the Japanese tea ceremony—*chado* he called it. He wore a crisp cotton wrap-around garment of midnight blue with those kimono sleeves in which anything could be hidden. Indeed, Ogata removed from one of them a stack of snowy handkerchiefs, which he placed on his low table. The traditional cauldron of water steamed on a hotplate with a bamboo dipper laid nearby. Rikyu Ogata, the master's nephew, wearing a similar coat of grass green, and another Asian passenger, a woman with a round gentle face wearing an aqua velour jogging suit, took their places on the side mats, *tatami*, bowing. Then Fiona made her entrance. We knew the moment she appeared that she had cloaked herself in full glamour, a Druidic talent of hers that the rest of us so envied. Whether mystique or magic, our matronly friend suddenly appeared taller, slimmer, and entirely regal, the coronet of carroty-gray braids encircling her head like a crown. Normally there would be a pencil or crochet hook stuck in those braids, but for this occasion she was wearing two elaborate ebony hairpins that crossed each other to create a decorative X. There was even the impression of a silver aura shining around her head and shoulders.

But I don't see auras, I thought. *Must be something to do with the afternoon sun.* "Holy Hecate, if it isn't the dragon lady in the flesh. I don't know how Fiona does that," muttered Phillipa.

"What's she's wearing?" Heather whispered. "A kimono or a muumuu?" Fiona's silken gray gown was decorated with an elegant spray of cherry blossoms from hem to bosom.

"Oh, be quiet, she looks lovely," Deidre said. "Wish I could look tall like that. Queenly really."

"I'm afraid you'll have to settle for princess-ly," Phillipa said. "You're just too cute and petite."

"Oh, thanks," Deidre said crossly.

"Fiona keeps trying to teach us the glamour but I still can't get it right," I complained. "Well, once almost." *That evening with Joe*, I remembered with a satisfied glow.

"So useful, too. Bewitching the beholder," Phillipa mused. "Do you suppose she's omitting one teeny-tiny instruction, you know like a chef giving you a secret recipe with the one vital step or distinctive ingredient left out?"

"You should know, dearie," Heather said dryly. "So now can we all just be quiet and respectful, watch, and learn?"

A meditative, meticulous ceremony was created before our eyes by the graceful master. After the official guests were served, two volunteer assistants came around with pottery bowls of the thick green tea and a box of bean paste dumplings.

Fiona and Ken Ogata moved toward us through the thirty or so people who comprised his audience. Others who had come to the Mayfair for British tea and the tempting pastry buffet were seated around the edges of the room.

"This is a new experience for me," Ken said. "Hosting *chado* on the high seas. Not as tranquil an atmosphere as the traditional tea hut in a Japanese garden, but the ocean is as beautiful and pure as one could wish."

"It was exquisite, and so fascinating," Heather said. "How long does it take to become a tea master?"

"A student is permitted to host a tea after three years but his education doesn't stop there. I've been studying tea for over twenty-five years, and I'm still learning. Japan—well, from my first visit, I've felt it's my spiritual home," Ken said. "Very few Asians in Bermuda, but one of the hotels features a Japanese restaurant, *The Mikado Ryotei,* with an authentic imported tea hut. I hosted teas there last year, and they've invited me to do so again."

"You must have been born Japanese in a former life," Fiona said. As she plumped down in a chair with a sigh, her glamour began to dissipate. "That was a unique experience."

"*Unique* is the right word. The tea ceremony symbolizes the ephemeral, never to be exactly the same again." With a wave and a smile, the tea master glided away among other guests.

"Do you suppose that means he took this same cruise to Bermuda last year, that he was on board *The Goddess* when Christy Callahan disappeared?" Deidre wondered.

"Yes. He mentioned that. Very upsetting, the whole incident. Threw him off his Zen for days," Fiona said. "Don't you just love this green tea?"

"Tastes like artichoke soup. Really more like a vegetable than a tea." Phillipa sipped thoughtfully. "But the bean paste dumpling had an almond flavor. Extraordinary."

"Tea is a healthy restorative," I said. "Probably why the British are so intrepid and stalwart."

"You have the makings of a true Anglophile," Phillipa said.

"Almond flavor? Ground up apricot pits, more likely," Fiona said. "Bitter almond, you know."

"Oh, great. Cyanide. Well, I suppose one little dumpling won't kill us," I said.

"Not to worry. I dowsed the dumplings just in case," Fiona said. "Low in fat as well."

"Okay, Fiona, I suppose now you're going to tell us that dowsing is part of a sensible metaphysical diet plan?" Phillipa said. Easy for her to make fun, with her perpetually slim, graceful body.

"Of course it is," Fiona said. "It's important, too, to carry a programmed crystal, and there are certain affirmative spells to say before meals."

"Like grace," Deidre suggested impishly.

"Exactly, my dear." Fiona was not to be joshed. "One must also include in one's diet the ancient staples like honey and garlic...barley and fish...cucumbers and melons."

Fiona had managed to capture Phillipa's attention. I could just see the wheels of her culinary brain turning. *Ancient Foods* could be an interesting cookbook theme.

"And if you're seriously dieting, place a whole empty eggshell in the north corner of your kitchen," Fiona said. "But speaking personally, I don't believe in dieting to achieve that emaciated look. A woman ought to have a gently curved abdomen, a natural bosom. And children need to be carried on a hip with some padding on it.

"No crated veal. No tortured goose liver," Heather added her own reflections on a healthy Wiccan diet.

"Perhaps we are all perfect just as we are, goddesses incarnate," Fiona said. "Look at Paige, isn't she the image of divine womanhood?"

"Oh, is that Paige over there, pouring her tea into the fern? And she's alone. I'd just have a word, as the Brits say." Just the opportunity I'd sought. I wandered over casually and sat down at the little tea table next to hers. She was drinking a bottle of Coors Light, and her expression was sullen and exhausted.

"Hi, how are you? We met at the Captain's Dinner. Cass Shipton," I refreshed her mind, which didn't appear at the moment to be firing on all cylinders.

"Oh, yes. Aren't you supposed to be an herb witch or something like that?"

I laughed more politely than I felt. "I have an online herbal business," I said. "*Cassandra Shipton, Earthlore Herbal Preparations and Cruelty-Free Cosmetics.*"

"No fortune-telling, then? Lindsay Grenville told me you're a whiz at fortunes."

"Just the occasional flash of woman's intuition, you might say." I signaled the waiter and ordered a pot of Earl Grey with two cups. "Would you like me to have a look at your hand? I know a little about reading palms." Not really, but I wanted the opportunity to catch the vibes and to ask some questions. "May I pour you a cup of tea?"

"Tea?" she said hazily, as if I'd mentioned some obscure native drink.

"A cup of tea will warm your hands, better for reading," I said.

"Okay. Awesome." She drained the bottle and propped it in the same standing fern plant that was recovering from Japanese green tea.

The Earl Grey arrived in a real pot with a little plate of cookies on the side. She stirred in lots of sugar and drank hers quickly, making a face.

"Now let me see your right hand please. You are right-handed?" She nodded and thrust toward me such a perfectly manicured, smooth-skinned hand that I wanted to hide my own under the table.

This little drama of mine would probably go straight back to Lindsay, but I couldn't resist such an ideal opportunity to pump the girl about her bizarre accusation on the night of the Captain's dinner. Taking a deep breath, I accepted her hand and peered knowingly at the palm.

Impressions flooded through me that had nothing to do with those clear, deep lines. This girl was not as wild as she seemed. I felt her vast insecurity, unexpected in one who presumably had just married the love of her life. Although, her touch was telling me something else. Holding her hand now, I would have put money on this being a rebound match.

"Ah, you have a water hand, I see. A tendency to operate by intuition rather than reason. Graceful and sophisticated, like Princess Diana's."

"I *loved* Princess Diana." Paige was clearly entranced. Hearing about oneself never lost its fascination, as every fortune-teller must know.

"Oh, my, see here? Such a well-developed Mount of Venus. And this Love Line. These tell me, no matter what has happened in the past, it's over. The future is a completely new chapter, which will be written by the choices you make now."

Paige smiled wryly. "I've already made that choice, Cass. Tyler and I have a lot in common, I guess. Our backgrounds and all. Our families are ecstatic. Mom and Dad have bought us a gorgeous house near all our friends in Greenwich."

"Hmmmm. Now this Health Line. See this tiny loop here? Shaped like a little bottle?" I pointed to a mid-palm wrinkle. "This indicates some kind of drug. Have you been concerned about a drug or medicine recently? Found yourself to be suspicious of doctors?"

A wary frown crossed Paige's perfectly tanned features but soon disappeared. The *trust-me* glamour Fiona had taught us (so useful for cashing checks in strange cities) must have been working.

With her free hand, Paige pulled off her headband and tucked her long straight hair behind her ears. It was that weather-bleached, multi-shaded blonde that could only be obtained by a summer on the water or very expensive salon highlighting. "I need another beer," she said.

"And down here below your Ring of Saturn," I hastened to reassure her, "this Fate Line clearly shows a chain of surprising events."

"No shit? Listen, about the drug thing. I didn't mean that like it came out. Something happened to my roommate at Vassar. She couldn't really remember, but she'd been to a frat party with some med majors. I've been nervous about being dosed with drugs ever since."

"Really? At Vassar? That's unexpected."

Paige laughed darkly. "Hey, it's been a long time since you've been in college, Cass. These days a girl has to watch out for everyone. Ashley's clothes were practically torn off her body, semen stuck all over her thighs, and she couldn't remember a thing. Those bastards gave her some kind of drug, then dumped her on the dorm doorstep."

"A young woman can't be too careful," I agreed

Paige suddenly looked so young and vulnerable, I did feel a tad guilty to be playing her this way. Time to end this travesty. "Well, is there anything particular you'd like to know?"

"Will anything really *out of the ordinary* ever happen to me?"

I looked at that Fate Line one more time. At least I knew where it was and, in a general way, what denoted an event. It certainly zigzagged across her Life Line in a most unusual way. But more than that, holding the girl's hand, I opened the door of my mind to continued impressions. "Yes," I said with assurance. "This voyage...this voyage..." A sudden sharp pain shot through my midsection. I doubled over, unable to continue. *Must be that damned cyanide dumpling.*

Paige shrugged. "Well, so far... I mean, the Captain's Dinner was one big yawn, if you ask me." She stood up and looked down at me clutching my stomach. "Anyway, thanks. I believe I'll pop into the Moulin Rouge cocktail lounge for a real drink. Maybe you should do the same, Cass. From the looks of it, you've had one too many cups of tea."

"The Captain's Dinner was just the lull before the storm," I said through teeth gritted against the pain in my gut. *What does that mean?* Sometimes the words that come out of my own mouth surprise me the most.

Paige strode off laughing, hair flying in the wake of her athletic stride.

Still prone to bending double, I noticed that her headband was under the table. I put it in my pocket to return to her later. Then I hobbled off in search of my roommate.

I found Phillipa sneaking a cigarette in the Promenade Deck games room, which at this hour was deserted. "Oh, be quiet," she said before I could utter a word. "Nicotine is like a lover you've given up because he's so bad for you, but every once in a while you can't help longing for one more kiss."

"Very poetic. Now stub out that butt, or I swear I'll tell Stone your amorous secret."

For a moment Phillipa looked confused, like a gal who might have more than one amour to conceal. Then she pulled it together and went on the offense. "Listen, never mind *my* little vices. What about that vision of yours. Shouldn't we be *white-lighting* the beautiful Calypso with a psychic shield."

"Absolutely. But right now I'm for the marble bathtub and my third-best cocktail dress, the black and white. Too bad about those shoes, though. I'll have to wear the back-up pair."

"Not flats, I hope."

"No, Heather made me buy two pair of spiky heels, the sadist. I don't think we can go into serious magic at dinner, though. Might be disturbing to some of the other guests."

"*You think?* After dinner, then. And I know just where Calypso will be later." She gestured toward a black sign with sparkling silver letters *Karaoke Tonight at the Moulin Rouge Cocktail Lounge.* "She mentioned it at the Blue Note last night, while you were hurtling across the room into Tony's lap."

"Karaoke?" I murmured weakly.

"For your sins," Phillipa said with a grin.

~

"I wonder who else among our fellow passengers was on this ship when the Callahan bride went over the side," Deidre said as the five of us were strolling downstairs together for dinner at *Le Consulat*. "Will we be at the same table as we were last night?"

"No, the Captain will be entertaining other elite guests like ourselves, but we will be invited to his private cocktail party and seated at a reserved table nearby," Heather said.

"Don't you just love traveling with Heather? It's always such a ritzy production," I said.

"Possibly just a tad *over*-produced, a la Busby Berkeley," Phillipa muttered..

"I go along with Auntie Mame's theory that *life is a banquet*," Heather replied.

"To answer Deidre's concerns, we ought to ask around." I got them back on track. "Fiona, why don't you see if Ken remembers who else has made both voyages."

"Ulla. Ulla might remember I'll check with her," Heather offered. "But what about your vision, Cass? What are we going to do about that?"

Ever since Phillipa had brought it up, that very concern had been hovering in the back of my mind like a monster in the closet. "Calypso will be at the Karaoke scene around nine. We'll join her there. Fiona, we'll need a dynamite protective spell."

"Karaoke? Are you kidding?" Heather looked incredulous.

"The girl loves to sing-along—what can we do?" Phillipa said. "Didn't you hear her the other night at the Blue Note, singing into Negrini's ear? *Belle canto.*"

"We'll just have to outface the music, then," Fiona said.

CHAPTER EIGHT

And now the storm-blast came, and he
Was tyrannous and strong;
He struck with his o'ertaking wings,
And chased us south along.

– Samuel Coleridge, *The Rime of the Ancient Mariner*

But we were spared the full impact of amateur hour by unforeseen (even by me) events. Tropical storm Ossie had veered off its plotted course and was barreling toward us with winds that were approaching hurricane velocity. But full information was screened from us passengers to avoid needless panic. Just as we arrived at the pre-dinner cocktail party, the Captain made an announcement on loudspeakers heard all over the ship that we could expect some minor turbulence later in the evening but stabilizers would be keeping the ship steady. There was no need for alarm. Docking in Hamilton the next day might be delayed by an hour or two.

But when the captain did not appear at his cocktail party or his table at dinner, it was an ominous sign indeed. Still, our last dinner together before arriving in Bermuda was a spirited affair.

Tony Grenville and Bishop Guilfoyle got into quite an animated discussion of religious archetypes, and for once Fiona managed to listen more than she lectured except to mention that the Green Man frequently found carved into church architecture was in reality a pagan fertility god.

Lindsay was so obviously bored that she was reduced to flirting with Rudy Koch whose wife was confined to her cabin with an iffy stomach. Rudy still has his eye on Calypso, however; his sly glances in her direction were not lost on me. Meanwhile, Rob Negrini, having torn himself away from casino Blackjack, was turning on his charm to lure Heather into a terrific fund that invested only in environmentally-aware and animal-friendly corporations and yet out-performed the leading competitors.

"Next thing you know, he'll be selling her the Bridge of San Luis Rey," Phillipa murmured to me. My cabin mate was rather out of sorts, having lost the flattering attentions of Dan Simic. He was again seated at the captain's table, this time pinch-hitting for the captain himself. Another group of Penthouse and Riviera Deck passengers and notables was being honored by dining with Dr. Simic looking very handsome in the white Norse Line uniform that flattered his swarthy good looks. The first evening's guests of the captain, including us five, were seated at a nearby table sans officers. All of the other ship's officers were on the bridge keeping their attention on Ossie.

As the Pain au Chocolat and Crème Brulee were being served, Jason Severin held us spellbound with legends of the Bermuda Triangle, the background for his next book. His mother Madeline, as always, was transfixed by her brilliant son. With her champagne hair worn in a pageboy, heavily accented eyes, high cheek bones, and enigmatic smile, she looked like one of those over-fifty models in Vogue as she assured us that Jason would be the rightful successor to the masters of the horror genre, "the heir to H.P. Lovecraft and Stephen King."

"What can happen in a fictional Triangle story that's more horrifying than fact?" I asked.

"It's a death knell to talk about an ongoing novel, but I can say this." Jason paused in a way that suggested he would dearly love to light a cigarette. He even raised a hand to his inside jacket pocket, then dropped it and picked up his espresso cup instead. "It's not the horror of *what* happens, it's *who* it happens to. In fiction, the carnage is reduced from an unmanageable number to just a few vulnerable characters. You care about those few. You're terrified when they're threatened. But it's okay, because you can be *safely* scared by fiction, unlike real life."

I knew what he meant. My search for one of Jason's books in the ship's library had been rewarded with *Skin White, Blood Red* but I'd not had a chance to read much beyond the ominous scene where a lonely teen-age boy named Randy, driven mad by subliminal messages programmed into his video game, grabs his father's hunting knife and slits the old man's throat. By page 3, Randy is stalking a family of appealing children playing in the park with their nubile blonde nanny.

As if echoing my thoughts, Phillipa said, "And then you horror authors contrive that some naive young thing will get slashed and disfigured in unspeakable ways. Mrs. Severin, please tell us, was Jason one of those little boys who pulled the wings off butterflies and tormented frogs?"

A strange look came over Madeline Severin's face. Her eyes narrowed, and she glared at Phillipa. I couldn't decide whether Jason's mother was repelled by my friend's rude question or by something in her memory that she didn't want to raise its ugly head. I had the urge to reach over and touch her slim elegant hand so that I could learn more about the two of them, mother and son, but I didn't want to add coals to the fiery moment.

In a voice that was both harsh and crooning, Madeline was saying, "Jason was the most beautiful boy in his school—we lived in New York City, of course—with an I.Q. in the genius range. All his teachers said he was an enormously gifted child, and I could tell they didn't quite know what to make of him. There were many other mothers who envied me."

Her son was still beautiful, clean-cut in the way of matinee idols of the Thirties and more youthful looking than his bibliography suggested was really the case. *Fifty, it's the new forty,* and so forth.

"He's always adored Bermuda," Madeline rattled on. "And I adore the island, too, although I often end up playing bridge while Jason disappears for hours and hours on the pink beaches. My delicate skin simply won't take that much sun." She touched her fine high cheek bone with a scarlet-tipped fingernail that matched her slash of lipstick.

Phillipa raised an eyebrow at me and mouthed the words "Lucky for him."

~

I'm not a fan of Karaoke. To me, it's an amateur hour run amok not *America Has Talent*, but Calypso really did have a high, sweet soprano that caused a hush to descend on the crowded Moulin Rouge cocktail lounge full of raucous performers.

"What did I tell you," Phillipa whispered. "Jenny Lind performs for the P.T. Barnum crowd."

"I'm thinking more in terms of one of the sirens of the sea," I said, but my attention was elsewhere. I could feel a curious vibration in the ship, something I hadn't felt since we'd steamed out of New York Harbor. An ominous note, a sonar warning from the ocean to the ship to me. How I wished I'd contacted Joe earlier when I had the chance. Phillipa had suggested I join her at Sinbad's Cyber Cafe where she planned to send an e-mail to Stone, but I had decided to wait until we reached Bermuda. Now, for some reason, I kept thinking, *too late, too late.*

The evening's songfest had hardly got underway when we began to feel Ossie's turbulence in earnest. One buxom woman in a low-cut white tank top and pink capri pants, who was just in the throes of belting out "I will survive," went flying off her bar stool and had to be carried to the infirmary with a wrenched ankle.

Just about then, the bartender began serving free drinks to take the passengers' minds off the rocking and rolling of the room. A frequent cruiser at my elbow informed us that it was the cruise line's policy to open the bar when the going got rough. Someone turned up the music louder to drown out the angry clamor of the ocean getting more riled up by the minute.

"I don't like this," Fiona said, gathering us together at a round table against the wall. "Let's do our white-lighting thing for Calypso and get the Hades out of here. We need to secure things in our cabins. I have some duct tape in my reticule."

"Of course you do," Phillipa said.

"We may want to tape up our luggage, especially your laptop, Phil," Fiona said, pulling her coat sweater of many colors more closely around her bosom. I noticed there were two *Norse Goddess* pens and a swizzle stick stuck in her coronet of braids. It boded ill.

"Hey, you guys carry on with the good spellwork," Deidre said, "but I've got to get back right now to check on Jenny and Willy. They may be getting frightened, or queasy." With a worried frown, she hurried off to her suite where one of the ship's childcare personnel was tucking the youngsters into their beds. Deidre told us later that she had decided not to alarm the children by making them don their life jackets, but she had the jackets ready, just in case.

Meanwhile, Fiona, Heather, Phillipa, and I were murmuring words for ourselves as well as Calypso. *We are one with the Goddess Tara, She Who Protects, we are defended by her peaceful energy, we are surrounded by her light and love, nothing can frighten us, nothing can hurt us, Calypso is one of us, safe from all harm, safe in Her arms.*

Then we held hands and raised the power by chanting and passing energy from witch to witch until it could barely be contained. Karaoke aficionados, if they happened to glance our way, befuddled as they were by free drinks, probably thought we were having an impromptu prayer meeting. In a way, we were. Visualizing the embrace of the Great Protectoress surrounding the girl, we threw our hands upward to release the power of our wishes into the Cosmos. Fiona's hand, I noted, held a pinch of corn pollen that descended through the murky air of the lounge like a small shower of gold. A collective sigh rose from us as a palpable peace descended.

"So must it be," sang out Fiona. "Now let's vamoose."

Heather and I each took one of Fiona's arms. She wasn't as steady as she used to be before osteoarthritis set in. We had to watch our own footing as well, for the ship's floor was really swaying now.

As we made our way up the stairs, Fiona mumbled a pagan fisherman's prayer from a book she had given me earlier, *"O Father Neptune, I fear no storm when Thou art with me. Steer my small boat into gentle seas and safe harbors, and I will sing Thy praises forever."*

My stomach was registering a slight disquiet. It was time for me to nibble some more candied ginger. I thought longingly of my pleasant single bed with the two fluffy pillows and the nautical blue blanket, which I just wanted to pull over my head. But that was not to be.

When we got back to the Penthouse Deck, the water in our private pool was sloshing onto the courtyard, and we slipped and slid our way to our rooms. Heather took charge of Fiona, but not before our resourceful friend had pressed a roll of duct tape into Phillipa's hands. Then Fiona insisted on blessing all of us with more pinches of the corn pollen she'd carried with her ever since her healing trip to the Navaho reservation. *Any blessing in a storm*, I thought.

"I could use a cigarette right now. And a blindfold," Phillipa complained when we got back to our own suite. She taped up her laptop and put it away in the top of her closet. Although it was late, we were both yearning for a boost and decided that caffeine would do the trick. Our little coffee set-up provided us with two steaming mugs of the black stuff in short order. Not surprisingly, we found we were no longer sleepy. Actually, we were more uneasy than we even admitted to each other. So instead of getting into bed, we changed into jeans and sweatshirts; we sat up reading and occasionally dozing in easy chairs.

"Just to be ready for whatever..." as Phillipa put it.

It was in one of those dozes that I jolted upright with a wrenching fear in the pit of my stomach. My heart was thudding against my ribs and perspiration sprang out on my forehead. In my mind's eye, I was seeing an immense wall of water towering over our ship, a wave higher than the highest deck of this floating hotel. I felt that I was looking death in the eye. Surely we would be swamped!

"We've got to get everyone up," I cried out rather louder than I had intended, shaking Phillipa's shoulder for emphasis. "And I mean, like, right away. I think the safest place will be the Atrium, away from the windows."

She took one look at my face, stricken with fear and the wave of nausea that always accompanies a major clairvoyant episode, and never uttered a single smart remark. Fifteen minutes later we had the whole family of us on the move, wearing the life jackets I had insisted upon. Fiona was wrapped up in her tartan shawl, dragging along her green reticule. I took her arm to help on the stairs, although truth to tell, I was still somewhat woozy from my clairvoyant episode.

Phillipa said, "Here, lean on me," and I put my hand on her shoulder gratefully, since her arms were full of supplies. Heather and Deidre, in sweats and sneakers, were each holding the hands of Deidre's two cranky children in jammies and life jackets.

We made our way carefully down to the Atrium with its giant columns and winding staircase, the heart of the ship. No one else was there except one elderly couple who seemed to have fallen asleep in the comfortable recliners, clutching the two paper buckets holding the handfuls of quarters they had been using at slot machines in the casino. Phillipa shook out the stack of light blankets she'd liberated from the Penthouse Deck's private fitness room. There was an awful chill in the air. We wrapped up in those blankets appreciatively. And we waited. And waited. Ossie could be heard raging outside, but the *Goddess* seemed to be handling the rough waters just fine.

"What did you say you saw again?" Deidre asked after a long silence.

I never got a chance to answer that one. Or rather, the ocean answered for me. They told us later that what came at us was a rogue wave over 50 feet high. But we should feel thankful, because rogue waves often register 83 feet in height, which would be something like being smashed into by an eight-story building.

Just before impact, all we knew was that the ship suddenly tipped crazily to one side. As the wave roared toward us, first we sank into its deep trough. Everyone and everything slid down in the direction from which the wave was coming. The elderly lady, now awake, would have gone right out the door that banged open if Heather hadn't seized her and flung the door shut. The couple's gambling coins spilled crazily in all directions. I put my arms around Deidre and the children, Phillipa grabbed Fiona.

Slowly, amid our involuntary screams, the ship righted itself and seemed to be holding its breath for one calm instant. The elderly couple clung to each other, as we, too, held tightly arm in arm, a defensive circle like the tortoise formation of an ancient Roman army.

The massive wave of my vision slammed into us with a dreadful fury. The shock was like being hit by a falling tower. All of us shrieked, our voices lost in the cacophony of angry seas. Windows broke under the pressure, soundless in the general racket, and sent a spurt of salt water into the room. Any chairs not bolted down slid around dangerously, smashing into walls like crash dummies.

After that colossal wall of water passed over us, the ship's alarm bells began to ring in earnest. The loud speaker instructed us to don life jackets and, using interior stairways, make our way to the Atlantic Atrium or the restaurants (there were three) on the Atlantic Deck, deck eight, or to other public places on the Caribbean, deck nine, but to stay away from any broken windows. We were advised to keep calm, these measures were simply routine precautions. The emergency was over, and everything was under control. I marveled at one more classic example of how those in charge inevitably deny the true nature of a danger. They wanted us to assemble where we could easily be herded into lifeboats located right outside on deck eight and nine if the need arose.

Captain Johansson's hearty voice assured us that we were still steaming toward Bermuda where any damage would be repaired and we would be reimbursed for any inconvenience or loss. No need to be anxious, just follow directions given by the ship's personnel as they moved among us.

As befuddled passengers, many in bathrobes, began to crowd into the Atrium where we were, workmen were already mopping up salt water and boarding up broken windows.

Madeline Severin appeared at Heather's elbow clutching her arm anxiously. Although her pageboy was still perfectly smooth, her eye make-up was sooty and smudged. In narrow-legged tights, a voluminous shirt, and silk flats, she looked like a distraught ballerina doll. "Where is Jason? *Where is Jason?*" she demanded. "I can't find him anywhere."

"Take it easy, Madeline," Heather said soothingly. "This place and the restaurants are getting so crowded, it's no wonder you haven't connected with him yet. He's probably searching for you right now. Perhaps the best thing would be if you were to stay here with us and let *him* find *you*. Otherwise you two may just keep missing each other."

The stewards and a few officers came through, distributing advice and assurance, along with soft drinks, water, apples, cookies, candy bars, and other solaces.

Tony Grenville strolled up to us wearing a Sherlock Holmes shawl over his life jacket. "When last seen, Lindsay was seeking safety with the jazz trio," he said. "I've been wandering from place to place with the refugees on this deck, surrounded by strangers. I have Xanax to trade for friendly faces and a little civilized chat."

What else could I do? "You've found five of 'em," I said. "And I think Madeline could use one of your inducements. The rest of us will muddle through on magic and amulets."

Deidre winked and pulled out a tiny replica of the Venus of Willendorf from the pocket of her sweatsuit and waved it at Tony. "Who needs Xanax when we have Mother Courage," she said.

Fiona spritzed us all with a lavender restorative, saving a few squirts for Madeline and Tony. Tony dodged, muttering, "Good Lord, I've stumbled into a snake's nest of magical thinking."

"Magical thinking is like anesthesia," Fiona said. "No one knows how and why it works, but we wouldn't want to operate without it."

The look on Tony's face made us smile for the first time since the Rogue (as we called it later) hit the *Goddess*. Fiona's logic could blow fuses in any brain.

A short time later, we were advised that some of the suites on the Penthouse Deck had been damaged, as had as the Blue Note bar on the Blue Vista Deck, but it would be safe now to return to our cabins and suites for some rest, using interior stairways and staying off the water-soaked decks. Broken windows would be boarded up, and breakfast would be served as usual in the restaurants and at the buffet. Ossie had passed to the south of us toward the mainland, and that extraordinary wave had been a unique event, not liable to be repeated.

Rogue waves may form in any region swept by powerful currents, such as the Gulf Steam that flows through the Bermuda Triangle, Dan Simic explained when he materialized later in the Atrium, most solicitous of our well-being (especially Phillipa's). Although he looked a bit banged up himself, our ship's doctor had been occupied with myriad small injuries, assisted by the young officer Gerry Leary, who'd had paramedical training, and Kirsti Hansen, the ship's nurse, toting a large white plastic first-aid kit emblazoned with the Norse Line insignia and a red cross.

"We've been all over the ship dispensing first aid," Simic said. "Lost my cell phone in the big splash and couldn't get in touch with my team. My bag, too. Luckily, Kirsti ran into me, and she'd brought hers. It's sure been a busy night—bashed heads, sprains, nervous palpitations, and the usual stomach woes. If you guys are okay, then, I guess I'll have to move along." He cast a regretful glance at Phillipa and hurried away, closely followed by Kirsti Hansen.

What greeted us when we made our soggy way to the Penthouse Deck was rather a mess, but the kind of mess that a seasoned crew could soon put in order. Except for Deidre's suite. In the freakish way of storms, her rooms had taken the brunt of the wave on this deck. The furniture in her suite had been turned into pick-up-sticks; her clothes, luggage, the kids' toys, the handcrafts she took everywhere with her, and even her cosmetics and medicines were washed away or damaged beyond use.

Deidre's face blanched when she saw it. "Good Goddess," she exclaimed, turning over a dripping drawer, her clear blue eyes filling with tears. "What if we'd been in here sleeping?"

Thank you, I said silently to whomever or whatever was guiding me. For once clairvoyance had been a blessing. And to think this trip had been dreamed up by Heather to lift Deidre's spirits!

"Do you think this suite was targeted because of the ghost," Deidre wailed. She wasn't making sense, but sometimes when common sense flips out that's when the psychic sense kicks in. "Am I being cursed by the bride of voyages past? The ill-fated Callahan couple did stay here, you know. I got Ulla to admit that much. Some film star and her guy had opted for the Romance Suite, so the Callahans got second choice. Ulla and Fibonacci the butler have seen something weird around here, too, like a shining form moving right through the stateroom door, but they thought it best to keep quiet about it. We even discussed asking the Bishop to do an exorcism."

Heather appeared undaunted. "Now, now. This is a perfectly horrid thing to have happened," she said, firmly hugging Deidre's thin shoulders. "You naturally feel shaken and bereft. Perhaps you could have a little chat with the Bishop tomorrow about The Curse of Bridal Suite or whatever. But there isn't a thing you've lost that we're not going to replace with our shopping trips in Hamilton, that I promise you. No, don't protest, the bill will be paid by the Norse Cruise Line, I'll see to that. Your new wardrobes will have the cachet of being very, very British. And as all us Anglophiles know, the British mystique can be very classy stuff."

Hanging onto their Mom tearfully, Jenny and Willy were not to be easily mollified.

"I've lost my Star Wars Yoda Action Figure and my Game Boy with Marty the Zebra," Willy wailed.

"My new red dress with the red and white boots," Jenny cried.

"You just wait until tomorrow," Heather said. "There's a game shop in Hamilton that will knock your socks off, Willy. I think they have action figures, too. And we'll shop dresses, as well! Jenny, you'll look like a little princess."

"Princesses are so boring. I want to look like Madonna's daughter Lourdes. But where are we going to sleep?" practical Jenny wanted to know. She'd picked her way to the closet, the door of which was hanging open in a most unpromising way.

Deidre opened the little safe inside. Her papers and a few pieces of jewelry put away in the lockbox had remained secure. "Where indeed?"

"You and the kids take our suite, Dee. At least it won't be haunted. Phil and I will move wherever there's an empty cabin." A noble offer, but I did hate the thought of packing up those excesses of wardrobe we'd brought and unpacking them in a new cabin. I glanced at Phillipa for affirmation, and she nodded approval.

Heather was on the phone and on the case. Who can deny the magic of big bucks? Within ten minutes, Phillipa and I had been moved to a suite on the deck below, the Riviera. It was a deluxe two-bedroom, two-bathroom accommodation with its own miniature library, a wet-bar, and a veranda, exactly as the Severins had described their suite on the Penthouse Deck. Not only that, but Fibonacci and two chambermaids moved all our clothes for us.

It was the butler who told us that the New Jersey politician who'd reserved and paid for our suite had got involved in a scandal and checked himself into an expensive rehab instead. As if that would keep the press off his trail! Still, good fortune for us.

"I could get used to this royal treatment, Phil," I said as we settled into our new quarters. Phillipa was busying herself opening the complimentary bottle of Amontillado sherry. By now it was three in the morning, and we were much too wired to go right to bed. I almost wished I had availed myself of Tony Grenville's Xanax.

~

Some time later, I was sitting up in bed sipping the sherry and trying to get sleepy, when there was a sharp knocking on the door. "Let me in," Heather whispered urgently. "Something weird has happened."

Phillipa popped out of her bedroom and flung open the door. "You mean something *else,* weirder than a rogue wave in the Bermuda Triangle?" she demanded.

"Yes. I thought you'd want to know," Heather said. "The thing is, Ulla came looking for you two and found you'd decamped. Fiona's still asleep, and Deidre's watching over her little ones, so I volunteered to find you. Here's the problem—*Paige Bratton seems to have disappeared.* Simic's had to sedate Tyler. The doctor and Ulla are checking with everyone who was at the captain's dinner that first night, on the off-chance that Paige is having a late-night chat with some new acquaintance. But from the look on Ulla's face, she must fear that something terrible has happened to Paige. An accident, perhaps, when the monster wave hit us. I offered to check that the girl wasn't with you two. But I rather knew she wasn't."

"You've got to wake Fiona, then," Phillipa said. "I mean, if finding is to be done, she's the gal to do it, you know that."

"I suppose you're right," Heather agreed. "But she looked so peaceful after all that stress, I didn't have the heart."

"Never mind," I said, as cold as the ice that was freezing my blood. The insight came and went in a flash, leaving me chilled and faint. It was not exactly a vision, more an inner knowing beyond any doubt. A sure thing. Remembering the sharp pain I'd felt when I'd pretended to read the girl's palm, I berated myself. I should've realized then that she was in danger. We might have been able to protect her. "Paige is gone. I mean over the side, into the ocean, drowned. And I don't for a minute think it was an accident."

"Are you saying that beautiful girl is dead? Assaulted and drowned?" Phillipa, who is naturally pale, got paler and sank back down onto one of the small easy chairs in the sitting room. "Who would have done such a thing, do you know, Cass?" Phillipa asked.

"There's someone on this ship who likes to kill young women, and he's going to continue doing it—oh, not now—he's lying low now. But I feel his sick need, and it's very strong. And he'll do it again, unless someone stops him," I said, collapsing into the other easy chair.

"That would be us." Heather was still leaning in the open doorway. Two spots of color splotched her cheeks. Her patrician profile took on the resolute look of her seafaring forebears. "Thank the Goddess I brought a few candles."

"Oh, no. What we *don't* need is to have to explain to the steward why you're burning a black candle," Phillipa said. Candle magic was Heather's special province, and she had been known to stray onto the dark side.

"Oh, don't fuss, Phil," Heather said. "I'll just light one all-purpose candle, very dark green, a triple Hecate, incorporating a few raven feathers. She who assures safe travel and guards Wiccans from harm from evil types. If the steward asks, I'll tell him she's a Holy Virgin of the Islands."

CHAPTER NINE

Full many a gem of purest ray serene
The dark unfathomed caves of ocean bear...

– Thomas Gray

Fiona dangled her crystal pendulum, holding its chain between thumb and forefinger, over a diagram of the ship's decks spread out on our breakfast table. Although her arm never moved and the silver bangles she wore were silent, the pendulum was describing erratic circles and figures eight, never settling above any one place. Every once in a while, the crystal would execute a swift skip to the right or left into the blue borders of the diagram. We watched miserably. Even though I knew better in my gut, I'd hoped against hope that Fiona's dowsing would find Paige in an overlooked obscure corner of some deck, possibly passed out but at least alive.

"Does that crystal thing have a motor in it?" Willy asked. The children seemed to be in no hurry to join the kids' morning program, t-shirt painting and Indian headband making. They were standing close to Deidre soberly watching our finder at work.

"The crystal is moving all on its own, honey," Deidre explained. "It's a magic way of finding lost things. And people.

One of our friends is missing this morning, and Aunt Fiona is looking for her."

"This could be a great show-and-tell for Sunday School, kids," Phillipa suggested, winking at me.

"Why can't Aunt Fiona find where my Yoda and Game Boy are," Willy asked.

"Oh, honey, we already know what happened. Poor Yoda and your Marty the Zebra game got soaked and sunk in that storm last night," his mom replied. "But Aunt Heather says we're going to buy other great stuff when we get to Bermuda because she knows just where to shop."

"Sunk in the storm, indeed," Fiona said, laying her crystal pendant to rest. "And so, I fear, did the young woman we're seeking here. The pendulum simply wants off the ship and onto the surrounding ocean. It's just as Cass has been saying. Paige is gone."

"More than that. Someone deliberately dispatched her to Davy Jones' locker, I'm sure of it," I said. "As I told Phil and Heather last night, he'll do it again. Oh, not this voyage, but somewhere, sometime. No idea who, though. Except I know it's not Tyler," I said. "But I fear the Bermuda police are going to give Tyler a hard time this afternoon. The spouse is always the chief suspect. Remember what happened when that bride disappeared off this ship last year? The husband was held for ten days by the Brits."

"Who's Davy Jones?" Jenny asked. I realized with guilt that I'd been babbling too freely.

"Davy Jones is another name for the devil, dear," Fiona said. "who doesn't exist but is used by some religious teachers to frighten the impressionable."

"Let's not talk about this now," Deidre suggested. "Let's walk the kids over to the t-shirts and headbands workshop first."

The sky was soft and hazy, the ocean misty blue, the sea air refreshing—hard to believe how black and wild the night had been, except for the evidence of damage here and there that members of the crew, like a swarm of industrious worker bees, were busily repairing. After the reluctant children had been deposited in the arts and crafts class, we settled wearily in the Mayfair Tearoom for a quiet conference.

"Will we continue the cruise on this ship, do you think?" Deidre asked, stirring sugar and milk into a mug of coffee. After a nearly sleepless night, we were all overloading on caffeine.

"I had a talk with Ulla before breakfast," Heather said. "Apparently, we were lucky in one regard. The damage could have been a great deal worse. Just a half dozen outside cabins and Deidre's suite flooded. Bummer, though. My hope had been that Deidre and her kids would enjoy a stress-free idyll. Well, chalk that up to another hope dashed. But we'll be four days in Bermuda, plenty of time to get shipshape. Ulla believes we'll be making the return voyage on the same ship, which is good in a way. Maybe it will help Cass catch some vibes. At the very least, we won't have to move all that baggage."

"Well, I guess the Norse Cruise Line isn't going to be a favorite with honeymoon couples anymore," Phillipa said. "No bride will want to make 'three' in 'things always happen in threes.'"

"The queer thing is, I was so sure it was going to be Calypso," I said.

"But we evoked Tara, we cast a protective light around Calypso," Fiona reminded us.

"Coincidentally," Heather said, "Ulla told me that Calypso was called away from her karaoke evening immediately after Fiona shooed us all back to our suites. Rob Negrini got into a scuffle at the casino, fell and hit his head on a slot machine. Ulla didn't say, but I heard from Lindsay who heard it from the jazz trio that Negrini was suspected of being a card counter. When the casino manager asked him to leave, Negrini got all huffy and aggressive. He says they pushed him, they say he lost his balance. Whichever, Calypso had to help Negrini back to their suite and minister to him for the rest of the night, until everyone was called to the public places for safety. So she was unavailable as a target. Perhaps our spell actually worked."

"Faith is so important, dear," Fiona said. "I find faith and corn pollen to be the most important ingredients in any blessing. But if you don't happen to have corn pollen, faith alone will do."

"Not everyone carries around a medicine bag of corn pollen blessed by some Navaho shaman," Phillipa pointed out. "And faith, I find, is an incalculable quality that varies in mysterious ways, like love. Still, Calypso *was* called away by serendipitous events, so I guess we can take credit where credit is due. If the killer planned to lure her away after the karaoke program, he never got the chance."

"Of course, Calypso isn't a bride," Deidre remarked.

"I don't think our attacker has a thing for brides per se," I said. "It's more like a thing for beautiful young women who might be having one drink too many." I felt the back of my neck tingle, and I listened to myself in surprise. The words just tumbled out of my mouth without ever passing through my censorious brain. "He'd arrange a meeting with his victim on deck—on what pretext, I don't know—knock her out, I'm not sure how, probably rape her, then hurl her over the side. Last year and this year. Such a nice clean kill, no forensics. Goddess help me, this whole situation is messing up my spiritual equilibrium. How I wish Joe was here!"

"You can call him with a credit card," Phillipa suggested.

"I tried that twice. But I couldn't reach him aboard the Greenpeace *Gaia.* So I guess I'll try e-mail. I know the crew gets to check their e-mail. On the other hand, what am I going to say? That our vacation away from our usual sordid pursuit of criminals has brought us into an isolated situation with a killer? Is it fair to worry him when he's cruising the coast of Africa looking for illegal loggers?"

"I'm not telling Stone, either," Phillipa said.

"If I may say so, my dears, this murderous character seems to prefer younger women than ourselves, so we are probably perfectly safe," Fiona said. "Well...until he catches on that we're after him."

"So the killer's among our fellow passengers now, whoever he is," Deidre said. "And will probably be with us on the trip home. But he won't kill another girl the same way, too obvious. If he did, can you imagine? Every passenger on this ship would be questioned by the police in New York, and we'd be stuck there for hours and hours."

"Depends on his appetite, which I feel is very intense," I said. "Maybe he'll go after someone in Bermuda, and no one will make the connection."

"Oh, I wouldn't say that," Phillipa said. "You already have."

~

Despite everything, when we sailed into Hamilton Harbor we were in irrepressible good spirits. It was so exciting to steam toward that picturesque island of tropical trees and pastel dwellings. Especially to Deidre and me, who had never before been on a cruise. The children, of course, were jumping up and down with ecstatic abandon, wearing their Indian headbands with feathers dancing. Deidre and I felt like doing the same but were more discreetly gleeful.

Deidre had called home and was assured by her mother-in-law Mary Margaret Ryan (called M&Ms by her grandkids) that the two youngest Ryans, Bobby and Baby Anne, were perfectly fine and impossibly adorable. Which was why she and the au pair Betti had taken it upon themselves to enroll the youngsters in a talent contest for photogenic toddlers.

"Suppose the little cuties win!" Deidre said. "I hope Mom Ryan won't be on her way to Hollywood with my kids by the time I get home. Well, one good thing, it's taking her mind off gambling for a few days. Say, look at that. Isn't that the prettiest little city you ever saw!"

"We're late," Heather said. "I sure hope the good stores on Front Street are still open. We have everything to buy, and it's going to be such a blast. We've got to go to Archie Brown's for woolens, Cecile's for drop-dead evening dresses, and Marks and Sparks, of course, for the kiddoes and what-have-you."

"Sounds like a late buffet on the boat for you guys," Phillipa said smugly. "I, on the other hand, have a dinner date for Aqua at the Ariel Sands Beach Club."

"Dr. Simic, I presume? That explains your splashy outfit," Deidre said. "And I must say, it's nice to see you in something besides black for a change."

"You really look terrific in red," I agreed. "Okay, Fiona, I guess that leaves you and me. Where would you like to dowse your food tonight?"

Fiona smiled serenely. "Don't forget, Samhain's just two days away. You and I, Cass, will take a taxi tour of the beaches to find a suitable place for our celebration. And then, what would you say to fish 'n chips at the Hog Penny Pub?"

~

I don't know by what sixth or seventh sense Fiona chose that ancient cab. Perhaps because, although old and battered, it was polished to the nines, which said something about the owner's character. Or perhaps she knew that our elderly Bermudian tour guide and taxi driver, Bert Swan, could be thoroughly charmed. Patiently he drove us from beach to beach on narrow roads bordered by extravagantly blossoming hibiscus bushes until she found the very rock-secluded cove that would do us nicely.

Fiona had cast her glamour on the poor chap, all right. When Swan braked at the pub door, he leaped from his cab to open her door and swept off his captain's cap with a flourish. "No, no, my honor," he insisted, refusing to take the bills I handed to him. "Please, what time shall I call for you after dinner? Not good for fine ladies to walk to the harbor alone."

"How very sweet of you!" Fiona exclaimed, casting the trailing MacDonald tartan back over her shoulder. I looked at her more closely, noting the noble tilt of her chin, the glowing rosy cheeks, the dazzling blue of her eyes. And of course, her regal figure."Give us about an hour and a half then, thank you, Mr. Swan."

The lingering affects of glamour got us seated immediately at the crowded bar. "You've completely befuddled that poor man," I said after we'd been served pints of ale.

"Don't be concerned, dear. I'll see to it that he has a handsome gift when we leave Bermuda. Meanwhile, we won't have to worry about transportation. I don't think I'm up for racing around on a moped, how about you? Oh, look...isn't that Lindsay Grenville?"

It was she indeed, leaning back against the dark smoked wood of a booth, her eyes narrowed sensuously, her face flushed. Surrounding her were the jazz trio from the Blue Note, two flashy Jamaicans in tropical shirts and a grizzled guy with a Willie Nelson pony tail. We waved. She waved back, her hand holding an American Express card. *Her party.*

Our delectably crusty, fragrant dinners were served at the bar. "I never feel the need to dowse fish and chips. Something about the deep fat negates...well, unless it's fugu of course, or as the saying goes in Japan, 'I want to eat fugu but I don't want to die,'" Fiona explained. As I struggled to follow the connections, Lindsay paused beside us on her way out of the pub. The trio had preceded her in a hurry, no doubt late for their gig. Her pale aristocratic beauty blurred, she was anesthetized but ambulatory. Pulling herself onto an empty barstool, she crossed her legs with an actress's automatic grace, her tangerine silk skirt sliding up to her thighs.

We persuaded her to wait for us so that we could all share a ride in Mr. Swan's taxi. It wouldn't do to leave her on her own in this condition.

While we threw ourselves into our fish feast, Lindsay drank an Ascot Martini (made with a dash of sweet vermouth and Angostura bitters) and then another, prattling on about how much she despised cruise ships but for Tony's sake she'd agreed to make another blasted trip to the isle of boredom, and then what does the bloody man do but desert her during that awful storm. Fiona and I looked at each other.

"We saw Tony later that night, after the rogue wave incident. He told us you preferred to seek safety with the young jazz musicians," Fiona said.

Lindsay laughed raucously, spraying us with a fine mist of Grey Goose vodka. "Safe? *Safe? As if!* We got swamped up there in the Blue Note. It was one of the hardest hit places on the ship, as you may have heard. I nearly slid over the rail to a watery grave when we sank into that trough, but dear Jacques hung on to me." At this point, her voice was getting higher and louder. "Then we had to sprint for our lives before that colossal wave smashed into us. The guys grabbed their precious instruments and shoved an armful of their arrangements at me. And where was Tony in my hour of need, I ask you? My devoted husband had disappeared, as always in times of trouble. The Elusive

Pimpernel, as I call him. Or Pimp, for short." She smoothed her skirt and grinned at her lap as if enjoying a private joke. "*They seek him here, they seek him there...*"

"So, you never saw Tony at all last evening?" I asked.

"Oh, is that funny little bloke peering in the door your driver?" Lindsay asked. "Do let's go then. I'm feeling absolutely knackered. Must be this entrancing island air, ha ha."

I was feeling a bit "knackered" myself, just from trying to kick in my visioning, which is as shy as a wild thing when hunted.

Mr. Swan conveyed us back to the ship as majestically as if he were driving the Queen Mum's limo. At the dock, Fiona arranged for him to meet us at ten the next morning. He nodded, bowed solemnly and turned smartly, a knight errant accepting his mission.

"Well, it appears that you've made a conquest," cackled Lindsay. We helped her up the gangplank and into her suite, where she fell on the bed face down. *One Ascot Martini too many.* There was no sign of Tony. I turned her over into the recovery position with a pillow on each side, so that she couldn't turn over and choke if she vomited.

"A sprinkle of corn pollen wouldn't hurt," Fiona said, suiting action to words. She drew out the small deerskin pouch from her reticule and flicked a pinch of the silky stuff over Lindsay Grenville. "It will be all right," Fiona whispered. "Whatever you're afraid of, it will be all right."

"Lindsay's afraid?" I asked as we headed to the buffet set up in an anteroom off the Atrium where Heather and Deidre had planned to get a late supper.

"A pistol shot in the dark," said Fiona. She patted her reticule in an absent fashion.

CHAPTER TEN

On life's vast ocean diversely we sail,
Reason the card, but passion is the gale.

– Alexander Pope

The Ryans were exhausted, practically falling noses first into their supper plates. Heather, however, was blithe and bonny after a flying trip through the British shops on Front Street. "Duty-free, what a lark," she cried. "You've absolutely *got* to buy yourselves some lovely expensive perfumes while you're here. *Chanel* or *Joy*—you're worth it. Of course, Deidre still needs so much more than we managed to scrounge up today, but I've hired a shopper to forage for the routine stuff, kids' underwear and the like. She'll be delivering everything on our list by noon tomorrow."

Willy closed his eyes and leaned his cheek against a dark-skinned Bermuda traffic cop doll, helmet, white gloves and all. Half-asleep, he blew the action figure's tiny whistle. Jenny was enraptured with her new aqua patent leather boots, matching handbag, and studded belt spelling out GIRLS RULE. "just like Lourdes! " she exclaimed. Willy also had new boots, suitable for playing polo with the royal princes.

"Jenny wishes her mom were Madonna." Sipping tea laced with Irish whiskey, surrounded by boxes and bags, Deidre rolled her eyes and shrugged. "Have you ever tried to convince our friend Heather to go easy with her spending? She storms through stores like Shelley the Shopping Goddess."

"Is that a real goddess? Are you all set with what you need tonight, then?" I asked.

"Throughout all of time, new deities have been created to reflect our changing images. I may have heard Fiona say that. Amazingly, yes, I'm richly outfitted with the Heather basics. Now I've got to put these two in bed before they fall asleep standing up in their brand new boots." Deidre ran a hand through her blonde curls, hugged a "thank you" to Heather, and hurried off, lugging the new purchases with the help of her weary children.

"You did well," Fiona said. "Deidre's looking much less forlorn, poor baby. There's no antidepressant like a clothes-buying spree, don't you think?"

Forlorn described me, too, as I realized that I'd again failed to get in touch with Joe. Only three days but it seemed like a year since we were last together. *Mea culpa,* Sinbad's Cyber Cafe would be closed now until morning. I supposed that events on the *Goddess of the Sea* will have been reported on CNN World. Joe—and my family—must have caught news of the rogue wave, the swamped cabins, the missing bride. Good Goddess, *the second missing bride!* The Norse Line had better be prepared for a media blitz. Gorgeous Ulla Nobel might get her chance to appear on the Larry King show.

They'd all be expecting to hear from me. Joe, Becky, Adam and Freddie...Cathy, too? Yes, any media attention could be exciting to those star-struck hopefuls. The whole family would be worried that we were involving ourselves in another crime. I'd have to downplay that. Not that I'd ever fool Freddie.

Another unhappy thought—I missed my doggies terribly. But at least Scruffy and Raffles didn't watch CNN.

To stave off the blues, I got a coffee and an outrageous chocolate raspberry napoleon at the buffet, where I found myself elbow-to-elbow with the elusive Muffy Koch who was piling her plate with pastries.

"Tummy feeling better, then?" I asked.

She started like the doe she resembled, all timid brown eyes and soft gray dress buttoned up to the neck and fastened with a simple silver brooch. "Oh. You're...?"

"Cass Shipton. We met at the Captain's dinner, such a lovely occasion. Have you ever tried candied ginger? I think it's the best for minor nausea."

"Thank you, but now that we've docked I'm feeling so much better. Not quite well enough to go on shore yet, though. Rudy's gone off to some primitive festival or other. Santeria, you know? He's working on an article. But that's all right, I have stacks of organizing and typing to finish. I thought maybe the dessert buffet would give me a boost of energy, you know?" Much of what Muffy said was voiced in the questioning tone favored by insecure females. If she consumed all the sweets on her plate, she'd surely be flying.

"Since you're alone, why don't you join our circle. That's our table over in the corner among the potted plants. I'm glad you decided to take a break." In my mind's eye, I was getting the fairy tale image of the girl who was locked up by her prospective husband and ordered to spin straw into gold—or be executed. I put down my tray, shook my hands and stamped my feet to get rid of such a negative image. I got a few curious looks, but I was used to that.

Still, I wondered. "So...you must be a great help to Rudy then?" I probed as we carried our desserts to the solarium corner amid ferns and palms. Heather and Fiona had their heads together over Samhain. Using pastel chalk and a sketch pad she'd taken out of her bottomless reticule, Fiona was drawing a map of the pink-sanded cove surrounded by rocks.

"Oh, just some minor editing of that article I mentioned, 'The Sounds of Santeria: orishas and steel drum music.' And the research, of course. It's so important for Rudy to have his name in the right journals. 'Publish or perish,' you know? Golly, I've really missed our computers, but I do spend a lot of time at Sinbad's Cyber Cafe. It's not the same, though. Oh, that's pretty." Muffy admired the sketch of the beach, which I was rather hoping Fiona wouldn't explain—but of course, she did, and in full detail—while Heather went in search of a bottle of Sambuca to liven up our coffees.

"Oh! Does Rudy know you're going to have a real Wiccan Sabbat?" Muffy breathed in an awed tone." He does so love those kinds of 'boil and bubble' things."

"Muffy's been helping Rudy with his writing," I said, hoping to change the subject.

"Oh, my, just deep background, nothing really important. Rudy's the scholar. I don't know how he does it, just comes up with one brilliant insight after another. I only help with the organizing and typing, you know? Sometimes I write out a few possible connections as minor topics. Keeps me busy. We don't have any little ones to worry about. Rudy doesn't want the distraction, you know? He says, maybe someday, when he's not under so much pressure to succeed, you know?"

Heather had come back with the liqueur and poured it liberally into our coffee cups, except Muffy's. The pale young woman had laid her slim white fingers over the cup's top. "Oh, no, I must keep a clear head for later, you know? I'm in the middle of outlining the principle points."

Heather cast a smoldering glance at me that summed up wordlessly her feelings about Rudy and Muffy. Her handsome chum from Vassar was fast losing the esteem in which she had held him.

"Perhaps you should write something of your own, my dear. Or—to Hades with it!—have a bit of a lie down with a racy novel," Fiona suggested, reaching into her reticule and pulling out a thick paperback. I glanced at the title. *The Outlander*. "Here, give this one a try. Guaranteed to transport you to another time," Fiona crooned, patting Muffy's arm. "I'm sure there are typing services at Vassar that Rudy could use. After all, this is supposed to be a vacation, is it not? Oops, what's this?" Fiona lifted the girl's arm to examine a long scratch on the soft pale underside.

Muffy blanched. "Oh, that dreadful wave, you know? Threw me right across the stateroom, and I grazed my arm on the desk's edge. Unbelievable force, you know. I was terribly worried about where Rudy might be, was he in danger? I went looking for him and for some antiseptic, but there was no one in the infirmary, so I just helped myself to the First Aid Cream. It's better today, really. Shall I tell Rudy about your Halloween thing? Although I think there's some rooster sacrifice service that night that's a *must-see*." Muffy trailed off uncertainly.

"Better not distract him, dear. Still, be sure he wears an old shirt to the ceremony, won't you? When he gets back to the ship, put it right into a basin of cold water. You know how hard it is to wash out sacrificial blood," Fiona said. "But *you* may come to our Sabbat, if you like. We're going to evoke the thirteen powers, do you a world of good."

Heather smiled and winked at me. A little consciousness raising was in order for poor Muffy.

∾

I was perusing the books in our suite's tiny but delightfully apt library—*Moby Dick, Robinson Crusoe*, Sabatini's *The Sea Hawk, Treasure Island, The Old Man and the Sea, The Caine Mutiny, The Search for Red October, Life of Pi*—when Phillipa returned, sighed deeply, and flung herself into one of the easy chairs, legs sprawled straight out like a castaway doll.

"Oi, what a dinner!" she exclaimed. "And the wines weren't too shabby either."

"What about the company?"

"The roasted salmon stuffed with lobster mousse in puff pastry with a piquant sauce of pink peppercorns and sherry vinegar was *divine.* The Chateauneuf-du-pape was *exquisite.* And the company, since you press me..."

"I only asked."

"The company was attentive and entertaining. And yes, he did make a pass, but in my considerable experience, it was not a serious one. *Pro forma.*"

"That will be such a comfort to Stone when you tell him about your date."

"*Are you out of your mind?* Stone's still a bit upset about the Cuban poet. And you, Cass, are never, never to breathe a word, right?"

"Oh, right. What are friends for but to keep secrets to their graves. Speaking of which, Fiona has invited Muffy Koch to our Samhain. And Fiona's found an idyllic secluded cove, not to mention a devoted slave named Mr. Swan to ferry us there in the oldest taxi on the island. What's that on your dress? Not a spill, I hope."

"Well, the pass wasn't *that* halfhearted. I guess I was holding a glass of wine at the time. How fortunate that the dress is red, too. I suppose he'd spent a fortune, and after all, how much can a ship's doctor make?"

"So? *You* spent a fortune, too, on that *haute couture*. I take it you won't be seeing him again?"

"I didn't say that."

"Uh oh."

"I can handle Dan Simic, don't worry. *Girls just want to have fun*."

"Fine. Then you can have lots of good clean fun by joining us for the aquarium excursion tomorrow. There are literally hundreds of fish species, a living coral reef, and if we get there at the right time, we can watch the seals being fed."

Phillipa groaned. "What no sharks? I don't believe I have the naturalist's mind set. When you rave about fish, I dream only of Trout Almondine or Shrimp Fra Diavolo."

"That's okay. Heather is naturalist enough for all of us. She's as addled as Joe, ecstatic over some program to preserve the Bermuda whistling frog."

"Ah, yes. Batter-fried Frog Legs!"

"And the day after tomorrow, it's the crystal and fantasy caves. We're all going, and that's that."

"No Merlin in that crystal cave though, right? Hardly worth the trouble, then..."

"Okay, Phil. *Get with the program*. After the aquarium tomorrow, we have an early dinner reservation for all of us, including the youngsters, at former President George Bush's favorite restaurant at the Fourways Inn. "

"What kind of a recommendation is that for a restaurant? What, do they serve Barbecued Dolphin and Wahoo Chili?"

CHAPTER ELEVEN

I stood by the shore at the death of the day,
As the sun sank flaming red;
And the face of the waters that spread away
Was as gray as the face of the dead.

– Paul Laurence Dunbar

Before our excursion the next morning, I got copies of the *Bermuda Sun* and *The Royal Gazette,* scouring them for some report of a grisly murder, but the island paradise had had an untroubled night—or else the victim hadn't yet been missed. I hoped it wasn't too depraved of me to be disappointed. At the lowest level of my consciousness, I was sensing the killer's craving growing within him like a malevolent cancer.

Confessing all this to Fiona, I got a spritz of invigorating lavender on my wrists and pep talk. "Averting harm is one of the thirteen powers."

"What thirteen powers?" Heather mouthed at me, her back turned to Fiona.

"The thirteen powers of a witch, but they are not exclusive, they exist for everyone to attain," Fiona said, just exactly as if she'd seen Heather's pantomime. "I will bring them forth at our Samhain, and you'll see. Some of you are already quite proficient." And that was all she would say about the powers then.

~

Returning to the dock after the exhaustive and exhausting Bermuda Aquarium, Museum, and Zoo—known as BAMZ—we were feeling British enough to be longing for a restorative cup in the Mayfair Tearoom, not to mention a chance to ravage the vast array of tea goodies. I was growing quite fond of the smoked salmon and watercress crustless triangles.

As it was, however, we had to push and shove our way "home" to our ship-hotel. Perhaps we shouldn't have been surprised to find the rapacious media and TV camera crews waiting to waylay us as we attempted to board. The few passengers who paused, like deer dazed by headlights, were instantly beleaguered with shouted questions. The five of us formed a tight-knit wedge with the children at the center and attempted to bull through. But a particularly aggressive young woman with wolfish eyes managed to cut me out of the herd. My friends kept rushing forward, however, abandoning me to my fate without a backward glance.

Instantly I was peppered with shouted questions from the insensitive reporters. *How did you feel when you were nearly capsized by a giant wave? Weren't you and the other passengers terrified that you'd all be drowned? Did you realize that Paige Bratton was the second bride to disappear off the* Goddess of the Sea*? How is Tyler Bratton holding up under questioning by the Bermuda police? Does he know the girl's parents have flown in, demanding action? Has Captain Johansson really cooperated with the authorities, or is he holding back evidence to protect the Norse Line? Has the FBI arrived yet? Aren't you anxious about sailing home on such an "ill-fated" ship? What compensation is the Norse Line offering? Are you going to demand a refund?*

I mustered as much aplomb as I could and looked my attackers coolly in their blinding camera lights. "It's true that there have been some worrisome events," I said, "but I have every confidence in Captain Johansson's ability to handle the situation and to sail the *Goddess* safely back to New York." Even to myself, that speech sounded rather unctuous. TV cameras don't bring out the genuine in people.

But what about Paige Bratton? Was she the victim of a tragic accident or did someone...? Why is her husband being questioned by the FBI? Is he a suspect? Do you know if an arrest is imminent?

"Oh, for goodness sake, what is the matter with you people?" I found myself addressing the gal with wolfish eyes, brandishing her microphone like a baseball bat. "No one has a clue yet what happened to Paige. Experienced people are working on it, though, and no doubt answers will be found. Meanwhile, it's not really helping for you folks to whip up the passengers' anxieties and throw around unfounded charges. Tyler Bratton deserves sympathy not a barrage of innuendoes."

I realized I was rattling on a bit. Simultaneously I felt a hand pulling me off my soapbox and away toward the ship. A harsh voice whispered, "Holy Hecate, Cass. *What do you think you're doing?*" It was Phillipa who'd come back to rescue me from fame. Somehow it had always been my karma to be the one in the limelight dodging tough questions.

She pushed me none too gently onto the ship. "*Come on.* We're all perishing for our tea. As soon as I noticed we'd lost you to CNN, I got worried about what you'd say. Like, *don't worry, guys, although there's a serial killer of young women on board, we're keeping it quiet because we intend to apprehend him ourselves.*"

"Now, Phil. You're exaggerating."

"Not by much. I believe I heard you say, 'answers will be found,' with all the assurance of a law enforcement spokesperson, which you are not."

By then my escort had muscled me into the tearoom where the others were waiting in various attitudes of sightseer's fatigue. Ever the mommy's helper, Jenny took Willy back to their suite for a rest. Having visited the gift store with Heather, the little boy was waving a cuddly stuffed shark, and Jenny had a video of *The Little Mermaid* to watch. Deidre sank gratefully into a small soft chair and put her feet up on a banquette.

The tired little feet went right back to the floor as soon as Deidre spotted the Bishop. I would hardly have recognized him in "civvys," if it were not for the black caterpillar eyebrows.

Fiona immediately invited him to join us.

He'd been to BAMZ on other vacations, he explained, so had not joined that excursion, but instead had visited The Devil's Hole, the oldest tourist attraction on the island, a natural pond aquarium where the fish and resident turtles were nearly tame. While the Bishop was holding forth on these aquatic delights, eyebrows wiggling, Phillipa organized the delivery of pots of tea and plates of scones, tarts, fairy cakes, and little sandwiches.

"I was so sorry to learn that your stateroom was flooded." The Bishop leaned toward Deidre and looked into her face keenly. "So many troubles, my dear. Have they found new quarters for you and the children? And how are you coping? Any return of the..." He paused a moment and looked around, but Deidre nodded to indicate that we knew all about it. "... spectral phenomena?" he continued. "Perhaps I can help."

"No, no, Your Excellency," Deidre said. "I seem to have left the specter in the flooded suite. Now that we've been moved next door, it's been quiet as the.... Well, very peaceful. My friends have been extremely supportive, and I am getting along just fine. Despite everything, the children and I managed to have a great time today. And I don't miss the mysterious vision draped in white lace and seaweed one bit." She shuddered expressively.

"Good, good," Bishop Guilfoyle said. "Remember, if you need any counseling concerning your recent spiritual experience..."

"Oh, thank you, Your Excellency."

"We're on vacation, Deidre. Call me Aiden. Listen...some of us are getting together for a rosary later. After the close call we've all shared, a very pleasant group of people from the Holy Cross parish in Springfield have asked me to lead them. You're welcome to join us. About nine. Ulla Nobel has found us a conference room on the Promenade Deck. My traveling companion, Father Dunn, will be there with me."

Phillipa cast a worried glance my way, but I felt quite confident that Deidre would know whether saying the rosary with a simpatico bishop would bring her comfort. If so, why not? Many Wiccans followed other paths without any feeling of conflict. In religion as in pantyhose, one size does not fit all.

If only Fiona had remained as reticent about powers as she had been with us, but no, she began chattering about the ability to perceive the world of spirit, "one of the glamourous powers that the adept may possess."

Naturally that caught the bishop's interest, considering his own experience with spirits of the dead, as he had revealed to Deidre. (And to tell one of us was to tell all.) A forceful and formidable man, Aiden Guilfoyle's attention moved like a searchlight in a dark room. Deidre seemed content to escape into the shadows for the moment while Fiona got the full glare of his interest.

"Yes, I'm familiar with the notion of glamourous powers," the Bishop said. His nostrils quivered as if he were already catching a whiff of burning sulfur a.k.a. brimstone. Poor man—imagine having to exorcise one's own demons! "And you're acquainted with those powers yourself?"

"Of course. I find there are thirteen, and they're available to all, just as music lessons are available to all. But they're not easy. Anyone can learn to play "The Happy Farmer," but only a few are blessed with true talent in one or more of the powers."

"And you're personally acquainted with some of these talented persons?" the Bishop persisted.

"Oh yes," Fiona beamed. With her round rouged cheeks and coronet of braids, she looked like The Happy Farmer's wife herself. Her plump hands moved expressively, bracelets tinkling, to include all of us, at which point Phillipa strongly changed the subject by tipping her cup of tea across the table, most of which funneled off onto my lap.

"Oh, thanks," I whispered. "Was that the best you could do?"

In the resulting confusion of exclaiming and mopping up, the Bishop seemed to be looking at each of us in a most speculative way, either as a nest of vipers or a parish of the self-deluded.

"It would have been better if Fiona had not brought up a word like 'powers,'" Heather said later.

"You think?" I said.

~

Tea time that had begun as an oasis of calm after a busy excursion had ended soggily. I hurried away to change my long flowered dress (the Laura Ashley afternoon look) for chinos and a t-shirt with Cass Shipton Earthlore Inc. emblazoned on it in green and brown, then headed for Sinbad's Cyber Cafe on the Lido Deck. I'd have to change again for dinner at the Fourways Inn, but hey, that's cruise travel. Nothing to do but fend off reporters and change outfits.

The Cafe was crowded with folks on the same placating errand. As I waited for my turn, I noticed Rikyu Ogata working intently at one of the computers, a *JAWS The Revenge* cap shielding his eyes. Seemingly satisfied, he signed off and looked around. When I waved, he motioned me over to take his place.

"Oh, great," I said, ignoring some outraged looks as I pushed my way into the vacant seat. "How are you, Rikki? I haven't seen you or your Uncle Ken since the storm. Did you both weather that incredible wave okay?"

"Awesome, wasn't it!" He smiled cheerfully. He was wearing low-slung jeans, a Nike scorpion t-shirt, and black leather running shoes, also Nike. Everything he wore appeared to be brand new, but then his uncle's outfits always looked as if they'd just come out of the box. Must be an Asian thing. "I ran into some of my mates when the crew herded all of us into Atrium, and we had a blast." He glanced at his watch, an expensive-looking wood-paneled timepiece. "We're meeting in a few minutes at the Starfish to patrol the ship looking for clues on what happened to Mrs. Bratton. We're calling ourselves the *Bermuda Sharks*. Awesome, huh? Oh, and the night of the storm? Uncle Ken was off on some Buddhist retreat—with a Korean lady he met on board, Seamoon Iseul. You probably saw her at the tea ceremony? Anyway, we never connected until breakfast. I guess he and Ms. Seamoon took quite a bashing when the ship practically tipped over. Uncle Ken has a black eye."

"Oh, the poor man. I wonder if he knows that a wet tea bag makes a wonderful eye poultice. Black tea, though."

"Hey, don't worry about Uncle. He looks cool in those Ray-Bans, anyway. You need some help there?" When he grinned, I realized how much Rikyu reminded me of Tip when he was younger—the troubled Native American boy I had once fantasized about adopting. Rikyu had the same Asian eyes and straight dark hair that reflected red glints under the bright lights of the cafe.

I would have loved to gossip a little, find out more about Uncle Ken and Ms. Seamoon, and about the boy himself, but that impulse got shelved by my need to understand how to use the ship's computers to send e-mails. For that, Rikyu Ogata was a Goddess-send. Suddenly the grinning youngster became methodical, intent, and almost too quick in his tutorage.

"And if you need to hack into anything, like for research or whatever, just call on me. I've already got into some pretty tight sites," Rikyu bragged.

"I'll keep that in mind, Rikki, but I sure wouldn't want to see you get yourself into hot water. So be cautious, you hear? Will we see you and your uncle at the formal dinner on the night we start for home?"

The boy rolled his eyes heavenward and shrugged. "Uncle Ken will be there, that's for sure. I suppose I'd better. After he took me along on this trip and all. I thought it might be boring, but hey, no way. Being swamped by a Godzilla wave, and Mrs. Bratton getting murdered. How cool is that?"

"Yes, murder is very cool indeed." I couldn't blame the kid. My own morbid interests had definitely been aroused. I wanted to know what happened, and I would do anything to find out.

Rikyu was about to run off when he seemed to remember something. He paused and looked at me seriously. "You and your gang...what do you call yourselves?"

"Just...the Circle."

"Uncle Ken told me that you guys were mixed up in an arson case recently. Said he read about it in the *Boston Globe*."

"Just happened to be there, you might say. Why, what's on your mind, hon."

"I saw her, you know. Paige Bratton. Must have been just before....the thing that happened. Ossie was blowing up crazy, so I thought I'd better head back to our stateroom. We're on the Riviera Deck. So I, like, happened to look out onto the deck when I was running upstairs, and I saw Mrs. Bratton hanging onto a column with one hand and laughing. Her hair was all plastered down wet, and she had a drink in her other hand. I wondered if she was all right, but then I saw there was a guy with her. I couldn't make out *who* because he was, like, standing in the shadows. Could have been anybody. But I wonder, now, if I should have gone out on deck, see if she was okay. Maybe I could have..."

"It doesn't do any good to think that way, Rikki. What's done is done, and nothing can change what happened. Sometimes fate is as inevitable as that awful storm. No one can alter it. I'm sure you did what you were supposed to do, which was to return to your stateroom and stay safe."

"Yeah. I guess you're right." His solemn expression turned devilish and grinning again. "But it sure would be awesome if we find, like, a vital clue! I think I'd like work in law enforcement some day. Computer forensics maybe."

"Awesome," I agreed. Looking at the boy's eager, hopeful, open face, I felt a frisson of worry. If Rikyu's goal was the FBI or something of that order, he ought to avoid getting any illegal hacking on his record now. Maybe I would mention that to him later.

Oh, don't get involved again! I chided myself. Joe always said that I was as drawn to lost boys as Peter Pan.

After Rikyu ran off to join the Bermuda Sharks, I got busy sending e-mails to Joe aboard the Gaia, to my oldest, Becky, at her law firm, to Adam and the very pregnant Freddie at their new place in Hingham, and to Cathy on the West Coast, all of which said more or less the same thing. *No matter what you've heard on CNN about the rogue wave and the missing bride, I'm fine, we're all fine, and we're not getting involved. REPEAT: not getting involved. Bermuda is gorgeous, and we're having the time of our lives. Looking forward to a non-eventful trip home. Anything that could have happened already has, LOL. I miss you. I love you. Take care of yourself.*

I thought maybe I'd follow up with a call to Becky after dinner tonight to make sure the e-mails had arrived. Joe would be impossible to reach by phone on the *Gaia,* alas. Maybe just as well, as I was surely due for a serious lecture.

So imagine my surprise when Joe called *me.* "*Jesu Cristos*, sweetheart! Are you all right? What a thing to happen on your first cruise!"

"Which thing, honey?" I asked cautiously.

"The rogue wave, of course. Why, what else?"

"A girl is missing off the ship. We don't know if it was the wave, or... Haven't you been watching the news?"

"Ah, no. I've been rather tied up..." Joe's voice told me that he wasn't telling me much. "Haven't *you* seen CNN?" he asked. Tossing my own question back to me seemed odd.

"Okay, out with it, honey. You tell me what I missed, and I'll tell you," I offered.

"You mean, you show me yours, and I'll show you mine?"

That sexy tone wasn't going to divert me this time. "Something has happened aboard the *Gaia*—what? You know you can't keep stuff like that from a clairvoyant wife." Actually, I hadn't a clue. Too many distractions had been keeping my several senses in turmoil.

"*You first.*" Joe could be tough, and a good thing it was, too.

"Okay. Not only is the missing girl a bride, but she's the second bride to disappear from this particular ship, *Goddess of the Sea*. Talk about déjà vu. So no one seems to think that she may simply have been swept overboard by that freak wave. The general consensus is, Paige was a victim of murder, and although there's no logic to it, the husband Tyler Bratton is the chief suspect. With all of that, the media, who aren't being allowed on board the ship, are swarming around Hamilton like killer bees trying to suck up information from passengers. And..." I paused.

"And they caught you?"

"Yes, I'm afraid so. It was just a little interview. I did my best 'we are not amused' Queen Victoria impersonation. Okay, *now you*! What's been going on there?" I was getting more and more uneasy at Joe's reluctance to explain. He must really have thought I knew already, but in truth I hadn't heard or watched world news since I left New York. The aliens could have landed in those UFOs perched on stilts and begun the War of the Worlds, for all I knew.

"It wasn't an alien abduction, was it?" I prompted.

"It might as well have been. The *Gaia* is out of commission," Joe said slowly.

"Oh, Good Goddess! Why? Spit it out..."

"Someone sabotaged the engine. Blew it up actually."

"Oh, honey. Didn't that happen before, to the *Rainbow Warrior*?"

"This wasn't quite the same, but totally crippling anyway."

"Is it fixable? Who was on watch? How did the saboteurs get past him? Aren't you absolutely wild?"

"The answers are yes, Heidimarie, she's been flown to hospital in Germany, and if I get my hands on those bastards, I will certainly kill them."

"*Belay that thought*. What did they do to Heidimarie?"

"Coshed her on the head and threw her overboard. Fortunately she got caught up on a hook and so didn't drown. Leg's in bad shape, though."

"Those logger guys play dirty, don't they? I'm just grateful that they didn't blow up the whole ship and you with it."

"According to Heidimarie, the guys who attacked her looked more like army guerillas than loggers. The bootleg logging operation has been funding a kind of civil war between the rebels and the government."

"Didn't you swear to me you'd probably only be painting slogans on logs? I might have known this would turn out to be a dangerous mission. What's next? I hope you're getting out of there."

"We'll be towed in for repairs. Some nice safe, sane port. Most of the crew will be flying to the States for the time being. I'm staying, at least until we know what's what. You'll probably be home before me. But now I'm worried about you."

"Oh, don't worry about me, honey. We witches are definitely on vacation. We're letting the police solve this one, honest," I lied. "Say, sweet as it is to hear your voice, how much is this call costing you?"

"I think it's sixteen a minute."

"Sixteen *dollars?*"

"Yeah, but who's counting. I'm loving hearing your voice, too, sweetheart. Now I want you to promise me that you'll stay out of trouble. Absolutely no amateur sleuthing."

Who are you calling an amateur? "I absolutely promise. And you absolutely promise not to kill the guys who blew up the *Gaia?*"

"Absolutely."

It was no use trying to fool one another. We chuckled at each other's attempts and lapsed into some serious sexy love chat, couched in innuendoes, but very sweet. And worth every penny of Joe's money.

∾

Talking to Joe put me in such a good humor, nothing could diminish my buoyant mood, not even the company of Tony and Lindsay Grenville, who were also dining at the Fourways Inn, and at a table so nearby, we were like one extended party. They were dressed to the nines as stage Brits, Tony in a flawlessly tailored navy blazer with muted gold buttons, a genuine cravat tucked into the neck of his silk shirt, and Lindsay in a nautical blue silk blouse and crisply pleated white skirt. I almost wanted to ask them what play they were performing. I just hoped it wasn't *Who's Afraid of Virginia Woolf* again.

"So, what do you think of our tragic little murder drama," Tony asked me, leaning over confidentially as if to spare the children's innocent ears. "Did the bridegroom quarrel with the bride over some guy she was flirting with—Paige was quite the swinger, you know—and accidentally whack his lovely wife over the rail?"

I wondered when Tony had run into Paige in her swinger mode. I thought about when I'd last seen the girl, so bored and despondent about her future. Not knowing that there wouldn't be one. If only I had seen *something*. Could I have prevented that tragedy? I shuddered. I knew just how Rikyu felt, not sensing the girl's danger. "Sounds as if you're writing a play based on Paige's death. What's it called: *The Bermuda Love Triangle?*"

"I'll leave the recording of our adventures to that creepy writer Jason Severin and his weird Mommy Dearest. Bizarre events in the Bermuda Triangle are rather his specialty, not mine." Tony smiled at Phillipa and me with a devilish gleam in his eyes as if to draw us into some gossipy clique, *if you can't say anything nice about anyone, come sit by me.* "They look as if they're on something, the two of them. What do you think, Phil? Cocaine perhaps?" His dramatic voice was irresistibly conspiratorial.

"I put down Jason's otherworldly manner to the Creative Coma, or Socked by the Muse," Phillipa said, toying with her dessert of Champagne-Strawberry Soup. "I'm familiar with the effect."

"As a cookbook author?" Tony's tone was dismissive.

"As a poet," Phillipa said tartly.

With her usual talent for a rousing interruption, Fiona announced, "All right, ladies, Mr. Swan is waiting!" She glanced at the brooch watch pinned to her muumuu. "I told him we'd be ready by eight-thirty, and here it is quarter to nine already. The kiddoes must be exhausted, poor little tykes, and we have a busy day ourselves tomorrow, between the crystal caves and Samhain."

"*Sow –win?*" Lindsay sounded out. "What's that?"

"Oh, it's sort of a Halloween thing," Heather explained airily, and more or less pushed us all out of the way so that she could grab the check. After she'd signed for it and we moved outdoors, she muttered to me, "If we didn't get out of there, we'd have had Fiona inviting the psychiatrist and his hissing wife to our Sabbat."

"Personally, I feel grateful that she didn't invite Aiden Guilfoyle."

It was rather a crunch, getting all of us into Mr. Swan's taxi, but since it had been built with one of those gracious interiors of yesteryear, we made it—with petite Deidre and her children perched on laps.

Fiona rode beside Bill Swan. "I have everything you asked for, Madam," he said, his face crinkled with sheer pleasure.

"Oh, dear," Phillipa whispered in my ear. "What do you suppose...?"

"Torches? Wood for a bonfire? A steel drum band?" I speculated quietly.

Fiona, who always heard the sotto voce, turned around and replied, "Just a permit for a tiny altar fire, my dears. And some exotic flowers, indigenous incense, and pure white candles to send our heart's wishes off on a magical breeze to the God Neptune himself."

CHAPTER TWELVE

O listen to the sounding sea
That beats on the remorseless shore.
O listen, for that sound will be
When our wild hearts shall beat no more

– George William Curtis

Many Wiccan groups have names, the *Something Coven*, but we have preferred to call ourselves simply *The Circle.* As I looked around at us on Samhain evening, with our eclectic styles of dress, *Chameleon Coven* came to mind. Phillipa, the traditionalist, was wearing her signature black, in this case narrow black pants with a black poncho. Since cruise ethos invites excess baggage, I was able to swirl forth in the forest green hooded cape with pewter clasps that Joe had given me early in our relationship (to "match those enchanting eyes") over a paler green ankle-length travel dress. Deidre looked sharp and cute in brand new British clothes: navy slacks, silk blouse, and tweed jacket. Heather was dramatically robed in plum velvet. Fiona wore her favorite coat sweater of many colors, a rainbow striped skirt, and carried, of course, her green reticule.

We were a far cry from the peaked hat, green-skinned, warty caricature witches who ride their brooms over mundane Halloweens. Although we may not be able to turn the odd luckless adversary into a frog with a *pouf* of our wands, we did make another kind of spiritual magic, especially on Samhain. We connected with the energy of the Cosmos, seeking to bend reality into the shape of good wishes. "To bend" is the operative phrase, spelled *wicce* in the Old English.

This particular Samhain, however, was to prove one of the most challenging we had ever celebrated. We'd always been careful not to invoke and provoke the dark entities, but this was not our home ground of quaint, quirky Plymouth. The mythic culture of Bermuda was an unknown quantity, and we were working magic in unfamiliar territory. Perhaps we should have consulted Rudy Koch, who'd spent some time studying the Bermudian *old ways*, before we'd ventured to open a door to the local spirits.

Yet, what could have been more perfect for an outdoor Sabbat than the cove Fiona had found on the pink sands of Bermuda! Secluded by a ring of boulders and earthen banks, it was presided over this night by a maiden moon, newest of the new. The dark of the moon, with its attendant dangers, had just passed. I hoped that would be a good omen for the rest of our voyage, that the perils we'd encountered were all behind us now.

This Samhain, we'd welcomed two guests into our circle, the repressed Muffy Koch and the gorgeous Calypso, who was wrapped in even more shimmering colors than Fiona. Calypso had been Fiona's last minute invitation, and to my eyes she looked distinctly uncomfortable. I wondered why she had accepted. It might have been quite a squash if Mr. Swan hadn't recruited another cabbie, his nephew Horatio, a dark-skinned giant with a gleaming smile, to transport the girls. Fiona glanced at the brooch watch pinned to her sweater. It was just going on eight. "Come back at ten, please," she instructed her devoted driver. He doffed his captain's hat and bowed. As they were trudging back to their cabs, I thought I heard the nephew mutter "voodoo women."

Although we turned first to her, Fiona declined the priestess role. "We five wouldn't be here if it weren't for Heather. It's fated that she be the one who casts the circle and calls the quarters for our Bermuda Samhain," Fiona decreed.

I swept the area clear with a long frond of palm. From the varied supplies provided by Mr. Swan, Phillipa lit candles on our impromptu altar, a large flat rock. We invited Muffy and Calypso to participate in this part of the ceremony by igniting the sweetbriar rose and freesia incense. Heather herself held a flame to the squat green, raven's feather candle dedicated to Hecate that she'd made for this occasion. Fiona rang the bell (carried in her reticule, of course.) Now we were ready to begin.

Heather drew her athame from its ceremonial leather sheath. Its ivory handle had been decorated with scrimshaw, another treasure from her sea-going family. Glancing at her wrist compass (this wasn't home, after all, where the Atlantic was always east) she welcomed the North and its connection to our mother earth, the East and its spirits of transcendent air, the South and its fires of transformation, the West and its healing waters. Representing the quarters were fragrant incense, candle flames, pure consecrated water in a silver-chased bottle, and an enameled box of crystal salt.

While Heather cast the circle, Deidre used the altar candles to light four more, one for each of the elementals. The pink-sanded cove was beginning to resemble a spooky ancient church of trembling flames. Although the evening was mild and still, occasionally a riff of breeze would blow out a candle, which Phillipa would then relight with the cigarette lighter she just happened to have in her pocket.

"Oh dear," said Muffy. "I hope Rudy won't be cross with me for having this exciting experience—all on my own, you know?"

"Sometimes it's a kindness not to burden a husband with too much detail," Fiona said, slipping her plump arm around Muffy's shoulders and giving her a supportive hug. "Especially when he has so much of himself on his mind."

Then we each lit small white candles, standing them in a long wooden tray filled with pure white sand, to honor the beloved dead, most recently Deidre's husband Will. As always, I lit a candle for my own dear Grandma whose influence had led me into the heady world of herbs when she bequeathed to me the precious Shipton notebooks as well as her cottage and gardens on the Plymouth shore. At Samhain, the veil between the worlds is thinnest, and those who guide us and speak to us from Summerland are closer then. Under the bright starry sky of this island, the swirling misty shapes of those others seemed almost visible.

Calypso crossed herself and started away from the altar fire at the center of our circle. Deidre took her hand. "Let nothing disturb you, let nothing frighten you, all things are passing, Goddess only is changeless." She'd adapted the prayer of St. Teresa, perhaps without intention. Her expression was wistful, openly waiting to sense the presence of her husband Will.

"And now, Fiona, lest you forget, we're all waiting to hear about those thirteen fabulous powers which we may or may not possess," Heather urged, taking on the authority of the high priestess she represented this night.

"*Dying* to hear," Phillipa amended. "This is, after all, the Feast of the Dead."

It's always so fascinating to watch Fiona take on her full glamour. Our plump, slightly frowsy, pixilated friend drew herself up and became before our eyes a full-figured, handsome wise woman of inscrutable charm and goddess power. "Yes, this is the time, end of the old year and beginning of the new," she said. "I'll recite them for you. When one of you accepts a particular power as natural and inevitable to her, she will light a candle to claim it, understood?"

Fiona's glamourous voice was something else, melodic and irresistible. Never to be gainsaid. "Understood," we murmured.

"To begin, I will speak of the power to transform reality, which is called magic. Since magic is the province of us all, our Samhain priestess will take the first candle."

Heather smiled and nodded. She lit the white candle and stood it with others in the sand tray.

"The power to change appearance, which is called glamour or shapeshifting. So convenient. You should all practice glamour more." Fiona herself lit the second candle.

"The power of visioning, which is called clairvoyance," she continued. That was me, all right. I lit the third candle for my own gift, which I would not wish on another soul.

"The power of mind over matter, which is called psychokinesis," Fiona said. I lit the fourth candle for my daughter-in-law Freddie, whose amazing energy could bend locks, addle delicate machines, and spin the devil out of slot machines. *What a worry!*

"The power to avert harm and attract good fortune, which is called luck." For some reason, possibly for her partner Rob Negrini, this fifth power moved our guest Calypso, who gracefully joined our lighting ceremony.

"The power to understand and communicate with all earth's creatures, which is called empathy." Me, again. As I lit the sixth candle, I realized how much I missed that communication with my own dogs and wondered how they were faring while they boarded at Heather's. No doubt Scruffy would have many vociferous complaints on my return.

"The power to perceive the world of spirit, which is called channeling." Deidre, our newest ghost-hunter, took the seventh candle as her own.

"The power to bless and heal, which is called prayer and the laying on of hands." Heather, probably thinking of Dick and his Wee Angels Animal Hospital, lit the eighth candle.

"The power of finding, which is called dowsing." Fiona claimed the ninth candle, then went on. "The power to read thoughts, which is called telepathy."

We looked at each other uncertainly. Fiona smiled. "That could be any of us, dears, but let's ask our guest Muffy to light the tenth candle for telepathy." The girl moved forward uncertainly, but it was clear that she was feeling a touch of circle empowerment herself at that moment and enjoying it.

"The power to divine the future, which is called prophecy." Phillipa of the tarot accepted her right to light the eleventh candle.

"The power to bend time and space, which is called relativity." Stretching time to fit her needs was Deidre's specialty, one we all envied. She lit the twelfth candle with a gamine grin.

"And the highest power of all, to align with the divine: raising a cone of power, drawing down the moon, invoking goddesses and gods." Fiona paused, looking around at our firelit, intent faces. "Heather, our priestess, will light that one on behalf of all of us."

Heather smiled enigmatically, lighting the last. I knew what she was thinking, that she would create her own version of our thirteen candles of power in her home workshop at the

Morgan mansion. "May the Goddess and the God bless us with these powers, each according to her ability and inclination."

Now that the thirteen candles were flamed, plus the earlier tributes to the dead, the long box tray bloomed with a garden of light. After which we each gave a moment to our hopes and dreams, some spoken, some silent, then raised a cone of power in the way that had become traditional with us. Standing in a circle with our guests, holding hands under familiar starry skies on an unfamiliar foreign island, we passed the energy from woman to woman until at last Heather gave a quick upswinging signal with her athame and we threw out hands toward the Cosmos.

There was a collective "ahhhh," a wonderful feeling of relaxation and completion.

Diffident Muffy and doubtful Calypso had felt the power, too. Their faces were shining and accepting. I wondered how much our spell of protection was responsible for Calypso being here tonight so vibrantly alive while Paige Bratton's blonde beauty was food for the sea worms. I shuddered.

Gazing fixedly at the fire, I reached out deliberately (something I generally try to avoid) to Paige's spirit, because it was Samhain when such communications are the most possible, and because I had failed her and she deserved to be avenged. "*Paige, tell me who, tell me who killed you*," I whispered.

Surprised at my own ability to jumpstart a vision, I felt that familiar fading away of my surroundings. The starry, candlelit cove disappeared, and again I found myself on a dark deck of the *Goddess of the Sea.* Paige Bratton was leaning on the ship's rail watching the storm roil the waves. Someone put a cocktail glass in her hand. It sparkled in the reflected light of one of the lounges; I wasn't sure which lounge or even what deck, but I could hear dance-band music. It seemed to be growing louder to match the rising wind. Paige drained the glass and smiled at the cacophony. The storm screamed more fiercely, whipping her blonde hair over her face, causing her to cling to a column. She turned toward the light then, seeking safety within. But something was wrong, something had happened to her ability to move, she was helpless. A terrified expression came over her face. Her mouth opened but she couldn't speak. Slowly she slumped against the column as if she were fainting. I could only see the back of the man she was with. He was laughing darkly—a laugh that ended on a particular high note—as he helped her to walk, moving her into the shadows away from the lounge door. He couldn't wait. He was already ripping down the front of her dress. I couldn't see his face, but suddenly I knew what deck they were on and just where he was taking her, pushing her now, into a passenger restroom tucked under the stairs. The storm grew even wilder. Everything was banging, flapping, blowing in the rising storm. The lights went out, total darkness.

The next thing I knew was the disgusting taste in my mouth and the sharp scent of smelling salts. A circle of concerned faces. The familiar nausea and disorientation. How many times would I put myself through this! Heather came running up with a cloth dipped in cold sea water for my forehead. Looking over her shoulder, I could see Muffy and Calypso clinging to one another.

"The odd couple," Phillipa whispered, echoing my own thought. "What did you see, girl? Do you know the bastard?"

"I only saw his back, damn him. But I heard him laugh. I think I'd know that laugh again," I whispered back. "Every time I go through this, I get another glimpse, never the whole picture. This time it was auditory—the sick laughter. *I'll remember that.* Listen, Phil—she drank something that affected her. She must have been drugged. I'll give you all the details later. We'd better finish our Sabbat now. The girls are looking pretty anxious. Probably think you're about to make a human sacrifice...of me."

By this time, the fast-burning candles we'd lit for the dead and for the thirteen powers had melted down into white puddles and were guttering out on their bed of sand. Heather got ready to close the quarters, indicating that Fiona, Deidre, Phillipa and I should each extinguished one of the elemental candles in the order in which we'd lit them, North, East, South, and West. But before we could conclude our ceremony in the traditional way, a freakish gust of wind rushed at us from over the waves and put out all the lights, even the altar fire which was hit by an unexpected spray of water.

"Uh oh," said Fiona. "Someone or *something*'s here."

"Jesus, Mary, and Joseph," Deidre exclaimed. "What's that?"

Even the usually unflappable Phillipa gave a little shriek. "Hey, Fiona, did you, maybe, whistle up a wind right then?"

Panic is contagious. Calypso began to laugh hysterically. Muffy seemed to be having a difficult time getting her breath.

Despite the absence of light, Fiona managed to find a paper bag in her reticule. "Here, breathe into this," Fiona ordered the gasping girl. "No, Phil, I did not whistle up that wind. Don't you sense....well, never mind. Remain calm, all of you. Very soon your eyes will adjust to the blackness."

"Yeah, yeah," said Heather. "Personally I'd rather *light one candle* etcetera than put up with this shit. If I could only find the matches." Phillipa flicked open her lighter, whose flame promptly blew out.

Fiona brought forth a flashlight from her reticule, a small powerful one she swept around the circle, the bangles on her arm tinkling, a small familiar sound against the wildness of the rising wind. Our faces looked eerie and frightened in its singular light.

"Holy Hecate, what a Girl Scout that Fiona would have made," Heather exclaimed.

"U.S. Coast Guard, maybe," Phillipa said. "*Semper Paratus is our guide*, and all that."

"Light a candle by all means, dear," Fiona replied reassuringly to Heather. "If you'd rather have a flashlight of your own, I have a few pen lights in the bottom of my bag somewhere."

"Naturally," Phillipa said.

While Heather tried, and failed, to light her green Hecate candle, the mysterious wind swirled around us in a cyclonic fashion, spattering us with stinging wet sand.

Perhaps it was only the curse of a vivid imagination (which at times can be a blessing, but not now) that it seemed to me a chorus of impish voices was in that wind, screeching some insistent warning in an indecipherable language that made a chill of horror run down from the back of my neck to the bottom of my spine.

"Hey, gals, this is really creeping me out," Deidre said.

Fiona had found her clutch of penlights and began passing them out to us. Soon it looked as if we were mounting an amateur laser light show on the beach.

Then as suddenly as that bizarre wind had rushed at us, it calmed to a gentle, not unpleasant breeze that felt as if someone were stroking my face. I smelled a familiar scent, a particular medley of mints that had belonged to only one person in my life. "Grandma?" I heard my own inadvertent question.

Immediately, we were again enveloped by the strange phenomena, not shrieking not-quite-human voices this time, but nocturnal animal sounds of a thousand-thousand scratchings, scrabblings, squeaks, and whispering wings. Fancying that I was being nipped by some new species of no-see-'em gnats, I wrapped my cloak closer around me. The lovely fragrance of mint gardens was replaced by a whiff of decaying flesh.

"Did someone just open Pandora's box?" Heather asked in a quavering tone.

"Good God, what's happening to us! Are those *evil things* going to *eat* us?" Calypso's lyrical voice was reaching a high C scream.

"I'm still having trouble breathing. I think I'm allergic to the smell of death, you know?" Muffy said in a small, scared voice. "I'd like to go back to the ship now, please,"

"Eeeek!" Phillipa screeched, throwing her poncho over her hair. "Are those *bats* whizzing around us?"

"Cease and desist!" Fiona commanded.

My eyes *were* adjusting to the minimal illumination of our penlights, because I could see our intrepid friend, with her back to the water's edge, addressing the darkness of the rocks. She flung up her arm in an imperious hand gesture. *"Begone, you creatures of the underworld! Begone, and let the spirits of Summerland pass over the dark waters! Begone, and let those we love return to us!* Her commanding voice pierced the night, not shrill but distinctly, penetrating every shadowy nook on the beach.

The screeching, shivering sounds of unseen creatures gradually subsided.

"Ceres save us, we've been mobbed by spawns of darkness, guardians of the veils between worlds," Fiona said, wonderingly, as much to herself as to us. "I've known about their existence, of course, but this is my first....*well, well, well.*"

"What do they want of us?" Deidre asked in a worried voice. She'd put a motherly arm around each of our trembling guests who huddled against her petite frame.

"Ah, they want nothing, in the sense that they are made of something like anti-matter themselves, in other words, they want *no-thing*. If they wanted anything it would be to keep us from reaching across to Summerland, and to prevent those we love from speaking to us. Because then we would be breaching their chasm of no-thingness. One might call them *strangelets*, in the non-scientific sense.

"Strangelets? There's a scientific sense?"

"Look it up, dear," said the eternal librarian in Fiona.

Fiona's banishing cry had been powerful indeed. The bat-like squeals of the "strangelets" subsided into the distance, as if the siege wasn't weakening but was moving away from us slightly, hovering just off-stage. *The farther away, the better!*

A soft gray luminosity that was none of our penlights shimmered above the beach. Hardly discernible and in no way as dramatic as the preceding events, it caught our attention with its quiet advance.

"Oh," Deidre exclaimed. "Oh, it's you, dear. Are you all right?" She untangled herself from Muffy and Calypso and walked forward toward the water.

She was not speaking to us. Her face, which I could barely see, was upturned to the sky where the wisp of new moon caught her smile. *She was talking to Will.* Deidre really did see the dead! Judging by the silence on the beach, everyone else had the same impression, and none of us wanted to break the spell.

But a moment later, I did. I screamed blue murder. Because a wet, clammy hand shot out of the night and grabbed my arm. A gurgling voice in my ear whispered, "*Help me, help me, the water's freezing, I can't breathe...*"

Even as it seemed to be drowning in a clamorous ocean, I knew that voice. It was Paige Bratton.

~

I can't remember how we ever pulled ourselves together to get off that secluded, rock-ringed, haunted beach. Shaken up as we were, it was all Heather could do to open the circle properly.

Phillipa took around a large plastic bag and unceremoniously packed up all of our paraphernalia.

Deidre was in a world of her own, of course, wrapped in the ethereal experience of encountering her dead husband. "He didn't speak, but I could see him clearly," she whispered. "And I felt such love and forgiveness. For all my follies, you know. I never valued Will enough, I realize that now. Oh, it's true, it's true. Spirit lives!" Her voice trailed off, and we left her to bask in the wonder.

We'd brought several bottles of fine wines personally selected by Heather and a hamper of goodies for the "cakes and ale" conclusion of our ritual. Most of us weren't hungry—too much adrenaline coursing through our veins. Muffy and Deidre, however, really had an attack of the munchies. "Comfort food," Deidre explained, practically inhaling a slice of the *Goddess of the Sea's* excellent chocolate bread.

All of us swigged down those wines in rather unappreciative haste, which helped a little. After a healthy share of the red, Muffy got a case of giggles that soon became unstoppable hiccups. And Calypso danced around the beach dangerously close to the rocks in the darkness, her gold hoop earrings catching occasional glimmers of light from the new moon.

Phillipa glanced at her watch. "Where the hell is Mr. Swan?" As if on cue, the two venerable black taxis eased into view on the road above us. We didn't say much to one another driving back, conscious of Bert Swan, erect and dignified, steering the ancient vehicle over the dark walled roads to the port at Hamilton as if he were driving the royal limousine through the streets of London.

Later, Muffy told us that Horatio Swan had been in high spirits, singing native songs to entertain the girls on their trip back to the ship. Calypso had sung along in her pleasing soprano voice. Then the dueting couple switched to hymns, so Muffy had joined in. They'd arrived at the *Goddess of the Sea* with a rousing rendition of "Nearer My God to Thee."

"Shades of the Titanic," Phillipa commented. "How appropriate, *I hope not*."

CHAPTER THIRTEEN

There is one knows not what sweet mystery about this sea, whose gentle awful stirrings seem to speak of some hidden soul beneath.

– Herman Melville

We held a kind of debriefing at the midnight buffet, an event we'd avoided so far, being well fed enough on three meals and a pastry-laden tea time every day. The fantasy feast was spread that evening in the swank *Le Consulat.* In the midst of the Halloween party mood that prevailed, surveying the pyramids of shrimp and lobster, the sumptuous arrays of imported cheeses and exotic fruits, our haunted Samhain seemed more like a dream than a real happening.

"A true experience of the weird," Fiona declared. We'd commandeered the kind of round table in the shadows that we preferred and were huddled together over plates of delectable cold foods and pots of hot black coffee. Even Heather didn't suggest liqueurs. We were already drunk on the night's excitement and fear, augmented by bottles of wine consumed on the beach.

Surprisingly, Muffy hung around with us, round-eyed, listening, saying little. I wondered if she were storing up a bizarre tale to one-up Rudy when he returned home from the rooster sacrifice.

Looking quite recovered now, surrounded by the bright lights, music, and crowded tables of midnight snackers, Calypso smiled ruefully. "I have an elderly great-aunt who would have loved the voodoo stuff that went on this evening, but the rest of my family would be horrified. Aunt Callie. I was named for her in hopes that she'd make me her heir. Perhaps one of these days I'll tell her about those black 'no-things' of yours. No one else would believe it—I'm not sure I do myself." She moved to leave, but then turned back to look at each of us seriously. "Somehow though, I feel as if I owe you ladies—I don't know what. Good vibes, I guess." Then she dashed off in a rainbow swirl to find Rob, who was probably in the casino, if he'd been allowed to return after the recent fracas.

"Little does that girl know, we may have kept her safe from the murderer among us," Heather said. "Oh well, *to keep silent* is always the hard part. Now Fiona, tell us. What do you mean by *experience of the weird*? Is that like *fated*, or *destined*?"

"There's another concept of weird—Robert Graves writes about it—*the dark other*. The shadow twin of ourselves. Osiris and Set. Able and Cain. Jeckle and Hyde. Maybe even...I wonder...does everyone have a doppleganger?" Fiona rambled on from reference to reference, leaving us all to scramble after her as best we could.

"Yes, but you said *experience* of the weird," Heather persisted.

"Those things we encountered, the guardians of the deceased, like whispering black holes, gave me quite a turn, I confess. *Bean Nighe*, we Scots call them. *Banshees*, the Irish say. Messengers of death. Washers of blood. It's important to stand between the Bean Nighe and the water."

Muffy took a little leather book out of her shoulder bag as if to jot down a note, but Phillipa scowled at her darkly, and she put it away.

"We noticed you looming large at the water's edge," Phillipa commented dryly. "When you banish an evil spirit, it practically vaporizes, you know. I have to admit, you have some psychic authority, lady. But in what sense were those *things* our evil twins?"

"We are matter, they are anti-matter. If we worked on the dark side, those 'things,' as you call them, would be our companions. Makes the hair stand right up on the back of your neck, doesn't it?"

Deidre, who'd come out of her beatific trance, was listening now. "Golly, how does anyone work on the dark side, then?"

"*Very, very carefully*," Phillipa said, with a look at Heather, who'd been known to light a black candle or two in her time.

Heather turned her patrician head away from Phillipa's meaningful gaze. The granddaughter and great-granddaughter of sea captains would chart her own course, *thank you very much*.

"What a Samhain this has been!" I exclaimed, if only to veer away from troublesome waters. "Fiona, you must have accidentally chosen one of those sacred sites of great power. Not only was I able to envision the murder of Paige, I actually felt her hand and heard her cry out to me for help."

Muffy uttered a little cry herself, then clapped her hand over her mouth. Deidre passed the girl a plate of miniature cream puffs—more comfort food, I assumed.

"That was no accident," Fiona said. "The natives are aware of the places of power on this island. Mr. Swan knew what he was about when he took me there."

"Oh, capital!" Muffy exclaimed. "Do you think he'd, like, give Rudy a tour of those places?"

"Not a chance!" Fiona said emphatically. "What happens at Samhain, stays at Samhain," she warned the girl, at the same time patting her hand in a kindly fashion.

"And what happens at Beltane, ditto," Phillipa smirked.

"Beltane?" Muffy looked totally confused.

"May Day. Love in the woods," I explained. "A fine way of shaking off the winter blahs." I lapsed into smiling silence, remembering certain pleasurable outdoor interludes with Joe on Beltane and other warm nights.

Fiona waved her arms at us, silver bangles jangling. "No digressions, ladies, please. And in return for your caution, Muffy dear, you shall have as a memento a charming amulet that will work wonders for you in your relationship with your husband. Dee, you do have one of those Willendorf Venus thingies, don't you?"

Deidre grinned. "They don't make female idols like the Willendorf anymore." She reached into the pocket of her smartly tailored British tweed jacket and drew a small clay replica of the goddess with the pendulous breasts and bulbous thighs. "Here, you take this, honey, and stand her in the bedroom overlooking your bed. Or in the dining room, watching your table, if you prefer, but really the bedroom is best. The eternal mother, emblem of female rule. Look to her when you are in need of a little reinforcement, so to speak."

"Oh, but I couldn't take your very own goddess, you know?" Muffy said, reaching out her hand nonetheless to touch the lavish little curves of the ancient madonna. The young woman's wan complexion had taken on an attractive rosiness, and her doe's eyes shone with hope.

"Not to worry. I make these ceramic replicas myself, you know, in my spare time."

We all chuckled at Deidre's *spare time*, of which there didn't seem to be any, but somehow she continued to stretch hours to create new crafts prodigiously anyway. She ignored us and continued, "And I put a little special magic into this one. You'll be surprised..." Deidre let the matter trail off right there, knowing that Muffy would find strength in the mystery of it. Magical power! It's what every young woman longs to possess. What was that old Ladies Home Journal slogan? *Never underestimate the power of a woman.* Especially if she's a witch.

After Muffy had scurried off with new verve, the amulet clutched in her hand, Phillipa said, "One small step for a woman, one giant step for womankind, wouldn't you say?"

"Now, Cass, tell us, for Goddess' sake, what you've learned about Paige's murder!" Heather demanded.

"There was a man. I could only see his back," I reconstructed the scene slowly in my mind, knowing I would have remembered more details if I'd been able to speak about the vision immediately after it occurred. "He gave Paige a cocktail, and after she'd consumed the drink, it was obvious that it had been drugged. She lost control of her body and her speech. He ripped her dress down the front and dragged her away to that little passenger restroom under the stairs outside the ballroom on the International Deck. Oh, and he laughed. I won't forget that laugh, a nasty dirty laugh. And that's how I'm going to identify him. When I hear that laugh again."

"But we're leaving Bermuda tomorrow morning. We only have three more days. Well, two and a half, really, to catch him," Deidre complained. "Let's not forget poor Christy Callahan, the first bride to be drowned by that beast, whoever he is. And it's me she's been haunting, all dripping with lace and seaweed. I mean, *do I need that?*" She reached for a tempting little cream puff.

I put my arm around her shoulders with a supportive hug. "It hasn't happened since you changed suites, right? Listen, Dee, I know just how you feel, having your life disturbed by an uncomfortable and unwanted psychic talent. I'm not too fond of my visions, either. But I have to accept my gift, especially when it may help to save future victims. If no one stops him, this psycho will go on raping and murdering more young women like Christy and Paige. And that's insupportable."

"Bravo!" Phillipa applauded my speech. "So one thing we know about this killer, he's not a first-time cruiser. He was a passenger on the *Goddess of the Sea* last year when the Callahans were on their wedding trip."

"The Kochs are frequent cruisers, although I would be loathe to accuse a Vassar professor," Heather said. "Lindsay said that she and Tony had made the voyage before. Ken Ogata mentioned a previous tea ceremony demonstration at a Japanese restaurant, *The Mikado Ryotei*. And that's just the men we know about because they dined with us at the Captain's table."

"What about Jason Severin?" Deidre asked.

"Him, too—don't you remember?" Phillipa said. "His mom mentioned being left high and dry while he pursued his own pleasures on the beach. Lure of the islands, and all that. I suppose he couldn't very well search for a date with Mom trailing along."

"Well, my dears. We'll just have to get them all laughing," Fiona said.

"Laughing?" Deidre looked puzzled.

"Fiona means so that I can listen for the sick laugh I heard in my vision," I explained. "If it *was* someone we know."

"What an awful responsibility," Deidre said. "At least I saw...I think I saw...Will's spirit while all those bizarre events were going on tonight. That's the good side of my new... what?"

"Power," Fiona said.

"My new power," Deidre echoed. "I think I'm going to talk to Aiden about seeing Will, if you all don't mind."

"Oh, it's *Aiden* now, is it?" Phillipa said. I gave her a sharp nudge not to tease Deidre, who to my eyes was rather keyed up and distraught. So what if Dee might be seeking the solace of her childhood beliefs? Perhaps there are times when a bishop in the flesh is more comforting than a goddess in the spirit. There was no reason on earth why any of us should feel confined to one doctrine. I certainly didn't think the Creator of the Universe herself favored one sect over another.

"Capital idea, Dee. Any altar in a storm," I said. "Now I'm going to my comfy bed because I'm getting very sleepy."

Just the very mention of sleep brought on a round of yawns, and we trudged wearily away to our suites. Hot showers and cool pillows were calling us.

Later, as I fell on my perfectly turned-down bed with its silky blue coverlet and gold-wrapped chocolates, Phillipa called out from her room, "I wonder if traveling about with wise women to distant places is always so dicey."

"It's not the foreign shores, it's the foreign demons that are the problem," I answered. "I'll never forget that plague of scavenging black imps on the beach. It's all very well for Fiona to call them *no-things*, but I actually felt itchy."

"A friggin' bunch of bats. That's what they were."

~

At breakfast the next morning, Deidre was absent from our table.

"She and the children breakfasted earlier with the Bishop and Father Dunn. What a handsome young fellow that Michael Dunn is, such a waste," Fiona said. "I saw the young priest leading the children off to the games room, while Dee and the Bishop had their heads together over coffee cups. No doubt she was pouring out her troubled heart to the dear man. It will do her good, but her return to the catechism of her youth is only temporary, ladies. Dee will never give up her faery life for second place."

"Second place?" Heather looked confused.

"Surely you're accustomed to Fiona's verbal shorthand," Phillipa said. "She's commenting that an orthodoxy that denies the priesthood to females would never hold a young woman who'd felt the power of magic and a touch of the faery."

"Amazing," Fiona said, patting Phillipa's hand. "The woman is a poet, by Brigid. But I can't imagine that any of you have a real problem following my train of thought."

"Well, it's a bit like jumping from ice floe to ice floe, but we manage to keep up most of the time." I said. "Not to change the subject, but does anyone know what happened to Tyler Bratton? Is he going to sail with us when we leave for New York this afternoon? Maybe if I questioned him, you know... about who Paige was pals with. Delicately, of course. I wouldn't want to be the one who suggests..."

"Tyler will be staying in Bermuda," Heather said. "I heard this straight from our knowledgeable social director Ulla. Paige's parents, the Davisons, have arrived and are throwing their weight around with the Bermuda police, the Norse Line reps, and the FBI, who are putting in a *pro forma* appearance, because what can they do when all the forensics are at the bottom of the ocean? Tyler, who is now the sole owner of a mansion in Greenwich that was a wedding gift to the happy couple from the Davisons, naturally must hang around to be supportive."

"Do you think there's a chance that he..." Phillipa let that thought trail off and poured us all another cup of coffee.

"No," I said firmly. "I took advantage of his grief and confusion to give Tyler a sympathetic hug before we docked in Hamilton and the Brits dragged him off for questioning. He was as clear to me as a glass of spring water. Blunderer and incipient alcoholic, yes. Murderer, no. It wasn't a passionate love match, but Tyler and Paige had known each other since childhood and could have settled down together amiably to the usual over-indulgent Greenwich life and produced the desired grandchildren. Poor Paige. Did I tell you that I read her palm shortly before...?"

"I didn't know you read palms!" Heather said.

"I don't. Well...I know the general stuff, Life Line, Love Line, Fate Line, and what have you. Just an excuse to hold Paige's hand because it's *touch* that informs me. And also, the reading itself gave me a chance to ask some pertinent questions. I wanted to see what was up with her weird outburst at the Captain's Dinner," I said. "Turns out Paige was simply drunk and confused, remembering an incident that had happened to her roommate at college. Rape, possibly drug involvement. But then, you know, I looked at the way her Fate Line crossed over and cut through her Life Line, and it gave me such a pain in my midsection, I just doubled up and fled. That's why I feel so guilty about Paige. I was on the verge of *knowing*. I could have warned her."

I seemed to be working myself into a depressed state, but Phillipa reached over and gave my shoulder a sharp shake. "Hey, come off it, girlfriend. Many's the time I've seen something horrid in a tarot spread, which I then prettied up for the petitioner. It's just natural, even if you *are* named Cassandra, not to be clobbering everyone you know with doom and gloom. I, too, have kicked my own ass later. Not an easy maneuver. In fact, that's why I'm so reluctant to read for any but the strongest of psyches. I see too much, too much."

Now Phillipa was getting in a maudlin mood.

Fiona clapped her hands sharply, bangles jingling. "None of that Monday morning second sighting now! Has it occurred to you two that there are fates which cannot be changed, no matter what you say or do? There may be karma at work in someone's life that is stronger than any of our manipulations of events, or even our magic workings. That's why we always leave our spells open to interpretation by the Cosmos. Even if you had flat-out warned Paige to beware of male companions bearing cocktails, she might have walked right into danger anyway. And in a way, she had been warned, by the experience of her college friend."

"Yeah, maybe," I said, still unconvinced. "So...isn't it time we worked a spell to banish that psychopath for good? On the white side, of course."

"Well, personally, I'm ready to resort to something stronger," Heather said.

"There are no gray areas in magic," Fiona warned.

"Okay, then," Phillipa said. "How about this? We'll magic the bastard into revealing himself."

"Perfect," I said.

CHAPTER FOURTEEN

The real voyage of discovery
consists not in seeking new landscapes
but in having new eyes.

– Marcel Proust

It was past three in the afternoon when we sailed out of the harbor at Hamilton and headed toward New York. Little remained of the damage suffered by the *Goddess* from the disastrous rogue wave, just the smell of fresh paint and new wood. Deidre's old suite was still not operational, however, fixed up with a new door until the interior could be extensively redecorated. But that freak storm belonged to the legends of the Triangle now. To our small party, it seemed both memorable and unreal. Some other passengers, of course, were talking litigation.

The weather on our departure day was clear, breezy, and chilly, turning too cold, as November began, for the sun-seeking tourist trade; this was the last voyage the Norse Line would make to Bermuda until spring.

Tomorrow night would be the final formal dinner for which I'd been saving my knock-out green silk Caroline Rose tunic with cape. Tonight we were gathering for an early supper with Deidre's youngsters at the Terrace Cafe. Once they were settled in bed, we would meet in Fiona and Heather's suite for some serious spell-making. It was our intention to give the murderer a psychic push that would cause him to reveal himself before we docked in New York.

"To know, to dare, to will, and to keep silent." Deidre quoted the age-old formula for spellcraft and took up a spoonful of her Crab Bisque.

The children, busy arranging pickles on their Burgers Deluxe, paid no attention, but I did, concluding that their mom had recovered from her chat with Bishop Guilfoyle and was ready to invoke some serious magic.

"How'd it go this morning in the confessional?" Phillipa asked, lifting the puff pastry on her Beef Pot Pie with a suspicious fork.

"Confessionals are always secret," Deidre replied pertly. "But for your inquiring mind, I'll say that I've been enjoined against glamourous powers, fortunetelling, graven images—can you imagine? There goes my poppet business straight to hell!—and, most urgently, I was urged to foreswear *consorting with witches*. For my own good. Really, I felt about six years old."

"What's consorting with witches?" Jenny asked.

Deidre picked up her lobster sandwich thoughtfully. "It's like hanging out with your girlfriends," she explained.

"Sister Firmina says a witch is a soccer...a saucer...a *sorceress*, and 'you shall not let a sorceress live.'" Willy Jr. said.

Fiona raised her eyebrows. "Exodus 22:18," she identified the damning quote in a fairly tranquil mood. Only a single *Goddess of the Sea* pen stuck into her coronet of braids. "It is high time these youngsters had some remedial religious training, don't you think?"

"The trouble is my mother-in-law, Mary Margaret. Gives her some comfort, you know, that the kids are going to Will's church," Deidre said.

"It's a problem," I agreed. "I bet Sister Fermina knows right well about Willy's mom."

"Not too shabby," Phillipa murmured, still poking around in her dinner casserole. One assumed she meant what was under the puff pastry not damnation by the clergy.

"A bit fruity," Heather said. "Rather a peach finish, don't you think?" She swirled her glass of chardonnay in the approved manner, holding only the stem. "Children can be deprogrammed just like military dogs."

"Wait until you have had the care of small children before you equate their education with training canines," Deidre suggested.

"As a matter of fact, Dick and I have been thinking of..."

"Can we have one of Aunt Heather's extra doggies? *Pul-eeze*, Mom?" Willy interrupted as he constructed a log cabin of French fries held together with ketchup.

"Of course you can, honey," Heather replied. "Dee, we have some darling pups at the Animal Lovers sanctuary that would be perfect for your family."

Deidre's eyebrows shot up toward her fringe of blonde curls, and she shook her head emphatically at Heather's suggestion. "Hey, sweetie—we already have two darling little poodles, and Geronimo the Gerbil," she reminded the boy. "Perhaps when you're a bit older and can take over training a new pup. Right now, you and Jenny come with me and get settled in your room. Mommy has *work* to do." As the three Ryans left the supper table, Deidre called back over her shoulder, "Goddess will get you for that, Heather. See you ladies in a few minutes. Warm up the wands!"

~

"I sure miss *Hazel's Book of Household Recipes*." I referred to a decaying volume of unknown origin, black leather with title in tooled purple letters, which Fiona had found at a yard sale of "attic treasures." Besides stews, soaps, sachets, cough syrups and other staples of life in the early 1800s, the "Household Recipes" had included formulas with magical ingredients and intentions that had proved to be worth its weight in frankincense. *Hazel's Book* had been our group grimoire ever since we'd formed the circle.

"Not to worry. I never leave home without it," Fiona said. She marched over to the closet and stood on tiptoe to take down a rather ancient briefcase of many buckles. Whipping a Japanese scarf out of her bureau drawer, she laid it on a round table situated near the window. Then the venerable book of household magic, which she placed reverently on the silk dragons.

"Nice scarf," Phillipa commented. "A gift from anyone we know?"

Fiona, who never blushed, reddened and twinkled. "It was a 'thank you' from Ken Ogata for some little finding I did for him. A missing tea bowl. Very valuable some of those old bowls, even the mended ones. Who would believe that a proper lady like Seamoon Iseul would do such a thing. Well, I left the matter to Ken to handle in his own Zenish way. *But now,* let's see what we've got to help our evil genius reveal himself." She opened the book with infinite care. *Hazel's Book* offered no Contents page or definitive Index.

Fiona turned the pages, and the rest of us watched in absolute fascination as evocative recipes appeared.

"Ooooh," Phillipa squealed. "*To Increase the Blood in a Male Member*. Early Viagra?"

"Hey, Fiona, I want to go back to *Calming a Child in Church with Chamomile Chews*," Deidre said.

"Later, later, dear. We must stick on the point," Fiona cautioned.

"Look at this one," Heather exclaimed as Fiona continued resolutely paging through. "*To Open Locks without Alarm*. Holy Hecate, I could have used that one when I was going through my animal activist phase. *Moonwort!* She used moonwort!"

"It's a good thing Dick persuaded you to quit raiding labs," I said.

"Yeah, well I'm getting a little too old to be climbing over wire fences—although I must say it was a challenge! We'd back up to the fence with a pick-up truck and lay a sheet of plywood across the barbed top. Scramble right over it like a bridge. And I know people who are still in the network. If a really egregious case comes to my attention, I have only to call," Heather said. "One simply cannot allow strayed and stolen dogs to suffer for medical, cosmetic, or, worse of all, military experiments concocted by humans."

"One ought to stick to picketing Provimi veal and keep one's ass out of Federal prison, that's my advice," Phillipa said.

"Here's something!" Fiona exclaimed, just in time to veer away from one of our perennial topics of disagreement. Phillipa's fondness for veal and Heather's anarchical impulses were sore subjects.

"*To Reveal Hidden Matters of the Heart*," Deidre read over her shoulder. "Sounds more like a Valentine trick. How to see the face of your future husband in a soup pot or some such folk lore."

"Keep reading," Fiona said. "Hazel was careful in her wording, I suspect on purpose. In those days, discretion was the better part of reputation. But look here where Hazel has written, 'a man will unburden the sinful secrets of his heart if…' That's not a love spell. It says we'll need a 'neckerchief belonging to the injured party.' *Injured party?* Definitely a spell to identify an attacker. Is Paige Bratton's luggage still on board? And what about these herbs, do you have them on hand, Cass? Periwinkle to unclothe evil, dried toadstool for the emergence of hidden matters, angelica to dispel untruths, turmeric for cleansing, and sage—well, we all have our sage, don't we, ladies? Sage and lavender, the all-purpose protectors."

"*Toadstool!* What no eye of newt?" Phillipa demanded.

"Yes, as a matter of fact, I do have everything *except* the toadstool and eye of newt." I said, feeling rather proud of my prescience. "Along with all that candied ginger, I packed a kind of herbal first aid kit. You never know..."

"Can't we make do with a plain old mushroom?" Deidre asked. "It seems to me I've seen you, Phil, chatting up that cute French chef in his snug little office, no doubt attempting to pry out of him Goddess-knows-what culinary secrets...why don't *you*..."

Phillipa demurred. "You think an innocuous button mushroom can possibly sub for a nasty wild toadstool?".

"Oh, he must have something more exotic than button mushrooms in his stores," I said. "What about some dried porcini? Those babies still have the sand of Italy clinging to their gills."

"Yes, that might do it," Phillipa agreed. "Okay. I accept your *mission impossible*, Cass. I shall obtain some dried shreds of porcini from Henri. I'll tell him I need porcini to use as an aphrodisiac."

"Henri?"

"Henri Beauveau. Which means *beautiful veal*, and he does have those eyes like a moonstruck calf."

"Can you never stay out of trouble with men?" I complained.

"And veal," Heather added. "But how do we work this? Any candles?"

Fiona scanned the page. "Basically, Hazel instructs us to make a medicine amulet out of an item of the injured party's clothing, fill it with a pinch of each herb, and bring it into the presence of the suspect or suspects, making certain that their eyes fall upon it. Then we are to say the words, *by this token, now reveal secrets that your heart conceals.* Apparently the guilty party then gives himself away."

"Oh, sure. Shall we all wear our peaked black hats while we're at it?" Phillipa said. "Everyone will think we're a few straws short of a full broom."

"Say, never mind trying to purloin something from the Bratton luggage, which is probably locked up in the evidence room in Hamilton anyway. I just remembered that I have something of Paige's," I said. "I meant to return it to her but then the storm...and everything."

"What!" Phillipa demanded.

"Just a headband. Will it do?"

"Sure it will. I'll make it into a bag," Deidre said. "Doesn't have to be big, right?"

"And I'll put the herbs in it." I said.

"Damn," Heather said, still pouring over the page. "This doesn't seem to need any candles. And things always work so much better with a candle dedication."

"What worries me is how we're going to set the spell in motion without giving ourselves away," Phil said.

"Don't worry about a thing, Phil," Fiona said. "I'll carry the spell to the formal dinner and make sure everyone sees it."

"And say the weird words?"

"Trust me," Fiona said.

And, of course, we did.

~

The next day at sea was dazzling with sunshine but cold with a wind that cut right through our jackets. Nevertheless, Heather and Deidre marshaled all of us, including the children, for a brisk after-breakfast walk around the Promenade Deck. Despite the stabilizers, one really needed so-called sea legs to keep from falling on one's face. Phillipa and I each took one of Fiona's arms and bundled her along after the fitness twins who were leading the way at a vigorous pace, albeit Deidre's strides were much shorter than long-legged Heather's.

"Isn't it glorious to be out here gazing at a limitless horizon," Fiona exulted. "So transcendent, such a lift for the spirit."

"It's a trip, all right," Phillipa puffed. "Hey, look, here comes the esteemed professor and his handmaid."

Rudy Koch and Muffy were tilting along the rail; he was a couple of paces ahead with Muffy hastening after him holding a notebook. His Donegal tweed suit and plaid scarf looked much warmer than her pink parka.

Pausing for greetings (and a few deep breaths) seemed like a good idea. Deidre and Heather had ducked into the Games Room to drop off Jenny and Willy where they would join the other youngsters for lessons in table tennis.

"Hi. How was that Santeria thing the other night?" Phillipa asked. "Bloody good sacrifice and all?"

Rudy stopped so short, Muffy nearly plowed into him. "Oh, it's you, Phil," he said, warming slightly, staring into her dark eyes with his hypnotic ice-blue gaze. "It's a powerful ceremony. A shame we've left the island. I would have enjoyed introducing you to Santeria. Both of you, of course. After all, you were good enough to introduce Muffy to Wicca. Although she claims that nothing much went on."

I smiled warmly at Muffy and winked. *Good girl!* Fiona had warned her that "What happens at Samhain stays at Samhain," and apparently she'd heeded, even though she'd obviously been eager to impress Rudy with her adventures.

"Yes, I'm sure the dancing and drums and dead rooster and so forth evoked some nifty weird stuff," Phillipa said. "I'm desolate to have missed it for a hum-drum girlie thing. So... Muffy...how are you getting on with your chores?"

Muffy smiled shyly. "Rudy's decided to include a credit line for my assistance in the Santeria article we're...he's...preparing for the *Journal of Cross-cultural Psychology*. Isn't that generous?"

"Yeah, sure is," Phillipa said. "You still have that little memento that Dee gave you?" Muffy nodded and grinned. The first genuinely impish look I'd ever seen pass across her face.

"Well, keep it dusted, honey," I said. Deidre and Heather had emerged from the Games Room and were power-walking their way toward us. "So, we'll see you all at the formal dinner tonight? Ulla tells us it's going to be quite the swell affair. I saved my most special dress for the occasion—how about you?"

"Oh, Rudy has his own tux," Muffy said. "For presentations and such. He'll be very handsome."

Leaning against the rail, Rudy looked out at the roiling waves, giving us his handsome profile. The wind gave his scarf a dramatic flair. Feminine admiration, his nonchalant stance suggested, was only his due.

Heather had reached us and was jogging in place. "And how about you, Muffy? Got some designer outfit to dazzle us?" she asked.

Muffy looked uncertain and did not reply.

"Tell you what," Heather said. "They have some class A stuff in the *Goddess* shops. Why don't you and I go rifle through the racks in, say, an hour from now? We could catch a bite of brunch together." She glanced at her Cartier watch; its diamonds caught the sunlight brilliantly.

"Talk about Breakfast at Tiffany's," Phillipa said.

CHAPTER FIFTEEN

Rowing in Eden!
Ah! The Sea!
Might I but moor
To-night in Thee!

– Emily Dickinson

The "mojo bag," as Phillipa insisted on calling it, was prepared. It had been sewn by Deidre, filled with herbs by me, the dried porcini added by Phillipa, and was now secreted in Fiona's reticule as we departed from our suites that evening for the last fancy-dress occasion on board the *Goddess*. No event was so formal, however, that it would induce Fiona to swap her miraculous reticule for an evening bag. She did, however, clip a jeweled thistle brooch to the moss green suede. Other than that, she was in full glamour, wearing an ankle-length lavender velvet outfit we'd never seen, a sheath with a long graceful over-jacket; judging from a certain shine here and there on the folds, it was hardly new.

Although we weren't invited to dine with the Captain on this occasion, we found ourselves at an adjacent table with precisely the same dinner companions that we had dined with on our first evening, except for the lamentable absence of the Brattons. As if to jolly us out of that depressing emptiness, Ulla Nobel in a peacock-blue cocktail dress and Gerry Leary, the young officer who'd had an eye for Deidre, took the missing couple's places at our round table. Deidre, who'd lost all her cruise clothes by that ill-fated rogue wave, had been outfitted by Cecile's in Hamiton with an adorable, pale yellow, full-skirted dress that made her look about sixteen. Even Ken's elusive nephew Rikyu had torn himself away from his buddies and was dressed up in leather blazer over a 5-toed dragon t-shirt. In the way of shipboard relationships, we were all old friends now. A lovely champagne was served with the appetizers, and we, too, sparkled as we chatted with new interest and enthusiasm, having our varied experiences in Bermuda to share.

Muffy was the biggest surprise. I wondered if I, too, had changed that dramatically when Heather got her shopping hands on me. Sometime during the afternoon, Muffy's thin mousey hair had been given an attractive ash-blonde rinse and fluffed into a gamine style, and she was wearing one of those deceptive "little black dresses" that confer instant sophistication. Around her shoulders, she had draped a silk scarf with soft rose accents that brought out her subtle skin tones. Unobtrusive eye make-up made the most of her soft brown eyes.

"Jumpin' Green Jacks," Phillipa murmured to me. "That Heather can sure work magic. I wonder how the Kochs will survive us, don't you?"

"What's that, princess?" Dan Simic inquired, leaning over Phillipa's décolletage somewhat more than was strictly necessary for conversation.

"I said, I wonder when the clowns will arrive." Phillipa smiled alluringly. Her olive skin exuded the faint fragrance of almonds, and I could have sworn his nostrils flared. Although stately Ulla, the quintessential Nordic beauty, was seated on his other side, he seemed almost perfunctory with her. Perhaps they'd made so many voyages together she had begun to seem like family.

On my right, Rob Negrini, wearing what appeared to be a classic Armani suit and that fashionable shadow of a beard, was praising a global environmental fund that specialized in emerging markets, clean energy, and responsible forestry, addressing Heather and Jason Severin across the table. Jason, however, was more interested in talking to Tony Grenville about the "Triangle trauma," as he called our adventures with the rogue wave, while Tony, of course, was trying to attract Calypso del Mar's attention with the possible added benefit of seriously irritating his wife. Lindsay gave him the back of her cool blonde chignon and addressed herself to Madeline Severin. The two consummate travelers were enthusiastically comparing ports of call where jewelry, handwoven fabrics, and leather goods could be bought for a song.

Fiona and the Bishop duked it out over communication with the dead. She was for welcoming them into our lives *whenever they wish to come to us through the veil between the worlds.* He was for convincing the dearly departed to leave this plane of existence for good, even giving them a push "upstairs" with exorcism if necessary. But Aiden Guilfoyle was smiling broadly and seemed to be enjoying himself. I suspected Fiona was playing his devil's advocate, putting into words the Bishop's own repressed beliefs. After all, he did see the dead himself, as he had confessed to Deidre. Now he was telling Fiona about seeing his own father standing in the corner of the bedroom while the family was gathered around the bed weeping over his dead form.

I contributed my own experience with the spirit of my grandma and how she had led me to notebooks of herbal recipes and wisdom developed for generations by the Shipton family that I might never have discovered without her guidance. "If there are earthbound angels, she's mine," I said.

"Angels, is it?" the bishop said with a superior smile. "Surely angelic beings are not part of the Pagan panoply?"

"Indeed," Fiona retorted, "I believe we had them first."

Rikyu Ogata was eager to learn more about the behind-the-scenes running of a cruise ship, and Gerry Leary was fielding a barrage of animated questions, tossing an occasional query to Dan Simic. Meanwhile, Rikyu's uncle Ken Ogata explained the Japanese way of tea to Ulla, who seemed genuinely intrigued. I wondered if his valuable tea bowl had been retrieved from Ms. Seamoon.

So we spent a pleasant two hours with good food, good wines, and good company, enjoying each other and ourselves dressed to the nines. I liked the way cruise travel encouraged elegance and grace. It was almost a shame that it was all ending so soon, especially as we had not solved the mystery of Paige as we had determined we would.

"Now here's something that will interest you, Aiden, and perhaps everyone," Fiona said in her magical glamour voice. It's not that she speaks loudly when she adopts that irresistible tone, but in a low, melodious way that somehow rivets everyone's attention.

"Oh, here it comes," murmured Phillipa, gazing at the tablecloth and turning her gilded cup of after-dinner coffee in circles.

"As you all know, certain mysterious troubles have been associated with this voyage. Oh, yes, Ulla, despite having an outstanding captain and dedicated crew, some unsettling events have occurred. So my friends and I have made a charm, simply to bring light to the dark corners of our experiences, to elicit the Word of Truth, *Ma'Kheru* as the Egyptians call it. Logos, you might say. A charm to us is like a medicine bag to a Native

American shaman, a source of great power. And the more we believe in it, the more powerful it becomes. That will surely intrigue Tony from the point of view of psychiatry. Jason, you, too, as a novelist, and Rudy with your anthropologist insights. The rest of you because you're high-seas adventurers, and you've had quite an adventure on this voyage," she continued in that hypnotic tone from which no one at the table seemed able to turn away.

Fiona reached into her reticule for the amulet we had made according to Hazel's instructions. It was, after all, a rather small and unimpressive object, just a small cloth bag stuffed with an earthly bouquet, and yet I could have sworn there was a glow emanating from the pale blue fabric that had once encircled Paige Bratton's long blonde hair.

"Shades of the Shechinah," Phillipa murmured.

"Holy Mother," Deidre said, "the blessed thing looks radioactive."

"Now here is the rhyme that cinches the spell," Fiona said. I noted that the person watching her most intently was Aiden Guilfoyle. *Now that was interesting!*

Implacably, Fiona continued. "*By this token, now reveal secrets that your heart conceals.*"

There was a wild shriek at the other end of the table. It was Madeline Severin. With her whitened face and white hair, she looked like a death's head. Jason put his hand over hers in a tight grip, silencing her instantly.

"What rot," he exclaimed with a black look at Fiona.

"Hey, there, better give your mom a shot of something strong," Lindsay advised. "Pull yourself together, Mad. You don't believe that thing actually *works* do you?" She laughed a brittle British stage laugh. "Heaven forbid! If our innermost secrets are to be revealed, what will become of us? Tony, for one, will never be able to show his face in public again."

Fiona laughed, too. Rather a spell-breaking, contagious chuckle. "Calm down, everyone. Just sharing a bit of Wiccan myth-making I thought would interest you. Here, I'll tuck this away now before you have me locked up in stocks like the ones we saw in St. George."

"Thus always to witches," Jason muttered, ministering to his distraught mom. You didn't have to be a clairvoyant to perceive that Madeline Severin was not too tightly wrapped. I wondered what "secrets of the heart" had set her off on that tizzy. But wherever Mad was, I did not want to go there. I shook my hands and feet to shake off her frenetic vibes.

"What are you *doing*, Cass?" Phil asked. "The hokey-pokey?"

Soon we were all laughing. Probably our dinner companions were feeling relieved to be let loose from Fiona's spell-weaving grip. There was a shuffling and scraping of chairs and a desultory exchange among the people at our table and others nearby for the rest of the festive evening ahead. Some were opting for the musical that was playing on the stage of the Broadway Ballroom, a version of *42nd Street*. Others were heading for the casino (last chance to lose their shirts!) or the jazz trio at the newly-repaired and painted Blue Note or "Dancing to DooWop" in the Moulin Rouge cocktail lounge. I noted that Deidre had taken Gerry Leary's arm, and they wandered off in the direction of the dancing on the deck below. Phillipa and Dan were going for a walk on deck "to clear our heads."

Rudy Koch suggested that Heather join him at the Blue Note so he could regale her with his hopes and plans for the anthropology department at Vassar. I had the feeling that he saw her as one of the alumnae's possible big donors. The Grenvilles had already taken charge of Muffy and insisted she join them there, also.

"Uncle and I are going to the Starlight Cinema," Rikyu enthused. "It's Oceans Fifteen, George Clooney and his pack of cool guys hack into the casino computers in Monaco and do this amazing bank transfer thing. They don't have to blow up the vaults or anything. They're not even *in* Monaco at the time. They're in Paris, living it up on the Le Rive Gauche. But then Oceans has to rescue Julia Roberts from a convent in Nepal."

Ken Ogata raised his eyebrows at Fiona and me and shrugged. "I've visited a Buddhist monastery near where the Himalayan scenes were shot. It's located in the midst of a pine and rhododendron forest, at a precarious altitude. 3,800 meters, as I recall. I'll enjoy seeing those mountains once more."

"Sounds great," Fiona said. "Shall we, Cass? We can go to the Blue Note afterwards and catch up."

"Oh, why not," I said rather sharply. Not that I wanted to be involved in a shipboard romance, being so happily married and all, but *really,* the last night of the cruise and the best I could do was a movie with a teenager, a Japanese aesthete, and a pixilated pal. I supposed my frisson of regret was disloyal to Joe, my dynamic and lovable husband, and I certainly hoped he never entertained similar remorseful feelings.

We started down to the little theater on the Atlantic Deck, passing Phillipa and Dan leaning on the rail outside *Le Consulat*, head to head. She whispered something in his ear, and they laughed together. "Whatever you say, princess," I heard him reply. I didn't pay much attention because Fiona was holding forth on the quirks of spell-making. She insisted that we should not be too disappointed if our charm didn't have an immediate affect on someone (other than Mad Madeline!). It takes time for magic to do its stuff, and sometimes it even takes distance as well. "*Murder will outsource* as the poet says," she mused.

I trudged downstairs with the cinema party, listening glumly.

The theater was half-full, the film about to start. We helped ourselves to the free buttered popcorn in the foyer and found seats near the front row. There was something to be said for being able to enjoy a movie theater without worrying about tickets, seating, and the inflated price of snacks.

The house lights dimmed. The camera panned over a starry sky gradually growing lighter in the pre-dawn hours. Then a magnificent range of mountains came into view just as the sun began to rise, a glory of vivid crimson and gold. The chanting of monks could be heard in the distance. The musical sound of their voices lifted and fell. A temple bell rang. A single great-winged hawk flew across the cinemascope horizon. Ken Ogata sighed.

Slowly the camera panned away from the monastery to zero in on a Buddhist convent on the other side of the mountain. Entering one of the crumbling huts, we saw Julia Roberts, with a shaved head, dishing out some kind of gray legume porridge to a long row of elderly nuns holding wooden bowls. Her saffron robe sported a deep cleavage. A heavy medallion with a curious etching that looked like a many-armed woman dangled from a chain around her neck,

"Ah, morning gruel at the nunnery," Fiona whispered. "I wonder who, in the Goddess's name, was their technical advisor on this segment, because already I'm seeing several errors. I mean, what in Hades is the Goddess Kali doing in a Buddhist sanctuary? I have a pamphlet on Buddhist nuns that would have explained how to do this scene with a modicum of authenticity."

I was half-listening. Some idea as dark as one of the *no-things* on the beach in Bermuda was tugging at my consciousness.

Like a rocket, that realization zoomed up into the light of consciousness. I stood up, dumping my popcorn on Ken's lap.

"*That laugh! I remember that laugh*," I screamed. Probably I upset everyone's concentration on the gruel queue and Roberts' half-exposed breasts but I hardly noticed. "Come on, Fiona. *I know who did it!* And he's going to try it again. He can't help himself." And all the time I was sobbing these words, I was climbing over theater-goers and empty seats, heading for the exit. Fiona hurried after me with questions I couldn't take time to answer.

"We've got to find Phil," I yelled urgently to Fiona, who was stumbling after me, her plump and arthritic form unable to quite catch up.

"What...what...what..." she yelled back breathlessly. "Are you saying that he...that Dan...what *do* you mean?"

"It's his damned laugh. That laugh I just heard when we passed them on deck. I remember now. Same predatory laugh as I heard at Samhain when I summoned Paige and that vision came to me."

"Ah, ha! So he did give himself away!" Fiona puffed. "Praise Hazel!"

We had reached the place on International Deck where Phillipa and Dan Simic had been talking, but now they were nowhere to be seen. The long deck stretched backward and forward from where we stood, implacably dark and empty. *Le Consulat* was nearly deserted now, but the Broadway Ballroom was filled with passengers enjoying the dancing feet of *42nd Street*. I shivered in the chill wind that blew in from the ocean.

"Oh, shit, shit, *shit*," I wailed. "Where can they have gone? I really think she's in danger from that bastard."

Fiona was leaning over, trying to catch her breath. "Wait, let me think," she said. "Didn't they say *anything* to give us a clue?"

I struggled to remember conversations to which I had hardly listened. "I'm not sure if they said dancing or they didn't say dancing. The ballroom's set up for the show, but there's dancing at the Moulin Rouge. Yes, let's try that...the Promenade Deck..." All the while I was struggling to talk sensibly to Fiona, I was rushing toward the stairs.

Fiona followed me, painfully, and I fought with myself to slow down for her.

"Leave the damned reticule, Fiona!" I screamed, too terrified to hide my exasperation. "That thing is too heavy for you to be toting. We're in a hurry here. Throw it in the corner there, and we'll pick it up later."

Leaning against the stair rail, she breathed raggedly and hugged the reticule to her chest protectively. "No, Cass. We might need something. You never can tell. What about a cell phone? I don't suppose you have your cell phone, do you, in that antique evening bag?"

My evening bag, a gift from Joe, dated back to the twenties. It looked like an oversize gold compact, oblong, barely room for cosmetic necessities, a hanky, and a few bills. "Did you try calling Phil?" I demanded.

"Of course I did. Left a voice message, too, but her cell, like yours, is probably back in your suite. I believe her bag was a sequined silver and black thing about the size of a sandwich."

I groaned. "So, let's go then. I don't dare sound an alarm that might cause Simic to act rashly. Here's the stairway. Hurry... hurry...we'll have a look near the Moulin Rouge."

Soon we were moving down a stairway crowded with other passengers who all seemed to be in a silly, festive mood. How could they be so carefree when Phillipa was in danger? As I pushed by and pulled Fiona after me, I wanted to slap each one of them on the side of the head.

There were various clusters of people on the Promenade deck, braving the nippy ocean breezes on their last night of sailing, but Phillipa and Dan Simic were nowhere to be seen. In my mind's eye, I had watched Paige as she drank that numbing cocktail outside a place where there was dancing and laughter. Heading straight for the Moulin Rouge, I spotted a passenger restroom that opened onto the deck just like the one where the rapist had dragged Paige. Without conscious thought, I found myself attempting to bust into it. First I tried to kick it in, as I'd often seen in the movies, cracked the heel of my second pair of killer heels, and barely made a dent. Then I hit the door with my shoulder, which hurt like blazes, and when that failed, with a wooden deck chair. Finally! One good smash on the lock was enough to spring it. But I only rousted a very irate drunk, who stumbled out half-zipped. Valuable time had been lost, my shoulder throbbed painfully, and I was hobbling like a troll on my broken shoe.

Fiona was wheezing, so I left her to catch her breath and keep watch on deck while I limped onto the small dance floor of the Moulin Rouge. "Earth Angel" was playing on some kind of souped-up electronic system, while a male vocalist from the ship's crew sang mournfully. The floor was thick with romantic couples as I wedged my way hastily back and forth looking for Phillipa.

I thought I might run into Deidre and Gerry Leary, and get them to join the search. Of course I'd have to make up a story for the Norse Line officer, and I was fresh out of inspiration. But I had no luck finding anyone in that crush of Doo Wop fans. After a number of futile forays, I ended up at the bar. "Has any of you seen Dan Simic in the last hour?" I demanded loudly of the three bartenders.

They shook their heads disinterestedly and went on mixing and shaking drinks for thirsty customers crowding the bar stools.

"Are you sure? It's very important," I screamed over the din.

"Hey, watch it!" one of the cocktail drinkers exclaimed. "You just jolted my arm, Sister."

"You need the doc? What's the problem?" a woman in a bright red dress asked anxiously. "Is it that cruise virus? Everything else has gone wrong on this trip, so it wouldn't surprise me one bit if we all got the trots next."

"Oh, Simic, the good doctor," said her companion, whose nose and cheeks matched the woman's dress. "God bless him for helping me to recover from that nasty bout of seasickness. You just missed him. Pleasant chap. I believe he was ordering two stingers."

It was all I could do not to shake the man for more details. "Was he with a woman? A dark-haired woman wearing a black and dark purple gown? Where did they go, did you see? Did they head toward the elevators or the deck?"

"He was alone at the bar," the red-veined man said. "Must have had some hot chick waiting for him somewhere. Kind of a sly smile, you know. Didn't see where he went. Could be anywhere."

No, he'd have to join her outside, keep her away from other passengers, I thought. *Nothing else made sense. On his way outside, he spiked her stinger with some date rape drug so he could drag her off.* I heard a sob and realized it was mine. *But where else could he have taken her?*

"He was here," I said succinctly to Fiona whom I found collapsed in a deck chair, shivering. "He ordered two stingers at the bar. And I don't know where he might have met Phil after that."

"Do you want me to alert the ship's crew that there's a missing woman?" Fiona asked, fishing for her cell phone. "Get them searching all the hatches and cubbyholes?"

"Last resort," I said. "I'm afraid of what will happen if we sound a general alarm. Remember this guy is really good at getting rid of his victims."

"Let me call Heather, then," Fiona suggested. "On the off chance that she wasn't seduced into carrying a useless toy bag. It's so important to have one's cell at all times."

"Okay, good idea," I said. "Tell her to come alone. But never mind calling Deidre. I don't want to have to deal with Gerry Leary."

While Fiona made the call—and did, indeed, reach Heather, who had a rhinestone-studded cell phone strapped to the matching belt she was wearing with her Chanel evening suit. "Tell her, as long as she's at the Blue Note, to start searching on the Blue Vista Deck and work her way down. We'll move toward her," I said. "He'd have her outdoors, away from everyone, the damned creep."

As we hurried forward, Fiona talked earnestly to Heather, explaining about the nasty laugh that had alerted me, and the subsequent disappearance of Phil with Simic. She clicked off breathlessly. "Heather's starting at the Blue Note. Don't worry—she's a gal who can cover a lot of territory fast. She said she'll meet us...wherever. Oh, I do wish there were time for me to dowse the deck plan." She reached under her velvet gown for the crystal that was hanging on a chain around her neck.

"No time, no time," I cried, forging on.

There were five decks between us on the Promenade Deck and the Blue Vista at the top of the ship. The Penthouse and Riviera Decks were less public because the upper class suites were located there, but that would suit Simic perfectly. He might know about some empty suite where he could drag Phillipa and do what he wanted with her undisturbed. I wanted in the worst way to kill that murdering pervert.

"Listen, I'm at my wits' end here. I just don't know where to go next," I confessed to Fiona. "I feel that Simic would have sought out some empty suite, but where?"

"What about the one that Deidre and her children occupied before the rogue wave wrecked it?" Fiona said. "All they did was put a new door on it. I believe the interior is still a shambles. Dan would know it's probably dark and empty."

Yes, yes! Why hadn't I thought of that!

CHAPTER SIXTEEN

I shall go the way of the open sea,
To the lands I knew before you came,
And the cool ocean breezes shall blow from me,
The memory of your name.

– Laurence Hope

I couldn't wait for Fiona this time. "You take the elevator," I said. "I'm going to run up those stairs. It's faster." And I did, all three flights. I had to kick off my shoes, because of the broken heel, and run in my stocking feet. The frequent beach walking I did at home stood me in good stead, pumping my leg muscles as I sprinted upward to the Penthouse Deck. Still, I was almost a grandmother and not fit for much by the time I reached the entrance to Deidre's storm damaged suite. The door was new all right, but the lock hadn't yet been installed. I pushed inside. Compared to the well-lit decks, the interior was darker than a mountain cave. Once out of the light that fell through the open door, it was too dark to see anything at all. I banged my shin royally on some jutting timber. Invisible objects fell over with a loud clatter.

I heard someone curse in the interior of the suite, what would have been the bedroom if it weren't wrecked. *It was Simic!*

"Leave her alone, you sonofabitch!" I demanded. "I know what you're up to. You have Phil in there. I've alerted the captain, and they're on their way to arrest you, so you'd better let her go." I tried to sound authoritative and convincing although I really had no idea how I was going to deal with Simic and save Phillipa. In really tight spots like this, there's not enough time (not to mention mental serenity) to wrap oneself in the white-light cloak of spiritual invincibility. Still, I gave it a shot.

"Oh, it's you, the witch," he called out to me. "And you're alone, aren't you? Don't try to tell me you've called for help. You're afraid I'd dump your friend over the side before they got here." Although I still hadn't seen him, I recognized that same dirty laugh that I now associated with Simic. "So why don't you come on in, and you can watch."

I groped around the floor for a piece of wood or metal, anything I could use as a weapon. In that blackness, I had no sense that Simic was creeping up on me until suddenly I was tackled from behind and shoved onto the floor. I screamed in pain as my arm struck something with an exposed nail, which I wished I'd got hold of when I was looking for a club. And where was my white light when I needed it?

I lay prone, winded. If I could get my limbs working, I thought, maybe I could scramble up and confront my attacker. But right then, Simic jumped hard on my back, riding me like a horse. The wind was knocked out of me in an instant. I thought I heard my spine crack. The vivid pain made me shriek. Straddling me with his muscular legs, Simic held me down while his hands, closing around my throat to strangle me, silenced my scream. I fought him with all my strength, twisting and turning to get away from those throttling fingers. But no matter how I struggled, I couldn't break free. His hands were unbelievably strong. I felt myself slipping away. *Goddess help me...*

"Let her go!" ordered a deep, powerful voice in the open door.

That moment of surprise and distraction loosened his grip. Air rushed back into my lungs. I gave a mighty heave to free myself from his weight and succeeded in rolling away, scrabbling to my feet. I guessed my back wasn't broken after all, just aching like hell.

Looking up, I saw Fiona looming in the doorway. She appeared tall and square-shouldered, like a gunman in a Western movie, holding a pistol leveled directly at Simic.

"Good, stand away from him, Cass," Fiona said, taking careful aim. "Now you, Simic, step out here onto the deck or I'll shoot you down right there like the wild beast you are." I could see that her hands were steady, not trembling at all, and her voice was strong. She was a force to be reckoned with—I knew it, and so did Simic.

He left off trying to grab me again and stood up in one swift graceful movement. "Fuck you, you bitch," he said. But Fiona still held the pistol with a resolute aim, and there was steel in her stance. Simic didn't feel that lucky. He moved to obey her command, no doubt planning to get the upper hand on these two middle-age ladies somehow.

"Watch out for him, Fiona. He's going to try something," I warned.

Fiona moved aside to allow Simic to step through the door. He walked cautiously forward, reaching the doorway, only an arm's length from Fiona. Suddenly he dove toward the pistol. But our plump, arthritic friend was in her glamour mode. She stepped back with graceful ease, never taking her sight off the mark. Off-balanced by his lunge, Simic staggered across the deck, stumbled against a deck chair, righted himself, and dove toward her again.

Fiona fired. Simic went down like a felled tree.

It was quite a loud noise.

I thought people would come running, but evidently, passengers in neighboring suites were all down below whooping it up in their last night on the high seas. Not a single head appeared out the impassive closed doors, not even a steward's.

Frozen in place, horrified, I stood staring at Simic's collapsed body, limp as a fallen puppet. I felt certain that he must be dead, but where was the blood that should be oozing out of his head?

Then I was conscious of someone running pell-mell toward us. It was Heather, who had sprung out of the elevator, taken in the scene at a glance, and raced down the deck, her bronze braid swinging like a bell rope. "Great Goddess," she exclaimed. "Fiona, what have you done now?"

Fiona suddenly looked bewildered, visibly shaken, her old small round self. "*Oh, dearie me,*" she said in a plaintive tone.

Gently Heather pried the pistol out of Fiona's hand and ran to the rail. Like Diana getting ready to cast a silver spear, she pulled back her arm, then cast the pistol upward, a strong, curving throw into the air. It made a perfect arc, then plummeted straight down into the black waters rushing by the ship. Evidence gone forever. *Good!*

"Rob Angus Ritchie gave me that pistol, Heather," Fiona wailed. "My late husband pressed it into my hands just before his last fateful voyage on the *Fiona Fancy*. 'Walk softly, darling,' he said, 'and carry a forty-five.'"

"Do you want to be arrested for carrying a concealed weapon onto a cruise ship, charged as a terrorist?" Heather demanded.

"I loved that sweet *memento mori*," Fiona insisted, staring down at the water as if hoping the sea might disgorge the lost item.

"Oh, leave it be, Fiona. Phil will get Stone to provide you with another piece," Heather said coolly. "Did you kill him?"

"Oh, it's not that, it's the sentimental value. You don't have to bother Stone," Fiona said. "I have plenty of other weapons."

"How reassuring. Sometime you really must tell me how you got that handgun past the port authorities." Heather was squatting down to examine Simic. "Thank the Goddess, you merely creased the bastard's skull. We'll say he hit his head on the rail. Cass, look around for a shell casing, will you? As long as he stays unconscious, let's not call for help until the wind blows away the stench of gun powder. But the instant he wakes..."

Removing her rhinestone-studded cell phone from the matching belt, she held it at the ready. One high-heeled shoe she placed on Simic's chest, looking down at him as if he were a temporarily immobilized snake. "Give me something to use as a club," she said. "Anything."

Fiona looked around in a bemused fashion. Just inside the door of Deidre's old stateroom, a few new planks were leaning against the wall. Fiona handed one of these to Heather. Although it was heavy, the way Heather held it, there was no doubt she could smash it down on Simic's head if he sat up and threatened us. But from the look of him, slack and unconscious, there was little danger of that.

"Have you checked on Phil? Is she all right?" Heather asked. "What did that pervert do to her?"

The deep freeze that seemed to have afflicted me during these events finally thawed. "Phil!" I screamed and sprang back into the cabin. My unshod feet seemed to bang and stub into every piece of broken wood in that darkness.

I found Phillipa in what had been the bedroom, lying on the sodden collapsed mattress of one of the stateroom's twin beds. Her black eyes were open and pleading but she seemed paralyzed. Her beautiful black and purple gown had been ripped straight down the front, but it appeared as if that's as far as Simic had progressed before I disturbed him. Her lacy black underthings were still in place.

I lifted her up into my arms. "Oh, Phil, dear. It's all right now. Fiona shot the sonofabitch."

Her lips moved but no sound came out. I leaned over, hoping to hear her first faint words. Fiona rushed in after me, smelling salts at the ready.

"Tell me...tell me..." Phillipa whispered. "Tell me the bastard is dead. Never mind that '*harm none*' shit. Just look what he did to my Versace gown! Cover me up and get me the hell out of here."

~

After Fiona had wrapped her long velvet jacket around Phillipa, we managed to pull her up between us. We walked her around in the cold night air, hoping it would clear her head of some of the drug's affects. That brisk ocean breeze, I noted, had blown away most of the acrid odor that hung over us. Still keeping careful guard on Simic, Heather called the ship's emergency center and reported her version of what had occurred.

She told the officer to whom she spoke that Dr. Daniel Simic had given a passenger, Phillipa Stern, a knock-out drug and dragged her into an empty stateroom where he had sexually assaulted her. When we—the three of us, as she explained it—had come searching for Phil, interrupting Simic's attack, he'd struck me down, then rushed on deck to escape, where he'd slipped and fallen against the rail, scraping his head against the metal cross-piece and knocking himself out. Considering his attempted rape of Phillipa, we were convinced that Simic had drugged and raped Paige Bratton as well, then thrown her overboard during the storm. We wanted him arrested and locked up immediately. And Phillipa needed medical attention. Could they bring the nurse, too?

While we were waiting, Heather pulled a white linen hanky out of her pocket and wiped it across the bloodied gun crease on the side of Simic's head. At first I thought she was trying to bandage him, but then she smeared a good swab of his blood on the cross-piece between sections. Hiding the bloodied cloth in her pocket, she went back to holding the plank over Simic.

Soon two worried officers were pounding toward us, and behind them came Kirsti Hansen, the ship's nurse, carrying a first aid kit. She blanched when she saw Simic and immediately knelt to assess his condition. Fibonacci came running up after the officers, and Ulla followed him, looking like an avenging angel in her shimmering blue gown. But as we soon learned, it was the ship's good reputation she was intent on protecting.

"Oh, never mind Simic," I said crossly to the nurse. "He seems to be breathing okay, doesn't he? See what you can do for my friend here, whom the doctor poisoned with some sort of central nervous system depressant. Knocked her out temporarily, but she's coming around now."

"Are you sure? Are you sure that someone drugged her?" Ulla asked sharply. "I've seen plenty of passengers get themselves in this condition with too much alcohol. She certainly looks drunk to me. Drunk and incoherent."

"You're kidding, right?" I said hotly. "Don't you get it? If Phil can't even trust her feet or talk right yet, it's because she's been drugged into a coma so that Simic could drag her into that empty suite. Just look at how her dress is ripped open. You've been harboring a psychopath in your medical team, Ulla."

Ulla uttered something in Swedish, which, judging from the tone, was fairly nasty. "What's happens here," she continued icily in English, "is that we find Dr. Simic lying unconscious on the deck while your friend holds up a plank with which she probably has already bashed him on the head. I can see the bloody mark right there beside his ear. Have a look, Kirsti, for wood splinters in Dr. Simic's wound."

Fibonacci sniffed the air with a curious expression on his face. He leaned over Kirsti's shoulder and considered the open crease on Simic's skull. I could almost see the wheels of his brain turning. He looked at Heather and raised an eyebrow. "Dr. Simic would have had to slide across the railing on his head," Fibonacci murmured, "to sustain this particular injury."

"Yes, he did hit the metal in a rather freakish position," Heather agreed. "I believe the ship lurched just as he fell across the deck. Amazing that he didn't go right over the top into the ocean, wasn't it?"

At that moment I noticed something metallic gleaming dully near one of Ulla's metallic blue high heels.

What we needed here was a distraction.

Which was nicely provided by Deidre, mistress of good timing, who popped out of the elevator and uttered a piercing Fay Wray shriek that made even the dignified butler leap back a bit. She raced toward us followed by Gerry Leary still holding the cell phone on which he'd received a garbled trouble report. "Oh, Phil, you're alive. Thank the Holy Mother for that! Gerry got a call that someone had been raped and someone was dead, and I thought...I was afraid...."

"The only thing that got raped was my beautiful dress," Phillipa assured Deidre who was still sobbing. "Unfortunately, the beast who did it isn't dead after all. Until I get my hands on him, that is." Obviously Phillipa was recovering.

While everyone's attention was riveted on Deidre's dramatic outburst, and Ulla had moved to lay a reassuring hand on her arm, I was able to bend over and snatch the cartridge casing off the deck. Seeing my maneuver, Heather held her hand out surreptitiously near her leg.

I dropped the casing into her palm. Unfortunately, it bounced off, back onto the deck.

"Oh, darn, that must be my missing earring," Heather exclaimed, swooping it up in a flash. She stuffed it into her pocket with the bloody handkerchief. One thing about Coco Chanel suits, they always have decent pockets.

Ulla looked at Heather speculatively, her eyes narrowed. Heather was wearing gorgeous rhinestone drop earrings, both ears.

"My *other* pair," Heather said. She continued her crime reconstruction. "Off-balanced by his frenzied attack on Cass and an unexpected pitch of the ship, Simic hit his head on the rail right there." She pointed to the smear she had contrived, now barely visible and brownish.

Simic chose that very moment to regain consciousness. "That dumpy Annie Oakley over there was packing a pistol. And the bitch shot me," he said, pointing a shaky finger at Fiona who was still helping me to keep a drooping Phil on her feet.

He tried to sit up but the nurse held him in place. "Jesus, what happened to my head? It aches like blazes. Let me up, will you, Kirsti," he insisted.

"You'd better not try to talk right now, dear," Kirsti warned. "Reports of what happened have been quite contradictory. You may want to speak to a Norse attorney. There is someone on board, you know. I'll give you some Tylenol with codeine for the pain."

But Simic ignored her. "These women tried to kill me just because *that whore* got drunk and attempted to lure me into the empty cabin." He waved an accusing hand toward Phillipa.

"Simic is suffering delusions from that crack on his skull. How do you suppose that any passenger could have carried a handgun on board past Customs in New York, let alone an elderly little lady like Mrs. Ritchie?" I said, avoiding Fiona's eyes. "He gave Phil some date-rape drug and forced her into a dark, abandoned suite. Take a good look at her dress—it's torn all the way down the front! When we confronted this pervert trying to rape Phil, he attacked us. Pushed me down and throttled me. Look at my neck right here? You can see the bruises, right? I had to shove him away, and that's when he fell and hit his head. We all saw it."

"Yes," Phillipa whispered, her head still hanging down limply. "That Fiona! Jane Wayne to the rescue." She wasn't thinking clearly yet, but fortunately no one could hear her except Fiona and me.

"Right," Heather said loudly as if Phillipa hadn't spoken. "Cass is telling you exactly what happened. I insist you arrest this man and keep him locked up until we dock. And tomorrow morning, before we reach New York, I am personally going to notify the FBI that we have apprehended a suspect in Paige Bratton's murder."

"That's a load of crap," Kirsti said. She smoothed Simic's forehead and looked down at him fondly. "Dan was with me the night Paige disappeared off the ship. We were together treating passengers injured by that freak wave."

"Bollocks!" exclaimed Deidre. "All of us were in the Atrium, and we saw you both that night. You were *not* together. Simic came in later claiming he'd lost his cell phone and first aid case, and that's why he hadn't been in touch with the rest of his team. It's obvious now that he'd taken advantage of the storm to have his way with Paige Bratton and dump her overboard. Then that monster wave hit us and everyone thought she'd been swept off the deck. Pretty damned lucky for this bastard."

"That little blonde bitch must have fucked the Blarney Stone," Simic growled.

Deidre glared down at him. "May the curse of Mary Malone chase you so far over the hills of Damnation that St. Brigid herself cannot find you."

"The Irish are so colorful," murmured Heather.

"Yeah," I said. "But better the FBI than the hex. Banish those words, Dee!"

"Don't worry, dear," Kirsti said to Simic. "I don't believe a word of it. I'll watch out for you." She glared meaningfully at her two accompanying officers who had been looking back and forth at each speaker as if they were at a tennis match, obviously becoming more and more confused with these conflicting versions of events. "I want you guys to search that old woman's tote bag. Maybe she's hidden the handgun in there. Do it now before she gets the chance to ditch the weapon."

"Not without a search warrant, they won't," Deidre shouted.

But Fiona drew herself up with great dignity and, in a queenly flourish, lifted her arm, silver bangles jingling, and dumped the entire contents of her reticule onto the deck. What followed was a cascade of keys, change purses, passport, books, pamphlets, flash light, duct tape, medicines, hankies, keys, herbal refreshers, amulets, goddess and angel figurines, butterscotch candies, and assorted small tools pouring across the floor. Shamefaced young officers, including Gerry Leary, hurried to assist her in returning these innocent articles to her handbag.

Heather and I simply could not look at each other or it would have been all over.

"This is harassment, you know," Deidre continued angrily. "You are harassing my elderly friend who is a paying passenger on this cruise ship. We will be seeking legal advice on this matter as soon as we have disembarked.

"Hey, who're you gals calling elderly?" Fiona complained.

"Let's not be hasty now," Ulla said in a placating tone. "The lady herself indicated her willingness to have her tote bag searched."

We might have gone on wrangling with one another until dawn if Captain Lars Johansson himself had not come striding onto the scene with thunderbolts in his eyes, like the god Thor in a bad mood. It was understandable; one had only to reflect that this particular cruise had been more than ill-fated from a captain's point of view, what with the missing bride, the freakish weather, and now these troublesome accusations.

"Quiet down, all of you. We will settle these matters later. Right now I have a ship to run," he boomed. "Tonight everyone will cool their tempers, and tomorrow we shall see what is made of these incidents by our Norse executives and the duly authorized law enforcement officials."

The captain had us all sorted out in short order, Simic carried off to the medical facility, and the rest of us back to our quarters. Not that any of us could sleep, except Phillipa whom we dared not allow to do so until we were absolutely certain that she was no longer affected by the drug. The circle gathered in our suite for a war conference on how we would proceed tomorrow.

~

Kirsti's obvious bias toward her boss, or maybe it was infatuation, poor addled girl, must have been her motivation for fiddling with the tests. The urine sample that Phillipa provided later that night was mysteriously altered to prove negative for drugs but with a blood alcohol level that suggested she must have been dead drunk. Obviously there had been some kind of substitution, a sick drunk had been talked into peeing into a cup for the nice nurse.

When we were told these suspect results, Phillipa demanded a second urine test by an outside lab, but that wouldn't be possible until the next day when we docked in New York. By then, too many hours would have elapsed. The drug Fiona was sure Simic had used, Gamma Hydroxybutyrate, would no longer be detected.

According to the pamphlet on popular recreational drugs that Fiona was so fortuitously carrying in her reticule, "G" was sometimes taken to bring on a euphoric state and help a person to lose their inhibitions. It was used medically to treat depression and narcolepsy. Given in an inappropriate dose or combined with alcohol, G induced muscular fatigue, passing out, and memory loss.

After we'd insisted on a search of his pharmacy, Simic admitted that he had "G" on hand, for cases of severe, unresponsive sea sickness, he claimed, to help the victim sleep it off.

But it was simply our word against his. The whole *Goddess* team closed ranks behind their colleague. They'd seen enough drunk, neurotic women on their voyages to doubt our vociferous complaints. Captain Johansson did agree, however, to keep Dr. Dan Simic under a form of honor-system house arrest until these matters could be investigated in New York. The doctor was confined to his own quarters adjacent to the medical facility, located on the Mariner Deck, which was at least quite a distance below the Penthouse Deck.

It was late in the afternoon when we sailed into the Port of New York, so we'd had plenty of time for good-byes and (in some cases) an insincere exchange of addresses with our shipboard friends. Oh, maybe we'd get in touch, sometime, somewhere.

Everyone wanted to know about the Phillipa Stern-Dan Simic affair, of course. In fact, Lindsay and Madeline were nearly avid for scurrilous details. So were Tony and Jason, but they hid it better.

The bond we'd formed with Muffy and Calypso at Samhain still held us, and we parted with affectionate hugs. Muffy was looking surprisingly radiant, and Heather promised to visit her with a "goddess refresher" the next time there was an alumni weekend at Vassar.

With a gambler's irrepressible optimism, Rob Negrini pressed his business card, "Negrini Financial Services" into Heather's hand. A sad expression passed over Calypso's beautiful face. In my heart, I wished her free of the uncertainty and worry that Negrini would always evoke.

Surprisingly, after shaking my hand, Rikyu Ogata gave me a sudden awkward hug. "I'll come and see you, if you like," he said. "Uncle has me enrolled in Phillips Exeter, and it's not that far." I hadn't even realized that the boy and I had connected, but I was warmed and pleased.

"Come at Yule, if you like, Rikki. Christmas, I mean. You'll have to meet my son Adam," I said. "He's a VP at Iconomics, Inc., and they're always on the lookout for great new talent." I knew that Ken had to be in Japan in December, and although I didn't know the boy's home situation, my sixth (seventh? eighth?) sense told me there was something missing or wrong there.

Ken smiled broadly at me over his nephew's shoulder. "Your invitation is a perfect way to get this computer nerd off campus for the holidays. My brother, Rikyu's father, is in San Francisco, and the mother is remarrying. If you ever need a tea master, I owe you one. Just give me a buzz," he said.

"You never can tell what karma has in store. I feel we will be brought together again," I said.

"Yes. I, too. Looking forward to our next meeting, then."

~

Heather did report our suspicion (for us, of course, it was more than suspicion, it was conviction) to the FBI. Our interviews after we disembarked in New York took place in a shabby green room right in the port area. They were not very satisfactory. We were exhausted, and the wooden slat chairs were uncomfortable. Special Agents Frank Frost and Esther Thouless questioned each of us alone in turn, Thouless taking a few desultory notes.

Comparing our experiences later, we were pleased that our stories were in agreement. We'd all voiced vociferous complaints to the FBI interviewers about the ship's doctor attempting to rape Phillipa and our urgent concerns that he may have been responsible for the deaths of other young women, the most recent being Paige Bratton. We'd all denied having seen or used a handgun during the incident. I would have liked to be present when Fiona was interviewed, but I was reassured to see, as she passed me in the doorway, that her glamour was firmly in place. It would have been like questioning Queen Elizabeth. As I left and Fiona entered, I saw Special Agent Frank Frost spring to his feet and pull a chair out for her.

That was not the end of our discomfort in skirting the truth. Our concerned welcoming committee—Phillipa's husband, Detective Stone Stern, and my Joe—had us fielding a bunch of embarrassing questions once we were all safely ensconced in the Hummer limo and the driver was conveying us and our copious luggage back to Plymouth.

Only Heather was perfectly relaxed, smiling, sitting at a small table in the front of the limo to play a game of *Fish* with Jenny and Willy. Her husband Dick having been called away on a veterinary emergency, she wasn't about to let anyone else subject *her* to a family inquisition.

"What I want to know," Stone said severely to Fiona, "is how you got away with shooting Simic, as he is claiming. Yet no handgun was found at the scene or in your reticule. Very strange. Very strange indeed."

Fiona took a sip of the excellent scotch that the limo's bar had provided and gazed out of the dark glass window. "What would life be without that occasional streak of strangeness?" she countered. "Like raspberry ripple ice cream without the ripple. Plain old vanilla."

"That wound on his head was only a scrape," Heather said, rearranging her hand of cards. "Barely knocked him out for a few minutes. Just long enough for us to get help. If Fiona had shot the guy—you know Fiona—the guy would have suffered some real damage."

"Did Auntie Fiona shoot someone?" Willy asked.

"Auntie Fiona is an awesome lady," Jenny commented. "She knows how to do almost everything."

"Of course Aunt Fiona didn't shoot anyone, dear. We are only speaking hypothetically," Heather said.

"What's hyper...hypo...thet...? What's that?" Willy persisted.

"It's like making up a story," Deidre explained. "Talking about something that never happened, but what if it did? Just keep your mind on the card game, honey, and stop interrupting the grown-ups, please."

Stone was not so easily diverted. "Simic claims that Fiona was aiming a handgun at him, that what creased his skull was a bullet." He ran his long fingers through the fine brown hair that often fell into his eyes. "And as you point out, Heather, this wouldn't be the first time that Fiona has discharged her weapon, which has only recently been made legal."

"Thanks to you, darling," Phillipa said. "We're all so grateful for that." She did not add that Fiona's legal handgun was now at the bottom of the Atlantic Ocean.

"Mind you, had I been there, I would have shot the degenerate bastard myself, with pleasure," Stone said, tightening his hold on Phillipa. She was sitting very close to her tall, serious husband, whose sheltering arm was around her shoulders and whose scowl was black.

"As I recall, this cruise was supposed to have been arranged especially to provide a cheerful change-of-scene and relief from stress for Deidre after all she's been through this past year," Joe continued the third degree. "Yet apparently you gals embroiled her and yourselves in a murder investigation *again*. What kind of anti-depressant therapy was that?" He winked at me. Not much got by Joe, who understood better than anyone how my crusading nature led me into these situations, and that my friends of the circle were irresistibly drawn to follow me into dangerous waters, so to speak.

"Nonsense. I wouldn't have missed it for the world," Deidre declared loyally. "I saw my first ghost, so I am now the Circle's official ghost whisperer. Not that it's an experience I care to repeat very often. But now I have Bishop Aiden Guilfoyle of Boston to whom I can turn at any time for spiritual comfort and a quick exorcism. A bishop, mind you! Just think how thrilled my mother-in-law will be! Also, the kids had a *ball.* After that rogue wave hit us in the Bermuda triangle, Jenny abandoned her plan to become a pop singer like Madonna and has quite made up her mind to study weather science instead. *My daughter, the meteorologist.* Also, I danced with this really cute guy, a ship's officer, who begged for my phone number so he could keep in touch. He's only a baby, though. Nice for a shipboard fling and all that, but the holiday is over now. Best of all, I've helped to rescue Phil and expose a serial rapist and murderer, if we can just convince the FBI of it. Did anyone mention that the Paige and Tyler's families have put up a $50,000 reward for information leading to the conviction of her murderer? So what's not to like?"

"Glad to have added another fillip of excitement to your trip," Phillipa said acidly.

"But why did he target you, Phil," Stone asked. "I just don't understand it. Not that you weren't the most beautiful woman on the cruise—I'm sure you were—but as I understand it, his usual victims were girls in their twenties."

"I haven't the slightest idea why he went after me," Phillipa said, allowing a faint moue of indignation to cross her face. "I never gave the man even a hint of encouragement."

The rest of us busied ourselves with looking elsewhere so as not to betray our incredulity. But Joe felt my reaction and studied me closely.

"Don't look at me," I whispered. "We'll go into all this *later*. I feel that I spent all my time watching out for everyone else. There's quite a variety of temptations to resist on a cruise." I was thinking of Heather pouring after-dinner libations, Deidre having a fling of orthodoxy with the bishop, Fiona smuggling contraband in her reticule...and Phil, of course.

Fiona glanced at me sharply. There was never a whisper low enough for her not to hear it, or sense it, or whatever she did.

Louder, I said, "Now tell me everything about my daughter-in-law, honey. Is Freddie still enjoying the euphoric hormones of pregnancy?"

Joe laughed. "I've only been home two days myself. Yes, she's feeling fine physically but worried that her special talents have deserted her and may never return. She can't even addle a slot machine any more."

"It's nature's protective chemistry. She'll be her old self again after the birth, I'm sure. And what about Scruffy and Raffles? I've really missed the little guys, you know."

"This was going to be such a long day of traveling, I figured it was best to leave them where they were, with the Devlin dog pack. So if Scruffy's going into his usual complaints, you'll get to hear them first hand."

And so I did.

PART TWO – THE HOMECOMING

CHAPTER SEVENTEEN

Home is the sailor, home from the sea,
And the hunter home from the hill.

– Robert Louis Stevenson

Ack! Ack! Ack! Hey, Toots, I got a real bad case of kennel cough from being herded in with that mangy pack of low-class mongrels. That old duffer who lives there fed us nothing but tasteless gritty stuff and a few fish scraps. Never had one decent bowl of stew the whole time you were gone. Then he let that green feathered freak of his tease us, but don't worry, I jumped up and nipped his ugly tail. And that girl who comes in to throw spongy balls and entertain us didn't seem to understand that it's against all nature for us canines to be immersed in a tub of disgusting water. She even attacked me with those scary clippers.

"Oh, come now, Scruffy, it wasn't that bad, was it? You're quite trim from all that exercise and low-calorie food, and you smell good, too. I bet Honeycomb noticed how spiffy you look."

That blonde bitch has some attitude. Wouldn't stand still long enough to get herself a friendly greeting. Grabbed the kid's leg and toppled him right over on his ass.

Scruffy allowed himself to be hugged and kissed while coughing and hacking to make the point that he'd been vastly neglected and abused while I was away.

I'm practically fainting from hunger. Can't you see I need building up? I sure could use a pork chop. He snuggled under my arm and looked up at me with the canine equivalent of a winsome smile.

Raffles, on the other hand, dashed around with youthful abandon, nosing all his old haunts in the backyard and chasing the odd squirrel out of his domain. *Home! Home! It's good to be home!*

Actually, I felt the same as Raffles, reveling in my return to familiar sounds and scents. Outdoors, there was the blend of salt air, singing waves, pine trees, and the remnants of my herb garden, the staunch perennials like rosemary and sage still fragrant in November. Indoors, I was greeted by a whole array of drying herbs hanging from the kitchen rafters within my snug saltbox cottage, not to mention scented candles and potpourri. As soon as I walked in the door, I experienced afresh my heady romance with herbs. Not so much as to be overwhelming, but it was sensually embracing.

The strange and vivid adventure we'd experienced on the cruise was ebbing into unreality. Everything that had happened—the characters we'd encountered, the violent storm and the shock of that incredible tall-as-a-building wave, Paige's tragic disappearance, the otherworldly intruders into our Samhain, even Phil's narrow escape, and our dangerous confrontation with Simic—all took on the quality of fiction. Surrounded by the comforts and pleasures of home, I almost felt as if I'd never been away. I breathed in the pungent atmosphere again, deeply

"Wow! Do you ever feel rather bowled over by this effulgence of herbs?" I asked Joe.

"Nope," he said, swinging me into his muscular arms, rubbing his neat beard softly against my cheek. "I just take the dizzying atmosphere of this place as part of your intoxicating personality. Want to go check out those provocative dream pillows in the bedroom right now?"

The feel of him against me was intensely promising. "Alas, we'd better take care of the dynamic duo first," I suggested, "fill up their bellies so they'll be ready to nap. But hold onto that thought you've got there. You and I can dine later."

"Much later," he growled. "Okay, guys, let's go check out the property and make sure the raccoons haven't taken it over. Meanwhile, Cass, you get those dinners ready pronto."

"Don't get chilly out there," I admonished.

"Not to worry, honey. Not with this torch I'm carrying."

Afterwards, leaving the pups snoozing off their welcome-home banquet on their kitchen bed, we hungry humans stole away quietly to the bedroom and firmly shut the door.

At first we were as impetuous and breathless as if we'd been separated for years not days. But later, we were relaxed and sensuous as if we were making lazy love underwater. Either way, Joe filled me completely, leaving nothing more to want.

So it was indeed much, much later, when we finally dined on Joe's specialty *Pasta alla Pesce* (with enough crushed hot pepper to necessitate the drinking of much cold white wine). The scene was set with my very own bayberry candles, and the mood was romantic and magical. Another honeymoon in our marriage of parting and coming together.

Right now, in the coming together phase, I wouldn't have traded our relationship with any other in the world.

∾

Joe's mission to protest illegal logging on the Ivory Coast had been as ill-fated as our so-called "rest and relaxation" cruise to Bermuda. But he'd abandoned the *Gaia* to its extensive repairs at an Egyptian port so that he could fly home and meet our ship in New York. Well, not exactly abandoned. Rather, he'd arranged for some other Greenpeace watchdog to fly out and replace him. Meanwhile, his injured shipmate Heidimarie had been transferred to a hospital in Germany, where she was receiving rehabilitation for her injured leg. The rebels suspected of attacking the Gaia were never caught. Presumably, they continued to profit from the logging enterprise that funded their arms imports.

It was a wonder that Greenpeace didn't throw up its hands in despair and let the whole planet deplete, poison, and destroy itself as it wished. Not so, though. There would be other attempts by Greenpeace to expose and thwart the illegal loggers, and many more canvasses for donations to continue their efforts. I hoped Joe would be called upon in future more as a good will ambassador to big contributors rather than as a knight errant tilting at dangerous windmills.

That fictional feeling distancing us from our *Goddess* adventures , however, disappeared in a splash of cold water when we learned that Simic had not, after all, been charged with the murder of Paige Bratton or even (at least!) the attempted rape of Phillipa. The voracious defense of Simic by his friends on the *Goddess* crew had weakened the case considerably. Kirsti Hansen was still insisting that she and Simic had been together throughout the storm Ossie and rogue wave ordeal, treating the injured without regard to their personal safety. By the time his nurse got through with her deposition, Simic appeared more deserving of a medal than an arraignment.

We seemed to be the only people who'd noticed that Simic was on his own for quite a while, that Kirsti was lying out of friendship or even love.

Tony Grenville, who was there with us in the Atrium during the storm, who saw and heard what we did, must have realized she was lying, too. I wondered what had come out in his deposition. Apparently, no one was taking our accusations seriously enough, not even crediting Phillipa's report of sexual assault with no evidence other than a ruined Versace gown.

It was special agent Esther Thouless who called the Sterns to update them on the situation. She was sorry that the ripped gown affair had degenerated into a "she said, he said" impasse, but Thouless wanted all of us to know that the FBI was still working on the case as a possible serial rape/murder, collecting evidence on the disappearances of both brides, Paige Bratton and Christy Callahan. Murder of US nationals on the high seas was their responsibility. The Bureau had not given up on prosecuting Simic, but it was not their way to bring charges without sufficient evidence to gain a conviction. If the Bureau did assemble a strong case, however, they would be calling on Phillipa as a material witness, and perhaps others in the party who could discredit Kirsti Hansen's testimony that she and Simic had never been separated on the evening of Paige Bratton's disappearance.

Phillipa suggested checking Tony Grenville's deposition as well. Since he was there in the Atrium, too, he should have noticed that Simic came in separately with a flustered air, complaining about the loss of his cell phone. As a professional man, a psychiatrist, Grenville would be an eminently believable witness.

Special Agent Esther Thouless said that Grenville's deposition made no reference to having noticed Simic's solo appearance in the Atrium. When made aware of Kirsti Hansen's report, he had not refuted it. Grenville claimed he'd been unwell himself, anxious about his wife, and rather "out of it" regarding what was going on around him. He'd confessed to having taken a maximum dose of Xanax to calm his nerves and that he'd administered the drugs to the five of us as well. In his capacity as a physician, he'd felt it wise to prescribe a calming agent to these excitable women traveling alone who were so obviously suffering from fear and mental disturbance.

At that point in the conversation, Phillipa had had to turn away from the extension on which she was listening intently and utter several pithy pagan oaths—not exactly curses, in the sense of being hexes, she assured us later. We were all aware that whatever we sent out on the karmic waves of the universe, good or evil, would return to our own doorsteps. It had been one of those days, however, when it was a real struggle to be Glenda the Good Witch of the West. Tony Grenville deserved a good psychic kick in the ass.

Although she was counseling patience, what Esther Thouless got from Stone Stern was an earful of abuse. He was hopping mad that Simic was still at large, but as a local detective in a rural area, there was little or nothing he could do. It really was up to the FBI to assemble a case against Simic, and we had no idea how thorough and persistent they would be about it.

"We are totally in the dark," Phillipa summed up our situation angrily, handing around perfect cups of coffee from her Miele wonder machine. We were gathered in her kitchen for a post-cruise and pre-Thanksgiving conference. "Meanwhile, that pervert may be stalking another innocent victim to brutalize and drown like Paige."

"Oh, he won't be able to attack another passenger," I said. "Not after the fuss we've made. Whoever he's going after now to feed his sickness will have to be accosted on one of the islands among the Norse Line's ports of call."

"Well, *don't you care*? Shouldn't we be doing something?" Phillipa demanded.

"We *did* do something," I reminded her. "Our spell surely helped to expose Simic for a rapist and a murderer. It's not our fault that the law has been slow to follow up on our good spellwork."

"Time wounds all heels," Fiona said absently. She was looking rather depressed, chin sunk into her coat sweater of many colors, and we all knew why. Her adored grandniece, little Laura Belle with the morning glory eyes, was not here to bring joy to her heart and a ray of sunshine to her little fishnet-draped cottage in Plymouth Center. Laura Belle was slated to spend the holidays with her mother, Attorney Belle MacDonald, and Mommy's parents, Fiona's uptight brother Donald and sister-in-law Viv. The distraction of the cruise had evaporated, and Fiona was as deeply gloomy as only a Scot can be.

Affectionately known as "Tinker Belle," the child had once been afflicted with *elective mutism*, meaning there was no physical reason for her not to begin speaking at an age when other children were babbling away to the delight of their families. Even now, when she was old enough for pre-school, Laura spoke very little, and only what was implicitly true. Fiona said that Laura had been gifted with what the ancient Egyptians called *Ma'Kheru*, the word of truth, a state of grace. "And if she *is* Ma'Kheru," Fiona would affirm, "according to the old beliefs, whatever she says will come to pass in the world."

"Your little Laura will be back in your arms before you know it," Deidre told her softly. "Her mom will be returning to her position with that International Court in The Hague right after the first of the year. And your brother and his wife have never felt comfortable taking charge of Laura in her mother's absence. Personally, I don't think they know what to make of her, do you? Smart as a whip, yet so quiet and good. Mother Ryan would say the child has 'an old head.'"

"An old soul, really, my dear little lamb," Fiona said mournfully.

"I don't know—it wouldn't surprise me a bit if little Tinker Belle turned up on your doorstop earlier than you imagine," Phillipa said. She passed around a tray of perfect Danish pastries, and none of us could resist their sugary comfort. "I got the impression that Laura's grandparents, your dear brother et al, are fairly nervous about the kid's penchant for disdaining childish prattle in favor of the occasional truthful pronouncement."

"Yes," Fiona said, nibbling an apricot pastry with her first little smile of the afternoon. "Apparently Laura has come out with some rather 'inappropriate' remarks in the presence of my brother Donald's business associates."

"Oh, good fun," Heather said, passing around a bottle of Sambuca to enliven the coffee. Deidre and I declined, but Phillipa and Fiona added a healthy dollop to theirs. "Was it the 'I saw Grandma kissing Santa Claus' kind of thing?"

"And the guy kissing Grandma Viv wasn't Grandpa?" I hoped.

"No, the guy in this case was the choir director at their church—Episcopalian," Fiona smirked.

We all laughed, the comfortably wicked laugh that a circle of women friends will sometimes enjoy.

"Speaking of church, what's new with Patty Peacedale?" Heather asked me. Since the Garden of Gethsemane Presbyterian church was right around the corner from my place, the reverend's wife often visited me with her perpetual knitting and scatterbrained problems, not the least of which concerned the Maine Coon Cat who called himself Loki of Valhalla, an autocrat I'd foisted upon her care.

"Patty appeared at my door the day after we returned to Plymouth. She was knitting a longish bottle-green thing as part of her project Hats for the Homeless."

"Shouldn't that be Homes for the Homeless?" Heather suggested.

"Perhaps Patty feels that 'any place they hang their hats is home,'" Phillipa said with a grin.

Ignoring them both, I continued. "Patty said that knitting helps her concentrate on her other Christmas project. She's in the throes of writing a script for the Christmas pageant. It's called *A Star from Afar* and composed entirely in blank verse, 'similar to Shakespeare,' she tells me. She's been looking for a mentor, so I suggested that she ask you, Phil, since you are a fine poet yourself, to listen to her read the script aloud and to offer a critique." I hadn't really. I'm not that cruel. But I was terribly afraid I'd be skewered for the task myself.

"*Hecate, preserve me!* Goddess will get you for that," Phillipa said darkly.

"You know, this is going to be my first Thanksgiving without Will." Deidre changed the subject just in time to prevent an exchange of hexes. "And I'd dearly love it, Fiona, if you'll come and spend the day with us. Otherwise, the children and I will be in the sole clutches of Mother Ryan who will turn the holiday into a flag-and-crepe draped memorial. We all miss Will intensely—you know that. Willie's especially. His schoolwork's been affected, and there's the bedwetting. So I really want the kids to have a happy turkey day not a funeral feast. "

"What you need, Dee, is a cute little puppy to take Willy's mind off sad stuff during holidays," Heather suggested. As the guiding light (and purse) behind Animal Lovers Pet Sanctuary, Heather was always on the lookout for kindly adoptive homes, which was how I had come to bring home the redoubtable Scruffy when I'd first moved to Plymouth. "

"Oh, *give me a break*, not that again" Deidre protested. "Willie will have to make do with our present menagerie. And I don't need to worry about housebreaking a pup."

"Okay, how about a tiny kitty then? Entirely litter-box trained," Heather persisted.

Deidre scrunched up her pixie face and shook her blonde curls in a way we had learned was adamant and final. "Try me again in twenty years or so when the blessed empty nest syndrome kicks in. Now, back to you, Fiona...will you join us for the holiday?"

"Oh, bless you, my dear. Of course I will. But had you given a thought to poor Mick Finn who'll be hanging around the firehouse all by himself again? I mean, if his presence won't bring back too many painful memories."

Deidre's eyes shone with that special twinkle reserved for her matchmaking schemes. "Oh, yes, let's invite Chief Finn. He won't dwell on the past glories, will he? No, he does seem like a tactful soul. What fun for Willy and Bobby to have a fire chief to pester! And the poor man is simply besotted with your charms, Fiona. You must tell us someday what kind of a love spell you've woven around Finn."

"Sometimes the best love spells are not spells at all. They are simply vibrations of one's psychic being." Fiona's smile was enigmatic. It was good to see her round cheeks growing pinker. "What about you, Cass?" She looked at me over her granny glasses with that faery-godmother gleam in her eye, ready to wave her witch hazel wand if I needed help turning a pumpkin into a pumpkin pie.

"Patty's invited us to join the volunteers in dishing up turkey at the Gethsemane annual Thanksgiving Dinner for the Lonely and Elderly," I said. "Joe thinks it's a grand idea—well, he would, wouldn't he? His whole career is about caring for the world's well-being. And my family doesn't seem to mind dining late on a turkey roasted at Forker's Turkey Farm instead of by my own loving hands. Phil's offered to bring an array of homemade pies. So I guess Joe and I will spend the day helping out at the church."

"I'd do the whole shebang but we'll just be getting back from visiting Stone's mom in her new assisted-living apartment in Brewster," Phillipa said.

"Sara Lee Frozen Pies can be quite tasty, you know," Deidre said.

Phillip rolled her eyes heavenward. "Sara Lee?'

"Don't be such a food snob, Phil. We're not all masochists who revel in making pastry from scratch. And Sara Lee's pies are baked fresh in one's own oven. Makes the whole house smell like the First Thanksgiving," Deidre retorted.

"No kidding? Well, that's something then," Phillipa said. "And I bet you're making that green bean casserole with cream of mushroom soup, too."

"So? That casserole is a family favorite and much tastier than those weird spindly green beans from France that you serve half-cooked," Deidre defended her menu hotly.

"*Haricots Verts*," Phillipa murmured. "What else are you having, dear. Candied yams with marshmallows?"

"Leave Dee alone, Phil," I said. "She's serving America's favorites, and this is a totally American holiday not *A Day in Provence*."

"*Nobody doesn't like Sara Lee*," Phillipa sang softly, and went on to tease me instead. "So, Cass, would that church dinner be the same lovely Thanksgiving event at which the Reverend Sylwyn Peacedale once got poisoned by a hemlock-laced chocolate cake?"

"If only you'd get into the practice of dowsing your food for wholesomeness," Fiona declared, "you'd be safe as if you were in church."

"We *were* in church then, and we will be this time," I reminded her. "It's no safer than anywhere else. Take it from one who's had her stomach pumped out after a Presbyterian hospitality hour. But you know the Peacedales. Forgive and forget. Their good heartedness is quite persuasive. And admirable."

"Hmmmm. I wonder if I could talk Patty into fostering another sweet kitty then," Heather mused.

"Not after we stuck her with Buster a.k.a. Loki of Valhalla," I said. "He's a full-time fussbudget. He thinks the Peacedales are his personal staff, and I feel certain he wouldn't want to share."

"Oh, okay. Maybe later then. We'll be home, if you'd like to leave Scruffy and Raffles at our place for the day. We're hosting Dick's family this year," Heather said. "Captain Jack has agreed to roast a turkey—free range, of course—providing he can stuff it with oysters." The Devlin's cook-and-houseman (a retired fisherman whose feisty parrot named Ishmael so annoyed Scruffy) could rarely be persuaded to cook anything that didn't come fresh from the ocean, which suited Heather's brand of occasional vegetarianism very well. Of course, she *meant* to give up meat one of these days, but so far had only managed to rule out veal and baby lamb.

"Oh, the pups will be fine on their own," I said hastily. I couldn't have taken the canine abuse that this plan would have stirred up. Scruffy was looking forward to dining on turkey scraps not the Devlin's nutritionally complete doggie diet of dry stuff. "Joe will slip home once or twice to take them for a run. And we do have that pet door on the porch."

"So...so..." Phillipa had her hand on her hips, her expression fierce. "I'm asking you ladies once again, *what are we going to do about Simic?*"

Deidre sighed, the sigh of a mom who just wanted to mother her little family not hunt down a dangerous murderer. After all, she'd fallen into peril herself in a similar pursuit not so long ago. "How about if we just let the FBI handle this one? Agent Whatshername did say they would be assembling evidence. Your point was that we don't *know* what they're doing, but that could just as well be a good reason for not interfering with an operation we don't understand."

"I tell you what," Heather said, "why don't we all think about this until the full moon esbat after Thanksgiving, and *then* we'll decide how to proceed."

"As a circle. No Wiccan vigilantism," Fiona added, a steely glint of glamour in her gray eyes, a resolve not to be argued against.

Now it was Phillipa's turn to sigh. "Oh, very well. But be warned, I won't give up easily. I'm the one that was drugged out of my mind and dragged into a cold wrecked cabin. I'm the one whose beautiful Versace was ripped down the front by that bastard's scrabbling hands. And I'm the one who saw his eyes, his sick, sick eyes." She shuddered, remembering.

"I think what we must do today is a simple little purification ceremony," Fiona said thoughtfully. She reached into her green reticule and took out a packet of white stuff, which she proceeded to sprinkle in a circle around us. "I'm sorry, dear, if I've been insensitive to what you've been through."

"What's that you're sprinkling, Fiona?" Phillipa said, eyeing her spotless ceramic tile floor. "Nothing poisonous for Zelda to pick up with her paws, I trust?"

"Just salt, dear, common blessed salt." Fiona lifted one beringed hand and with her index finger drew a pentagram in the air over Phillipa, silver bangles tinkling. "Let's all hold hands and do a white light blessing for Phil right now."

Phillipa struggled to look cool and amused, but I could tell that underneath the pose she really needed and appreciated the healing boost. We held hands around her grand marble table, sending our loving strength and the dazzling light of pure spirit to surround our troubled friend. The blue-white energy swirled around us all, taking every one of us into its embrace, and for a few moments we truly were "out of this world."

"Wow!" Deidre said. "It's like downing a double shot of good Irish whiskey after a wake."

CHAPTER EIGHTEEN

We rest here while we can, but we hear the ocean calling in our dreams,
And we know by the morning, the wind will fill our sails to test the seams…

– Michael Lille

After our long day of helping the Peacedales and the other volunteers at the Garden of Gethsemane Thanksgiving Dinner for the Lonely and Elderly, it was rather daunting to trudge home (just around the corner) to thoughts of serving yet another feast to our own hungry family, although delightful, of course, to enjoy their company. I only wished my younger daughter Cathy with her partner Irene could be with us, too, but as aspiring actors, they were across the continent on the opposite coast, probably standing in line at some casting call for extras in *The Thanksgiving Story.*

The church dinner had been early, so it was still on the good side of five o'clock, but dead dark and windy, with the manic howling that is particular to a home on the Atlantic shoreline. I leaned on Joe's arm, grateful for him above all other blessings, but especially at that moment, for his sheltering warmth. I hunkered down and let him take the icy blasts on his broad chest.

"Thank the Goddess I set the table last night. I'm bushed, aren't you? And so weary of smiling. A whole day of smiling really gives your facial muscles a workout. Hey, do you hear a flute? Oh, good. I was hoping Tip would come by for dinner." Thunder Pony Thomas, known informally as Tip, the young friend who had a special place in my heart, was studying Native American music while finishing high school in Wiscasset, Maine, but he was nonetheless a frequent visitor. "I smell wood smoke, too, don't you?"

"Yes, and I think it's ours," Joe said, pulling me closer into his shoulder. "I imagine someone's lit a fire in the fireplace. Nice thought."

We met Tip on the chilly porch. He'd sprouted up a bit taller than Joe, but he hadn't got too big for one of those manly slaps-on-the-back greetings. His gray eyes turning Asian with his wide grin, he hugged me with a shy kiss on the cheek. He smelled of pine, cinnamon, and pepper. I noted that he'd grown his crow-black hair long and was wearing it in a pony tail. "I've been staying at Plimouth Plantation with friends, helping out with the so-called authentic dinner for tourists, but that was served early today. After we cleaned up, my buddies went out to watch football at the Bert's Cove Sports Bar, but I remembered your invitation and snuck away. Your kids are all busy in the kitchen with food prep, so I stayed out of the way, came out here to practice. Spooked Scruffy and his pup. Guess they're not into this Indian flute stuff."

Busy in the kitchen? I left Joe on the porch and rushed inside to see what was going on.

There are few things in life more gratifying than discovering that one's children have not only grown up but also are perfectly capable of thoughtful efficiency to relieve their mom of home-keeping chores. Not only was there a toasty warm blaze in the living room fireplace, there were appetizers on the coffee table, bottles of white wine in an ice-filled tub, Forker's turkey heating up in the oven, and vegetables in covered dishes ready to nuke in the microwave. And the house itself, which might be described by a real estate agent as "a snug and cozy Cape Cod treasure" (meaning ancient and small with low ceilings) seemed filled to the brim with laughter and chatter. What a pleasant realization that there was nothing I had to do, or even supervise. A glad day on the parenting scene!

My oldest, Becky, her shining chestnut hair cut in the latest asymmetrical style, wearing jeans and a stylish big shirt, was in the kitchen tending a vat of soup. With a sly smile, she introduced her newest squire—*esquire* really, an attorney like herself—Johnny Marino. (That smile, a challenge for me to "read" the new man.) The soup was Johnny's contribution—cannellini and mushroom, redolent with onion, garlic, fresh sage, and rosemary. Earthy, like Johnny himself. Stocky build, baritone's chest, big smile, square jaw, and intense dark eyes. Something about him reminded me of Joe, but this man would be much less open and accessible. My senses were quite won over, however, before I'd had a chance to grill Becky's companion properly. "You're a cook, too, Johnny! Smells heavenly. Especially after that cold dark walk home," I said appreciatively. Somehow I'd missed shaking hands with this guest. Touch always gave me the most direct psychic impressions. *Oh, well...later.*

Since her divorce from Ron Lowell, there had always been some needy character or other hanging around Becky, drawn to that remarkable life-giving energy that she radiated without really knowing she was doing so. I wondered what Johnny Marino needed. That last man of hers had been an artist in search of an approving mom.

Scruffy and Raffles were holed up on their kitchen faux-sheepskin beds, watching every move toward and away from food. Somewhat intimidated by high-pitched plaintive music on the porch and the presence of a strange man at the stove, they could only manage little moans of hunger accompanied by flopping over from time to time as if overcome with weakness brought on by starvation. *Are we never, ever going to have food in our food bowls? A canine's lot is not an easy one. So often our loyalty and protection is taken for granted, and our poor bellies go empty.*

"Oh, sure, you faker. Would you like me to play a violin?"

"Violin?" Johnny Marino looked around uneasily for the mysterious instrument, then turned to stir the soup. I went in search of Adam.

I found my son standing by the fireplace mantel, drinking his favorite single malt Scotch and gazing dotingly at his wife Freddie reclining on the sofa. I hugged the splendidly tall, expensively-attired stranger (a stranger with my green eyes!) that I was astonished to have given birth to so many years ago, and my dear daughter-in-law who was soon, very soon it appeared, to make me a grandmother. She was drinking "a Virgin Mary, so appropriate, considering my due date, don't you think?"

That hug had told me more than she realized, but as is usual with clairvoyants, I was careful not to spoil the surprise.

"Ha ha. Not your style, that immaculate stuff," I said. "So have you got The Name picked out? I need to know what name you're fixing on. Tell me it's not a trendy Hollywood one like Apple or Hermoine or Phinneas."

"*Names*," Freddie cried with a triumphant smile. "*Two* names. His and hers."

"*Great goddess!* Why didn't you tell me? What's the purpose of all this instant electronic communication, if I'm not to know about the... twins...*twins!* How miraculous!" I thought I was making rather a good show of incredulity.

"Sorry. It was me, not your son," Freddie said. "I wanted to see your face. When the doc detected two heartbeats, I broke down and went for the sex sonar thing. So beautiful. So fragile." She gazed down and patted her stomach fondly. "Bound together in shared space like the celestial twins. What were *their* names, Adam?"

He smiled ruefully. "Castor and Pollux. That won't do for Ma."

Before we could get too embroiled in the name wars (actually, I'd be happy with anything as long as they didn't name the boy after my ex-husband Gary, the nuclear engineer and all-around jerk), I went through the downstairs like the town crier announcing the news of my forthcoming grandcutenesses, only to discover that everyone else already knew, even Joe who'd been filled in by Tip.

"Now, Mom, we have dinner completely under control," Becky said firmly, taking my favorite wooden stirring spoon out of my hand. "You and Joe have a nice sit-down by the fire and let Adam pour you drinks while Johnny and I finish up here. I'll call you when the soup's on and the turkey's out of the oven."

Although it felt strange—*shouldn't I be mashing or seasoning something? how could they possibly get on without me?*— after an afternoon of serving at the church, resting our feet on hassocks with glasses of Moselle wine in hand, Joe and I smiled at each other, silently counting our blessings.

Gazing into a hearth fire, especially when one is a little tired, watching those flames leap, spark, and fall back, constantly shapeshifting from one nearly recognizable form to another, is a mildly hypnotic experience and, for a psychic, very conducive to second sight. *Jack*, I was thinking. *She'll name the boy Jack, for her brother who disappeared in a fishing boat off the Florida coast last year. My grandson will have Freddie's midnight hair and tiger eyes. When he's older, he'll be called Black Jack. But why? Oh dear. I wonder if he'll be the inheritor of his mother's spooky abilities as well as her coloring. Or my psychic talents. Talk about a double-whammy of quirky genes. And the girl? Jonnet? Janet? or is it Joan? Something like that. Lighter hair and my green eyes. Well, Adam's green eyes, but I had them first. I must remember to react with amazement and pleasure when they tell me the true, plain names they've chosen! Thank the Goddess for ordinary familiar names, no Chastity or Lourdes or Banjo or Aspen. Still, I could have gone for a Rosemarie or a Rosamund. Suppose I lit, say, one little rose-colored, rose-scented candle tonight and let it burn down to its last bit of flame? No, no...it's not nice to tinker with your children's and grandchildren's lives. Two babies! I'll need two cribs in one of those guest rooms.*

All this and Phil's pies, too.

Phil and Stone arrived just before the soup. That made nine of us squashed around the dining room table. We seated Freddie at the hostess end where she could spread out a little. She was so big, she had to turn sideways to reach her plate.

"You realize, don't you, that this is our second Thanksgiving dinner of the day." Phil sampled the cannellini and mushroom broth with an educated palate. No way was she about to ask for the recipe when it was so satisfying to guess—and guess right. "Hmmmm. The rosemary and sage are perfect. Fresh herbs are so important, don't you think? But really, at this point, Stone and I should be eating no more than a turkey sandwich. The traditional Thanksgiving Eve supper."

"You barely ate anything at the William Brewster Inn," Stone pointed out. "If ever someone could be said to be toying with her food."

"Well, my dear, on the one hand, I always feel that a traditional turkey dinner is the one entrée that few restaurants can ruin. On the other hand, there's something so dispiriting about those slices of breast meat artfully arranged to hide a sodden lump of bland stuffing. I mean, there we were on the

Cape—couldn't the chef have tossed in a few oysters and a handful of chopped sage?"

"I really enjoyed that Austrian Reisling," Stone protested.

"Yes, I noticed you did, and that's how I became the designated driver. At least, the Inn's wine cellar was decent. Still, two turkey dinners in one day is so *Lucullan!* This is a marvelous soup, though. But a mere sandwich should have been sufficient for us. I usually make lemon mayonnaise and slice the turkey breast very thin. Sprigs of watercress, of course."

"I have Hellman's, if you insist on slapping your supper between two pieces of bread," I offered.

She ignored me and skewered Johnny instead. "Marino... Marino...of the sea, of course. Isn't your family in the fishing business out of Boston? Oh well, no matter. What kind of law do you practice exactly? Family law? Becky's firm?"

"General practice. Why, are you in need of a good attorney?" Johnny said smoothly.

"I don't know, maybe" Phillipa replied. "I don't seem to be getting anywhere with the FBI."

Stone gave Phillipa a look designed to suggest that our present worries were not a proper subject for holiday dinner table conversation.

"I can handle the FBI," Johnny Marino said. A dark curl fell attractively on his forehead, and his smile was self-assured but modest. "That was quite a mess, that cruise. Rebecca told me some of what happened. There's always civil court, you know. Deep pockets, those cruise lines."

Too late, apparently, to caution Becky, I gave Phillipa a warning look. This was not the time, the place, or the person, I felt strongly.

"Yes, well...that's something to consider, isn't it? For the present, I will probably follow my husband's counsel to be patient. Stone's in law enforcement, and he understands these things better than I do." She smiled ingenuously at the young man.

Joe had disappeared into the kitchen to carve the turkey. Although it was a gloriously crackling-brown bird, we were much too crowded to gaze upon its noble presence at table. Becky and Johnny cleared the tureen and soup plates and followed Joe out of the room.

"A civil suit would be my last resort," Phillipa said, "but I'm not abandoning the notion altogether. Dear Tip, you're looking ever so puzzled by the lot of us."

Tip grinned. "Not at all. You medicine women took a vacation cruise, so naturally Coyote, the trickster spirit, went right along with you to stir up trouble. I don't know all the details, but I get the picture. Aunt Cass, I'm going to be in Plymouth for the rest of Thanksgiving vacation. You'll tell me if you need any muscle, right? In case, the human trickster , whoever he is, follows you here."

Phillipa and Stone and I looked at each other. Somehow the words "follows you here" jumped out at us in an alarming new way.

Out of the mouths of babes...

"Good man, Tip," Stone said. "I remember your superb tracking skills. But don't worry. Unlike the rest of the company, I have great faith in the FBI's ability to collect and process evidence. I have to admit I was furious at first that no charge had been brought, but now I feel the longer they work, the more solid the case will be."

"Okay. I guess. Even after I go back to school, Aunt Cass, just give me a call if you need me. You have my cell number, don't you?"

"How did we ever manage to get through high school without personal cell phones?" Phillipa asked wonderingly just as the kitchen crew returned with turkey and fixings.

There were deep sighs under the table, but I was ready for that. With two dog dishes at the ready, I selected a few delectable shreds of meat and skin from the turkey leg and slipped them into the bowls, which were emptied before I got them down to the floor.

Hey, Toots, what about a little gravy? Or stuffing, if it's sausage. And that big old liver? And the gizzard? Gizzard is traditionally saved for us canines, you know. Not for the kid, though. Gizzard's probably too rich for Raff. You better leave the turkey innards for my mature digestive system. Also gristle.

Hey, Da...I can eat anything you can, anything you can, and faster, old guy. My teeth are sharp and white, sharp and white.

"You two just be quiet and mannerly until it's your turn, or you'll be dining on Alpo," I said firmly.

Johnny Marino glanced at me strangely.

"It's okay," Tip explained. "Aunt Cass is just putting Scruffy and Raffles in their place. Scruffy's liable to talk fresh when he's hungry."

"Scruffy and Raffles?"

"The dogs, Johnny. The furry people under the table." Becky explained with a winning smile. "My mom talks to dogs, and that's not all. She reads minds, too."

"Ah, *strega*," Johnny said.

"Exactly," Becky agreed.

~

We five met again in the first week of December, Esbat of the Oak Moon, at Heather's. It was cold, of course, but not too cold to draw down the moon outdoors, warmly wrapped in new-for-Yule wool cloaks. Phillipa had felt that five hooded long capes made us look conspicuously witchy, but we pointed out that she was the only one of us who had chosen unrelieved black.

Fiona's was the MacDonald of Isles hunting tartan, subdued greens and blues, Deidre's navy, and Heather's plum. Rather than ordering new, however, I'd preferred to wear the forest green that Joe had given me when we were courting. It was embroidered with a border of leaves in vivid shades of green with tiny pink and yellow flowers.

"A rainbow of witchiness, then," Phillipa said.

"A unique aspect of Wicca is that *there is no dogma*," Fiona said. "We can please ourselves, create our own ceremonial robes and our own rituals. *There are traditions*, of course, and I honor them, but not to the point of restricting my wardrobe to medieval garb. And besides, I don't look my best in black." Fiona's cheeks were pink with defensive zeal; none of us cared to argue with her.

"When the moon rises, we'll all appear to be in shadowy black anyway," Heather pointed out. "Dick says when he looks out the conservatory window and sees us silhouetted up here on the hill dancing, he feels as if he's got into a time warp, watching some ancient Women's Mysteries ceremony."

"And right he is," Fiona said. "Women have always had their Mysteries."

Heather had laid out a great stone circle in the pine and oak grove on her considerable acreage. The more esbats and sabbats we'd held here, the more sacred the space had become. At the center, a flat-topped glacial boulder served as a natural altar, imbued with all our spiritual yearnings. The good vibrations of our own personal "stonehenge" drew us to freeze a little for the sake of celebrating the glorious full moon. The silvery green light it cast on haphazard tree limbs leaning this way and that made them look like fingers reaching for one another, a somewhat sinister take on the hands painted on the Sistine Chapel's ceiling.

"Look at that!" Fiona exclaimed at the crisscross branches. "The Lord of the Night, the Horned Stag of the Forest, is walking among those trees, our guardian and guide, infusing us with His life-force and fire, His wisdom, and strength, and above all His daring." She drew herself into the glamour of the Goddess, gesturing toward the woods, drawing us all with her. "His is the spirit we'll need to inspire us if we are to follow Phil's plan to bring in Dan Simic. Let us appeal to Him tonight. At the still point of the darkest days, when the sun and moon are born, we will apply our magic to end the terror on which that evil doctor thrives."

"Geeze," whispered Deidre to me, lighting incense on the altar. It was too breezy for candles, but a small cheery fire blazed in the fire pit. "Is Fiona ever impressive, and we haven't even cast our circle yet."

"Shhhh," I said. "Here we go now."

Heather stepped forward, and with her ivory-handled athame, marked our circle with an imagined blue spear of light. She welcomed the spirits of the four quarters by name, drawing pentagrams in the air. At Fiona's instigation, Heather invited also the Lord of the Forest, whose presence filled the star-silent woods, to lend His boundless energy to our quest. The strong scent of pine trees and the more subtle fragrance of frankincense and cinnamon perfumed the air; salt and water were sprinkled around the circle. Now we were in the space between the worlds where magic can be made. In due course, we raised energy by dancing and chanting until at last Heather drew down the Goddess of the Moon into our arms.

Then we got down to work. There was a spell to be cast.

Earlier that week, Phillipa and I had paged through Fiona's arcane texts looking for an appropriate ritual.

"Think what it is you want to do, exactly," I'd said.

"Kill the bastard," she'd replied.

"Well, you know that won't do. What about, drive him into the arms of the FBI?" I'd suggested.

"*Ha ha. Drive him into the ocean* is more like it. That's where he dumped his victims."

"Your capacity for revenge makes me a bit nervous, Phil," I'd cautioned.

"All right, all right. Oh! How about *this one!*" She'd laid a triumphant finger against a page of the dark, moldering *Book of Shadows* Fiona once had found in a box of donations for library sale. How it ever ended up there was a mystery. Inattentive heirs, one assumed. This decrepit handwritten volume, some long-gone witch's grimoire no doubt, had been our source for a water misdirection spell, and others. Its craft was somewhat darker than the recipes in *Hazel's Book of Household Recipes*, which was my personal favorite.

"*To Summon a Villain to His Just Desserts*," I'd read aloud. "The word *Summon* is what makes me nervous in this one, Phil."

"Nonsense," she'd said briskly. "Now let's see what we'll need..."

So here we were at the Esbat of the Oak Moon, summoning danger with herbs and chants and burning intentions, with the Lady of the Moon and Lord of the Night to give us their wisdom and strength. In some ways, I found this a deeply disturbing spell, but since Fiona had given it her *imprimatur,* I joined in with my whole heart and energy.

Summon a Villain was simpler in many ways than some of our other magical efforts. It called for Dragon's Blood Ink, which I'd prepared from Indonesian *Daemonorops draco,* or Gold Seal, a pinch of *Pimpinella saxifraga* or Blessed Herb for its power and truth, and pure alcohol. (Well, of course, it's impossible to get pure alcohol these days, so I used vodka. I don't think that minor deviation is in any way responsible for the slight skewing of the spell that resulted later.) The ink was dark red with a spicy fragrance that enveloped us as soon as the bottle was opened. Using a new quill pen which we had purified by drawing it through incense, fire, salt water, and fresh earth, Phillipa wrote Simic's full name inside a dry piece of willow bark. We placed that in a cast iron cauldron and, with the aid of a few dried pine needles, burned the name until it was reduced to ashes. These we cast to the prevailing wind. Each of us then called out the name and chanted the rhyme Phillipa had improvised.

Daniel Marko Simic, Daniel Marko Simic, Daniel Marko Simic...

Ashes in the air, early or late, Hecate calls you to meet your fate.

It was an intense effort that actually made me shudder. We were all glad afterward to open the circle and run back to the house for warmth and light. Dear Dick, that great teddy bear, had a roaring fire blazing in the fireplace of the Victorian red parlor, a sumptuous room which was large enough to accommodate a grand piano in the bow window without in the least seeming crowded. Fiona, as was her custom, fell gracefully upon the velvet fainting couch and allowed Heather to pour her a dram of Drambuie. Deidre requested hot coffee with whiskey, and the rest of us had glasses of the excellent Merlot that Dick had opened for us.

The Devlin's eccentric houseman, Captain Jack, with Ishmael on his shoulder, brought in a tray of boiled coffee in an enamel pot, spicy shrimp sandwiches, and sliced Dundee cake. That was about as fancy a spread as the captain cared to prepare in what he referred to as "my galley," Heather's gorgeous kitchen (rebuilt after being bombed out during an earlier investigation) that even Phillipa envied. Bypassing Heather's Royal Doulton, the grizzled old fellow had provided us with thick white plates and mugs along with checkered napkins.

"A bit nippy out there tonight," the captain commented. "Wind's edging around Nor'east." He thumped the heavy tray down on the carved teakwood butler's table.

"Nippy, zippy, Ish wants a nip of whiskey," the parrot screamed, leering at Deidre.

This little tableau, complete with dancing firelight, made me feel I'd just stepped into the pages of *Treasure Island.*

"Oh, that looks lovely. Thank you, Captain," Heather said. "Dick and I will take care of the cleanup. You go ahead home now and get some rest."

"Doggies are all tucked up in their beds, Mizzus Devlin. Ish and I will be following shortly. Might be snow in the morning. I got the shovels all waxed and ready." The old man trudged off to his snug apartment above the garages-converted-to-kennels.

Dick Devlin followed closely on the captain's heels, mumbling something about patients who needed checking in his Wee Angels Animal Hospital. Actually, I think that the five of us in concert made him a tad uncomfortable, even though we weren't humming. Joe was the only guy I knew who seemed unfazed by the forceful aura of five Wiccan women in the same room. His male ego was as strong as a Minotaur, and that was probably good fortune for me.

Heather sighed. "I've tried to convince Captain Jack not to shovel, but he turns his deaf ear to me. Literally. As a result, every time it snows, Dick and I do our best to beat him to it. We have the driveway plowed by a landscape service, naturally, but there are so many paths from the house to various outbuildings, plus the patio and the dog yard. I just tell myself that snow shoveling is wonderful exercise, for those who are young enough not to keel over."

"So many things are like that," Fiona murmured. "Grand if they don't kill you."

"I hope that doesn't include magic," I said.

"Of course it applies to spellwork," Fiona said. "That's why we say 'To know, to will, *to dare*, and to keep silent.' But if it's in a good cause, sometimes we have to spread our wings and fly forth in the face of disaster."

"The Icarus credo!" Deidre exclaimed.

"Oh, nonsense!" Phillipa said. "The spell we worked tonight may very well save some unknown woman's life—someone that Simic will never be able to harm because he's been terminated—by us."

"*Terminated*? Banish that thought," I said with alarm.

But the worrisome subject was changed by Fiona, who had begun reciting a ritual chant in a low voice. *There's a river of birds in migration, a nation of women with wings.* Soon we'd all joined in, gradually raising our voices louder, chanting faster, and clapping hands or drumming on the nearest end table. In the way of chants, we were lifted to new heights, feeling the force of our combined will. It even seemed for a while as if murder and mayhem could never touch us again.

CHAPTER NINETEEN

The waves that plunged along the shore
Said only: "Dreamer, dream no more!"

– George William Curtis

Yule, from the Anglo-Saxon *Yula*, meaning *Wheel of the Year*, has its own joyous magic. Soon we were caught up in preparations for that beautiful winter Sabbat, a festival of Light and Love whose purpose is to celebrate the return of the sun, growing stronger as the days grow longer.

Myths of the Goddess giving birth to the God at the winter solstice go back to prehistoric times. Thus "the Son is born" over and over again, time out of mind. But why should we not celebrate, I wondered, the birth of the Son *and the Daughter?* The creative force of the universe includes the divine female as well as the male. I was thinking about Adam and Freddie's twins, of course; they would be born very close to that sacred date.

Some say that those born in the winter solstice or on Christmas are believed to be able to see the Little Folk. Naturally, I knew in my bones that my grandchildren would be exceptional, with extrasensory powers on both sides of their genetic inheritance—and perhaps it *would* take the form of "seeing faeries." What an enchanting childhood they might enjoy! And what trouble would await them in the years ahead when those extra senses and unusual powers made them outsiders, different and suspect in ways that others viewed suspiciously. I vowed to teach them early to dissemble and conceal their psychic abilities.

Oh, isn't that great! Jack and Joan aren't even born yet, and here I am planning to teach them to lie. I shook my hands and feet, that little dance I do to rid my psyche of negativity. A sprinkle of cinnamon or cloves on one's shoes is good, too.

Immersed in the fun and furor of Yule, we of the Circle actually put the Simic spell out of our minds (well, maybe all of us did except Phillipa) which is exactly what one should do with spells once they are worked. *Let go and let Goddess.* We had summoned him to justice with dragon's blood ink and willow bark, but mostly with the energy of magical intention. Our spell would be swirling like a cloud of stardust in the Cosmos, and the Cosmos would answer in its own good time and mysterious way to end the man's evil. Even now Simic was moving toward his "appointment in Samarra" while we Yule celebrants ignored whatever it was we'd begun at the Esbat of the Oak Moon.

For one nanosecond, a secondary meaning of "appointment in Samarra" flashed across my inner eye, the notion that a deadly fate may turn up in an unexpected place. But that insight was instantly erased by my own internal message blocker. *Banish that dark thought and get merry*, it insisted. My half-realized thought faded more quickly than a dream.

Meanwhile, December went on, our restless energies were kept busy, and the short, dark days got absorbed in shopping, wrapping, decorating, cooking, and for me, filling Christmas orders that arrived steadily via my Internet catalog, an efficient program that my son Adam had set up for me. My herbal recipes were largely taken from spidery handwritten notebooks, passed down by Shipton women for generations.

At this festive season, some of my big sellers were the Love Potion Number Nine Kit (herbal blend for mulled wine, massage oil, and scented candles), along with Adam and Eve Apple-Scented Bath Salts, Less Stress Bath Oil (geranium, lavender, cardamom, patchouli), Incense to Attract Abundance (cinnamon and sandalwood), and Psychic Visions Dream Pillows (rosemary, lavender, aniseed, mugwort, wormwood, lemongrass, rowan, saffron, and other more esoteric herbs.)

The original Psychic Visions herb mixture had actually worked *too* well when I tried it on myself, so I immediately and deliberately adulterated and weakened my commercial formula. (Like, easy on the mugwort. And saffron, which is prohibitively expensive anyway.) It was still evocative but no longer a clairvoyant trip-out experience. The prototype pillow I kept hiding in various places, hoping I would eventually lose it before I would be called upon to lay my head on it again. Although I generally didn't find it difficult to lose my belongings—quite the contrary, my car keys and reading glasses wandered off on their own regularly—that pillow turned up relentlessly whenever the Cosmos decided to put my clairvoyant skills to work.

Speaking of divination, Yule is second only to Samhain and Beltane in being a perfect time to consult whatever oracles one fancies. At Yule, if Phillipa felt that her energy was high enough, she would read the Tarot for each of us during the "cakes and ale" conclusion of our private circle. That was often a rather raucous session. Last Yule, however, Phillipa had practically fainted when she read for Deidre, knowing that Winter Solstice predictions often proved to be uncannily accurate. She prettied up what she divined, of course, but later she told me privately that the real death card, the Ten of Spades (not the Major Arcana card that is called Death but is read as Transformation) had turned up in Deidre's family. And then the tragedy of Will's early death had followed. Sharing that sorrow, Phillipa had almost thrown her tarot deck to the four winds, but I managed to talk her out of such a waste. After all, if I had to live with the after effects of my clairvoyance, she could very well tough it out with the tarot.

In the midst of all this festive planning and activity, it came as a jolt when Special Agent Esther Thouless called the Sterns with news that the Simic investigation was moving forward and a couple of promising leads were being followed.

After the scandal on *Goddess of the Sea*, Thouless said, Simic still had a year of his three-year-contract to fulfill, so he'd been quietly posted to another Norse Line vessel, *Siren of the Sea*, for its winter cruise season. No, no more brides had disappeared, but a diligent computer surveillance had turned up two missing girls on dates relevant to the *Siren* schedule. The first was a twenty-year-old waitress, Enesha Cook, at the Sunbury Plantation on Barbados where a nostalgic 19th century English tea was served to tourists every afternoon. Her frantic parents reported that she'd failed to return to her home after work one night. Witnesses said she'd been last seen walking on the beach with a white man who was so ordinary in appearance, none could describe him with any confidence. *Average height or possibly shorter than average, jeans and a t-shirt or tan chinos and blazer, might have had brown hair or blond.* Despite a massive search of the island, Enesha had not been found.

The other was eighteen-year-old Beth Sweeting, who worked with her father on a glass-bottom boat at Stingray City, a popular excursion on the Grand Cayman Island. Three days after she disappeared, her father found her body at dawn one morning floating in the water, a victim not of stingray but of man.

Local police had made no connection between the presence of the cruise ship *Siren* at their docks and the fate of the young women. Since the victims were not American citizens, in the normal course of events, the FBI wouldn't have been involved in their disappearance or murder. But this time, Thouless and Frost were on alert for just such crimes, coincidental with Simic having the opportunity to commit them.

With the Sweeting case, the special agents had something they'd never had before—a body to autopsy. Even a three-days-in-the-water bloated and nibbled torso was useful evidence. Although Thouless didn't tell us until much later, the body of Beth Sweeting still had traces of DNA in its vaginal tract—a major breakthrough.

What the special agent did relay to the Sterns, however, was that Phillipa would be needed as a witness if and when a Federal Grand Jury was convened to charge Daniel Marko Simic with the murders of Christy Callahan, and Paige Bratton. Phillipa was the only witness who could cast suspicion on Simic in regard to the two missing brides by relating the details of his attack upon her.

It was a tenuous link, of course. But without telling us the rest of their plan, Thouless and Frost were counting on Simic's DNA to cinch the case, proving him to be the sexual predator and murderer of Beth Sweeting. But first they had to obtain a DNA sample from Simic.

Unfortunately, shortly after Thouless's report to the Sterns, Bess Sweeting's murder had turned up on the news—a small item of minor interest. The *Siren* was just docking in New York when the story broke, so to speak, on a CNN feature about "exotic island crime." Before Frost and Thouless could question him, and request a DNA sample on whatever pretext they might come up with, Simic had jumped ship and gone missing.

Normally, ship's personnel did not go ashore until all the passengers had disembarked, and they were due back on board well ahead of the next scheduled cruise. Simic had not reported to the *Siren's* captain as the medical staff was required to do twenty-four hours in advance of the subsequent sailing. Another doctor had to be hastily recruited for the Norse Line's "Christmas Cruise Caribbean" leaving December 21. If acting guilty could be taken as proof of culpability, the FBI had Simic right there. Only they didn't have him. New York is a great place in which to get lost.

Special Agent Thouless ought to have told us that Simic was on the loose. Whatever the FBI's reasoning may have been, a quiet search for Simic was mounted without a word to us. Perhaps they were worried that Detective Stern would bring in State and Plymouth Law Enforcement to clutter up the FBI's sophisticated surveillance methods, as if any local cop must be a yokel, Andy Griffith from Mayberry.

Believing Simic to be safely on board the *Siren*, we were looking forward to a pastiche of celebrations in these last days of December. As Wiccans, we'd celebrate Yule with evergreen, holly, ivy, mistletoe (cut on the sixth day of the moon with a sacred knife) and a *waes hael* bowl, Anglo-Saxon for *be well, be whole*. We'd light this year's decorated Yule log with last year's and burn it for twelve hours to bring luck. The Winter Solstice would be divided into a private ritual for us five, and the merry celebration for everyone afterward.

Christmas was traditionally celebrated with our extended families. Becky planned to spend Christmas Eve with Johnny Marino's family ("Feast of the Seven Fishes!" Phillipa declared enviously), and Christmas Day they would come to us. The romance was obviously still progressing, how fast and how far I refused to speculate upon, psychically or any other way. I even tried not to "read" Johnny Marino too closely, in case that might be an unfair intrusion. The temptation to protect one's child, however, was very keen. Becky had often commented on the drawbacks of having a clairvoyant mother.

To accommodate their soon-to-expand family, Adam and Freddie had decided to buy a town house in Hingham, a detached condominium in a gated community on 380 acres of the Wompanoag Country Club. The location was convenient to Boston and no more than a half hour's drive to Plymouth. They were on tenterhooks, of course, with the impending birth. The twins were officially due on December 28, but first babies are notoriously tardy. So if the weather was perfect, the roads impeccable, and Freddie in robust good health, they thought they might risk a short visit at Christmas. Although Adam hesitated, riddled with worry, Freddie was insistent, refusing to be hampered by pregnancy, or even imminent birth. "*Confinement*," she had declared, "is a Victorian bad attitude. Those uptight buggers simply didn't want to be, like, totally grossed out by the bloated appearance of girls who were preggers."

"Nothing about you is 'bloated,' Freddie," I'd replied. My amazing daughter-in-law was carrying her double burden high and neat, rather like a concealed ottoman. Her features had softened a bit due to those happy-hour hormones of late pregnancy, but her skin was still fresh and bright. She continued to bemoan her diminished skills, but I kept assuring her that psychokinesis would return (alas) about a month after the birth.

Wonder of wonders, Cathy and Irene were arranging to fly East for Christmas this year but wanted to time their visit so that they could meet their new niece and nephew in person, whenever that would be. They would trust to stand-by tickets. *Ah, my whole family will be together again,* I thought, *albeit in the hospital waiting room.*

Religious roots drew us back to our childhoods. Deidre never missed a Christmas Eve Midnight Mass, and this year she planned to attend accompanied by the oldest child, Jenny, and her Ryan in-laws. Phillipa lit menorah candles for each of the eight nights of Hannukah. Fiona was invited to attend Episcopal services with her brother Donald and his family, which gave her a chance to visit with Laura Belle bringing hugs, gifts, and love. Heather was organizing a God-Is-Love Pet Adoption Day for the holidays under the auspices of the Unitarian-Universalist church. And Joe and I found ourselves recruited yet again by the Peacedales for their Garden of Gethsemane programs for needy parishioners—to help distribute the "Jesus Delivers" food and gift baskets and serve a holiday meal to those who had no other place to go, the annual "Plenty of Room at the Inn" dinner.

The Solstice arrived in wintery splendor. A fall of bright, light snow touched the trees with crystal magic. Pines and firs dusted with frosty white made our town look like a Currier and Ives print, and we celebrants of Yule were in a festive mood. It was Fiona's turn to act as hostess/priestess for our Sabbat ritual. With Laura Belle absent, however, Fiona's place had slowly but surely reverted to Chaos Cottage; it would be difficult indeed to find a nine-foot space in her living room in which to cast our circle. Fortunately, she herself decided to pass the athame to another.

"I'll do it," Deidre offered. "Let's save Heather's for our outdoor rituals when the weather allows. Her ring of stones is so perfectly set on that hill surrounded by pines, I wouldn't mind making it our permanent altar. And have you noticed what good vibes that place gives off? Woo...eee! Positively *em*powering." She pushed the bottle of Irish whiskey across her yellow formica kitchen table, and I poured a slug into my coffee. The sun was over the yardarm, and Deidre's coffee tended to be both weak and tepid.

Salty and Peppy, the Ryans' little poodles, came hurtling into the kitchen with an on-going game of tug-of-war. With a practiced hand, Deidre recovered the chewed tan thing they were using for a rope. "M & Ms' support hose," she explained, smoothing it out in her lap. "Now a bit aerated."

"If I were you, I'd throw that chewed-up thing away before your mother-in-law sees it, Dee. She probably has plenty of others," I advised. "It may be that Heather intuitively arranged the stones in a place of natural magnetic power. Who knows what ley lines are converging in Plymouth? Tip calls them Serpent Power Tracks. Got that from his uncle the shaman."

Deidre's smile was both impish and sad. "I know what you mean by ley lines. Will said his cousins in Kildare called them Faery Paths. The Old Straight Track it was to the Brits. But, ley lines on the old Morgan place? Could be. No wonder I get such a hit when we dance up there on the hill. If it's true, Fiona should be able to tell by dowsing. Ley lines draw the dowser like water does. Natural energy, what a trip."

"If it's energy they're emanating, you must have a couple of ley lines intersecting right here under this kitchen, Dee," I commented. While we were chatting and drinking coffee, Deidre's busy little hands also had been fastening wings to tiny flower faeries named Daisy, Lily, and Poppy, each accompanied by her own pet honeybee

"Aren't they the cutest? I've created a little garden for them, too. Just like a Barbie habitat. Did you know there's a faery Barbie? Yes there is. *Pink Sparkle*. Stealing my stuff, I call it. But look, the wings *I've* made can be moved without falling off!" Deidre flapped Lily's wings back and forth to simulate flight.

"Ingenious, Dee. As always. You'll sell a million. Well, all you can make, anyway."

She glowed, whether with my praise or her business prospects, who knew? Deidre clearly had the merchandising gene. "The only way I can sell a million in my home-grown operation is to sell the pattern to a toy manufacturer. And somehow that idea doesn't please me at all. I enjoy being small and select." My petite friend dimpled; she was indeed "small and select" to me. "But maybe one of these days, I'll hire a helper or two. But what about you...don't you sometimes have trouble keeping up with orders, especially this time of year?"

"Yeah. But when I run out, I just paste a "sold out" icon on my internet catalog and catch up later." I almost said that having a husband who insisted on paying household bills sure lifted the economic pressure off a gal, but I caught myself in time. Deidre no longer had that luxury.

"So we're set then for Yule?" she said. "I thought we'd celebrate here this year. Phil's offered to do a buffet for after the ritual, thank the Goddess. That will be a first class upgraded 'cakes and ale.' Luckily, M&Ms, who's practically moved in here since Will passed, will be spending the Solstice with her cronies at Mohegan Sun. Let's hope one of those Serpent Power Tracks runs through her slot machine. If she loses any more money, she'll be down to her social security, and then she may *really* take up residence with me. I'd feel responsible for her, you know."

"Bummer."

"You can say that again. But enough wallowing in worries. In fact, banish that thought. Back to Yule. I've decorated the log, you know. Just wait until you see it! Sea shells, sea horses, sand dollars, pentagrams, runes—and ribbons, of course"

"Perfect for a Plymouth Yule. This won't be too much for you then...I mean...."

"I know. It's my first Christmas without Will. I'm not so concerned about myself as I am about the children. Especially Willy—he's the one I worry about most. He really misses hanging out with a macho man. And Jenny, too, of course. She doesn't say much, but here she's growing up like a string bean, third grade now, and a girl needs her Daddy, you know. A male presence to make her feel special and cherished. "

A girl needs her husband, too, I thought. In my heart, I sent forth the prayer spell that there would be someone for Deidre when she was ready to love someone again. *No rush,* I told the Divine Spirit in all her forms, by all her names. *Things always go better when You do it Your way.*

"As for me," Deidre continued, oblivious of my psychic meddling, "I've been much more peaceful in my heart since what happened at Samhain. Having that experience of Will's spirit reaching out to me with such love. Love and forgiveness. For my carelessness, my neglect, my feelings of superiority."

"Hey, now, Dee. None of that upbraiding yourself. You were a fine caring wife to Will. And after all, you had all these children, as well."

"I know. The babies simply seemed to happen. Will was a party-line Catholic, but after Will Jr. was born, I went on the pill—seemed the easiest and least obvious method of family planning. Well, they do say that the pill is between 92 and 99 percent effective. I guess I'm the other 1 percent. Must be that my karmic profile intends me to be prolific. I'd be afraid to plant a real garden. Do you remember the time I threw a few sunflower seeds in the backyard?" Deidre grinned and offered me more coffee. I put my hand over my cup before she could pour in another tot of whiskey.

"Yeah, I remember. *The screaming sunflowers from Amityville.* I thought we were going to have to get you a botany exorcist."

"Speaking of exorcists, Cass, that was a ghost, right? Will, I mean. Oh, I don't like that word *ghost*, do you? *Spirit* is much more accurate. Have you ever had that experience?"

"Not exactly as compelling as yours, from what I could tell. But occasionally I do feel my grandma's presence, a fleeting warm touch, a sudden urge to sing some rollicking Victorian tune she loved. 'Never go walking out without your hatpin' was her favorite. Or even finding something unaccountable, something I feel she put in that place especially for me. Her creamy wool shawl that's been such a comfort at times. But *you*...you saw the ghost—spirit—of Christy Callahan while we were on the *Goddess*. Let's face it—*you see dead people*! A bona fide *spirit whisperer*. Will it happen again, do you think?"

A crash sounded overhead. That would be Bobby's tower of blocks. An imperative wail followed. Baby Anne had woken from her nap.

Deidre sighed. "It's a good thing I have Betti to take charge on weekdays. How I love escaping to the store every morning—it's so peaceful at the mall. Well, comparatively, you know. But to answer your question, the visioning thing *has* happened again."

But just then the busy mother had to rush upstairs to the rescue, and it was time for me to get home as well. My rampant curiosity, however, couldn't wait till later to be satisfied. I chased up the stairs after her.

"Who...what...did you see, Dee?"

She hurried into the nursery and swooped up her anguished, sodden toddler. I followed like another demanding child.

"Check on Bobby for me, will you?" Deidre ordered. Already she had the diaper removed and was administering a soothing warm wash to Baby Anne's bottom.

I found the cheerful, giggling four-year-old sitting in the midst of quite a mess. Not only his fallen tower of blocks. His brother Willy's gerbil cage lay on the floor, door swinging open.

"Oh, dear. Where's Geronimo, Bobby? We have to find Gerry before he gets too far away from us. Willy will be very upset if we lose his pet."

Bobby giggled some more and pointed to the open closet door. Well, that was something. I'd have the little bugger cornered in there. Cautiously, I peeked in among the folded clothes on the shelf above the hanging shirts and pants. Two eyes shown brightly under a pile of sweaters. Slowly...slowly...I reached for the gerbil.

Ouch! Damn it to Hecate!

Deidre appeared in the doorway, holding Baby Anne, whose head drooped on her mother's shoulder. "What happened?"

"Geronimo escaped. I tried to catch him, but he just nipped me and dashed into the hall."

"Oh, don't worry. He'll be downstairs at the dog dishes, looking for scraps. We corner him there all the time." She raced downstairs again; Bobby and I tagging after. He was over his giggling phase, now—a small hunter on the trail, all business.

Deidre pushed Baby Anne into my arms. She imprisoned the escape artist in an upside-down wastebasket, slipped a magazine underneath, and quickly turned the impromptu cage right side up. With the gerbil trapped inside, she allowed Bobby to convey the fellow back to his little home, but she watched him closely, keeping her hands free in case rescue was needed. I followed after Bobby, carrying the toddler, who was still half-asleep. Baby Anne was a pretty heavy bundle. Maybe it was time to stop calling her *Baby.*

"Okay then. You have to answer my question now, Dee. I'm dying to know. Who else's *spirit* did you see?"

"Why, Paige. Paige Bratton, of course. I was taking a little rest in the living room, looking over some new patterns while Baby Anne was taking her nap. And I must have dozed. In fact, it may have been a dream not a sighting." She helped Bobby to ease Geronimo into his wire crate and quickly latched the door. Overcome with so much stimulating activity, the gerbil dashed into the friendly darkness of his nest, a former Chef Boyardee

Ravioli can, which I hoped Phillipa would never see. She tended to get violent over feeding canned pasta to children.

"Yes...yes...then what?" I prodded.

"I saw Paige, plain as I see you, only transparent, you know, looking in the window at me. Maybe it was the afternoon sun playing tricks with my eyes."

"Did she say anything? Do anything?"

"She looked absolutely terrible. Her skin was pasty gray, her eyes resembled two burning coals in the back of a woodstove, and there was an ugly purple slash around her throat, as if she'd been garroted with a wire or thin rope. She kept trying to talk, and I could see her tongue—ugh! It was so black! No sound came out of her mouth, but I could hear her thoughts whispering in my head. It seemed that she was trying to warn me about something."

"Warn you about what? Did you have any kind of a clue?"

"About Simic, actually. But that's crazy," Deidre said.

"Yes, the FBI told Phil that Simic is on the *Siren of the Seas*. Probably perfecting his tropical tan and lining up his next bride." I relayed this comfort in all innocence. Thanks to the reticence of Special Agents Thouless and Frost, none of us knew yet that Simic had jumped ship. Later, Detective Stone Stern would raise bureaucratic hell about that lapse, but it would be too late. "You seem to be so cool about this, Dee. Weren't you frightened at all? I don't know what I'd do if I saw a *dead person* outside the window. Sounds like a vampire movie. I'd be waiting for her to turn into a bat with flapping wings and little fangs."

"I'm surprised at you, Cass. You've seen *actual murders* in that little film that plays in *your* head, which I think is far worse. Besides, we have nothing to fear from the spirits of the departed, whoever they are. These revenants are caught in their own time-warp, so the Bishop explained to me. They're not moving onto the next plane. If we can get them to move on to Heaven—well, he calls it Heaven, we call it Summerland—they won't be haunting us anymore. They will enter the light in the kingdom of God. And Goddess. You know what I mean."

"Guilfoyle may be right. It sounds as if he's had plenty of experience, what with all those haunted house exorcisms he's been called upon to perform for the Church. *Paige Bratton*," I said wonderingly. "That is odd. As you say, we have it from Phil who had it from the FBI that Simic is still sailing the Caribbean. Probably still murdering girls, too, but that's a long way from our purview. Why should Paige be warning us against him now?"

"That's another thing the Bishop said. Time has no reality in the life beyond. Dead people who don't spiritualize, who don't enter the eternal light, are still wandering in a timeless mist. So Paige may not know what's a past, present, or future danger. But a warning is not to be dismissed lightly. And it wouldn't hurt to have *you*, Cass, pursue this for us. You're our real seer. Maybe you should do your vision thing, get a line on that SOB's whereabouts and what ugly deeds he's perpetrating. Perhaps you could even provide leads for that Thouless gal."

"Oh, sure. Last I heard, the FBI does not solicit psychic testimony. Besides, my visions aren't voluntary, Dee. You know that. They come without warning and cannot be summoned at will."

"Yes, so you say. But *Fiona* says it's only a question of focus. That you're reluctant to move your psychic skill to the *next level*. And don't I remember something about a visions pillow you made that really gave you a buzz? What about that?"

"Oh, that. I never know where that damned thing is." My spirits sank as I recalled my earlier pillow visions. *Now I lay me down to weep...* Whatever I saw, it would not be pretty.

CHAPTER TWENTY

Along the sea-sands damp and brown
The traveller hastens toward the town,
And the tide rises, the tide falls.

– Henry Wadsworth Longfellow

"Dee has been seeing the ghosts of murdered brides?" Joe said in an skeptical tone. "And this soggy seaweed lady is warning her against that bastard from the *Goddess? Jesu Christos,* I wish I'd been there the night Simic tried to pull that stunt with Phil. I'd have given that pervert a dose of his own medicine." He brought the wooden mallet down with a mighty thump. Those would be some tender chicken cutlets.

"Stone has the same wish. And he carries a handgun."

"Apparently, Fiona carries one as well. Although how she got that Navy issue antique past Customs is still a mystery to me."

"Fiona has this way of sailing through inspections without the usual checks. But don't worry. She didn't bring that old thing back with her this time. Heather consigned it to the briny deep and tried to convince Simic that the bullet graze on his head was really caused by an encounter with the ship's railing."

Joe laughed and shook his head unbelievingly as he arranged another cutlet on waxed paper. The entree was to be Greek chicken with capers and raisins, he told me. He picked up the mallet again. His arms were sea-tanned and muscular under the rolled-up sleeves of his t-shirt. I admired his body as well as his cooking skills. This was the best of both worlds, and I knew it.

"I don't believe it's safe to let you and your friends out of my sight," he said.

"Yeah, yeah. How about when you go saving the environment in foreign climes for weeks on end? Abandoning us to our fate."

"It's my job, sweetheart. Once in a while I have to get out of here and earn some money. And besides, every Greek has the sea in his heart. Ah, *thalatta, thalatta..*" Two more cutlets were pounded into submission.

Scruffy and Raffles, who'd been lying under the table in hopes of a handout, hastened back to their kitchen beds. *Watch yourself, Toots. That furry-faced guy has always been a klutz in the kitchen.*

"Au contraire," I said. "I could as well say that *you've* always been a scaredy cat."

Hey, there's no need to be insulting. The kid and I are just getting out of his way before he runs amok with that mallet.

"You're talking to the dog now, right?" Joe raised his eyebrow and grinned.

"Right. Do you think I would impugn *your* bravery? Aren't you the same hero who crashed through a window to rescue me and Tip?"

"Our first misadventure. I never imagined *then* that you'd be making a career of crime."

"Crime-*solving,*" I corrected. "And I wouldn't call it a career. I'm an herbalist by trade. Bringing criminals to justice is more like...more like..."

"A hobby?" Joe suggested helpfully.

"That's too light a word. We're not talking quilting or painting trays here. It's more like an avocation. Or a calling. Yes, I like that better. A calling. Usually these things begin by my being *called* to help someone who is threatened. Which reminds me. Do you happen to remember where I left my Psychic Visions dream pillow? I've looked everywhere." *Well, not exactly*. Since I got home, I'd made a half-hearted kind of foray in the bottom of the bedroom closet and in my office, a former borning room next to the kitchen where I had a number of antique pine cabinets for stashing Stuff.

"Uh oh. This is getting serious. Have you looked in the freezer?"

"*In the freezer?* Surely you jest. Why would I put it there?" There were two wine glasses on the table and a newly opened bottle of a decent chardonnay. Nothing in Heather's league, but very pleasing nonetheless. I poured some into each glass. "Here's to crime," I toasted Joe as he thumped the last cutlet to tender thinness. "And to your very good health."

"And to yours. *Stin Eyiassou*!" He picked up his glass and drank. "I have no idea why you would hide a pillow in the freezer. I merely ask, have you looked there?"

"Well, no." We had a kind of coffin freezer in the cellar where I kept meats and other foods we might run out of in winter if the roads were impassable. But I couldn't remember the last time I was rooting around in there. With a sigh, I put down my glass and trudged down the cellar stairs.

When Joe was between assignments, he liked to tackle home "improvement" projects, although whether they were actually improving might be open to question. Therefore my cellar workroom, formerly a spooky, cobwebby den of herbs and essential oils that resembled the Wicked Stepmother's apple-poisoning catacombs in *Snow White*, was now a well-lighted cheery laboratory with sturdy shelves and an efficient worktable. I had managed to retain my old rocking chair and swinging green-shaded light, however, for when I needed "atmosphere" not florescence. I'd also hung onto the scarred gate-leg table missing its leaf and my big old wooden bowl, carved from some long-ago oak, so indispensable for mixing dried herbs.

The freezer was in the old root cellar, now shut off from the main cellar by a newly erected pine wall. The door opened with nary a squeak. I surveyed the gleaming white sarcophagus. Could it be? I lifted the cover. Yes, there it was, frozen solid, my blue-bordered, lavender-sprigged nemesis. I grabbed it.

As soon as I brought the thing upstairs, almost immediately, it began to steam and thaw. "How did you know where it was?" I demanded, shaking the pillow at Joe accusingly. "You're not getting psychic, too, are you? It never occurred to me that clairvoyance might be, well, *contagious*."

He laughed. "Don't flatter yourself. I saw it when I went looking for something to cook for dinner." The cutlets were being efficiently dusted with flour and oregano. Feta cheese had been crumbled for the sauce. Rice was steaming on the stove. A salad with big chunks of sweet peppers, onion, and tomatoes was already assembled in a bowl on the counter. I supposed I had just time for a quick rendezvous with the Cosmos before dinner.

Hugging the pillow worriedly, I said, "I'm just going to freshen up."

"Sure you are. The chicken will wait, don't hurry yourself. Something important is brewing in your pretty brain. You can tell me all about it over dinner."

I kissed him silently and stole away to our bedroom. Looking at the pillow with dismay, I placed it in the middle of our big bed, kicked off my shoes, and lay down. With a sigh, I put my cheek against the innocent pastoral pattern and closed my eyes. It was still damp, which intensified its herb fragrances, especially rosemary, lavender, aniseed, and lemongrass. But there were many other more subtle scents, usually quite a heady, potent aroma-cocktail.

Nothing.

I waited, breathing slowly and deeply, willing myself into that light trance state that is usually such a pleasant place to be, like a cool blue cloud of unthought.

I waited and waited. *Still nothing.*

I sat up and shook the damned thing with exasperation. "What's the matter with you! Don't you realize I don't have all evening. Joe's out there cooking his heart out to feed me some ravishing Greek dish, and you're not cooperating, you dummy." Nevertheless, I was secretly pleased that I didn't have to be subjected to some nightmare scene that would scar the inside of my eyeballs.

Oh well, what can I do about it? Even Pythia at the oracle in Delphi must have had her off days. I hopped off the bed, changed out of faded jeans and a flannel shirt into one of my "casual" cruise outfits, a flowered skirt with a solid green top and green suede shoes, preparing myself to appreciate the Greek chicken... and the Greek cook.

In the course of counting my blessings, I drank quite a lot of chardonnay and forgot all about the visions pillow in the middle of my bed. Forgot it so completely, that when I fell on that bed later with Joe for some amorous tussling, the pesky thing got shoved over to one side, my side.

I'm not as young as I used to be, but parts of me are still surprisingly energetic. By the time I was ready to sleep, I was enjoying the kind of exhaustion where you can't really feel your lips, fingers, and toes, as if your body were no longer separate from the floating world.

"Ah! *Sleep that knits up the ravaged whatever*," I murmured into my cool pillow.

In that instant, I was transported right away from my snug bedroom and my vigorous lover into the fastness of Jenkins Park. It was snowing heavily, a dark, silent, wet day in winter. Not a human sound, just the shriek of northeast wind through bare branches and the ominous howl of a dog in the distance. But I'd walked through there often enough in good weather for pleasure and the profit of wild plants, I knew the lay of the land like I knew my own herb gardens.

The park was a mile or so of conservancy pine and oak woods that lay between my property and Phillipa's place. And that's where I found myself, at the wood's edge, looking at the Sterns' home through a thick screen of young trees that had sprouted between the bare columns of the cadaverous old pines. I could see their back deck with Phillipa's elaborate grill, covered for the winter with green tarp. And I could also see Phillipa herself, through the large kitchen window over the herb planter. She was fiddling with her upscale coffeemaker.

Suddenly, I was overcome with inexplicable terror. Between me and the wood's edge, a dark crouching figure was moving toward the house. *Where was Stone?*

The figure uncoiled into a man shrouded in a dark parka crossing the lawn in slow motion, ducking from tree to tree. He flattened himself against the house, peeking cautiously into the window, then ducked away. Carrying some kind of sack or bag, like a rubbish bag, he crept toward the back door. *I hope that door is locked!* Oh, how careless we can be about locking our doors in these small towns where not much ever happens!

I tried to run forward, to shout at the man, to bang on the door and warn Phillipa, but as in a dream, I could barely move, my gait as slow as if my shoes were stuck in deep mud. I opened my mouth to cry out, but only an anguished whisper emerged. *He's here. Watch out, watch out!*

Just as suddenly as I had zoomed into my vision, I woke from it, crying, sweating, heart pounding. I jumped off the bed where Joe was still sleeping soundly and stumbled into the kitchen. It was just past eleven. On the kitchen phone, I punched in number three, which was set to dial Phillipa's landline home phone. Both of us had cell phones, but we rarely kept them on at night.

She answered on the second ring. "Hi. Cass? Is anything wrong?"

"Where are you?"

"At home. You just called me, remember?"

"Where exactly?"

"In the living room. Watching some dratted true crime show with Stone. Why do you ask?"

I breathed a deep sigh that felt like my first breath in several moments. "Goddess help me, I had this horrible vision."

"About me? Oh, peachy. Now what?"

"There was a man..." I slumped down into a chair, feeling unable to continue.

"Isn't there always? Now you're alarming me, and I see you're alarming Stone as well."

"I mean to alarm you. It was that damned Psychic Visions Dream Pillow. I lay my head on it and fell into a trance. It was daytime, but dark, snowing heavily, and I was looking toward your house from Jenkins' Park. I saw a man prowling around your house, and he seemed to be stalking you. He looked in the kitchen window, headed for the back door to your mudroom, but I don't know what happened afterwards, because that's when the vision ended. You *do* keep that door locked? It must have been Simic. And he was carrying something like a large sack."

"Maybe it was Santa Claus. Okay. Not to doubt your clairvoyant skills or anything, but we know that Simic's on the *Siren of the Sea*."

"Do you have a contact number for Special Agent Thouless?"

"Hmmmm. Yes. Office and cell."

"Call her now. Ask her if Simic could have left the ship. If so, he might be prowling around your house. Remind her that you're the only living material witness against Simic. And you're also the only 'girl who got away,' so to speak."

"Okay, worrywart. First thing in the morning."

"I think you should call tonight."

"Cass! What's all this about Simic." It was Stone's voice. He must have wrested the phone away from Phillipa.

In the background, I could hear Phillipa say, "It was only a vision, Stone." *Oh, ye of little faith.*

"Don't worry, Cass. I'll sleep with one eye open and a weapon on hand. And we'll call Thouless and Frost in the morning. *I'll* call. I promise you."

And I had to be satisfied with that.

When I went into the bedroom, Joe was still asleep, flushed and smiling in his dream, whatever it was. So infuriating not to have anyone on whom to spill my frustration!

Unable to sleep, I went down into the cellar and sat in my old rocker with only the light of green-shaded lamp swinging in the darkness. I paged through one of my Grandma's old herbal lore notebooks, her faded, scratchy handwriting always as calming as a cup of chamomile tea. Suddenly I felt that warm presence swirling around me, I inhaled her scent, a mixture of subtle herbs. The song came unbidden to my lips.

Never go walking out without your hatpin...

"I won't, Grandma. I won't."

CHAPTER TWENTY-ONE

Christmas is here:
Winds whistle shrill,
Icy and chill.
Little care we;
Little we fear..."

– William Makepeace Thackeray

Yule at the Ryan home was truly blessed, although as it turned out, a short-lived interlude of peace and festivity.

Four days before Christmas, the Winter Solstice, December 21, was the longest night of the year, sacred to all newborn gods and goddesses, a time of introspection and a time of looking forward to the gradual warming of the earth. Since the frightening appearance of a stranger, probably Simic, that I'd envisioned hadn't actually materialized, I tried to put those fears out of mind rather than to throw a bucket of ocean-cold water (39 degrees in December) on the celebration. We five wanted only to focus on the goodness and healing we hoped to manifest in our lives and to forget the terrifying aspects of our cruise. So we more or less put all negativity in the broom closet to be revisited later, if necessary, preferably after the first of the year.

Betti, Deidre's indispensable au pair, volunteered to keep the children occupied upstairs while we held our Yule ceremony in the spacious living room of the Ryans' garrison Colonial home. All its rooms glowed with her prolific arts and crafts displayed in samplers, embroideries, hooked rugs, pine furniture rescued from the town dump and refinished, plus cabinets and cupboards bursting with prototype dolls and magical poppets.

The doors, windows, and mantle were garlanded with evergreen sprays—pine, rosemary, bay, juniper, and cedar—filling the air with a spicy fragrance that wafted away winter lethargy and quite energized us.

Not the least of Deidre's handiwork was the great old Yule log she'd decorated with the traditional three candles embedded in it—white, green, and red—along with symbols of our seashore and a cascade of red and gold ribbons.

"I'm glad to see it's a proper ash log," Fiona said, nodding her head with approval, sprigs of holly stuck in her coronet of braids waving like a Victorian lady's feathers. "This is the sacred world tree Yggdrasil on whose branches we are hung with all our fates and futures."

"Pretty picture, that," Phillipa muttered, sipping the magnificent sherry Heather had brought for our Sabbat. She sat on the edge of her chair, ready to spring into action; her heart was in Deidre's kitchen. Although she described the stove as "primitive," she was cooking up a splendid Yuletide feast of chestnut-stuffed chickens and steamed plum puddings using Deidre's plain old (but reliable) Kenmore.

Fiona lit the three Yule candles and the Yule log itself with a shard of last year's. "*The wheel turns, the power burns.* But let us not be in a rush to wish away winter. May we use this time of reflection for deepening our inner strength to create good magic."

Heather tossed in a handful of pinecones that flared and sputtered. "*Bless all the small creatures out in the snow. Give them good faring and a warm place to go.*"

"*May our circle be solvers and healers of all that is ill,*" Phillipa said, tossing cinnamon sticks into the blaze.

I added sheaves of sage and blessed thistle. "*May sun and moon born in this sacred season thrive and prosper.*" *And*, I added in my thoughts, *may my lovely and exceptional grandchildren come into a world of welcome and joy.*

Deidre cast the circle with her athame, which was yellow-handled and painted with jonquils and daffodils. It reminded me more of a cake knife than a dagger, except of course that it was pointed at the end. As Deidre invoked the spirits of the four directions and elements to our ceremony, Phillipa, Fiona, Heather, and I lit the corresponding candles, which had all been created for this event by Heather. Her candles were always quirky in an interesting way. I noted the North candle sparkled with quartz crystals, and there were tiny fossils in the South candle.

After that we chanted and danced and raised a cone of power that was nearly visible as we released it into the Cosmos. Somewhere there was a full moon that had coincided with the Solstice, a rare galactic event, but it was hidden in this overcast night. The weather forecast was for a northeast blizzard bringing plentiful snow, our first big storm of the season. But *not yet, not yet*. We were still celebrating.

When Deidre opened the circle, she called upstairs to Betti, who brought the children downstairs along with their toy poodles. Then the wizened little au pair hopped on her moped and sprinted eagerly for home, a tiny cottage on Crooke's Land that looked like a kid's playhouse, where her sisters, Hilde and Trudi, were waiting. I imagined a doll-house Yule feast for three, with miniature mugs of grog.

Our husbands arrived, giving me a heart pang for the palpable absence of Will, but Deidre shouldered on bravely. To the delight of her boys, Mick Finn stomped in from his bright red Chevy bringing with him two young firefighters looking eager but ill at ease. With a shy, longing glance at Fiona, Finn gave Deidre a big warm hug. "Thanks for letting me bring along these homeless galoots to the feast. We're all on call, of course. May the Good Lord preserve us from faulty space heaters and careless candles."

"Amen," Deidre replied. "Aren't you going to introduce me?"

The gangling blond was Ernie Bird and the black Irish type was Terry Moody. Stone not only knew both of these awkward young fellows, he also knew their families and backgrounds, and he took it upon himself to help them feel at home while Deidre was busy helping Phillipa. Heather invited the three men to help themselves at a cooler that Dick had brought filled with a selection of chilled designer microbrews and imported beers.

Glancing at me meaningfully, Heather whispered, "What's Mick up to here? Has Dee, the inveterate matchmaker, met her match."

"Maybe. They're not as young as they look," I said while we set up cutlery, napkins, and plates. The blue-and-yellow checked napkins had all been hand-fringed by Deidre. "Moody is thirty-five, an Irish bachelor living alone with his mother, alas. Bird is engaged, sort of, to Miss Hassel, used to be Jenny's second grade teacher."

Even though the Ryan dining room had been designed to hold a crowd, it had been necessary to tuck a children's table into the corner, and a merry crowded time was had by all. Compliments to the cook flowed as fast as the splendid wines Heather kept pouring into ready glasses.

We spread out for dessert and coffee in the living room, where Joe and Stone went into a deep huddle, awakening my rabid curiosity. How unlike they were—solid, muscular Joe with his wiry beard beside tall, nervy Stone with that fine straight hair always falling into his eyes.

I joined them with the excuse of filling coffee cups, slipped my arm through Joe's. "Okay, you two. What's up? We're supposed to be jovial and jocular this evening."

"Stone's not into denial, sweetheart. He's been in touch with the FBI," Joe said.

Apparently Stone had pursued my vision with due diligence. It was a tribute to his faith in my clairvoyance that he became intent on shaking some information out of the FBI.

When he'd reached Special Agent Esther Thouless, he'd asked the straightforward question, "Where is Simic right now, is he on board the *Siren*?" But in return, the agent had been annoyingly vague on details, falling back on that old chestnut about not sharing details of a covert investigation. The only matter which she discussed straightforwardly was the likelihood that Phillipa would be called as a material witness when their case against Simic was ready for the Grand Jury.

"But that body... Beth whatshername...on Grand Cayman Island—were you able to get any DNA evidence?"

"Sweeting," Thouless had said, then hesitated too long. Finally she'd said, "A trace. Now what we need, of course, is a match with Simic."

"So, get a warrant and swab the bastard," Stone had said angrily.

"It's not that easy. As a matter of fact, when the *Siren* docked in New York, Simic seems to have defaulted on his Norse Line contract."

"Are you telling me that you don't know where Simic is right now?"

"Oh, we'll find him, we have vast resources. It's only a matter of time."

"Why didn't you say that in the first place? Simic has given you the slip then? That sleazy bastard. I would have thought, with those marvelous resources you're bragging about, you could have kept track of one ship's doctor."

"I don't think I care for your tone, Detective Stern. I'm under no obligation to provide you with any information on a crime that took place in our jurisdiction."

"And that goes two ways, *Special Agent Thouless*."

The call had not gone well and ended on a sour note, Stone admitted when he repeated to me what he'd already told Joe.

"Phil knows?"

"Of course. But I'm not sure she realizes the gravity... the danger... She's dead set against having a cruiser hanging around outside the house. Says the Plymouth police have their hands full already with rabid raccoons and suspicious parked vehicles." Stone frowned with deepening intensity. He wore glasses trimmed with thin silver rims and looked for all the world like a physics professor trying to get a difficult concept across to his freshman class. "Cass, I'm depending on you to help her see reason."

"I don't know, Stone. I don't think I've ever been able to...." Again that Victorian song came unbidden into my thoughts. *Without your hatpin...without your hatpin.* "So here's the thing. Why don't you equip Phil with a panic button. And a pretty little brooch with a GPS tracker. For that matter, why don't you see that she's armed with a ladylike but totally effective handgun. You know, something small enough to fit in pocket or purse." I was thinking that I wouldn't mind having something like that myself. Maybe I'd been hanging around with Fiona too long. Pearl-handled would be pretty, and silver, although that might clash with my favorite pendant, a gold eagle that Joe had given me, in memory of where and why we'd met.

I noticed that both men were looking at me with incredulous expressions. Well, I was used to that. I guess men are never too comfortable with the notion of a pistol-packing woman. Even gentlemanly men toward whom deadly force would never be directed.

Would I have shot anyone if I actually had a handgun of my own? I thought back on our several misadventures of the past few years. *Damn straight*, I would have. And then, how many lifetimes would it have taken to live down that bad karma?

"Okay, okay. But the panic button and GPS are perfectly sensible ideas. And much more protective than some doughnut-guzzling cop dozing in a cruiser. No offense."

"None taken," Stone said. He was smiling now. *Amused by the little woman's cute exaggerations.*

"Never mind the smirk. Take some measures to protect Phil when you're not home. That's when he'll break in. The guy I saw in my vision. Simic, I'm sure it was."

Stone turned serious immediately. "When, Cass? When is this break-in attempt going to happen?"

I looked away, chagrined. The clairvoyant's dilemma. We can see that something is going to happen, but who knows when? Being able to see into the future presupposes that there is a dimension in which events are not fixed to a past, present, and future, they are simply *out there*, floating in the primordial soup of timelessness. My grandma used to read fortunes in the cards, and she'd always weasel out of the time factor. "You will meet with surprising good fortune within a seven," she'd say. "Seven days, or maybe seven weeks. Possibly even seven months." *How about seven years, Grandma?*

"If only I knew, Stone. That's why I'm asking you...*begging* you...to protect Phil from that psychopath."

"I wonder..." Stone said reflectively.

"What?"

"Would Phil let me fasten a tracking anklet on her, do you think?" Apparently, he was unaware that Phillipa had slipped out of the kitchen and was standing directly in back of him.

"*In your dreams*," she declared. "Talk about invasion of privacy!" Her black eyes snapped as she shook her shining raven's-wing hair with dramatic negativity.

"Be reasonable, Phil," I said. "How about one of those brand new cell phones with a built-in GPS tracker? The tracking would be within your own control, you could shut it off anytime you wanted to." I didn't know if that were true, but I hoped it was.

"Hmmm. Maybe. But what I'd rather have is a *handgun*. Of my own. Remember what a farce it was when I tried to get Stone's gun out of his lock-box? I ended up having to wing the guy with the box itself."

Stone sighed, a sigh that my husband apparently understood completely. Joe jumped into the discussion in Stone's defense. "Stone is imaging a scenario in which he comes home late after a hard night spent fighting crime on the South Shore, and he's forgotten Phil's password of the day. As he enters the back door, what faces him is a distraught woman with a very effective pistol held in her trembling hands."

"Oh, bollocks, Joe," Phillipa said rather loudly.

"I don't know whether carrying a handgun is completely wise, dear." No matter where Fiona was in a room, she had a knack for hearing any conversation in which she took an interest. The holly sprigs in her hair nodded sagely.

"Oh sure, the pot calling the kettle *black arse*." Phillipa was getting distinctly defensive. The rest of us just laughed. I wondered if Fiona had replaced the pistol, now "lost at sea," which she had been accustomed to carry in her green reticule and to brandish at odd moments of panic. I had to feel grateful for that particular peccadillo of Fiona's—it had come in handy more than once, and had certainly saved my life in that confrontation with Simic.

"You're no longer carrying, then, Fiona?" I asked.

Fiona gave me a canny smile and said nothing. "Goodness me, it's a party. Let's have no more talk of *weapons*. And besides, we're peace-keeping, earth-loving Wiccans here. We have spiritual ways and means of deflecting threats. So before everyone leaves tonight, let's put our pointed caps on and summon new spells to keep Phillipa safe. In case there's a chink in her white light."

"Oh, good idea," Deidre enthused. Drawn by our heated discussion, she put in her own two pennies. "I've a new amulet that's just the ticket. I'll go get it now." She hurried off upstairs to her workroom.

I looked at Stone, and he looked at me. "See if you can legalize whatever Fiona's surely got in her bag these days, will you?" I murmured to him.

Heather, who had been half listening while pouring healthy dollops of Sambuca into unguarded coffees, soon joined the discussion.

"What you really need, Phil, is a trained guard dog, and I have just the bitch for the job."

Not being what you might call a professional "dog person" like Heather, I'm always somewhat taken aback by that word "bitch." To me, the female canine should always be referred to as a *lady dog* or some other refined term. Still I was interested in which of her resident mutts she had in mind.

"Stow it, Heather," Phil said. "You guys have already cornered me into taking in Zelda, and you're not putting one over on me like that again."

Heather laughed, a tinkling insincere laugh. "Oh, my dear, this wouldn't be a permanent placement. Just a temporary convenience. There is absolutely nothing like the confidence you feel when a truly well-trained canine is sleeping peacefully at your feet. You can feel perfectly secure that there is no one, *but no one*, trying to enter your home if a bitch like Boadicea is not alarmed."

"Boadicea?" we cried in unison.

"You don't mean that ferocious old boxer our neighbors used to keep tied under their deck, do you? They moved, you know." Deidre had appeared again, holding a small velvet pouch. "Remember the time Boady whelped that litter and wouldn't let anyone within six feet of her? And Bobby crept in under the deck to see the puppies? Oh, what a fright!"

"Yes, well, when your neighbors, those creeps, got ready to move, they dumped poor Boadicea at Animal Lovers Sanctuary," Heather explained.

"And now, in the middle of this dangerous situation, you're looking to unload her on me?" Phillipa's tone was incredulous. "Not to mention, she'd probably make a quick snack of little Zelda."

"Oh, so you do realize there's a *dangerous situation* here," I broke in, glad to hear her admit it.

"Your fat cat will be perfectly safe," Heather assured Phillipa. "Really, you should stop feeding poor Zelda those rich foods from your table. But dear Boadicea is quite used to feline companions. We've tested that at Lovers. And we've been training her in the rudiments of guarding property. Thinking that might be the ideal career for a bitch with her background. Nothing vicious, of course. Just the usual *Schitzhund* stuff."

"No, no, no, *a thousand times no*," Phillipa said firmly.

"I'll bring her over tomorrow for a visit," Heather said. "I'm sure you'll fall in love with her, she's such a sweetheart."

I guess I was the only one there besides Heather who knew that Boadicea had been rejected by every pet-loving soul who had come to her God-Is-Love Pet Adoption Day at the Unitarian-Universalist church. Boady was as tough and imperious as her name implied, a regular *alpha* female who wouldn't resort to pretty manners in order to curry favor with prospective adoptive families.

"Don't you dare!" Phillipa said.

"Ten o'clock okay?" Heather asked.

Before Phillipa could protest again, Deidre averted her attention by opening the velvet pouch and dropping a gleaming bracelet in her palm. "Put this on, Phil, and don't take it off until Simic is in jail," she ordered. "It's black agate, black obsidian, and black tourmaline. Deflects all harm."

"*Very* attractive, Dee. I adore black, and these stones are lovely. Maybe I'll keep it on until they execute the bastard." Phillipa fastened the bracelet and held up her wrist for the admiration of all. The stones matched her slim black velvet outfit beautifully. *Morticia*, I couldn't help thinking, but I had to admit Phillipa's chosen style suited her admirably.

Fiona zeroed in on my thoughts in that unsettling way of hers. "Wiccans traditionally wear black because it repels negativity and also because it lends the wearer a cloak of invisibility during night rituals."

"But isn't black the most unapproachable of colors?" I myself preferred green, although admittedly because it favored my eyes.

"Exactly," Phillipa snapped. "I'm counting on my sweeping black cloak to warn off all those negative mundanes who prate about evil witches."

"Now, now," Fiona said mildly. "Let's all shake those *negative* thoughts off our hands and feet." We obeyed, of course, even though Phillipa hummed *Doin' the Lambeth Walk* throughout the cleansing ritual.

Absolved and purified, we reinforced our earlier white-light thing for good measure. Ignoring the curious looks of the guys lounging around the fireplace, we five held hands, and with all our love and faith, visualized a sphere of impenetrable spiritual armor for our friend.

As we drove home shortly afterward, Joe said, "You know, maybe it's living with you that's getting to me, but I think I almost saw that light whatzit you gals were praying for."

"Of course you did. Because it was there," I said. *Everything will be all right now.*

CHAPTER TWENTY-TWO

The snow had begun in the gloaming
And busily all the night
Had been heaping field and highway
With a silence deep and white.

– James Russell Lowell

I looked out the bay window in our living room and groaned aloud in despair.

Oh joy! Fluffy stuff to jump in! Let's go out...let's go out, out, out. Scruffy had hopped up on the window seat to see what was troubling me, but the big wet flakes falling ever more rapidly looked like fun to him. Even though he now had a touch of elderly arthritis, snowdrifts still brought out the pup in him. Raffles pushed his cold nose comfortingly into my hand, suggesting that patting him would surely make me feel much better.

"What's the matter, sweetheart?" Joe asked me. "It's only snow. We'll shovel it. And what we don't shovel will melt in God's good time." There was a small gold cross on a chain gleaming under that fisherman's sweater he was wearing, and a faith to match, a sort of diluted Greek Orthodox. What a wonder that he was so tolerant of his wife's Pagan ways.

"I was counting on Adam and Freddie coming for Christmas, but they'll never dare drive on these roads. And I wouldn't want them to. She's due on the 28th, for Goddess' sake. But I will miss them. Becky and her new beau will be okay with the weather, I think. Johnny M. looks like the intrepid macho type, sort of like you, honey. But we have Rikyu coming, too, remember? And Tip."

"Sure I do. We'll just have to see what happens and play it by ear. It's only the 22nd. Rikyu's coming by bus from New Hampshire—arriving in Plymouth at four o'clock day after tomorrow, right? No problem at all. They'll have the roads plowed and sanded by then. And Tip's in Plymouth already with that buddy of his from Plimouth Plantation."

Come at Yule, Rikyu. Christmas, I mean. You'll have to meet my son Adam, I'd said in a mad moment on board the *Goddess.* Ken Ogata had been deeply grateful. Some business of his had required Ken to spend the holidays in Japan, and he'd have had to drag his reluctant charge along with him. Apparently, "Uncle Ken" was the teen-age computer whiz's caretaker while his father was in San Francisco and his mother was busy remarrying. My seventh or eighth sense told me that there was more to the Ogata home-life story than Ken was revealing, but I really didn't need to know. Rikyu had been invited, and he was welcome.

"Okay, I guess you're right. No sense worrying in advance. At least in New England we're prepared for snow and know how to deal with it. But the weather channel said it might be as much as *sixteen inches*."

"Metrological mayhem boosts their ratings. They love to sound the knell of doom." Joe put his arm around my disconsolate slumping form, edging out Raffles. I leaned on his comforting shoulder and breathed in his scent of spicy summer herbs. *As long as we're together, all's right with the world,* his presence told me surer than words. *Thank the Goddess he's not off on some quixotic mission.*

My cell phone rang. Although I keep it on in the daytime, usually it languishes in my handbag hanging on the office doorknob. Maybe I'll hear it, and maybe not. Fortunately, this time I was carrying my cell in the pocket of my flannel shirt just in case Freddie got started on the twins earlier than her due date.

"Boadicea is nervous," Phillipa screamed into my ear.

"What do you mean *nervous?* What's she *doing*, exactly. Barking?"

"No, for once she isn't barking. She's been prowling around the kitchen door with her ears pricked up, pawing the tile as if she wants to scratch her way to freedom. And she's already been out to pee and poop, so that's not it."

"Where's Stone?"

"At work, of course. He's still employed as a detective, you know. In Scituate today. Break-in and extensive damage at a posh condominium under construction.

"I don't suppose you'd call him to come home?"

"I hate to be a wimp. I wonder...is Joe there? Do you suppose?"

"Oh, sure. He'd love that. A chance to put my four-wheeler through its paces. Usually he drives some boring rental so he can take off for the airport at a moment's notice in case of an environmental emergency. And naturally, I'll come along for the ride."

"Yes, well don't be too long. I thought I saw someone ducking through the pines a few minutes ago."

"*Goddess help us!* Why didn't you say that to begin with? We're on our way. And *you call Stone*, Phil. Better a wimp than a victim. There must be other detectives who can take over for Stone when you need him at home to save you from some murderous creep."

Joe, listening to my end of the conversation, was already letting the dogs out to relieve themselves before we took off without them. "Bring your cell, Cass" he said, shrugging into his storm jacket. "And dress warmly. Even the dogs weren't too anxious to gambol when they got their paws in that sloppy snow."

"Of course. You'll drive, right? So I can call Tip." Unlike the rest of the world, I hadn't got the hang of driving with one hand while holding the cell up to my ear with the other, especially if I had to change lanes or turn corners or, Goddess forbid, park while conversing.

"Sure I will. Driving in this mess is no job for a lady."

How delightfully chauvinistic, as if I were wearing crinolines instead wrapping up in a quilted parka, an ancient striped school scarf of Adam's wound around my neck twice, knitted mittens with four fingers (a gift from Patty Peacedale), untied galoshes, and a hunter's cap with the flaps down, an outfit that required me to lumber about as awkwardly as a brown bear.

I pulled myself into the passenger seat of my RAV4 and stripped off the mittens so that I could call Tip at his friend's house. No answer. I left a rather lengthy message: "Tip dear, it's Cass. Joe and I are on our way over to Phil's. She thinks she saw a prowler. The guard dog that Heather loaned her thinks so, too. Boadicea. The boxer. Maybe you remember her? Anyway, I don't know if you're available or if it's possible in this awful storm, but if you can get over there safely, maybe you can follow the intruder's tracks. Before the snow obliterates them. Oh dear, I guess... Well, come if you can, but *be careful.*"

Even the main roads were slushy and treacherous. It took us three times longer than usual to drive to the other side of Jenkins Park. But this SUV was particularly steady in snow. Even in that short distance, we passed a couple of vehicles that appeared to have skidded into snow banks on an evil stretch of road near the Sterns' place, a sharp curve so shaded by pines that the ice had not yet melted before being masked with snow. I craned my neck to look into each car as I passed and reported to Joe that both were empty.

Phil's driveway was a long winding one. We parked off the road but near the street and walked in. What a surprise to find that Tip was there already! He was crouching over the back walk, wearing his red and black "Mountie" jacket, a pair of snowshoes slung over his shoulder, his long hair pulled back into a pony tail. He turned, grinned, and saluted us.

"Hi, guys. Step around this section when you go in, okay? It's filling in fast, but there's enough sign to follow."

"How...when...?" I sputtered.

Tip was now too intent to reply, moving slowly down the back walk to the pines beyond. Joe followed him, careful not to interrupt or disturb. I ducked inside.

"Well, if you aren't a sight for sore eyes!" Phillipa raised one winged black eyebrow at my outfit as I stripped off the mittens, scarf, and hunter's hat and stamped the snow off my galoshes. "Right after I talked to you, I did call Stone, just as you advised. You saw Tip out there doing the Indian-hunter thing? That was your work, but Stone thinks it's a dynamite idea." The back door attempted to blow free of its hinges with the blizzard winds, but she managed to pull it shut. "Stone's rather stuck where he is for a bit. I told him I would be all right because Joe was on his way. But Stone wants Tip to have a look around through the woods. He said there would be no one better."

"True. How'd he get here so fast?"

"Borrowed his friend Tommy Neptune's snow mobile."

"We didn't see a snow mobile, just a couple of abandoned cars."

"He parked in the neighbor's driveway down the road so he wouldn't disturb any tracks."

Boadicea was sniffing my feet and legs suspiciously. I let her get on with it until she was satisfied and allowed me to scratch between her ears. Zelda looked down on us and meowed a greeting from her lofty perch above the kitchen cabinets.

"How's she getting along with Boady?"

"Like cats and dogs. The minute they met, Zelda hissed and batted Boady across the snout, a pretty good whack. From then on, a kind of detente has been in effect." We peered out the long kitchen window over Phillipa's herb planters where basil, thyme, and rosemary were looking incredibly fresh and green as wet snow plastered itself against the glass. We could barely make out the two figures inching down the path to the woods, Joe still following Tip.

"What did you see, exactly?" I asked.

"Just a shadowy figure moving through the back yard. But I got this feeling, you know. The hair on the back of my neck literally stood up. Like Boady, I might say. And then, after I called you, I thought I heard someone trying the back door. And Boady confirmed it, sort of. She didn't bark, you know, although she sure is a barker. Just drew back her lip in a frightful low snarl and hurled herself at the door. If he was there, he heard her and made tracks. Literally, I guess, judging from Tip's fascination with the back step. Holy Hecate, Cass—what's going on?" Standing beside me, Phillipa shivered. I put my arm around her thin shoulders. "I feel *in my bones* that it's Simic stalking me. But why, in this storm? It's a dumb thing to do, and Simic's not dumb."

I was beginning to feel weird myself. "Wrong," I said. "I truly believe that criminals do dumb things or *they would never get caught.* Also, you recall that spell we did on board the

Goddess, the one that called for toadstools but we used some dried porcini instead?"

"Oh yes, so difficult to find toadstools on the modern cruise ship," Phillipa murmured. "I had to appeal to Henri the chef, what a cute little guy."

"You're incorrigible, my dear. Didn't you get yourself in enough trouble flirting with Simic?"

"Hey, real porcini mushrooms aren't easy to come by. I like to think I appreciate a good man the way I appreciate good wine."

"*One at a time* is a reasonable rule for wine appreciation. Well anyway, the toadstool spell was aimed at having Simic *reveal himself*. Then we did a second spell, that powerful dragon's blood thing, *To Summon a Villain to His Just Desserts*. Maybe Simic's here because those spells are *actually working*. I don't suppose you talked Stone into giving you a gun, did you?"

Phillipa laughed darkly and stooped to remove some big enamel Caphalon pot from the oven of her Viking range. When she lifted the cover to stir the dish, a rich aroma of simmering beef filled the room. She switched off the oven and turned. "No, and not for want of trying. It would serve Stone right to come home and find the two of us raped and garroted. Well, at least there'll be a good beef and barley soup for everyone's lunch. I always think there's nothing like a thick nourishing meat soup on a snowy day."

"Over our dead bodies? Rather an extreme way to make your point. Oh, look...they've reached the woods. Do you suppose they'll grab him if he's hiding in there?"

Phillipa was already opening the back door to have a better look. Not being used to canine companions, she flung it wide without blocking the escape hatch with her body. Instantly, Boady seized her opportunity to race out of the house and dash over the back yard, a tawny streak of pure muscle.

"Oh, shit," Phillipa said.

"Well, when Boady hits the trail, I guess that will be the end of Tip's careful tracking," I said. "Let's hope they've sighted Simic and are in hot pursuit. *Great Goddess*, you don't suppose he's armed, do you?" I leaned out over Phillipa and scanned the woods where Joe and Tip had vanished.

"*Shut the door, ladies.*" The voice behind us was low, menacing, and very familiar. "He *is* armed, so both of you turn around very, very carefully."

"*Oh, shit*," Phillipa said again, this time with more feeling. She slammed the back door, and we wheeled around to face the intruder.

"Where did *you* come from?" I thought of Joe and Tip and Boady all searching the woods for this monster. How could they have missed him?

"*No questions, ladies*, or I'll have to deal with you right here and now. Good thing you got rid of that filthy animal, princess. Well, well, I never thought I'd bag both of you together. Score two for the bad guys. Guess I won't be needing *this*, now that I have a *driver*. Our little escapade is going to be so much more civilized."

Simic let drop the heavy plastic bag he'd been carrying. He stood quietly, looking perfectly at ease, in the doorway between kitchen and living room. He was wearing a hooded jacket that covered his dark, tightly curled hair and holding some kind of pistol leveled at us, grinning with an evil glint calculated to give us cardiac arrest. Maybe it was the blood draining away from my head, but I had this one irrational thought, that I'd never noticed before how the swarthy doctor's canine teeth were rather pointed and vampirish. Was there some Transylvanian forebear on his Slavic family tree?

"You didn't think I'd leave you, princess, to swan into some courtroom and make up a lurid story about our romantic interlude on the *Goddess*, did you? *Now, grab your coats and get moving.* We're going out the front way before those white knights of yours return from their quest. You'd be sorry if I had to shoot them down, now wouldn't you?"

"Come on, Phil," I whispered urgently as I shrugged into my parka. "It's not going to take Tip long to find out this bastard's doubled back. And Boady!"

Without another word, Phil took down a black jacket hanging on a hook by the back door, put it on, and picked up a leather handbag on the kitchen desk. *Oh, good, I thought. She's got her GPS phone in there.*

"Ha ha. Drop that thing on the floor, Phil." Simic strode over and put his pistol against her head. "You, Cass," he ordered. "You bring your car keys and *nothing else.*" With my eyes on my terrified friend, I reached into my own handbag on the floor where I had dropped it and took out the jangling keys. Simic must know my car was outside. Had he watched us arrive? At that moment I realized my own cell phone was still in the pocket of my flannel shirt. *Chance favors the prepared witch.* I left my parka unzipped.

Simic motioned with his pistol that we should precede him through the living room and out the front door. At least he'd had to remove that nasty-looking weapon from Phillipa's ear in order to wave it around at us. Surreptitiously, I reached into my shirt pocket and pressed the *power-off* on my cell phone. What if someone tried to call me while we were being kidnapped by this thug? Simic would hear my ringtone, a tinny rendition of *On a clear day, you can see forever...*

"*Geeze, Phil, didn't you think to lock the front door?*" I whispered accusingly.

"*Oh shut up,*" she replied in a nasty tone as we trudged toward our doom.

Life-threatening danger doesn't always bring out the best in friends.

"Keep moving and make it faster," ordered Simic. His tone was even and calm. He wasn't even breathing heavily, unlike me. I was positively panting with fear. And sweating so much, I wanted to rip off the parka. What a time for a hot flash!

"Where do you think you're taking us, you bastard?" Phillipa snarled. Simic laughed evilly—that nasty laugh that had unmasked him on shipboard—and shut the door as we went outside to the front driveway. The snow would have been eight to ten inches deep now if it weren't blowing into drifts so that some places were almost bare, while others were piled with two feet or more of snow.

Phil was still wearing her house shoes. Her feet must already be freezing painfully. A problem she confirmed by high-stepping as gingerly as a dog on a new rug.

"Don't worry about your pretty little feet, princess. Look ahead of you. Your chariot awaits," Simic crooned.

The only chariot ahead of us was my Toyota. *Well, he can't manage both of us, even with a handgun. I'll think of something.*

"You're driving, Cass. I'll sit in back with the princess. We might want to make out on the way." He laughed again, a high-pitched cackle this time. Judging from that laugh, the man was teetering on the edge of sanity and soon would be falling into the abyss. "And drive carefully, no heroics, or I may be forced to end things before the princess and I have had our fun. *That* would be a shame."

I got into my car without delay, turned on the motor, and pressed the button that engaged 4-wheel drive. I could sense Phillipa shuddering. *What good was that cosmic light we'd invoked around Phil...and the black stone amulet...if here we were in the clutches of a sadistic rapist?* I concentrated on backing out of the slushy driveway cautiously.

"Which way?" I asked. I wondered how well he really knew this area and if I dared to drive him straight to the police station on Long Pond Road. Would he have the nerve to shoot us both in the parking lot among all those cruisers?

"South on 3A," he ordered. As he pressed the pistol to the back of my head for emphasis, any notion of taking brave action simply evaporated out of my brain. I turned into the main road and drove off at a reasonably slow speed, not wanting to skid and scare the maniac in the back seat. *Where in Hades is he bringing us? How can I take advantage of my cell phone while I have to keep two hands on the wheel so we won't end up in a snowbank? Where is Hecate when I need her? Maybe if I call on her right now. Oh dear Hecate, Queen of the Night, shining goddess of the crossroads, protector of women, please come to our aid, save us from this demented killer. Oops, that's a snow plow rumbling behind me, I'd better get out of his way.* Thus ran my incoherent thoughts as we followed the winding route south.

"Just keep driving," Simic told me. Not wanting to rile him, I did exactly what he said.

But I could hear Phillipa whimpering in the back seat. I stole a glance in my rear view mirror and saw that Simic was pressing the pistol into her breast, which looked agonizing enough, but his other hand was around the back of her neck in a nasty hurtful grip.

That decided me. I swung the car over toward the left of the snow-narrowed road, far enough to block any traffic, and stomped on the brake. The anti-lock brakes shimmied and shook, but the RAV4 didn't skid. "Let go of her, or I won't drive another foot." I was surprised at how forceful and confident I sounded, no matter how my knees were literally knocking against each other.

"Drive, you bitch, or I'll kill her right now," Simic countered.

Route 3A appeared to be deserted except for us and the snowplow rumbling along behind us. "I will drive as long as you're not hurting her. And look behind you. See that snow plow coming? He's going to stop and check out why I'm in the middle of the road, that we're not in trouble. And when he does, I'm going to scream bloody blue murder. Let it all end right here, I say."

I risked another glance in the rear view mirror. Simic was tipping some pills into his mouth, swallowing them dry, but he twisted around to peer through the rear window where a windshield wiper was valiantly attempting to sweep the snow off in a fan shape. I took one hand off the wheel. Slowly and carefully, I reached underneath my parka into my shirt pocket and lifted the phone out. I dropped it into my lap, where it fell between my legs, resting on my right thigh. If I pressed the control that turned the power on, a welcoming little tune was going to play, rather a dead give away. What I needed right now was some very loud distraction.

The oncoming plow and my stubbornness had given Simic pause. "Christ, what a bitch you are! Phil's okay, aren't you, princess? Tell your fucking friend that you're fine, and she'd better get going if she wants you to stay that way."

"Cass, he's let go of my neck. And I don't want you to get hurt because of me, so go ahead...drive."

"Yeah? Well, keep your hands off her, Simic. Now where exactly am I driving to?" I started the motor again, wondering if I could get traction in all this slush, but wouldn't you know, the car rolled ahead as readily as if it were a balmy day in May instead of a stormy mess in December. I pulled over to the right so that the snow plow could pass us.

Oblivious to our plight, the driver waved as he thundered by. He looked familiar. One of the young firefighters whom Mick Finn had brought to the Solstice dinner at Deidre's, Ernie Bird, was earning some extra bucks. Couldn't that dumb fool see by my expression that I was in distress? Did he at least recognize Phil and me? Surely Stone had issued an APB on my Toyota by now, but that was so routine. Oh, why wasn't there an Amber Alert for us older abductees?

Inching ahead, I peered through the windshield, my mind whirling through every possible escape scenario. What a dumb witch I was if I couldn't come up with some way to beat a sick guy like this. Okay, so he had a gun. *Better say your prayers, girl...* that was about the best I could come up with. I murmured a few more entreaties to the Great Mother by all Her names. *Perhaps if I said them in alphabetical order. Athena, Brigid, Ceres. Demeter, Diana, Gaia, Hecate, Innana , Isis...* I got all the way to Zoe and started over.

Maybe Phillipa would think of something, if she wasn't too paralyzed with fear. That last time I'd looked at her, she'd that frozen rabbit look in her eyes.

"Turn left here," Simic ordered when we'd reached the Plymouth Historic District, and I did. "Down one block, then around the rotary to Water Street."

Turning the corner, we headed downhill where some brave soul was trying to get traction to come up the slope by driving zig-zag from the snowbank on one side to the snowbank on the other. I sounded my horn and continued to honk more loudly and rudely than I ever have, while using the noise to cover turning on the cell phone in my lap. It played its merry melody, but Simic didn't hear it through the noise of my insistent horn. I eased around the rotary, holding my breath.

"Jesus Christ Almighty, what is *wrong* with you? If you think you're getting a message to that other car, forget it. He's far too busy trying to stay on the road. Was it supposed to be an S-O-S you were signaling?" He laughed crazily again, a sound that would freeze anyone's blood and certainly chilled mine. "You'd better brush up on your Morse Code. That was more like S-H-I-T."

He continued to laugh uproariously, fueled by his own humor, to the point of gasping. Of course he was taking some dangerous speed drug, an MD with access to everything a legitimate pharmacy had to offer. I'd seen him popping pills, and he'd probably taken a whole lot more of them earlier.

I took advantage of his hyper gaffaws to turn the volume on my cell phone down as far as it would go and punch in 911.

Fortunately, Simic's bout of laughter had driven him into a coughing spasm when a tiny voice between my thighs said "This is 911. What is the nature of your emergency?" I waited one terrified heartbeat, but there was no reaction. Simic's mindless coughing continued.

"Hey, *Simic,* what are we doing down here on *Water Street?*" I asked loudly, projecting my voice to carry over the sounds of the coughing, the car motor, and the storm. "*Detective Stern* is surely going to have the whole force out looking for us." I gave careful emphasis to the key words. The dispatcher might not know what to make of my code, but I hoped the call would be automatically recorded. I depended on Stone to be checking all possibilities. Not wanting to take a chance that Simic would hear the dispatcher's response, I shut off the cell before she could reply.

"Don't worry, Cass. I promise you'll be *long gone* before *Defective* Stern finds us," Simic said. Another nasty laugh at his own inane humor.

Simic's directions had brought us to a street that ran parallel to the ocean, normally a bustling avenue of seaside restaurants, but nearly deserted today in the blizzard. I could see a light gleaming in a window here and there, but it appeared that all places of business were sensibly closed for the day.

"Drive onto the Town Pier."

Athena, Brigid, Ceres, save us. He must have a boat. Of course, of course. I looked in the rear view mirror again to see if this notion had dawned on Phillipa. She still looked dazed with fear.

I inched along ever more slowly onto the pier past more harborside restaurants and the Harbor Master's office.

"Okay, stop," Simic ordered. "Stop right here."

As I had already imagined, he'd brought us to where the boats were moored. Many were attached to buoys in the water but a few of the boats were pulled up to the dock, mostly power-driven yachts but one a charter boat that I recognized. It belonged to Captain Billy Blume, a colorful old salt who liked to share yarns with Captain Jack, the Devlin houseman and cook. Captain Billy wouldn't be taking out amateur fishermen on the *Bluefin* at this time of year, but he might have rented his boat if he was desperate enough for money to refit it for spring.

We were nearly at the end of the wharf anyway. I slammed on the brake.

If we get on that boat, we're dead, I thought. I'd always vowed to myself that if I were ever the victim of a carjacking, I would not be forced to stay in the car. I'd roll out the door even at the risk of getting shot or run over by another vehicle. Because those who allowed themselves to be taken prisoner usually ended up dead anyway. Stuffed in the trunk and left in some abandoned lot. Only in this case, Simic would have the whole Atlantic to dump our bodies, leaving the fishes to dispose of the evidence, his usual modus operandi. *Better to take my chances right here. Hecate, Innana, Isis, help us. Light of the Cosmos, surround and protect us.*

"Get out of the car—*now!*" Simic snapped.

Looking back in the mirror, I could see that he was pushing Phillipa out the door, using the pistol as a prodding stick. *I sure hope Phil is reading my intentions by some psychic means.* The very moment that thought went through my head, she looked up at me and nodded ever so slightly. I reached under my seat and grasped the crowbar I keep there to break the window if

I'm ever trapped in the car when a bridge collapses. Sometimes paranoia turns out to be a survival tool.

But the crowbar seemed to be stuck on something, probably the seat adjusting bar. I lifted and pulled. *Nothing.*

"Move it, you stupid cunt, or I'll shoot you right now," Simic screamed. That speed drug he was on was making him more and more hysterical.

Hecate, where are you? One more urgent pull with all my panic and terror. The crowbar was freed! I held it down by my right side as I stood up out of the car.

"You go first," he motioned me toward the *Bluefin.* It looked like an ice sculpture, covered as it was with a film of frozen salt water.

Now or never.

I looked back at Simic and smiled as disarmingly as I could manage. As he came closer, preparing to drag Phillipa on board after me, I swung the crowbar at his head with all my might. Normally, I can barely lift the thing with one hand, but fright had given me the strength of ten.

He ducked and fired, but his gun hand flew up into the air. The bullet meant for me went awry, but my mighty swing had caused me to sprawl across the icy pier as if I were riding on a kid's flying saucer sled. Almost into the freezing water. Desperately, I grabbed onto the edge of the pier, wishing I were wearing those Peacedale mittens. I held on, but the crowbar didn't make it. A small splash and it disappeared.

Surely someone would be alerted by Simic's shot and call the cops! Seagulls hunkering down under an open shed squawked in protest and soared out of their shelter into the blowing snow.

"Get the fuck up, you stupid cunt," Simic snarled. "See that charter craft there? The three of us are going to take a little trip. Jump onto that boat, both of you. We've got to get out of here fast, thanks to your stupidity. Anyone hangs back, I'll shoot the other."

I got up off the pier, painfully aware of skinned knees under my jeans. "Okay, okay," I reassured him, trying to look cowed and sincere, which is hard to do when you've just tried to smash in someone's head with a crowbar.

"*You're not taking us with you, Dan,*" Phillipa said, her tone suddenly deep and commanding.

I jerked my head toward her in surprise. She had summoned her magical voice. It was low, musical, and incantatory, used mainly for rituals. Phillipa must have finally come out of her fog of fear to be using that powerful, hypnotic timbre. She was better at it than anyone of us except Fiona, of course, who had tried to teach us the skill as a vocal projection of the glamour. Oh, why didn't Phillipa croon something like, "*Wouldn't you like to jump off the pier, darling.*" I hoped we were on the same telepathic wavelength now.

More insane laughter from Simic. "That's the old spirit, princess. Fire and ice, that's you. A real ball-buster, if I gave you the chance. But you'll not be talking me out of my sweet plan. The *Bluefin* is not the *Goddess of the Sea*, but I think you'll have an interesting cruise anyway. And guess what, princess. I'm headed back to Bermuda. You two may disembark a bit earlier, however."

As soon as he got away from land, Simic was going to throw the two of us into the Atlantic. *Will he shoot us first, or will we die of hypothermia?*

While I was imagining us sinking into those freezing depths, Phillipa had succeeded in pulling Simic's attention toward herself. It must have cost her a lot of inner energy to summon his eyes with her seductive smile. "*Come over here by me for a minute, Dan.*" She was still using that voice, standing with her back to the moored boat and dangerously close to the pier's edge.

Simic turned toward her in slow motion, momentarily mesmerized. There would be no second chance. Crouching over, I rushed him in a move I had seen in many a football game but never attempted myself. A genuine tackle. If I had time to think, I would never have tried a maneuver that might have sent us both into the water.

But that wasn't quite what happened. Simic went sprawling into the *Bluefin,* and I went over the edge of the pier. As I plummeted downward, I thought I heard the sound of a distant siren. *Stone must have got our message. Phil will be okay now* was my last thought before I plunged into the icy water.

CHAPTER TWENTY-THREE

...what pain it was to drown,
What dreadful noise of waters in mine ears.

– William Shakespeare

All I remember was sinking into a cold that seared my body and my lungs with flaring pain. Instantly I surfaced, gasping and choking. Phillipa was lying flat on the pier. She'd pulled off her jacket and was waving it at me. "Grab it, grab it," she screamed.

And I did. I don't know how, but I did. That one breath of air was turning me to ice. Blackness was closing in on me. But maybe the blessed light was surrounding us after all. Or a few of those alphabetical goddesses. The problem was, I was so close to passing out, I didn't have the strength to pull myself up, and neither did Phillipa. In a moment I was going to have to let go. I couldn't feel my hands any more.

Just as I was sliding away, I heard the sound of cruisers skidding onto the pier. Stone, Joe, Tip, and an officer rushed over to help pull me out of the water. "Get blankets," Stone thundered at the officer.

"Simic," I said.

"Simic just took off in the Bluefin," Joe said, pulling the whole soggy bundle of me close. "Thank God, thank God we got here. But what happened to you, sweetheart? Did you slip on the ice? Did he push you into that freezing water?" He peppered me with concerned questions as he pulled off my soaked parka, putting his own coat around me. It didn't help much because the clothes underneath were also drenched.

"I tackled him," I explained. "It went wrong." My brain felt slow and befuddled. By then I was shivering so hard my teeth sounded like a pair of castanets.

I could see Stone holding Phillipa in an ardent grip. Looking over his shoulder, she grinned at me. "Hey, what a team," she called over to me in her normal Phil voice. "You okay?"

"Barely. You did good, Phil. Has anyone called the Coast Guard?" I asked, but then Joe was bundling me into a thermal blanket and helping me into the cruiser. The officer who was driving turned on the siren. Tip jumped into the front seat beside him. Phillipa and Stone got in the second cruiser.

"Don't worry about that bastard," Joe whispered fiercely. "Stone will get the word out about him. Let's just get you warm." Joe pulled off my boots, then reached under blanket and coat wrapped around me to remove my icy wet shirt and jeans.

Tip took off his Mountie jacket, reached over the front seat, and wrapped up my feet. Slowly, I could feel my blood moving again, but I hurt in every muscle and bone. "The pain is good, Cass," Tip said. "The pain means your body is coming to life again."

"Easy for you to say, Tonto."

"See, Tip, she's better already," Joe said.

"When did you miss Phil and me? How did you find us?" Now that my wits were operating again, I wanted to know everything.

"Tip saw where the footsteps had doubled back toward the house," Joe said, busily rubbing my shoulders and arms through the blanket. "By the time we'd raced back, we caught just a glimpse of you driving onto the main road. You were headed south. I couldn't be sure, but it seemed to me that Phil and *someone else* were in the back seat. The second person had to be the intruder Phil had spotted out her window. And he must be Simic. My heart sank, I'll tell you."

"I would never have left you guys with no word," I said, leaning weakly against the back seat.

"We knew that. I got in touch with Stone right away and told him I thought Simic had grabbed the two of you, and he put out an instant APB. But he didn't leave it there. He began checking with the 911 dispatchers, even the ones who were off-duty. One gal admitted to receiving a garbled, truncated emergency call in which 'Detective Stern' was mentioned."

"Did she remember anything else?"

"Nope, and I bet her ears are still ringing from what she heard from Stone. Anyway, he played back today's tape, and there you were, bold as brass, with your message about Water Street. Stone said, *I think that bastard's got a boat*. I said, *yeah, but he used a car to get to your house.* Tip had followed his track from one of those abandoned cars we passed on the road. Are you getting tired? Do you want to hear all this later."

"Are you crazy? Keep talking!" I demanded as strongly as I could in my half-fainting condition. Joe was vigorously rubbing my shoulders and back under the blanket. His brisk pummeling stung but I did feel slightly warmer.

"Stone dispatched one cruiser to pick up Tip and me. Meanwhile, he got another driver for himself and raced down to the pier," Joe continued. "He had a head start, but we were closer, so we both arrived at about the same time. And there was your RAV4, sitting empty with two doors open. Phil was leaning over the dock screaming, and the *Bluefin* was speeding off toward open water."

"Good riddance," I murmured. "But Goddess help the Coast Guard to overtake him."

Joe pushed back the hair plastered to my brow, sticky with salt water. "How you managed to make that call, I'll never know."

"The medicine women have shaman powers," Tip offered. "Also, Cass is a wicked resourceful woman. But you already know that."

"I do," Joe said solemnly.

I smiled beamishly and nearly dozed off despite the racket as the cruiser raced to Jordan Hospital, siren screaming.

It's always better to arrive at an Emergency Room with a police escort. No waiting at the desk to chat about insurance. We were immediately surrounded by efficient trauma personnel who whisked me off to a cubicle. I really felt I should have been complaining of something more critical, a knife wound at least, not just a dunk in ice-water. But green-garbed gals seemed to take my condition seriously, carefully checking my temperature and extremities and insisting on a period of inhalation rewarming, which normally would have been administered in a rescue vehicle, had we waited for one.

When Phillipa and Stone appeared through the curtain of my cubicle, he was still holding on to her as if she might be stolen away at any moment.

"Oh, Stone," she said impatiently. "*I'm* perfectly okay now. Why don't you take Joe and Tip down to the cafeteria for coffee while I talk to Cass. And find out, for Goddess' sake, if the Coast Guard has caught up with Simic. Well, one good thing... this should make the FBI's case for them."

After Stone had obediently dragged my two guys off for cafeteria coffee, Phillipa whispered to me urgently, "Cass, I want that son of a bitch Simic put away forever, *don't you?* So let's put the icing on the cake by testifying that he *confessed to us* about murdering Paige Bratton and that other girl, whatshername. What do you say?"

I was weakened by cold but my brain wasn't completely addled. "Not on your life, Phil. I think we've done quite enough meddling with that maniac, and it's time to *Let go and let Goddess.*"

"Always the most sensible idea, dear." Fiona had come bustling through the curtain with Deidre in her wake. Taking a medicine bag out of the reticule she was toting, Fiona set about sprinkling Phil and me with pinches of a golden powder. "Corn pollen. Good for what ails you," she said briskly. "Now don't you worry about anything, girls. Heather's got Dick's Wee Angel's ambulance and is driving over to your houses to take care of those dear doggies in case you're delayed." She placed one warm hand on my forehead, the other on my wrist, her silver bangles jangling softly. I could almost have slipped into sleep in the warmth of her healing touch. "Pulse is nearly up to normal," she said. "Praise the Goddess."

"Heather may as well collect Boadicea, then," Phillipa said. "I won't be needing a guard dog any longer."

Deidre winked at me over Phillipa's shoulder. *Fat chance* of Heather taking back an abandoned dog if she thought there was a prayer of permanent placement. "I'm giving full credit to my black stone amulet for saving your neck, Phil. I only wish I'd hung something potent on you, Cass. The ancient Egyptians used an amulet with the image of a fish to protect against drowning. My Irish mom would have inscribed it with 'May Christ and all His saints come between you and harm.'" She stopped suddenly for breath. "Oh sorry, here I am just rattling on. How are you doing now, Cass? Golly, you look a bit pale. In a greenish way."

"Thanks. Oh, damn and blast," I said. "I've lost my cell phone! How will I know if Freddie goes into labor?" I rubbed my forehead hard as if to wake up the "mind's eye" in my forehead.

"Dear Cass," Fiona said, gently taking my hand away before I could wear through the skin. "You're a clairvoyant. Trust me...you'll know, with or without a cell phone when your grandchildren begin to swim to the light. And besides, if Adam doesn't reach you, he'll naturally try Joe's phone."

"Listen to this, ladies," Phillipa suddenly announced in ringing tones, "If Cass hadn't been with me today, I'm afraid the evil doctor would have got me into that death boat. She was *amazing.* First she tried to smash him with a crowbar. And mind you, he was holding a pistol at the time. It went off, too! But he was so surprised, the shot went wild. All he did was fluster a few sea gulls. Then when that didn't do the trick, Cass tackled the bastard. I mean, literally. Of course, she missed him both times. But to me, she's a real heroine." She leaned over and kissed me on the cheek. "And I'll probably never hear the end of it."

"No, you won't, because you're a gal with a real penchant for getting into trouble. Why don't you tell them about that magical voice you summoned, just when it mattered most? Fiona, you'd have been so proud..." But I couldn't say more. There were tears in my eyes, warm and sweet tears that overflowed embarrassingly down my face.

I was glad enough for the distraction when the guys arrived. Joe handed me a mug of hot sweet tea. A real cup, not Styrofoam. And Tip opened a package of oatmeal cookies with his strong white teeth, insisting I take a few bites. "The more sugar you get into you, the better," he claimed.

"Did you go outdoors and check with the Coast Guard? What's the word about Simic?" Phillipa asked, eager for action.

"The storm is still raging, Phil. I'm afraid the Coast Guard isn't holding out too much hope of catching the *Bluefin* now."

Stone ran his long fingers through his fine brown hair in a distracted way.

"Everyone knows the madman is headed for Bermuda, right?" Phillipa said. "Surely they can track him once the weather clears."

Suddenly I got an attack of the shivers.

I felt myself plunging into that burning cold water again. My mouth filling. I sucked in a startled breath and it froze my lungs. A wave picked me up and smashed me against the hull of my capsized boat. Hands, I felt hands pulling me down into the gray icy depths.

"Cass, Cass, are you all right?" That was Joe. "Hey, Tip, run for the nurse, will you?"

"No, wait, don't!" I exclaimed. "It was just a passing vision. A very disturbing one, as if I were drowning in freezing water again. Only it wasn't me. Then I felt hands pulling me down, down into the ocean. I think it was Paige and Christy Callahan reaching out. I saw their hands—ugh! their fingers almost eaten away, white bony things emerging from the black waves."

"*Goody*," said Deidre with a toss of her yellow curls. "Then the murdered brides won't have to haunt *me* any longer. I don't want to be a person who sees dead people. Just give me my little poppets and charms, that's enough occult business for me."

"Now, now, Dee," Fiona said soothingly. "Once you've moved into another psychic dimension, you may not be able to unlearn what you've been called to learn."

"Yeah, join the coven," I said wearily.

∾

It was to be several days before the Bluefin was located by the Coast Guard. The terrifying memory might have begun to fade into a black, ugly dream if I didn't have a mean scrape on my left leg between knee and ankle that seemed still rather too painful to be simply a bruise. Meanwhile, the storm abated and left in its wake a mantle of white crystals on our evergreen landscape, the perfect decorative touch for Christmas Eve.

That afternoon we met our teenage guest Rikyu Ogata at the Exit 5 bus stop on Route 3. He jumped off the bus grinning uncertainly as if he hardly remembered what I looked like. But I would have known him anywhere, even without his Japanese baseball cap bearing the legend *Otaku* and Phillips Exeter sports jacket. For one thing, the look of him brought back the image of Tip when he was a couple of years younger and didn't have a pony tail. I introduced Rikyu to Joe, who managed his usual instant rapport with teenage boys. Perhaps it was that muscular Greek swagger, which I myself thought was rather cool—or the casual Greenpeace *We-Save-Whales* aura. They exchanged a manly handshake, and, with a show of great ease, Joe lifted the boy's humungous orange rolling duffle bag into the RAV4. Rikyu kept his laptop close at hand, however, in a smaller gear bag, electric blue.

"How's Uncle Ken?" I asked as I eased the car back onto the highway for the quick trip home.

"He's cool. He's in Kyoto taking this master course in tea," Rikyu said. "Me, I think it's totally boring. Uncle Ken's a pretty awesome guy, though. Did you know he's gonna get himself a place in Cambridge when I go to Harvard. Not that I'll have much free time, but... Good to have him in the neighborhood, know what I'm saying? Holidays and such."

Rikyu sighed and looked out the window at the white empty fields. I refrained from asking him about his parents. "Great hat. A gift from Uncle Ken?"

"Nah. The other way around. I bought one for him as well as me. *Otaku* is Japanese for a guy who's all wrapped up in one thing. Like a geek or nerd, you know. With him, it's this tea stuff. Me, I'm a hacker." He patted the gear bag. "But not one of those weirdoes who get into other people systems or send out monster viruses. Not that I couldn't. I wrote this cool program. Well, like you said, Ms. Shipton—Cass—if I want to, like, apply to the FBI or somewhere else when I'm through college, just as well if I don't have any run-ins with the computer cops on my record. You still seeing your cruise cronies?"

"Sure. Maybe you didn't realize that all of us live in Plymouth. So they'll be in and out of our house over Christmas week. We have another friend visiting, too, name of Tip. T. P. Thomas. Stands for Thunder Pony, a Native American name. He'll be staying with us tonight, and some of my family will visit tomorrow for Christmas Dinner. I hope. You see, the problem is, my daughter-in-law Freddie is having twins in a few days, due the 28th, but who knows what may happen? Anyway, I've asked Tip to show you around Plymouth—especially if Joe and I have to dash off to the hospital—and you couldn't have a better guide. You'll have a great time together."

I saw or sensed Joe raise an eyebrow, but his worries were not confirmed when we introduced the boys later. Rikyu was in awe of Tip's heritage. And Tip was enthralled with music contacts, specific to flutes, that Rikyu brought up on his laptop. That was all to the good, because I'd planned for the two boys to share the blue guestroom, saving the pink for whomever the Goddess would send to stay there, so much about my family arrangements being iffy this holiday.

∾

Hey, what's with this new boy, Toots? My pal who plays ball is supposed to sleep in this bed right here. He lets me snooze on his feet.

Scruffy was giving Rikyu's jeans a good sniffing from crotch to trainers. My older dog was used to having Tip bunk in the blue bedroom, snug under the eaves of the second floor. Tip had always been a favorite since I first hired him as a "handy man" who managed to combine stacking wood with throwing Scruffy's favorite orange squeeze ball.

I like this one, I like this one. Raffles bounced around with his usual gleeful welcome, then hopped up onto the bed. Scruffy snarled meaningfully, and Raffles promptly jumped off again, looking surprised. *What'd I do, what'd I do?*

"Raffles always says everything twice," I said, then realized that Rikyu was looking at me oddly. "I mean, he barks everything twice. I hope you don't mind having dogs around your room, because these guys are used to sleeping in here when Tip stays over. But if it bothers you, you can shut them out."

Hey, Toots, what do you think I am, chopped liver? No new boy is going to shut me out of my rightful room.

"Naw, dogs are cool. Uncle Ken said he might get us an Akita if he could find a good dog-walking place near that apartment he's going to get in Cambridge." Rikyu took the laptop out of his gear bag, flipped it open, and put it on the desk. A tenseness went out of his shoulders. With his computer up and running he could let himself feel at home.

"My son Adam was just like you, Rikki, when he was your age. *Otaku.* Another hacker, all wrapped up in his computers. His room used to look like a snake pit of connecting wires. I was always afraid I'd be electrocuted if I attempted to mop the floor." I showed Rikyu the closet where he could stow the orange duffle bag that otherwise would have taken too much of the available floor space. A veteran of changing custody and constant new homes, Rikyu must have adapted by traveling not light but heavy, with all his stuff at hand wherever he was. "I was hoping Adam and Freddie could join us tomorrow, but..."

Rikyu interrupted me as if suddenly remembering a mission. "Oh, whoa." He smacked his forehead with the palm of his hand. "Uncle Ken asked me to give you a message. He would have called himself but he got busy packing, and then he was late getting to the airport. Anyway, the message was about an earlier cruise he took. We missed you in Customs, but he knew, like, there'd been some bad, weird things going on with you ladies that last couple of days of the cruise, and that Dr. Simic was confined to his cabin. That social hostess *Ulla something* was running around trying to put a lid on the passenger buzz. Uncle Ken said to tell you he'd always had his suspicions about the doctor. The guy was, like, too friendly with Christy Callahan before she went missing on that other Norse Line cruise. Uncle Ken wanted you to know that he'd voiced his suspicions to the FBI, even back then when the first bride went missing, but their attention was concentrated on the husband. Uncle Ken said, with Simic wandering loose, you ought to watch out for yourselves even after you got home."

"Yeah," I said. "Timely tip. I'd like to talk to your uncle when he gets back from Japan. The FBI might listen to him this time."

Tip stamped into the porch just then, and the two dogs raced down the stairs to greet him. Rikyu turned his hat around backwards and sauntered after me.

Tip was standing in the kitchen looking tall and grown-up in his Mountie jacket. He wore a sturdy back pack and with a pair of snowshoes tied onto it; a flute case was tucked under his arm. Grinning his eye-slanting grin, he said, "Say, Cass, you look great. Guess you're all recovered from your tumble off the dock." I hugged him warmly, feeling that quick rush of love that is so close to tears.

"Tip, this is Rikyu, a friend from our cruise. You're sharing the blue guest room."

"Hey, man, is that a flute?" Rikyu and Tip saluted each other with studied nonchalance. "I got one of those, too. Bamboo. Shakukachi. Uncle Ken got me lessons when I was younger, with this old geezer, always half in the bag with sake. Haven't played in a while, though. "

"Practice, practice," I said. "Maybe you'll give us a Christmas duet. Well, not necessarily *Christmas*, but Solstice anyway..." I had no idea what spiritual path Rikyu was pursuing, but I knew Tip followed Native American beliefs and was not keen on what he called "white man's religion." Maybe the two boys would find some common ground in shared music. To my untrained ear, the Japanese flute sounded very much like the Native American. That wandering plaintive quality. *Is this the beginning of a beautiful friendship?* I thought of Humphrey Bogart and Claude Raines marching off into the night together.

When I mentioned this cinematic image to Joe later, he called me a complete romantic, but accompanied it with a hug so to soften any aspersion. Actually, I felt that he enjoyed my romantic fantasies but was loathe to admit it, being a macho Greenpeace hunk and all. Since my plunge off the pier, though, it seemed as if I could never get enough of Joe's enveloping warmth, so I just nestled in his arms and listened as he explained, "They're just a couple of boys who may never connect again."

"Right, honey. We'll see." I thought about that intuitive streak that runs through our veins like a river under the earth, deep and dark, yet nourishing all the green life above the surface. Obviously there were people who managed to live their lives without being in touch with that rich source of guidance, or, if they were nudged by intuition, weren't aware of it consciously. For me, it was always my "Amazing Grace."

CHAPTER TWENTY-FOUR

Christmas hath a darkness
Brighter than the blazing noon...

– Christina Rossetti

The days might be getting longer after the Solstice but the change was hardly discernible. December darkness came on at half past four as usual. A sliver of moon rode high in the black starry skies as we sat down to Christmas Eve dinner with Rikyu, Tip, Fiona, Joe, and me. Mick Finn, who hung around Fiona like some huge bumble bee in search of honey and usually cadged holiday meals from one of us, was for once visiting relatives in South Boston.

Joe was just bringing his Halibut *Spetsiota* to the table when I felt the first pain. Fiona saw my face and instantly reached over to squeeze my hand. "Shake it off, Cass," she whispered. "What's happening with Freddie does not require your labor, only your love."

Fiona was right, of course. The danger of clairvoyance was the urge to participate too keenly. I took several deep breaths, and the cramp eased. Perhaps it was only my imagination, I convinced myself. (Although I should have known from experience that what I imagine is most likely the case.) *Should I call? No, when we'd agreed that a Christmas visit would be too risky.*

Adam had promised to call me if Freddie went into labor, but he'd insisted that he could handle everything. He'd been to all the classes with Freddie, and he knew exactly what to do.

Mercifully, we got all the way through Joe's exotic Greek fish feast, and dessert was on the table before Adam called on the land line. "He sounds rather excited," Joe said as he passed me our new cordless phone.

"Ma, I couldn't get you on your cell!"

"Wow, is it starting then?" I glanced at the Delft clock that I kept on the sideboard for its musical chime if not its accuracy. Seven o'clock, if it was to be believed. "How's Freddie? Sorry about the cell. I lost it a few days ago."

"Geeze, Ma, what did you do that for? I need some help here. Talk to her, will you. She's having pains but she won't go to the hospital."

"Oh, Goddess help us. That stubborn girl. Put her on, please."

"Hey, Freddie. Ma wants to talk to you." Crunch time: a clear note of relief in Adam's voice.

Then Freddie was on. "Hey, Cass, Adam's going off the deep end. You'd better talk to him. Because it's, like, *way* too early. I just want to wait a little and see what happens. Hate to think that the poor little buggers will be born on Christmas, for God's sake. Think of always having to share their birthday parties with Jesus."

"They'll love it. It will seem to them that the whole Christian world is celebrating their birthday. So never mind this nonsense, dear. Here's what you must concentrate on. *You're having twins*, so they might weigh a bit less than other newborns. You need to be in a hospital where everything those little guys could need is available instantly. Especially at Brigham and Women's with its marvelous birthing center. But you know that, because you chose to go there. *Remember?* With all the expert care waiting to help you through, you don't want to take the chance of having the twins pop out in your Lexus. I can't quite see Adam as a midwife, can you?"

Freddie giggled. "You're his ma, so you know that Adam practically faints at the sight of blood. Oh, damn. I hate it when you go all sensible on me, Cass." She was wavering. I could hear it in her tone. "So, can't you good witches of Plymouth get together some little spell to make this—*ouch! Fuck it!*—this birth business go like a charm?"

"Of course, dear. Every easement in the grimoire. I'll burn herbs, say words of power, invoke Brigid as a saint and a goddess, the whole nine yards. Meanwhile, go straight to the hospital. You're having pains right now, aren't you?"

"Holy Mother of God! *Adam!*" Freddie, like Deidre, had been schooled by nuns, and in moments of great stress, had been known to call upon the whole Catholic panoply for strength.

"Okay, *you go, girl*! I'll meet you at BWH. I'm on my way now. *Everything is going to be all right*. You'll be fine. They'll be fine. And Freddie?"

"Oh *fuck, fuck, fuck*. Right. I'm going now. Adam's standing by the front door with my suitcase."

Their new condominium was in Hingham, rural and yet close to Boston. They could be at the hospital in a very short time. "Just one more word, Freddie. Don't be a hero. When you need drugs or anesthesia, make sure you get them. Shout the place down, if need be. I know you learned all about natural childbirth in your birthing classes, but don't feel pressured to go through with that. See you soon, honey." I hung up softly and reluctantly, trying to remember where I'd left my Wiccan first aid kit with all the little necessities of spellcraft-to-go. It had certainly come in handy during our cruise. *In the workroom.* I dashed down cellar and grabbed the kit, which I kept in a copious woven Libra handbag. Checking that it still contained essential oils of lavender, lemon, and sage (happy, peaceful thoughts and healing),I also crammed in a chamomile and rosemary dream pillow (calm courage) and ran upstairs again.

"What a lovely reticule, dear," Fiona said.

That gave me a turn. Was I getting to be a pixilated faery-godmother type like Fiona?—*have reticule, will travel*!

"Let's go, Joe. You'll drive, won't you?" I handed him the RAV4 keys. I wasn't sure I wouldn't suffer another bout of sympathetic labor pains while trying to negotiate Route 3 North to Exit 18.

"Wait, Cass," Fiona cried. "Do let me give you my smudging sage. And cedar. Cedar's very useful, too." She dug into the depths of her reticule. "Just light these, blow out the flame as you would with incense. Take the smoke in your hands and use it to waft away any negative vibes around our dear Freddie. A little dancing would help, too."

"Thanks, Fiona."

I didn't want to take time to reason with her that hospitals, as a rule, rarely allow smudging in their delivery room. It was a lovely thought. Perhaps I would smudge myself later when I was having my nervous breakdown.

൴

On the way to the hospital, I called Becky.

"Okay, Mom. Yes, you can leave it to me to call Cathy—it's about four-thirty on the West Coast. We're just finishing dinner at Johnny's. As soon as I can break away, I'll see you at BWH. Don't worry, I'll find you. I've been there before visiting traumatized clients."

As it happened, when Becky connected with Cathy, she and Irene were already at the airport, having decided that Christmas Eve was the perfect time to fly standby on the next available flight from Los Angeles. "Everyone who was going home for Christmas has already left," Cathy had said.

It would all be as I had imagined. A family Christmas celebration in the hospital. Adam, Becky, and Cathy all at once—that would be a Goddess gift in itself.

~

While Freddie was alone with Adam between contractions, I came in quietly just to give her a kiss and to slip a tiny Willendorf amulet under her pillow. I also put a few drops of sage oil on one of my grandma's embroidered handkerchiefs so that Freddie could whiff it for its calming influence. Then the nurse arrived on brisk white sneakers to check vitals and gazed disapprovingly at the dream pillow I was holding, so I stuffed that back in my bag. I smiled, imagining how Nurse No Nonsense might have reacted to smudging.

May Brigid, goddess of childbirth, ease this beloved girl through her labor. I did a little soft-shoe shuffle out the door that might have been a dance.

~

My incredible, adorable twin grandchildren, Jack and Joan, were born very, very early Christmas morning. Adam was semi-delirious with relief and joy. Although he'd stayed by Freddie through labor, usefully providing her with someone to curse and abuse as needed, he'd not attended the birth itself (that faintness problem) nor had anyone captured the marvelous event on video film, thank the Goddess. Freddie had been knocked out well and proper, only to come out of it groggily when the deed was done. An entirely normal birth, no C-section needed, no episiotomy, not even any tearing, Doctor Sharp told us, surprisingly easy in so narrow-hipped a young woman. A tribute to her muscle tone. Most likely, she could look forward to increasingly easy labors if she chose to have more children.

Of course, "easy" is a relative term. I'd heard some of Freddie's colorful expletives up until the time she was sedated.

When she was out of recovery and back in her own room, I tiptoed in for a short visit. My heart gave an eager thump when I saw the new mother and her twin miracles. The nurse had presented Freddie with the extraordinary reality of swaddled infants where there had only been dreams before. Freddie's short hair was spiked with sweat, and there were dark smudges under her eyes. "That wasn't too awful," she said faintly, forgetting already. "Aren't they perfect and beautiful?"

Adam ventured near and was allowed to hold them for a few moments. As the *grandmother* (incredible!), I, too, was given a turn to wonder at the amazing infants. How times had changed! Twenty-odd years ago, when I'd been in Freddie's place, no non-medical person was trusted with newborns, not even the new mother. I'd only been allowed to see my infants at feeding time, and no one else got to cuddle them.

Later Becky, Joe, and I viewed the darling duo in the nursery window, delineated by pink hat and blue hat, respectably weighing in at 5 pounds, 7 ounces (Joanie) and 5 pounds, 4 ounces (Jackie), squalling vigorously at the state of the world they were inheriting.

Imagining Cathy and Irene in some crowded airbus headed our way, I was reluctant to return home just yet. Instead I begged a blanket, laid my head on my own dream pillow, and stretched out on a convenient couch in the comfortable waiting room. After the earlier bustle of Christmas-baby relatives, the pace had slowed down and the room emptied out except for Joe and me. Joe turned off the annoying TV and slouched into what he calls his "seaman's alert napping mode." Working on merchant ships, then Greenpeace, he'd learned how to function without sleep or take instant advantage when the chance was provided to nap anytime and anywhere.

"Oh, what the hell," Becky said in a resigned tone. "Leave it to Cathy to travel in the dead of night. Might as well hang around here, then." She found a comfortable chair and stretched out, covered by her pink down coat, which was as close to being a sleeping bag as a coat could be.

~

When I woke, amazingly, Cathy and Irene had arrived! Those time-honored little squeals that mark female greetings pierced the silence. Cathy was being embraced by Becky. My ethereal youngest daughter with her pale gold hair and fragile figure was looking like the good faery come to bless the children. Soignée Irene stood near, watchful and protective. Neither one showed signs of having traveled the "red eye" flight. *Snow White and Rose Red* came to mind.

"*Mother!*" Cathy said, grazing my cheek with a butterfly kiss. "We were in *such* good luck. While I was talking to Becky, we were being boarded onto the *absolute next plane* East, which was—*tra la!*—a non-stop flight to Boston."

"Only two a day, morning and evening. Air Asia International, wasn't that exiting!" Irene continued enthusiastically. "Excellent tea, darling stewardesses, and an on-board film. Meryl Streep. You know, that one where she plays the U.S. President? Oh, we both *love* her so much."

"Then there was this *very kind* German gentleman, a middle-aged fish importer, who had actually met us backstage at the Golden Gate Theatre. *Cats.* Demeter and Bombalurina. Ages ago, that was, before we moved to LA. Anyway, *Bernie* got us upgraded to first class with him," Cathy took up the tale of their adventures.

"Bernard Von Wankel. What an old goat. But the accommodations were *très elegant!*" Irene enthused. "The airbus had been revamped very recently, and those first-class seats were fantastic. Each of us had her *own mini-screen*!"

"But then, there was one small *problem*." Cathy was suddenly looking very solemn. I had forgotten how quickly her expression could alter from one emotion to its opposite, that chameleon quality.

"Problem?" I was getting dazed as they fired lines off between the two of them.

"A tiny Chinese lady died in business class," Irene explained. "She was traveling with some family members. The stewardesses had no place to put her and her grieving relatives, so they wrapped her up and laid her over two other empty seats in first class right next to Cathy. I changed places with her, of course."

"*A dead lady was stored in first class next to you!* What if she'd had a contagious virus, like bird flu or something?"

"Oh, deliver me. Travels with Cathy are always so thrilling," Becky murmured in the resigned tone of the sensible older sibling.

"Now don't get all hysterical, Mother," Cathy said airily. "Bernie was beside himself, too, but it was *only* heart failure. The deceased lady's younger brother, a doctor, was a member of the party. He carried her entire medical history in a lizard briefcase. She was on her way to her grandnephew's Bar Mitzvah. Otherwise, we'd have put ourselves into quarantine before we came *here*."

"*Bar Mitzvah*!?" I took the sage oil out of my Libra bag and took a calming sniff.

"A blended family, apparently," Irene speculated. "Well, they couldn't very well put her in the galley, could they? Although, now that you mention it, I wonder why they just didn't seal her up in one of the rest rooms? But then the relatives might have blocked the aisles. The film was *excellent*, by the way. Took our minds right off it."

"So, as soon as we landed, and thanked Bernie, and took his card as if we might call him one of these days," Cathy giggled, "we grabbed a taxi at Logan..."

"*In his dreams*. Anyway, here we are, *right on time for opening night*," Irene exclaimed. "And I hope to God...Goddess...you're going to read my tarot while I'm here. There are some urgent issues."

"Tarot is Phil," I murmured faintly. "I'm the clairvoyant." I must have begun to pale, because Joe, who had been staying out of the line of fire, sipping a coffee, strode over and put a supportive arm around my shoulders.

"*Clairvoyant!*" Irene exclaimed. "That's right, I remember now."

"Never mind that," Cathy interrupted. "Here I've come all this way, and I think it's high time that my newborn niece and nephew met their new auntie. And it's been *ages* since I've seen Adam and his teen-aged bride!"

"Freddie is no longer a teen-ager," I demurred. "And she's always been quite mature for her years."

Cathy soon wheedled her way into the nursery to coo over the brand-new family additions, while Irene took numerous photos with her cell phone. I rather envied her that upgrade. Possibly a useful Wiccan sleuth tool, not that I would ever, ever get involved in a criminal investigation again. After all, I was a grandmother now. Not a *crone*, mind you, but definitely having reached the Age of Serenity and Dignity.

I ducked out of the photo session and popped into Freddie's room. This time I got to leave my dream pillow with her. Despite the deep circles under Freddie's eyes, her smile was triumphant, and Adam beamed like the sun. Afterwards, Cathy and Irene visited, but Becky had already warned them sternly not to stay too long, Freddie needed to rest after the intense hard work of bearing twins. Becky herself was heading back to her apartment for a hot bath and a few hours shut-eye.

So it was fully light before we finally returned to Plymouth to install Cathy and Irene in the rose guestroom. I'd been at the hospital all night, and I was absolutely bushed. This grandmother business was proving to be exhausting.

CHAPTER TWENTY-FIVE

Nothing of him that doth fade
But doth suffer a sea-change
Into something rich and strange.
Sea-nymphs hourly ring his knell.

– William Shakespeare

It might have been Christmas Day, but everyone was crashing in their various rooms. Except Rikyu and Tip, of course. Tip had borrowed his friend Tommy Neptune's old Chevy, and they were out seeing whatever sights of Plymouth that could be appreciated in mid-winter. Tip fully intended to sneak into Plimouth Plantation (closed for the season) to show Rikyu the Native American restoration.

Becky returned in the late afternoon with Johnny Marino and a hefty ziti casserole. The stocky, earthy, dark young man still reminded me of Joe, but so much less readable. *Interesting. When I have more time...*

Fiona appeared with a fruitcake soaked in Scotch. I removed a couple of fat pot-roasted, garlicky and lemony chickens from the oven. We nuked the side-dishes, and had a rather informal but delightful holiday dinner.

Hey, Sir...Hey, Sir... is this for us? For us? Raffles seemed to be inhaling his Christmas dinner with whimpers of delight.

Stop slobbering, kid. You're getting my paws wet. The two dog bowls of chicken and potatoes were licked down to the design before the two dogs switched places to check out any traces of greasy flavor left by the other.

Fiona's fruitcake was duly drenched in more warmed Scotch and set alight amid holly branches and cheers from the boys. After consuming a slice of it, I doubted I could have passed a breathalyzer test that day.

We'd decided to hold the gift-giving until we returned from the hospital. While Becky was packing up covered dishes for Adam and Freddie, unknown to us Rikyu and Tip had been upstairs surfing the Internet for news of the stolen *Bluefin.* So beatific was my mood, I had hardly given a thought to our close brush with Simic and a watery death. But the boys pounded downstairs just as we were getting ready to leave for BWH.

"Hey, Cass, the Coast Guard found the wreckage of the *Bluefin*," Tip cried. "Off the Carolina coast."

"No survivors, as far as they know," Rikyu added. "I guess CNN got ahold of the police reports. They're calling it The Demise of the Deadly Doctor."

"*Alleged* Deadly Doctor," Tip corrected. "No comment from the Norse Line, and no confirmation from the FBI. But that never stops CNN from putting two and two together. Two drowned brides, that is." He smiled wryly.

I was not surprised by the fate of the *Bluefin.* Not being surprised is often the lot of the clairvoyant.

"What *Demise* of what *Deadly Doctor*? Are you talking about a play?" Irene asked with a puzzled frown.

"Maybe Johnny can find out a few more details." Becky gave her escort an inquiring look. He frowned and shook his head negatively. She smiled and looked down at her hands. *Of course. She was wearing a new ring*, not engagement, wrong hand, but a knock-out ruby. This guy must see an entirely different side of Becky than the levelheaded, practical persona she showed the world. My daughter was so beautiful within, truly a rich, radiant ruby. *Good, he knows.*

No one else seemed to notice this quiet exchange. *He's got contacts at the FBI*, I thought. He'd described himself as an attorney in "general practice," which could mean anything, working out of a store-front with one partner in the North End. Not in the same league with Becky's firm of Katz and Kinder, an outfit that specialized in family law, civil rights, social security, and medical malpractice, but didn't take cases on a contingency basis, giving them a highly respectable, somewhat old-fashioned reputation. Somehow I knew Johnny's law practice took more chances, cut more corners, and possibly even specialized in criminal defense. But why then would Johnny have FBI contacts? Something to do with the Witness Protection Program? Yes, that might be it.

All this inner rumination went by in a wink. I turned back to Cathy and Irene to explain. "You remember the bride who disappeared off our cruise ship on the night of that rogue wave? I sent you gals and Becky and Adam an e-mail so you wouldn't worry about us," I said.

Cathy and Irene looked at each other blankly. "Was that the week we got a call from the casting director of that horror thing? Oh well, I didn't fancy myself as a vampire wood sprite anyway," Cathy said. "I think they were going to use real bats, too."

"They even had a bat trainer. Can you imagine being a bat trainer?" Irene giggled.

"Okay, possibly you didn't get a chance to read my message," I said. "I'll fill you in on our way to Boston while Joe drives, bless him."

"Think of the energy you save by not reading family e-mails," Becky remarked. "You never even had to worry that Mom and her companions nearly got capsized by a freak wave and friend Phil had to fight off a serial rapist on board the *Goddess.*"

~

The peace of Christmas. This moment in the cycle of seasons when the sun is poised on the threshold of rebirth seemed to act like a "cease fire" on the Christian consciousness. Even the halls of BWH had a relaxed air (but not *that* relaxed—it was still a model of efficient, safe birthing.) The nurse on duty pretended not to notice that we were exceeding the limit on visitors—although Joe and Irene volunteered to vanish if the crunch was on. Fortuitously, the new mother in the bed next to Freddie's had gone home in the late morning, giving us more space and less guilt.

"Oh, how delicious! I am *so* ravenous!" Freddie exclaimed, digging into her Christmas dinner with gusto. The shadows were still dark under her amber eyes, but she did seem less fatigued.

"She slept all day, only woke up when they brought in the babies," Adam volunteered proudly, scarfing up chicken and ziti. "I stretched out on the other bed and dozed a bit."

Freddie snickered. "Dead to the world," she commented. "Did you bring dessert, too?"

"Fiona's fruitcake might have been too boozy for a nursing mom, so I brought my own Pear-Ginger Crisp," I said. Noticing Freddie's quick glance toward Adam, I knew that she might be nursing now but not for long. What was she planning? Surely not a return to her government work!

"Thank Heaven the babes are big enough to take home with us. They're kicking me out of here the day after tomorrow. Clearing the decks for the New Year onslaught, no doubt," Freddie said. "But don't worry, Cass. We've hired a formidable

English nanny, Miss Minerva Sparks. Impeccable references, including some minor royals. Lured away to the Colonies by some wealthy French wine baroness. Our good fortune to nab her between gigs."

"When I had this lot," I gestured toward Cathy, Adam, and Becky, "new mothers were kept in the hospital for a week, or at least five days. Still, it sounds as if you'll be in capable hands with Miss Sparks." Then I stepped back and let the others crowd around Freddie. I was distracted by the onslaught of one of those rare moments in life that take one's breath away. Here I was surrounded by Adam, Freddie, Becky, Cathy, and Joe, most of the people I love squeezed into one room. Beneficence beyond all expectation.

Thank you, thank you.

CHAPTER TWENTY-SIX

And all I ask is a merry yarn from a laughing fellow-rover,
And quiet sleep and a sweet dream when the long trick's over.

– John Masefield

"Target practice!" Heather exclaimed. "But why?"

"Well, somehow the wreckage of the Bluefin not only remained afloat, wrecked but more or less intact, it was declared by the Coast Guard to pose a danger to shipping traffic in the area, so the government boys got to use it for target practice." Only yesterday I'd learned about this weird dénouement from Stone Stern.

"But what about poor Captain Billy Blume who owned the boat? Was there nothing to be salvaged?"

"The laws of salvage are like the laws of the jungle," I said. "The *Bluefin* had been picked clean by someone, maybe a passing fishing vessel. But don't worry about Blume. He was insured for full value."

"If the boat was still bobbing around out there, it's a wonder that Simic didn't survive. He struck me as a survivor type, like many another no-good bastard, don't you think?"

"I know it sounds a bit weird in the light of day, but I believe that the brides took Simic, reached right up out of that ghastly storm and pulled him over the side," I said. We both sighed and sipped our liqueur. "Of course, the brides weren't his only victims. There may have been more down there in Davy Jones' locker, just waiting for a wedding night with their seducer and murderer."

"Very colorful, Cass. Or it might have just been his guilty conscience giving him a sort of death wish," Heather suggested.

"Guilty conscience? That psychopath?"

"To think that we just happened to cross his path. *Kismet.* Ships that pass in the night and all that."

"What do you mean 'Kismet'? That ill-starred cruise was all your doing," I said.

"I refuse to feel guilty. Think of it this way, we survived those few little worrisome incidents that happened on board the *Goddess*, and now our Bermuda cruise is a wonderful memory that we'll always share, the five of us." She reached over to fill my little Waterford glass with *liquore di limone di Sorrento* "Let's toast to the Circle's memories. So many, so varied, so marvelous."

And we did. For the space of a thoughtful silence.

We were lounging in a favorite place in Heather's extraordinary home. The seafaring Captain Morgan who'd built the mansion, had of course ordered a widow's walk rising out of the top floor, but instead of being entirely open, it was like a small turret room with a walkway all around the octagonal sides. That became Heather's meditation room, furnished with rich velvet cushions and dozens of her quirky candles, and could only be reached through the trapdoor. Not even her canine companions were allowed up here in this rarified atmosphere.

This was the only room in the house which had a bona fide ocean view Apparently those old-time captains had seen enough of the sea and its ravages. They built their homes a little inland to avoid the worst of storms and wreckage, but they wanted their wives to be able to watch for their return (with three years of dirty laundry). Hence the widow's walk and its magnificent view. It was March now, and at this height, one could observe that the willow branches were thickening and yellowing, the first harbingers of spring in those desolate, snow-stained fields.

Then I said, "You know, for someone like me, time is not exactly ploddingly chronological. When I have a vision, it slips a bit, and the future is the present for a few weird moments. It's the same with memories. Sometimes when I forget and gaze too long into a candle or a sunbeam, I remember scenes of the past so vividly I can smell the flowers, so to speak."

"Once you've got a memory tucked away, it's a treasure that can never be taken from you, and there is nothing like travel to create the most exotic memories, don't you think?" she said softly.

Suddenly I was getting suspicious. "*What exactly* are you getting at, Heather?"

"Have you ever thought what fun it might be if the five of us rented a villa somewhere?"

"Yeah, like where?"

"Well, Florence would be nice. There's the Uffizi. Really educational. *See Florence and die.*"

"Watch it honey. *Thoughts are things.* And I believe that expression refers to Naples. *See Naples and die.* And besides, with our track record, we might end up beleaguered by some international crime ring and being chased by dark, slim Italian men brandishing Uzis on motorcycles. Besides, you're born under the sign of Cancer, supposedly the most home-loving of signs."

"Yes. Well. *Que sera, sera.*" Heather smiled a Mona Lisa smirk and leaned over to light one more candle, humming softly. I think the tune was *Come Back to Sorrento.* The candle was gold with tiny silver charms and bright pieces of cardboard embedded around the base. I looked closer. The cardboard chits looked like antique tickets, and the silver charms were boats and planes. "I'd never want to turn down a truly magical experience," she said.

"Listen up, girlfriend. Speaking of the truly magical, I don't want to miss a single glorious moment of my grandchildren's unfolding. They're growing and learning new skills every day now. It's such an amazing experience to watch them changing day by day," I rhapsodized.

"Kids are okay, I guess, but dogs are really so much more grateful for every kindness, and you can housebreak them in about six weeks. So...exactly how old are the little darlings now?"

"Three months. Completely adorable. I'm wondering really if they aren't going to turn out to be very highly evolved, maybe even a step in the next evolutionary plateau. Jackie, I believe, will inherit his mom's mind-over-matter skills, and that Joanie!"

"I don't believe what I'm hearing," Heather said. "You've gone off the deep end, and without your water wings."

"You see, the twins got a double-whammy of DNA from their psychokinetic mom and their clairvoyant grandmom. Jackie's extremely talented, of course, but Joanie...she always seems to know exactly what I'm saying to her. *What I'm thinking, even.* I can see it in her eyes."

"Listen, sweetie. Keep all this stuff for your grandbaby book of shadows, but I'm predicting that by next October... next Samhain, in fact...you're going to need a break. Badly."

"A lot can happen between now and Samhain," I said. And even as I said it, gazing out at the Plymouth shoreline, glinting with the reflection of lowering sun, gulls stitching through the rose-tinted clouds, the gold light entranced me, and I felt a strange visionary mood that sometimes comes over me. "It will be something like a trial."

"You mean like walking on a bed of hot coals, which I personally am never going to do," Heather asked.

"No, no. A real trial. Like at Plymouth courthouse or like that."

"No kidding! Well, in that case, I hope it's something juicy, like a murder."

"Be careful what you wish for. But it probably will be a murder, all right," I said. "That's *our* Kismet."

~

Ah, the caprices of spring! In New England, March and April are liable to be bone-cold with miserable wet winds right up until the brink of May. Rushing to get indoors, we hardly notice the grass getting greener day by day under those bleak, gray clouds. But occasionally, toward the end of April, there come a few blessed days of bright, clear skies and balmy weather, like a promissory note of better times ahead. Knowing that Mother Nature probably has at least one more blizzard up her sleeve, we native New Englanders tend to make the most of a few good days.

And so it was in such an April hiatus that I took Scruffy and Raffles for a long walk in Jenkins Park, foraging for willow bark, nettle shoots, tender young dandelions, and other goodies. I confess to treating the park as a kind of wildwood extension of my own cultivated herb gardens. Striding along in serviceable Wellingtons, armed with my hand pruner, spade, and sturdy basket, I allowed the dogs to run off-leash in what was a fairly safe environment. These expeditions were a special joy to Scruffy, who dashed and nosed and dug, circled and dove and barked, showing Raffles the canine ropes, the small life of the woods.

The memory of our Samhain cruise continued to fade fast in the way of dreams. I'd deliberately submerged the horror and dread I'd experienced, although I still enjoyed the vivid imprint of flowers massed on the roadsides and pastel houses clustered on the hill. So different than the gray-blues and bottle-greens of New England. I was glad, after all, to have seen tropical Bermuda. I should thank Heather again for shaking all of us out of our accustomed ruts.

I ambled toward the so-called wetlands, once a sand dig that had, in the course of time, metamorphosed into a marsh hospitable to black-bellied tree ducks, wood ducks, and even snowy egrets. There were some witch hazel trees bordering this former sand pit; I planned to harvest a few branches to make backup wands. The thick heavy marsh grass had occasionally produced a will-o-the-wisp, also called fool's fire or jack-o-lantern, possibly from gases released as the green reeds turned into rotting hay. Fiona called these moving fires *spunkies*, and decreed this place to be sacred ground, perhaps the home of faeries.

I'd never seen the faeries, but more than once I'd spotted the pair of bald eagles that had so fortuitously built their seven-foot-wide untidy nest in one of our highest pines, thus assuring "our" woods of a protected status. Signs were posted warning us to stay far clear of their home area lest disturbed parents abandon helpless chicks. I gave it a wide berth and moved to the far side of the wetlands, adding witch hazel to my already full basket.

Then I headed for the old log in a sunny clearing where I often rested, and the exhausted dogs sprawled beside me, panting. We were silent for a long time in the familiar way of friends who have no need of words. I closed my eyes and let the welcome sunlight warm me. Raffles dozed, but after a while, Scruffy quietly nosed my dangling hand. *Hey, Toots...do you hear that?*

I listened. At first I heard nothing but the silence. But in a short while I started to hear the small or faraway sounds that Scruffy must have been hearing all along. Wind in the treetops, splash of wings in the marsh, squabble of seagulls swooping inland, distant train—and then something quite extraordinary. A tiny silvery tinkling bell-like music that seemed to dance from reed to reed in the marsh.

"Yeah, I do hear that, Scruff, but let's be very quiet and not scare away whatever that is. A winged thing. Is it a dragonfly? A hummingbird? No, not exactly."

It was true, then.

This *was* a magical place, maybe even a crossing of ley lines, holy and powerful. Perhaps I'd make a small shrine here. Nothing too obvious. A flat rock, a few crystals, some herbal plantings. An offering of seeds and nuts.

Scruffy's nose swiveled in the direction of a gossamer being twinkling through the tall grass like a light ray. His watchful eyes followed every motion, but he moved not a muscle to chase whatever it was. That in itself was unusual.

No sense chasing one of those touch-nots, Toots. That's how many a stupid pup like Raffles here has ended up with his ass in the creek.

So many enchantments in this world! My amazing twin grandchildren flashed through my thoughts. When I closed my eyes, I could see them gazing at me, their eyes round with wonder as their new world came into focus, their mouths eager to smile, their minds open to marvels yet unknown. Someday I would bring them here, and we would see what we would see.

I sat for a while longer, lost in tranquil imaginings. Then we roused and started for home, Scruffy and I moving perhaps a little less gaily than when we'd set out earlier, but Raffles was still full of vigor. *I'm thirsty. I'm thirsty.*

"Okay, Raff. We'll be home soon. I wonder if I should tell Joe..."

It appeared as if Scruffy shook his head, or maybe he merely shook off a May fly. *We mature French Briards with our natural insight know when to leave well enough alone. Watch and wait, sense more, bark less, that's my advice.*

There's always some wisdom to be learned from one's canine companion.

The Circle

Cassandra Shipton, an herbalist and reluctant clairvoyant. The bane of evil-doers who cross her path.

Phillipa Stern (née Gold), a cookbook author and poet. Reads the tarot with deadly accuracy.

Heather Devlin (née Morgan), an heiress and animal rescuer. Makes magical candles with occasionally weird results. Benefactor of Animal Lovers Pet Sanctuary in Plymouth.

Deidre Ryan, recent widow, prolific doll and amulet maker, energetic young mother of four.

Fiona MacDonald Ritchie, a librarian and wise woman who can find anything by dowsing with her crystal pendulum. Envied mistress of The Glamour.

The Circle's Family, Extended Family, and Pets

Cass's husband **Joe Ulysses**, a Greenpeace engineer and Greek hunk.

Phillipa's husband **Stone Stern**, Plymouth County detective, handy to have in the family.

Heather's husband **Dick Devlin**, a holistic veterinarian. and a real teddy bear.

Cass's grown children

Rebecca "Becky" Lowell, the sensible older child, a family lawyer, divorced.

Adam Hauser, a computer genius, vice president at Iconomics, Inc., married to

Winifred "Freddie" McGarrity, an irrepressible gal with light-fingered psychokinetic abilities. **Jack and Joan Hauser**, their newborn twins.

Cathy Hauser, who lives with her partner **Irene Adler**, both actresses, mostly unemployed.

Thunder Pony "Tip" Thomas, Cass's Native American teen-age friend, almost family, whose tracking skills are often in demand.

Fiona is sometimes the guardian of her grandniece **Laura Belle MacDonald**, a.k.a. **Tinker-Belle**.

Deidre's family

Jenny, Willy Jr., **Bobby**, and **Baby Anne**

Mary Margaret Ryan, a.k.a. **M & Ms**, mother-in-law and devoted gamer.

Betti Kinsey, a diminutive au pair, a.k.a **Bettikins.**

The Circle's Animal Companions

Cass's family includes two irrepressible canines, part French Briard and part mutt, **Scruffy** and his offspring **Raffles**. Often make their opinions known.

Fiona's supercilious cat is **Omar Khayyám,** a Persian aristocrat.

Phillipa's **Zelda**, a plump black cat, was once a waif rescued from a dumpster by Fiona.

Heather's family of rescued canines is constantly changing, and far too numerous to mention, except for **Trilby**, an ancient bloodhound, **Boadicea** , a feisty boxer, and **Honeycomb**, a golden retriever and so-called Therapy Dog who is Raffles' mother.

Joe Ulysses' Halibut *Spetsiota*

A pot of rice pilaf will cook in the same time it takes to bake this fish—that's my idea of "fast food."

4 tablespoons olive oil, divided
4 scallions, chopped
2 pounds fresh wild-caught halibut
1/3 cup fresh lemon juice
2 cups fresh ripe chopped tomatoes (squeeze out the seeds)
1 clove garlic, finely minced (optional)
About ½ cup pitted, chopped Kalamata olives, or other olives of your choice
Oregano, salt, pepper
About 2 cups fresh bread crumbs

Preheat the oven to 400 degrees F.

Coat a baking pan with 2 tablespoons of the oil and sprinkle with scallions.Turn the fish over in the oil and arrange in one layer, ending with skin side down.

Pour the lemon juice over all. Sprinkle with tomatoes, garlic, olives, oregano, salt, and pepper. Top with bread crumbs and more oregano and pepper. Drizzle on the remaining 2 tablespoons of oil.

Bake 18 to 20 minutes on the top shelf or until the fish flakes easily in the center.

Makes 6 to 8 servings.

Phil's Snowy Day Baked Beef, Barley, and Mushroom Soup

Thickened by barley, this soup is hearty enough to be a main dish. Serve with a salad and a hot bread, such as cornbread.

3 tablespoons olive oil
1 pound stewing beef, preferably organic, cut 1-inch cubes or smaller
1 large onion, chopped
2 to 3 stalks celery, sliced
About 1 cup carrot chunks
1 (14-ounce) can stewed tomatoes
2 quarts water
½ cup pearled barley
2 teaspoons salt
Pinched of dried rosemary and thyme
Lots of freshly ground black pepper
1 cup fried mushrooms (not canned)

Preheat the oven to 375 degrees F.

Heat the oil in a large soup pot with heat-resistant handles and cover. Stir-fry and brown the beef on the stove top over high heat, adding onion near the end of browning. You want them to be quite brown, but not burned, to give color to the soup.

Add the celery, carrots, and tomato. Simmer 5 minutes. Add the water, barley, salt, and dried herbs, and bring the soup to a boil.

Cover and put the pot in the middle of the oven. Bake for about 1 ½ to 2 hours or until the beef is very tender. Check the water level occasionally, adding more as needed to keep the same level. When the soup is almost done, add the mushrooms.

Taste to correct seasoning; you may want more salt.

Makes 2 quarts or more.

Cass's Pear-Ginger Crisp

Easy as pie? This is much easier!

For the topping:

1/3 cup flour
1/3 cup firmly packed brown sugar
¼ teaspoon ground ginger
3 tablespoons butter
½ cup uncooked oatmeal (regular, not instant)
¼ cup finely chopped walnuts (or any nuts)

For the filling:

5 to 6 ripe pears (Bartlett's are a good choice, but any pears are okay)
About 2 tablespoons lemon juice or a mild vinegar
¼ cup firmly packed brown sugar
2 tablespoons flour
2 tablespoons finely chopped crystallized (sugared) ginger slices

Preheat the oven to 375 degrees F.

Make the topping. The easiest way is in a food processor. Mix the flour, brown sugar, and ginger. Cut in the butter until the mixture is crumbly. Add the oatmeal and nuts and just stir briefly to blend.

Peel, core, and slice the pears into a large bowl of cold water to which you've added the lemon juice or vinegar.

Mix the brown sugar with the flour using your fingers. Drain the pears well, and toss them with the sugar and chopped ginger. Press the fruit into a 9-inch pie pan or cake pan. Sprinkle the topping evenly over all, right to the edges.

Bake in the middle of the oven for 35 minutes or until the pears are tender when pierced with the point of a paring knife and the juices are bubbling around the edges.
Serve warm or at room temperature—possibly with ice cream!
Makes 6 servings.

Note: This recipe can be doubled; use 2 pie pans.

Made in the USA
Lexington, KY
18 January 2010